C000156098

A PASSION MORE PRECIOUS THAN GOLD

"You cannot have the treasure, Rafe Santana." The words came out much weaker than she intended. She tried to stir her anger. But his eyes caressed her, as did his hands, and her heart beat out of control.

"What treasure?" he mumbled, his eyes holding her captive.

"The cargo on the *Estelle*. You cannot have it."

"What if that is not the treasure I want?" His lips were so near hers she felt his breath whisper hot against her skin. Still his eyes would not release her.

Her body swayed against him, and she felt herself drowning in the desire in his eyes. She might as well have been swept overboard, for all the good her struggling mind was doing saving her from his seduction. Or was she seducing him?

SURRENDER TO THE PASSION

LOVE'S SWEET BOUNTY   (3313, $4.50)
by Colleen Faulkner

Jessica Landon swore revenge of the masked bandits who robbed the train and stole all the money she had in the world. She set out after the thieves without consulting the handsome railroad detective, Adam Stern. When he finally caught up with her, she admitted she needed his assistance. She never imagined that she would also begin to need his scorching kisses and tender caresses.

WILD WESTERN BRIDE   (3140, $4.50)
by Rosalyn Alsobrook

Anna Thomas loved riding the Orphan Train and finding loving homes for her young charges. But when a judge tried to separate two brothers, the dedicated beauty went beyond the call of duty. She proposed to the handsome, blue-eyed Mark Gates, planning to adopt the boys herself! Of course the marriage would be in name only, but yet as time went on, Anna found herself dreaming of being a loving wife in every sense of the word . . .

QUICKSILVER PASSION   (3117, $4.50)
by Georgina Gentry

Beautiful Silver Jones had been called every name in the book, and now that she owned her own tavern in Buckskin Joe, Colorado, the independent didn't care what the townsfolk thought of her. She never let a man touch her and she earned her money fair and square. Then one night handsome Cherokee Evans swaggered up to her bar and destroyed the peace she'd made with herself. For the irresistible miner made her yearn for the melting kisses and satin caresses she had sworn she could live without!

MISSISSIPPI MISTRESS   (3118, $4.50)
by Gina Robins

Cori Pierce was outraged at her father's murder and the loss of her inheritance. She swore revenge and vowed to get her independence back, even if it meant singing as an entertainer on a Mississippi steamboat. But she hadn't reckoned on the swarthy giant in tight buckskins who turned out to be her boss. Jacob Wolf was, after all, the giant of the man Cori vowed to destroy. Though she swore not to forget her mission for even a moment, she was powerfully tempted to submit to Jake's fiery caresses and have one night of passion in his irresistible embrace.

Available wherever paperbacks are sold, or order direct from the Publisher. Send cover price plus 50¢ per copy for mailing and handling to Zebra Books, Dept. 3366, 475 Park Avenue South, New York, N.Y. 10016. Residents of New York, New Jersey and Pennsylvania must include sales tax. DO NOT SEND CASH.

VIVIAN VAUGHAN

TEXAS GOLD

ZEBRA BOOKS
KENSINGTON PUBLISHING CORP.

With love and affection
To Kathleen and Son Vaughan
For thirty years
you have loved me like a daughter.

ZEBRA BOOKS

are published by

Kensington Publishing Corp.
475 Park Avenue South
New York, NY 10016

First printing: April, 1991

Printed in the United States of America

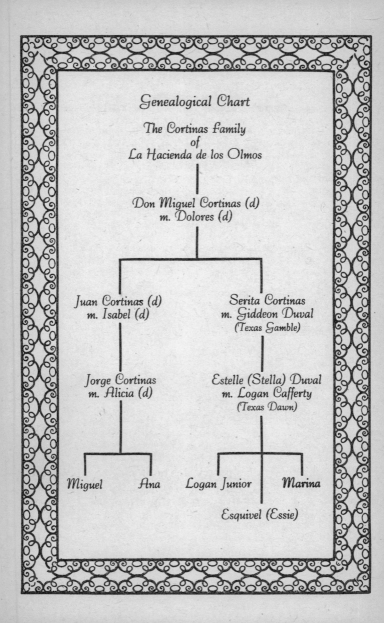

Genealogical Chart

The Cortinas Family
of
La Hacienda de los Olmos

Don Miguel Cortinas (d)
m. Dolores (d)

Juan Cortinas (d)
m. Isabel (d)

Serita Cortinas
m. Giddeon Duval
(Texas Gamble)

Jorge Cortinas
m. Alicia (d)

Estelle (Stella) Duval
m. Logan Cafferty
(Texas Dawn)

Miguel   Ana   Logan Junior   Marina

Esquivel (Essie)

Prologue

La Hacienda de los Olmos, South Texas
July 28, 1890

Fire ignited Giddeon Duval's green eyes. "I will not stand by—even with only one good leg—and let you marry some gotch-eared gringo who doesn't know his heart from his hind end," he replied to his granddaughter's announcement.

They sat in the restored ship's bridge atop the Los Olmos ranchhouse: Giddeon, his wife Serita, and their granddaughter, Marina Cafferty.

What began as a somber vigil, awaiting the arrival of Serita's nephew, Jorge Cortinas, and his son, Miguel, turned into a heated squabble when Marina revealed her plans to save Los Olmos by marrying Burt Wilson.

"I won't hear of such a thing!" Serita had responded.

"Never," Giddeon added. "We beat the sonsabitches once, and by God we will whip 'em again."

"It's no use, Tata," Marina argued. "Times have changed. They have the law on their side now.

7

Besides . . ."—she paused, trying to steady the tremor in her voice—". . . it won't be so bad. Burt is nice enough . . . we've been friends a long time."

Her grandfather fastened her with a hostile stare from his green eyes—eyes the color of her own, Marina thought, wondering what her eyes told him. *Not the truth, pray God.* Not the truth that she shuddered to think of Burt Wilson since his betrayal.

"I have nothing against young Oliver Burton Wilson personally." Giddeon looked toward Los Olmos Creek, a hundred yards or so north of the house, watching Jorge's wagon, driven by Miguel, ford the stream.

"At least I didn't have anything against the young man," he added, "until he showed himself kit and kin with his great-uncle and namesake. Your grandmother and I have tried to stay out of this until now. But—"

"Giddeon." Serita stopped her husband with her tone of voice. "Marina, dear, there is no reason to reconsider this marriage. It is plain to see you don't love Burt Wilson."

Marina felt her throat tighten. She tore her eyes from her grandmother's to stare at the approaching wagon, focusing instead on the elm trees bordering the creek, elm trees which centuries before gave Los Olmos its name. *Please dear God, don't let me cry. Not now.*

"Burt says love takes a while to grow," she answered. "He said that we . . . ah, that I live in a fantasy world here at Los Olmos. That I can't expect love to fall out of an elm tree and hit me on the head."

"Love does grow with time," Serita admitted.

Below them Miguel drew the wagon to a halt, set the brake, and helped his father down. Giddeon rose to go downstairs. Marina felt his eyes on her.

"But it must have something to start from," Serita continued, "an ember . . . something . . ."

"Sugar."

Giddeon's voice had softened. At his appellation—his name for both her mother Stella, his daughter, and herself—Marina glanced toward him. He held out his arms.

"Come here, sugar."

Almost eagerly she rose, crossed the room, and let him enclose her in his sheltering arms as he had done since she was a child. His hair was snowy white, but he was still tall and strong. He managed his peg leg so well strangers hardly noticed, and Marina had never known him any other way. She lay her head against his chest; as always his arms protected her—or promised to.

"You trust your ol' grandpa, don't you, sugar?"

She nodded against his chest.

"I have always told you the truth, haven't I?"

Again she nodded.

"Well, listen good." His hands slipped to her shoulders, and he held her back to stare solemnly into her troubled face. "That young man is wrong. Love can fall out of an elm tree and hit you on the head."

Her mouth fell open and she was sure she would have laughed, had he not studied her with such seriousness.

"Giddeon," Serita chided.

Giddeon Duval turned loving eyes from his granddaughter to his wife of many years. "It happened to us, *querida*."

As Marina watched, the look which passed between them brought a lump to her throat. They were alone,

9

the two of them, and she herself might as well have been outside with Jorge and Miguel. She sighed. This was where she got her fanciful thinking.

Giddeon returned his attention to Marina. "It happened to your mama and papa, too." That's when he told her, ". . . and I'm not about to stand by—even with only one good leg—and let you marry some gotch-eared gringo who doesn't know his heart from his hind end."

His jesting words soothed, but the truth brought her back to her own desperate state of affairs. Hadn't she herself accused Burt Wilson of not believing in love almost a year ago when he stunned her with his proposal of marriage? They had been friends, good friends, until then. She had never given thought to marrying him, and his proposal had come like a cold norther out of a crystal blue sky. She had protested that she didn't love him—not like *that,* and he had demanded to know what *that* was.

Then he chastised her for living in a fantasy world, insisting that love didn't fall out of trees and that she would die an old maid if she waited for it to happen. Afterwards he kissed her, and that night she had cried, thinking how his lips felt like a cold tortilla against her own.

Since she had never been kissed by anyone else, however, she finally came to believe he was right, so the wedding date was set for Christmas. Her parents went off to New England to visit her father's mother and her own two brothers who were following in their father's footsteps at Annapolis. Then she came to her senses and called off the wedding. After that she discovered the real reason Oliver Burton Wilson wanted to marry

10

her—so his father could gain control of Los Olmos, much like he controlled Burt himself.

Watching her grandparents now, as they gazed at each other across the small room, she conceded that they were partially right—love occasionally did fall from the trees, but to expect it to happen to three successive generations of women in one family was too much. At least, not soon enough to keep the roof over their heads. She had no time to wait for such an eventuality. Her own path in life led away from that cherished dream.

"But Los Olmos . . . ?" she whispered.

"You can't save Los Olmos by marrying Burt Wilson, sugar." Giddeon stroked her hair. "With you in the family, his case would only be strengthened."

"If I marry Burt, his father won't run you off the land. We don't live in the old days. We have laws."

Giddeon sighed. "Times haven't changed as much as we like to believe. Men who burn down courthouses to destroy tax records can do about anything they like."

"Perhaps not," Serita mused. "Let's see what news Jorge brings."

Marina and Giddeon followed her down the steep stairs leading from the ship's bridge. Over fifty years before Serita had this strange structure built to entice her sea-loving husband to stay at Los Olmos. During the War Between the States it had been mistaken for a real ship's bridge and was blown off the rooftop by a Union ship of war.

After the war Giddeon had the structure rebuilt. He had lost his leg in that war and claimed rebuilding the edifice would not only symbolize their determination to rebuild their lives, but the stairs leading to it would give him a place to exercise his one remaining leg.

La Hacienda de los Olmos had been in Marina's family since 1750 when the King of Spain granted these lands to her grandmother's grandfather. The ensuing generations had warded off threats from Indians, land raiders, outlaws, and Yankees. Now she had opened the door to a new breed of land grabbers who fought with weapons of a far different sort: weapons of the law and weapons of the heart. What choice did she have, except to fight them with their own weapons?

Downstairs a family ritual was in progress. Marina crossed the spacious parlor to sit beside her grandmother beneath the ancient shields which had belonged to their Conquistador ancestors.

Miguel Cortinas held the front door for his father Jorge, who strode to Serita, grasped her hands, and kissed them. He moved to Marina, kissing her hands, as well, greeting them both with *"Holas."* Then he crossed the room and took his usual place at the mantel beside Giddeon. So confident were his steps, so accurate his direction, no one would have suspected his blindness.

Like Giddeon, Jorge suffered his wounds in the war—a head injury which at first seemed minor, but later resulted in a complete loss of sight.

Like Giddeon, he had overcome his handicap with the determination Marina had learned to expect from her family. He had read for the law—rather, he hired someone to read to him—passed his exams, and set up a practice which had blossomed into a renowned business even before Miguel grew up, read the law himself, and entered business with his father. Today Jorge Cortinas and his son Miguel were considered

12

among the finest lawyers in South Texas.

Giddeon shook hands with this nephew of his wife's who had been more a son to both of them. "What news do you bring, Jorge?"

"I have been able to secure us three months, Tío," Jorge responded. "It is not much, but a start. I wired Logan and Stella. Since they are traveling by steamer around the Keys and up the Atlantic coast, it will be a few days before my message catches up with them."

"Three months . . ." Giddeon echoed.

"We visited the current tax assessor yesterday," Miguel added. "Now, we must track down Mrs. Raines, the tax assessor for the years in question."

"You won't find her," Giddeon said, "unless it's in an unmarked grave somewhere. These men play by the same rules as their ancestors—any way they damned well please."

"We will look, Tío Capitán," Miguel persisted, using the name Jorge, his own father, had coined for Giddeon when Jorge himself was but a boy.

Restless, Marina walked to the window and stared out at the family graveyard on the hill above the creek. Jorge's father was buried there. He had been killed in Texas's war for independence from Mexico. Serita had killed Oliver Burton, Burt Wilson's great-uncle, to keep him from murdering the lot of them in his personal war to take over Los Olmos. Giddeon had lost his leg in another war, and Jorge his sight. Would they never have peace on these lands?

"Logan paid those taxes," Gideon was saying. "I would not have turned the place over to him ten years back if I hadn't known he could manage the affairs."

"We do not doubt that, Tío," Jorge said. "But the

courts want records, and the present tax assessor claims never to have received payment. It is his word, an elected official, against Logan's."

"Elected," Giddeon scoffed. "Elected by his kinfolk who have coveted Los Olmos for generations."

The voices droned on behind her—talk of saving Los Olmos yet again, this time by selling cattle, paying taxes that had already been paid, but no receipts kept. If it would help, she would marry Burt Wilson despite her grandparents' wishes. She owed the family that much.

But she knew Tata was right. Marrying Burt Wilson would only play into their hands. On the other hand, it would take years, not months, to raise tax money by selling cattle and hauling goods from Mexico. If only . . .

Suddenly, she knew the answer. She twirled on her booted toes.

"We will salvage the cargo."

All eyes turned to her, all brows knit.

"The cargo," she repeated, excitement building within her. "Your cargo Tata, from the *Espíritu Estelle*. You know, the letter you received months ago from Tío Ignacio at the Hacienda de Vera Cruz in Mexico."

Light dawned on the faces before her, then as though rehearsed, the smiles faded in unison.

"It will work," she insisted. "We can salvage the cargo. Tío Ignacio said someone located the ship-wreck."

Serita crossed the room to her granddaughter. They stood eye to eye, and but for the silver streaks in Serita's black hair and the green eyes in Marina's oval face, they could have been sisters. Still trim at seventy-five, Serita wore the buckskin breeches and loose-

14

fitting shirt that had been a trademark costume for the women in this family since she herself was a girl.

"Marina, dear, that is a nice thought, but . . ."

"Do not belittle my intelligence, Grandmother, nor my determination. You saved Los Olmos from these *cabrónes* once before, now it is my time."

"Marina, I will not—"

"You might as well save your breath, *querida*." Giddeon rested an affectionate arm about his wife's shoulders. "I am afraid our granddaughter inherited much more from you than her beauty."

Serita sighed. "But . . ."

"I will take the *Stella Duval*," Marina continued as though she had not been interrupted. "Nick can come along."

"That's a fine idea, sugar," Giddeon assured her. "As soon as your papa gets back—"

"We can't wait for Papa. Didn't you hear Jorge? We have only three months—"

"And I cannot let you go alone. I will come—"

"No, Tata," she insisted. "You must stay here. If you leave, they might take over in your absence."

"Miguel . . ." Giddeon began, only to be silenced once more by his determined granddaughter.

"Miguel and Jorge must exhaust every effort to find Mrs. Raines, or any other witness who can verify the taxes. I doubt, like you, that they will find anyone who is both alive and brave enough to testify, but they must try."

"I can't let you go alone, sugar. Your papa and mama would have my hide—"

"And I must go. I'm sorry to disobey you. Truly, I am." She clasped an arm around each of her grandparents. "But don't you see? If there is enough gold or other salable cargo lying at the bottom of the Gulf of Mexico to pay these taxes . . . well, I must go. Besides, my mother could not in good conscience deny me this. Not after her exploits during the War Between the States."

Silence surrounded them for a moment, then she heard her grandfather sigh. "I insist on a few conditions."

A smile played on her lips. "What conditions?"

Giddeon pierced her with stern eyes. "You may take the *Stella Duval* to Tecolutla. We will send word to your grandmother's relatives at the Hacienda de Vera Cruz. You may discover whatever is known about the wreckage, determine whether a salvage effort would be feasible, and if it is, acquire the necessary crew and equipment. Don Ignacio will surely know whom to contact."

Marina could not contain her excitement. "Oh, Tata. Thank you. I know we will be able to salvage enough goods to repay the taxes."

"One more thing." Giddeon's voice held a firm warning.

Her smile died slowly. "What?"

"Even if the wreck can be located, I don't want you attempting to salvage that ship until I get there."

"But . . ."

"No buts, young lady. I mean it. Serita and I will wait here until your mama and papa return. Then we will come to Tecolutla and I will take over the salvage efforts."

That night when they had returned to their own

home on a hill overlooking what they called their Valley of the Mustangs, Giddeon cradled Serita in his arms, nipping at her temple with his lips.

"Are we crazy, letting her go off like this?" Serita worried.

Giddeon pulled at a strand of her hair with his lips. "She will be safer in Mexico than here with the Wilsons after her. And she'll be in good hands with Nick along." He leaned back and ran a finger lovingly over her face. "Not that she will listen to much he has to say. Beats me how three generations of women in one family can be so feisty and hard-headed."

Serita studied his eyes in the starlight which streamed through their open window. The years had done nothing to dim the intensity of their green depths, nor the desire with which they always melted her. "It must be in our blood."

"Heaven help the man who falls in love with Marina," he whispered. "I hope he loves adventure."

"He will," Serita assured him, then she sighed. "Oh, Giddeon, what if she meets someone in Mexico. I don't think Mexican men like independent women."

Giddeon squeezed her to him, running his hands up and down her bare back, feeling his desire for her push the bounds of containment. "Little choice he'll have if he falls in love with her. I will pity the poor bastard."

"Giddeon—" He silenced her with a kiss, after which her thoughts were only on him, her husband of fifty-one years, whose touch still sent her soaring to the stars.

"I'm excited, Giddeon," she whispered afterwards. "Aren't you?"

"Hummm," he mumbled into her damp hair. "The

treasure I gave up for love. Didn't think I would live long enough to have both."

"Did you ever regret your choice?"

"Does that question still trouble you after all these years?" His lips found hers again.

"No," she admitted. "But I have always wondered what lies beneath the sea. You said once we might look for it when we were old and gray."

He laughed. "I don't feel old and gray." His hands spanned her waist, cupped her breasts. His lips lowered to hers. "And neither do you, *querida*."

Tzintzuntzán, Mexico
August 18, 1890

The path threaded like a black snake through the dense undergrowth along the hillside then entered the mountains, leaving Lake Pátzcuaro shimmering below him.

Rafael Santana followed the trail as best he could in the pitch black night, kept on the path by the feel of ruts beneath his feet, by the snag of a branch from first one side, then the other. His breath came short in the thin mountain air, and he recalled the Indian belief that the spirit of the mountain sucked the breath out of intruders. In a protective gesture he patted the burlap bag hanging from his shoulder, then he grunted in self-rebuke. He should be in better shape. But he knew his shallow breath came as much from the fear of discovery as from the thin air. No spirits here, only irate Tarascans.

Chief Aztlán had offered a guide, but Rafe refused.

For his mission to succeed, no one must learn of it—no one. Otherwise he woud be considered no better than the thieves he was trying to protect against: grave robbers, he called them—greedy men who had begun scouring every Indian village in Mexico for pre-Conquest artifacts which they sold to foreigners at the highest bid.

Smoke hung suspended in the humid air. Although common sense told him it came from Tarascan kilns to the west, it nevertheless filled him with an urgency to be about his task and away before anyone in the village found him out.

The trail he followed was for the most part in his head—a drawing Chief Aztlán had prepared which he himself then committed to memory. It was quickly fading.

Suddenly he felt rather than saw the clearing. He tightened a fist around the burlap bag. Hair prickled along his neck. A breeze ruffled the sleeves of his shirt, then swirled around his legs. He froze in his steps.

He did not believe in ghosts, he reassured himself, neither the ghosts of men nor of gods. He clutched the object through the burlap bag.

Get hold of yourself, Santana, he commanded, creeping forward with tentative steps. You have hidden yourself in old ruins so long you're beginning to believe in their ghosts. What you need is a good dose of civilization—modern civilization with wine, women, and song.

All right, all right, he rejoined. Quit your simpering and finish this job. Then you can get the hell out of here. Just finish the damned job.

His little sermon worked, for he took a few more

19

steps, bumped into something big and solid, and jumped back as though he had stepped on a snake—or a demon. He chastised himself again. He didn't believe in ghosts, damn it.

Methodically, as he had trained himself, his brain itemized everything Chief Aztlán told him he would find in this ancient temple, called a *zácata* by the Tarascans. He had purposely chosen the blackest of nights, hoping to avoid discovery. Now he realized that to accomplish his task, he would need some light.

Producing a sulfur match from a rubber lined pocket of his jacket, he struck it. Around him all was silent, but inside his head the chants of a thousand Tarascan warriors reverberated. His skin prickled with the points of their obsidian-tipped lances.

Then the match spewed and flamed and the ghosts faded with his fears. Within the brush-guarded clearing a stone altar stood surrounded by offerings of various kinds. What he had stumbled over turned out to be a large clay pot, the kind for which Tarascans were famous. Other pots of varying shapes and sizes were lined up along the base of the altar; most of them held candles.

The flame licked his fingers. He extinguished it and struck another. This time he moved toward the altar and touched the match to one of the candles on the altar itself. Its glow revealed a wooden cross draped with fish net.

Candles and offerings which he could not make out in the dim light were strewn along the length of the altar, also draped in fish net, and interlaced with fish skeletons and flowers in various stages of deterioration. At the base of the cross stood the object he had come to claim.

In the old days Indians called turquoise the fire stone. Enthusiasm welled inside Rafe Santana when his eyes found the small idol, not over a foot in height. His hands trembled, not from fear now but with excitement, as he hefted the little goddess a couple of times, testing her weight. Since the Tarascans carried their gods into battle, the idols could not be made of stone. Rather, they had concocted a paste of ground cornstalk and orchid extract, which proved both lightweight and durable. Instead of being painted, this particular goddess was covered with copper and inlaid with turquoise. In the light of the single candle she turned a magnificent burnished blue-green.

Rafe bowed in an exaggereated gesture, awash with relief at arriving here undetected, at finding the idol to the water goddess unharmed. "Lady Chalchiuhtlicue, I presume."

At length the need for haste returned. Quickly he withdrew the package from his burlap bag and placed it on the altar, where he unwound the strips of packing cloth. Exposed, the idol he had taken from his sack resembled in every respect the one found here in the depths of the mountain forest.

His heart pounded when he stood the new Lady Chaly, as he had come to call her, alongside the old, but he didn't notice, so intent was he on the comparison. The craftsmanship of the new idol excited him, for it meant the chance of discovery would be slim. Beyond that he could hardly draw his attention from the old goddess of water. She took his breath away, and the fact that very soon now she would be safely preserved for posterity filled him with a thrill of satisfaction he rarely felt these days.

More than six months had gone into creating the new Chalchiuhtlicue, then aging her to resemble her three-hundred-fifty-year-old twin. Rafe leaned closer, comparing the two idols for wax drippings which Joaquin, the craftsman, had told him not to forget to apply. Joaquin was a master, Rafe discovered, not to his surprise.

He had spent months searching for the right man for this job. Joaquin, of Tarascan ancestry himself, proved his ability to work with the cornstalk and orchid paste, the copper and turquoise, and to age the finished product, but still Rafe had worried. To be convincing the new goddess would have to hold up under times of famine, as well as in times of plenty.

Reverently he removed the ancient Chaly from her place of honor at the foot of the Christian cross and replaced her with her twin. "We will pray for times of plenty," he mumbled. Lifting the lighted candle, he drizzled a few drops of wax onto the upraised hand of the new goddess. "Do your job, Chaly. Help the Virgin fill the fishermen's nets with white fish. Else they will dump you in the lake, and I cannot promise what you will look like when you come out."

After he wrapped the priceless artifact in the cloth strips, he slipped her into his burlap bag and blew out the candle, immersing himself in darkness once more. Patting the idol, he whispered, "I know it's outside your realm, sweetheart, but I would appreciate a little help getting out of here."

An hour later he walked, casually he hoped, into Tzintzuntzán, ancient captial of the Tarascan Indians. Here as in the other villages along Lake Pátzcuaro,

22

Tarascan fishermen used enormous butterfly-shaped nets to catch the little white fish city folks considered a delicacy.

Breathless from the excitement of his find, he stopped in front of Chief Aztlán's barracks-like adobe house. A hitching rail ran the length of the building, and for a moment he studied his own horse, tied at the far end. He was certain he had left the animal here in front of the chief's door. He shrugged and knocked.

Receiving no answer to a second knock, he pushed the heavy door open and stepped into the darkened room. The air hung heavy with copal, an incense Indians across the breadth of this country still used in worship.

"I am back, grandfather," he said quietly, addressing the chief with the time-honored title of respect. "The mission is accomplished."

From the far corner a rocker creaked on the dirt floor; "Good," an old man called in the musical Tarascan language.

A match scratched against wood and a candle flickered.

"I will go now," Rafe said.

"You must stay the night, my son," Chief Aztlán replied. "It is a long journey to the Valley of Mexico. And we must have a chance to thank you for saving little Chalchiuhtlicue."

Rafe tensed. The chief knew no one was to learn of the switch . . . didn't he? "Our agreement was to keep the secret between us. When I come to Janitzio to observe the Day of the Dead with my relatives, I will stop here. If the new goddess has not preformed well for your people, I will return the old one."

"Your secret is my secret, my son. Nevertheless I must show the gratitude of my people or the gods may not receive the new goddess with pleasure."

Rafe sighed. He wanted to tell the old man that the fish in Lake Pátzcuaro did not care whether the gods received the new goddess well or not. He wanted to tell him that all the thanks he needed was here by his side, riding his thigh, a solid and welcome presence in the night. He wanted to say that it was he himself who owed thanks—thanks to the old chief for helping him keep his country's artifacts, hence its history, out of the hands of thieving foreigners. But he didn't.

There were other treasures in danger across this land, other treasures about to be stolen by foreigners—or his own countrymen—for their own greedy purposes. And he, Rafe Santana, could not very well save them for posterity without the good will of men like Chief Aztlán. So, tired as he was, he simply mumbled, "As you wish, grandfather."

The old man clapped his hands together once, then spoke in the Tarascan language once more. He was answered immediately by a feminine voice. As the two conversed in the darkened room, Rafe was reminded that the name Tzintzuntzán meant Place of the Hummingbirds. Hummingbirds, indeed. The Tarascan language sounded like the fluttering wings of the little creatures.

Then Chief Aztlán addressed Rafe. "This is my youngest daughter, Juana. I give her to you for your bride in thanksgiving to the gods for their continued grace to my people."

When the shock finally died in Rafe's brain, he realized that the twittering of the female had come closer. His only coherent thought, however, was a warning expressed a couple of years back by his brother Chuy—Chuy, at that time a torrero-in-training, now a full-fledged matador.

"One day you are going to get yourself into something you can't get out of," Chuy had warned. Granted, the situation in which the two of them had found themselves when Chuy expressed the portent-filled warning was different from this. Instead of requiring the relinquishment of one's freedom, it had been merely dangerous and life-threatening. As he recalled, he and Chuy were hiding in a cave high in the Sierra Madres outside the colonial town of Real de Catorce. And instead of a bride twittering in front of him, they were being chased by irate bandits who thought they had absconded with a cache of stolen silver.

Come to think of it, he would take bandits to brides any old day.

"No, no . . . I cannot . . . absolutely . . . no, absolutely not. You are too kind, grandfather." Too kind indeed! He held his breath, willing the nightmare to disappear like the ghosts in the clearing.

"She is my youngest and most desirable daughter, son, the best in the village at making fish nets."

Rafe's heart thudded against his ribs. "I am sure she is . . . ah . . ." Youngest? The chief himself must be nearing a hundred. What could youngest mean?

"Her last husband was held in high esteem in the village because of her skills," the old man assured him.

"Skills . . . ?" Rafe strove to calm his mind enough to think of a suitable excuse for refusing this the most valued gift a chief could give—his daughter—his

25

youngest daughter. "Grandfather, I do not wish to give offense, but I am unable to accept a wife . . . ah, my profession forbids . . ."

"Forbids? You are not allowed . . . ?"

"Allowed, yes," Rafe corrected. "But it is not wise. You see my work is dangerous. I could be killed. I must travel . . . I will have no home . . . I cannot provide for a wife . . ." Breathless, his words ran out, and his mind swayed with the prospects. Still, he had not seen the bride. She could be fat or thin, smooth skinned or leathery, healthy or infirm, what difference did it make?

He strove to keep his temper. Why did the mountain people persist in following their primitive ways? Why did he always get himself caught in their webs?

"You misunderstand, son. You are not required to provide for Juana. She will not leave our village, and you are not expected to remain here. She will be your bride for tonight and when you return if you are so disposed. She is my gift to the gods and to you for tonight. Nothing more."

As he spoke Chief Aztlán had come forward, leading his daughter by the hand, and when he finished he held her hand for Rafe to take.

Properly chastised for the ungracious manner in which he accepted the chief's gift, Rafe bowed formally over the girl's . . . woman's? . . . hand, brushing it with his breath as he spoke. "A most gracious gift, grandfather. I am unworthy."

Without a word Juana led him outside and down the length of the gallery to a door in front of the rail to which his horse was tied. Inside he breathed a deep draft of flower-scented incense. Juana turned loose his hand and set about lighting the candles.

The cool air outside Chief Aztlán's house had cleared his head. He now resigned himself to a night with a woman and wondered at his sanity for being so hard to convince.

Glancing around the room, he found his saddle by the door and dragged it to the head of the sleeping mat in the opposite corner. Still he had not looked at his "bride."

That was the word that had troubled him—bride. He wasn't ready for a bride of his own choosing, much less one someone else pawned off on him.

Hearing her stoke up the fire, he surreptitiously removed the burlap bag from around his neck, patted the little goddess inside with true affection, and stuffed her beneath the arch in the saddle tree. The thought crossed his mind that this was all a set-up, that once he was sated and asleep, Juana, following her generous father's orders, intended to make off with his goddess.

He doubted that was the case. Chief Aztlán had been too agreeable to his plan for saving Lady Chaly. Nevertheless, he would take precautions.

When he turned around Juana stood over him, still wearing the loose white *huipil* women in this country had worn for generations. He tried to get a good look at her, but her dark skin blended with the adobe walls in the dimly lit room. She stared at him from large, dark eyes. Her twittering had stopped when they left her father's house, and silence now filled the room. He judged her to be ten or so years older than his own thirty-two.

"*Hola,*" he said. "Hello."

"*Hola,*" she responded.

27

And he wondered what to say next.

"Do you wish a bath?" she asked quite suddenly. Without waiting for a reply, she crossed the room and returned with a bowl and pitcher, which she placed on the floor beside the mat. She knelt before him. "I will bathe you now."

The next thing he knew she had his clothes off and was washing him, part by part, first lathering his skin with her hands, then rinsing the soap away with a rough cloth, after with she buffed him to a tingling shine. Several times during the process she left to throw out the dirty water and bring fresh.

Finished, she instructed, "Lie on your stomach."

He complied silently, having given up the notion that he might be required to carry on a conversation. When he lay stretched out on his stomach, hands folded beneath his chin, she proceeded to massage his shoulders and back until he felt his weariness dissolve beneath her skilled hands.

Skilled, her father had said, and indeed she was. If she wove fish nets with half the skill with which she soothed tense muscles, she must be sought after throughout the Tarascan lands.

Old Aztlán had also claimed her to be desirable, and just as Rafe decided he would have to leave that judgment until later, he felt her hands reach around his waist and shift him onto his back. When he opened his eyes, she leaned over him, all shining bronze skin. He wondered when she had removed her own clothing.

Even in the lovemaking that followed, nothing was required of Rafe—well, he conceded, nothing like the usual amount of attention he was called upon to give a partner.

Instead he was treated like a god to be placated, or at

the very least a king to be feted. She straddled him with her knees and after she had massaged him to the desired degree of readiness, she moved over him, filling her body with his. Then she moved along with him to reach fulfillment, after which she deftly slid to his side and promptly fell asleep.

Rafe was left to ponder the situation. Generally he was the first to fall asleep after lovemaking. Granted, what had transpired between them could not be termed lovemaking.

Although her performance had been flawless—he recalled again her father calling her "skilled"—he was left with a feeling of emptiness, of wanting something more.

Everything had transpired so rapidly, he had no chance to discover whether her father spoke the truth, calling her desirable. He would like to have run his fingers through her hair, but she kept it pinned out of the way; he would like to have kissed her, if not passionately, at least in a stimulating manner, but she had not given him the chance.

He sighed, feeling the fool. Here he had been afraid to accept Chief Aztlán's gift of a "bride," when all he was offered was a release from the day's more strenuous activities.

Perhaps that was it, he conceded, before falling asleep himself. He liked his lovemaking strenuous. And he liked control over the event.

Reaching behind him, he patted the little turquoise goddess. No use fretting, he had gotten what he came for . . . and more.

It was still dark outside when a pounding at the door

29

jarred them awake. Rafe struggled to clear his brain. Juana sat up on the mat and slipped the *huipil* over her head—expertly, as she did everything, he thought, struggling into his pants.

Before either of them was fully dressed, the door burst open and a slim figure barged into the room. Rafe reached for his rifle.

"Santana . . . oh, I'm sorry." The young man ran a hand through his disheveled hair, his black eyes round and wide. "Didn't mean to catch you in a . . . ah, in this situation."

Rafe Santana inhaled a slow breath, favoring his new assistant, Fernando Zamora, with a grin. "What's the all-fired rush?"

"I'm sorry, Santana, really."

"It's okay." Rafe stomped into one boot. "Okay." While he stomped into the other boot, he glanced back at Juana and shrugged. "Must be important," he said, returning his attention to his assistant.

Fernando nodded eagerly. "Remember the rumor we heard a few months ago about the shipwreck carrying President Bustamente's cargo from Veracruz back in the thirties?"

Rafe frowned, alert now.

"Yesterday we got a message from Tecolutla over on the Gulf. Someone is coming to salvage that ship. Zolic said not to concern yourself with it, he's on his way."

Rafe grimaced. They both knew what that meant. Zolic wanted the glory of an important find. Rafe had long suspected that was the reason Jesús Zolic joined the Ministry of Antiquities in the first place—glory. Well, he wouldn't be around long. Not when he discovered the glory consisted of little more than a "bride" now and again.

"Who's doing the salvaging?" he questioned.

The young man stared silently so long Rafe knew he intended his look to imply something meaningful.

"Well? Who, damnit?"

"A lady named Marina."

Rafe's mouth dropped open. His breath caught in his throat as though trapped there by memories—or, more accurately, he thought, by legends. Finally he managed a whisper. "Lady . . . Marina?"

The young man nodded animatedly. Behind him Rafe heard Juana hiss. "Malinche has returned. You will go to her, like before?"

"Do not worry," he assured his Tarascan bride-for-a-night. "It has been three hundred years since Malinche played her traitorous role in our history. This impostor will not harm you or your people."

He adjusted the burlap bag securely around his neck. Following his young assistant outside into the crisp morning air, he considered sending the little goddess back to the city with Fernando.

"You had best stop by your mother's house when you get to Mexico City," Fernando said. "She has dispatched messengers to the office daily for the past two weeks to ask your whereabouts. Yesterday she sent word that if you do not show up for the Independence Day celebrations you will be disinherited."

Rafe tossed his head back and stretched, studying the clear blue sky. He laughed. "She would do it, too—or damned well try."

Chapter One

Early one morning a week later, Jesús Zolic stumbled into the open-sided thatched-roof hut that served as a cantina along Tecolutla's short waterfront. He stared at Rafe Santana, rubbed the sleep from his eyes, then focused on Rafe again. "What the hell are you doing here? Didn't Fernando tell you I would take care of things?"

Rafe dropped his booted feet from the table, lowered the bottle of cerveza from his lips, and grinned—the last with effort.

Zolic continued. "I told that *lunático* Fernando to assure you I would handle this."

Reaching around the corner of the table he occupied alone, Rafe pulled out a chair and motioned Zolic to sit in it. Zolic, second-in-command at the Ministry of Antiquities, never failed to rankle him. Rafe strove to conceal that fact today. The man was quick to anger and held a grudge that would last through the next epoch. But Rafe needed him in the Antiquities department.

Jesús Zolic was Mexico's undisputed authority on ancient Aztec culture. If the cargo of the *Espíritu Estelle* turned out to be what was rumored, Rafe would need the man even more.

He waved a hand toward the bartender. *"Una más, por favor, José,"* he called, ordering one more beer.

"Hope you don't object to cerveza." He directed the conversation away from Zolic's obvious objection—his own presence in Tecolutla. "It's early in the day for tequila."

The bartender set the bottle on the rickety wooden table. In response to Rafe's comment, Zolic drew a long draft of beer, then slammed the bottle down, swiped the back of his ham-like hand across his mustache, and stared toward the dock.

"Problem with you, Santana, you want to do the work of the whole damned department. You cannot be in every mountain village with a goddess to save and salvaging a ship in the Gulf at the same time. Fernando was supposed to—"

"He told me." Rafe avoided Zolic's eyes, kept his voice light. "Did you expect me to give up a chance to meet the legendary Lady Marina?" He accompanied the name with a sneer and gained a grunt of approval. One thing they agreed on, he and his disgruntled assistant—their disdain for the lordly Conquistadors and their highfalutin' Spanish ways.

"Malinche," Zolic spat, reminding Rafe of the way Juana, Chief Aztlán's daughter, had hissed the word a week ago.

34

Lady Marina . . . Malinche. A lovely Indian woman, part Mayan part Aztec if the legend were true. Mistress and adviser to Hernán Cortés, conqueror of Mexico, defiler of all things Indian, Mexican.

"If she is after old Axayacatl's treasure . . . if it turns out to be Axayacatl's treasure—"

"If," Zolic interrupted. "You know the chances of that ship carrying Axayacatl's treasure are about as good as finding the temple where his son Moctezuma ripped out the hearts of his prisoners to feed to the sun."

Rafe sighed. Of course he knew the chances were slim, but slim chances were what an archaeologist's life was based on. The chance that the present discovery would be more important than the one before, and the next one larger still. Therein lay the road to piecing together the forgotten past.

He had long ago given up expecting anyone to understand his obsession with reconstructing the past in order that its secrets be preserved and learned from by present and future generations. His mother certainly did not consider his occupation worthy of the first son of a respected ranchero and government official. But precisely because his father was Mexico's Minister of Finance, Rafe had been able to help create the Ministry of Antiquities.

His brothers, including three natural and three brothers-in-law, worked in prestigious government positions or helped with the family's ranch holdings, which one day he himself would be expected to run single-handed. Even Chuy's love of the Plaza de Toros was accepted by their mother, who considered Rafe's chosen profession arcane, socially unpretentious, and totally useless. His dedication to it baffled and at times maddened her.

He smiled. Their latest encounter definitely left her closer to the state of madness. After Fernando awakened him at Tzintzuntzán, Rafe had gathered a tight rein on his urge to travel straight to Tecolutla. Instead, he rode to Morelia, then took the train across the mountains to the City of Mexico, where he deposited his newest goddess in a safe in his office. Afterward he paid a call on his mother at her townhouse. He had even promised to return in time for her Independence Day party, knowing all the while she would disregard the promise he elicited from her—namely, not to inflict upon him some air-headed female for the evening. Arranging marriages for her offspring was a mother's mission in life, he supposed.

So far he had managed to step out of every loop she cast for him, but his ability to out-maneuver her was wearing thin, given that she was assisted not only by his three sisters and three sisters-in-law, but also by the mothers of a number of the eligible señoritas, not to mention a few of the eligible señoritas themselves.

It never ceased to amaze him that a woman would want to marry as soon as she gained an interesting age. He had studied the situation at length, from a safe distance, of course. He watched his sisters bloom into lovely, independent-minded creatures who immediately forfeited their independence for the secluded life of a wife and mother. Why a woman would intentionally submit herself to an authoritarian husband and a house full of children he had not been able to fathom. But he had no intention of being caught by such a short-sighted person, one who would inevitably attach herself to him like a clinging vine.

Of course, the life of a married man was made more tenable by the social acceptance of mistresses. But that in itself posed worries a single man didn't have. Where, for instance, was he supposed to find time for a wife and family and a mistress to boot? From experiences of his brothers and friends, even mistresses were a hindrance to one's independence, becoming almost as clinging as a wife and often as hard to dispose of when one's fancy was run.

No, the single life was for him. Single, period. No wife. No mistress. He would never be able to find a woman who understood his line of work, anyhow, much less one who would willingly endure endless days and weeks in the field, often without even basic luxuries.

The Indians had the best idea. Not that they practiced it openly since the Spaniards sprinkled them with Christianity. Priests insisted not only on seeing the Indians baptized, they wanted them safely ensconced in the holy state of matrimony. Of course, like their religion, the Indians usually stuck with the old ways inside the sanctity of their homes and villages. Take the custom of giving their daughters as brides to favored visitors . . .

He inhaled a lungful of humid tropic air, recalled with longing the cool mountains he had left behind, then turned his attention to Zolic and the intriguing situation at hand.

"Tell me about our lady named Marina."

Zolic shrugged. "Not much to tell. Her name is Marina Cafferty. Comes from somewhere in Texas."

"Have you spoken to her?"

"Introduced myself, nothing more. I decided not to push her until I discover what she really wants."

"You didn't advise her that she is treading illegal water, salvaging off our coast?"

"I want to watch her a while," Zolic replied, as though the decisions were his to make. "Don't want to scare her off before I learn the whereabouts of that shipwreck."

"What has she been doing since you arrived?"

"She hired a salvage crew. A man called Ybarro."

"That was fast. Where is she now?"

Zolic nodded toward a three-masted square-rigger anchored at the dock fifty meters north of the cantina. "Sitting out there on that boat. Awaiting the arrival of her relatives."

Rafe studied the schooner, *Stella Duval* painted on its bow. He had figured that was the ship, but he wanted to talk to Zolic before approaching the namesake of a three-hundred-year-old legend. "Relatives?"

"Distant," Zolic supplied. "The Cortinas clan of the Hacienda de Vera Cruz."

"Vanilla planters," Rafe remembered. ". . . old Spanish."

"That's right. Hell of a coincidence, ask me."

Rafe slapped the empty beer bottle to the table and shoved back his chair, his eyes trained on the sailing ship. "Introduce me."

Zolic kept pace, although his legs were shorter than those of his boss and his energy level no where near as high. When they reached dockside, both men stared at the ship.

A half-dozen or so men, dressed more like vaqueros

than sailors worked around the deck, splicing lines, tarring rigging, polishing the teak wheelbox, and shining brass.

As Rafe and Zolic watched, a slight figure clad in buckskin breeches and knee-high boots climbed to the main deck and stretched toward the morning sun.

"Jesus Christ," Rafe whistled. "And I am not talking to you, Jesús."

It might have been a moment, it might have been an hour, but the first time Rafe Santana saw Marina Cafferty stretched back three hundred years in time. He had seen pictures of Lady Marina, the baptismal name the Spanish priests had given the Indian maiden who later became known as a traitor to her country. In some pictures she was clad in a native *huipil,* the loose fitting garment still worn by Mexican women of all rank and station; in others she wore elaborate costumes made of feathers and jewels; one particular painting had her clothed in no more than a brief circle of feathers which rode low on her hips, a towering feathered headdress, and some jewelry.

But even in that state of undress, no picture of Ce Malinalli, her original name, Christianized Lady Marina in order to bed the holy Spaniards, called the traitor Malinche by generations to follow—no likeness Rafe had ever seen did justice to the Lady Marina who stood before him in the flesh, exuding passion as bewitching as the original, enticing him as surely as her predecessor must have done the conqueror Cortés.

Marina Cafferty climbed the ladder from her accommodations beneath the quarter-deck and strode across the planks to face the morning sun. Although anxiety stirred in the pit of her stomach, she was content at the same time. Content and in charge, and she loved it. Her parents' cabin was luxurious, Cookie's food delicious, and she felt herself on the verge of a great adventure to equal those of her mother and grandmother before her.

After the decision had been made to sail for Tecolutla, it took two weeks to fit out the ship and assemble a crew for the *Stella Duval*. The usual crew of Los Olmos vaqueros had to be supplemented, since with the trouble at home, she could not sail away with the bulk of Los Olmos's protection.

Nick had come, of course. Son of Felix, one of her grandfather's own mates, Nick had served as the family's first mate since his father's death ten years back. Four of the other twelve crew members were from Los Olmos, with family members from Corpus Christi making up the remaining eight. Eager for the adventure to a man, each nonetheless considered his first duty to see to Marina's safety. In essence she had thirteen *dueños*. She might as well have her two brothers and Miguel along, she thought.

The fact, however, did not bother her, since everyone aboard was here for one purpose: to salvage the cargo of the *Espíritu Estelle*. No time to worry about parties or beaus.

Facing the golden glow in the east she raised her arms above her head and stretched, limbering her neck, flexing her limbs, inhaling deeply. How lovely to be on the precipice of such an adventure! Even if the weather was the most abominable she had ever experienced.

She had thought summers at Los Olmos hot and

humid, but Tecolutla was truly the tropics. Already her linen shirt clung to her skin, and her chemise beneath it. As soon as they put out to sea, she would exchange her buckskin breeches and boots for canvas pants and rubber shoes. Until then, surely she could bear the heat another day or two.

Tío Ignacio had sent word he would come for her today, but she had no intention of returning to the hacienda with him. Since she had been fortunate enough to engage the services of Pedro Ybarro and his salvage crew, the only reason she even waited for Tío Ignacio was to quiz him about the sunken ship. No one in Tecolutla could give her the headings to where the fishermen had discovered the wreck.

Nick came to stand beside her, but before he could speak Marina lowered her arms, stretching them toward the sea. "Look at that, Nick. See how it sparkles, like it is full of jewels. What do you think it is, the cargo?"

"I don't know," he sighed. "But it stirs the blood, for sure. Or is it the sea itself that does that? It is in our blood, both of us, the sea."

"I think it is more. Last night the setting sun turned the sea blood red, like rubies with golden highlights, and this morning it sparkles like diamonds."

"Last night the natives claimed it resembled a bloodstone," he told her.

"A what?"

"A bloodstone . . . an omen."

Marina laughed. "Not an omen, Nick, a promise."

"I hope you will not be disappointed."

She clasped her arms about herself. "I won't be. None of us will be."

41

Turning then she saw two men standing on the dock. She smiled and waved, recognizing Jesús Zolic who had referred Pedro Ybarro to her yesterday. "Señor Zolic," she called. "Come aboard. I would like a word with you." He could tell her where to find Pedro. And she must speak to the man before they set sail to be sure he brought the necessary equipment. She was courting her grandfather's displeasure as it was; she certainly must be able to prove herself responsible when he arrived and found she had disobeyed him.

"*Buenas días, señorita,*" Zolic greeted her, calling again, "Good morning," when Nick had lowered the gangplank for him and Rafe Santana to come aboard.

"*Buenas días . . .*" She strode forward, extending her hand in greeting, but her words died on her lips when she saw the man accompanying Zolic aboard. Recognizing Zolic, she had paid no mind to his companion, but now . . .

Zolic shook her hand then introduced Rafe, who had not taken his eyes off the lady named Marina. For a moment Rafe Santana felt himself lost in the depths of her dancing green eyes. He bowed low over her offered hand, brushed it with his lips, and muttered, "My lady."

After which he felt the complete and utter fool, much as he imagined Cortés floundering in the presence of the former Lady Marina. Her laughter fell about him like raindrops on a high mountain lake, clear and musical.

"What a gracious welcome, Señor Santana. What brings you to Tecolutla? Do you live around here?" Her tone was light, and she hoped it did not betray her sudden case of jitters. She recalled her conversation

42

with Nick concerning omens and promises and she thought how Rafael Santana's black eyes sparkled as much as a sea full of diamonds. Or bloodstones, perhaps?

Rafe released her hand, gripping instead his own runaway emotions. "No, señorita. I am here for the same thing as you."

She studied him, waiting.

"The cargo of the *Espíritu Estelle*," he added.

Grasping his words but not their meaning, she seized the opportunity to turn from his disquieting eyes. "Señor Zolic, where might I find Pedro Ybarro?"

Zolic frowned at her question. "I would not know, señorita."

"But you referred him to me—"

"I assure you, I do not know the man. If he used my name, it was not with my knowledge. The first I heard of him was yesterday when you mentioned him."

Their exchange had given Rafe time to regain his senses. "Ybarro? The salvage man?"

"You know him?" Looking back to Rafael Santana, Marina concentrated on his broad forehead to keep from looking into his unsettling black eyes.

Rafe shrugged. "What do you need with him?"

His words were all business, but his tone strummed some need inside her completely unassociated with salvaging the *Espíritu Estelle*. She started to retort that her business was none of his; instead she replied simply, "I want to check the equipment before we get under way—"

"You will not be needing the equipment," Rafe interrupted. "Nor Ybarro's services."

Although she would have understood his words had

he spoken in Spanish, he used fluent English. His words were not the problem. The problem was his tone which simmered inside her like a spring of hot water. The problem was his presence.

"I'm sure you have no idea what you are talking about," she retorted. "I certainly do not."

"Allow me to explain. You are planning to salvage a ship in Mexican waters—"

"My grandfather's ship."

"Carrying a Mexican cargo."

"Which my grandfather was engaged to carry."

"A cargo belonging to Mexico, nonetheless."

She stared hard at him now, forgetting the sparkle in his eyes, seeing instead an adversary whom she intended to dispatch forthwith. "Who are you to come aboard my ship and question my right—?"

A grim smile etched his fine-featured face, but it did not reach as far as his stone-cold eyes. "I, señorita, am Mexico's Minister of Antiquities, and I can not only question your rights, but I can damn well *tell* you what to do and make you do it."

Her eyelids flared wide. The simmering warmth inside her boiled into hot anger. "Go ahead, tell me," she said. "Tell me anything you like. Then get off the *Stella Duval* and leave me alone. I will salvage my grandfather's ship when I please, wherever it rests, and you will not scare me off with empty threats."

His smile broadened.

The arrogant *cabrón*, she thought, the word her grandfather had taught her coming easily to mind . . . a word to replace the more crude words she heard daily slipping from the tongues of their vaqueros.

He ran a lazy tongue around his full lips, while his

eyes roamed her face, her stance, then returned to hers. "I do not issue empty threats, señorita. And do not doubt that I can—and will—stop you from salvaging a ship in Mexican waters or retrieving any cargo from such a ship. Whatever lies at the bottom of this sea belongs to my government, and I will not stand by and let some bored little rich girl indulge a whim—"

His words died abruptly when she slapped his face.

"*Cabrón,*" she hissed. Then her voice gained strength, control. "Get . . . off . . . my . . . ship. Now. This instant."

"I do not require so speedy an exit, my lady. You may remain in port until tomorrow morning. At that time if the *Stella Duval* is not out of Mexican waters, I will instruct the Federales to arrest everyone on board."

She stared at him so hard her eyes felt permanently attached to him and him alone. Her heart pounded in her throat. "On what grounds, Minister?"

He returned her stare spark for spark. "How about grave robbing? Or perhaps international thievery?"

While they glared at each other, Nick cleared his throat beside Marina. "Perhaps if we invite the gentlemen inside we can work things out."

Rafe turned to Nick. "Are you the captain of this vessel?"

"No!" Marina shouted. "*I* am the captain of this vessel."

"You?"

She wanted to spit in his face. She wanted to reach over and pull his thick black hair by the handful from its roots. She settled for a sneer. "What is the matter, Señor Santana? Do you not credit *bored little rich girls* with having brains enough to sail a ship?"

"But you are—"

"Do not say it, señor. On this ship my authority exceeds yours. The *Stella Duval* belongs to my family. They are aware of my presence here and of my mission. Do not doubt that I search for the wreck of the *Espíritu Estelle* with the most serious of purposes."

"To hell with your purposes, señorita. As an official of the Mexican Government, I forbid you to pursue— what did you call it?—your mission."

"To hell with the Mexican government," she spat.

Later when Zolic chided him for losing control, Rafe blamed it on his long-held opinion of a lady named Marina. Certainly, he argued, no mere slip of a girl, not even one who called herself a captain, could rile him to such a degree.

Certainly not. Yet, after a bottle of tequila and half a dozen limes he came to his senses and realized the best thing for the Ministry of Antiquities would be to let Marina Cafferty, bored little rich girl or not, salvage the wreck of the *Espíritu Estelle* . . . for Mexico. Funding for his department was woefully slow and hard to come by. Even though his father was Minister of Finance— perhaps because of his father's position—he had difficulty prying money from the government coffers without proof a venture would succeed. At this stage of salvaging the *Espíritu Estelle*, nothing was a certainty. He could take money from his personal estate, of course, as he had done in the past. But why should he, when she blatantly admitted that her family was willing to foot the bill?

The problem now was not so much what to do, but

46

how to go about it. He did not relish the idea of returning to the *Stella Duval* only to be turned away in full daylight by its diminutive captain.

"You're too hung up on ancient history, Santana," Zolic told him.

Rafe grunted. "Me? What about you? At least I don't go about with one Christian name and one Aztec."

Zolic shrugged. "Call it homage. Seriously, you're confusing that girl out there with the legend. Even if they turn out to be related, it would have to be by a good six or seven generations. Over such a span of time, even the blood of a traitor must surely be weak as ewe's milk."

Rafe concentrated on pouring salt on a spot on his fist he had wet with his tongue. Satisfied, he downed a shot of tequila, licked the salt off his hand, then squeezed a splash of lime juice into his mouth. After the amount of liquor he had consumed over the last two hours, his throat no longer burned with the sensation but his mind blazed. "I have it, Zolic. *Por los dios viejos,* I have a solution."

Zolic took a pull on the bottle of cerveza he had nursed the last hour. "I would leave the old gods out of this, Santana. If you want to do business with that little señorita out there, you will do well to keep your wits in present time."

Rafe let his chair drop back to all four legs. He leaned over the table, crossing his arms for support. "You're the one who's going to do business with her."

"What do you mean?"

"You don't rile her. I want you to go out there and pave the way. Tell her I . . . ah . . . I have had a change

47

of heart. Hell, tell her whatever you want, but get her to talk to me. Tell her I can fix it so she can salvage that ship, but she will have to hear me out."

After Rafael Santana had finally spun on his heel and left her ship, Marina was hard-pressed not to pick up a bucket of tar and throw it after him.

Nick put a restraining hand on her arm. "Cool off, Marina. We may need his approval before this is over."

"Never. Never will I seek his approval."

Nick shrugged. "Let's go below and consider our options over a brandy."

The brandy burned her throat, her stomach, and brought beads of perspiration to her forehead. "That *cabrón!* He cannot stop me . . ."

"If he is with the government as he claims, he can stop you."

Marina paced the floor in the teak-paneled Captain's dining room, running her fingers nervously beneath her collar, loosening it from her sticky skin. "I hate this place. How can any one live here? You can scarcely draw an ample breath."

"Marina, I think we can work things out. Likely this man Santana is angered because we didn't ask his permission. If we fill out the necessary papers, file a petition, then, perhaps, he will allow—"

"Allow?" Marina stormed. "That is Tata's ship at the bottom of the sea. Who is Rafael Santana to prohibit us salvaging Tata's ship?"

"He told you who he is," Nick replied gloomily.

"I know, I know." Suddenly she stopped pacing and whirled to face her first mate. "I know how we will whip him." Her pulse quickened, but curiously her body began to cool. "As soon as Tío Ignacio arrives, we will discover the location of the shipwreck, then—"

Clapping her hands, she threw her head back and laughed at the low ceiling. "Nick, how are we for drinking water?"

He shrugged.

"Well, find out. Send someone ashore to replenish our stock of water and any other supplies we are low on. I will wait here for Tío Ignacio."

Nick frowned. "What are you cooking up, Marina?"

She laughed again. "With the exact location of the wreck, we can slip out of the harbor under cover of darkness." She threw her hands in the air. "We will be gone in the morning, just as Señor Santana ordered us."

Nick needed no further convincing, so while he saw to reprovisioning the ship, she went above deck to await the arrival of her family.

Instead, early in the afternoon, she was surprised by a visit from Jesús Zolic.

"I come on behalf of Rafael Santana."

At her silent frown, he continued. "He has instructed me to invite you to . . . ah, to dine with him."

"Then you instruct him I would rather dine with a javelina hog."

"He . . . ah, I think it would be in your best interest to meet with him, señorita. He has a plan for allowing you to salvage your grandfather's ship."

Marina studied the mild mannered man a moment, then looked out to sea. "I have so wish to deal with such an arrogant man. You may acquaint me with his plan."

"I understand your feelings, after the way he shouted

at you today. That is not his usual manner. You must understand . . . you affected him—"

"I bring out the worst in him?"

"No, señorita, it is not you. I mean, not you personally. It is your name."

Brows knit, she beseeched him silently. "My name?" she asked at length. "It is a practice in your country to verbally abuse a person with an unattractive name?"

"No, señorita," Zolic denied once more, his brown eyes warm. "Your name is not unattractive. If I may say so, nothing about you is unattractive—"

"Apparently Señor Santana thinks otherwise."

"It is not personal," Zolic assured her again. "It is something in his past . . . in our past. It happened long ago."

"It concerns my grandfather's ship?"

"No. Well . . . ah, you would not understand."

"Enlighten me, señor."

Zolic shook his head. "I will leave that for Santana. Remember, when he speaks to you in a rough manner, it is another lady named Marina he is seeing. If you hear him out, you will have your way; he will return to the City of Mexico and you can salvage your ship."

Chapter Two

It was a spur of the moment decision designed, Rafe assured himself, to save his own honor, concocted when he saw Marina Cafferty step off the gangplank of the *Stella Duval* dressed more like a nun than a ship's captain. He could never take her inside a cantina. Where were Zolic's brains, anyhow?

After speaking quickly with José, the bartender, he waited for her beneath a banana tree in front of the hut. The late afternoon sun cast an elongated shadow of the tree, enveloping him in its dark umbrella. Aggravation smoldered in his belly like an ancient temple fire as he watched her proceed toward their rendezvous.

Earlier, when Zolic reported he had invited the señorita to dine with him, Rafe had exploded.

"You did what?" He had flung his arms wide, encompassing the entire village in one sweep. "Where the hell will we *dine?*" He emphasized Zolic's own word.

Zolic shrugged. "I told her to meet you here at the cantina."

"A lady does not *dine* in a cantina. She does not *enter* a cantina."

Zolic surveyed the hut casually then stared at Santana. "Think of her as the captain of a sailing ship."

"Easy for you to say," Rafe had retorted. "Your reputation is not at stake. I would be the laughingstock of the village if I took a woman into that cantina. Why, José would likely refuse to serve us."

Watching her approach now, Rafe knew his decision had been right. In her previous attire of boots and breeches, she would have been gaped at. Garbed as she was, José would bar the door. Prim and proper carried to the ridiculous on one so young and pretty. Even her hair gave offense, drawn into so severe a knot at the top of her head that her eyes were stretched at the corners. Her eyebrows met in a frown over her petite nose, and her small chin jutted defiantly. Her stride told him she thought about as much of their dinner engagement as he did himself.

So much the better. It would soon be over. José had agreed to fetch them some tortillas and a crock of *pozole* or whatever soup his wife had on the fire. They would eat at his camp, away from the scrutiny of José's customers.

Earlier while Zolic had gone to the *Stella Duval* to soften up the lady captain, Rafe had taken his advice and headed for his camp along the Río Tecolutla. The place afforded a measure of ventilation, if not a direct breeze. *Por los dios,* how he hated the tropics at sea level!

He watched the water lap against the trunks of several cypress trees, while his head pounded with more than his irritation over a female captain. He had known better than to down a whole bottle of tequila at one sitting. At the time, however, it added welcome fuel to his anger at both the lady—*capitán,* he corrected—named Marina and at himself.

So he had stripped off his clothing and submerged himself in the cool waters. After a bit, he settled into the lea of a cypress root and let the water rush over his body. The afternoon sunlight sifted through feathery leaves high overhead, sprinkling the water as with diamonds. After he stopped splashing about birds returned to the trees and resumed their animated chirping. His lids fluttered shut and he felt the tension drain from him.

He had been hard on her. She hadn't deserved it. He rubbed his jaw where the sting of her palm still prickled. Grimly he knew that though she slapped his face, the sting had gone much deeper—to his pride. He had pushed her too hard.

But damned if she wasn't annoying! If she wanted to play a man's game, she should learn to conduct herself like a man. Toward that end she had a lot to learn.

Of course he hadn't conducted himself with much more acumen. Opening his eyes he stared into the green canopy above him. Perhaps he had become so enmeshed in antiquities his emotions emanated from somewhere back in time.

His decision to let her salvage the ship should appease her, though. The cool water eased the heat from his body, stilled his pounding head, and after a while he began to think his solution not only right, but simple.

Then he returned to the cantina and learned of Zolic's dinner invitation, issued in his name to the lady named Marina.

By the time Marina dressed for her meeting with the Minister of Antiquities, she was in a state of agitation greater than anytime since she discovered Burt Wilson's true reason for wanting to marry her. This abominable weather. How did anyone live in such a stifling place? Especially when one was required to dress as a *lady*. Not that she wasn't prepared with numerous gowns; her grandmother had seen to that, saying folks in Mexico looked even more askance than those in Texas at women in pants.

Her irritation grew, thinking about the place that arrogant man had chosen for their meeting. A cantina! What did he think she was, anyway? She had considered inviting him to the *Stella Duval* instead but quickly changed her mind. If he was testing her mettle, she would show him.

Examining her costumes, she discarded one after the other as being too formal, too fussy, too hot. With the latter in mind she finally settled on a white batiste waist and simple black skirt of wool twill.

She secured her hair in a tight knot, then opened her box of jewelry. No, she would not adorn herself.

Already that wretched man thought her nothing but a frivolous woman. She would show him. Plain, simple, and unadorned. That's what she would be.

And she would not slap his face again. Ship's captains did not slap men's faces. Perhaps a punch to the jaw.

She smiled in spite of her dismal mood. Of course that was out of the question, but never mind. She knew something even more damaging to a man—and his pride. She would ignore every barb he threw at her. Nothing difficult about that. Then, come nightfall, she and her crew would sail away. And in the morning he would be left with nothing but a red face to show for his patronizing invitation.

At the bottom of the gangplank, she turned and called to Nick. "If Tío Ignacio comes, tell him where to find me."

Rafe watched her walk toward him with a deliberate, no-nonsense stride. Studying her severe coiffure again, he realized she was bareheaded, of all things. He could not recall when he had seen a lady deliberately go out without a fancy hat or at lest a pretty rebozo framing her face. His mother would be horrified.

He grinned sardonically. Her lack of headcovering was the least of the things about *Capitán* Cafferty which would horrify his mother.

Standing deep in the shadow of the banana tree, Rafe was hidden from Marina's view until she stopped in front of the hut to peer inside.

He pushed away from the tree. *"Capitán?"*

When their eyes met he thought instantly of the little turquoise goddess. If the Indians had looked into Marina Cafferty's eyes, they would never have called the turquoise "green fire." Her eyes gave true meaning to the term.

And the fire in their depths raged at him. He watched her struggle to contain it, suddenly regretting his earlier behavior. Surely he could uphold the laws of the land without playing the pompous bastard.

As if privy to his thoughts, her eyes darted to the spot on his cheek she had struck this morning on board ship.

When they spoke, it was in unison.

"I'm sorry—"

She stopped, sighed.

He stopped, astonished at the words which had fallen unbidden from his lips. He felt Zolic's eyes on his back and hoped the man had not overheard his slip of tongue.

At length Marina tore her attention away from his intense appraisal. Once more she looked into the cantina.

Rafe quickly stepped in front of her, extending both hands to thwart her entrance. "Wait here. Right here. I'll be back."

His mouth had curved in a grin, the first she had seen on him, and his eyes twinkled with mischief. She watched him disappear into the depths of the hut, leaving her with a peculiar fluttering in the pit of her stomach.

In no more than a moment he returned carrying a pail, took her arm and guided her toward a path which led away from the settlement, disappeared beneath a canopy of vines, and opened into a glade beside the riverbank.

"Welcome to my humble home." He released her arm.

She watched while he set down the pail and dragged a log closer. Glancing back at her, he nodded toward the log.

"Have a seat. Dinner is served."

That he had brought her to this secluded place should have troubled her, she knew, but it didn't.

Instead of being threatened, she was comforted somehow that he had considered her reputation. Comforted, while at the same time the fluttering inside her stomach increased.

"Zolic didn't consider the lack of proper dining places when he issued his invitation." He began unloading the bucket.

She watched him remove a cloth and take out bowls, spoons, a dish with tortillas inside, then a larger bowl which he handled as though it were both hot and liquid.

Marina knelt on the ground beside him and spread the cloth. Without speaking he placed the bowl in the center.

She glanced around the secluded glen. "If you were concerned about my reputation, we could have taken supper aboard the *Stella Duval*."

He eyed her briefly, pouring coffee into two tin cups before he settled back. "It wasn't your reputation, *capitán*. It was mine. I would never live down taking a lady into a cantina."

Suddenly the evening became unbearably warm, stifling. She ran a hand inside the high collar of her dress. It was this man, she told herself. This despicable man. Likely his arrogance stemmed from his uncommon good looks. He had pobably had women fawning over him his entire life and as a result had become a singular bore. She started to tell him so, but recalled her promise and her problem. Let him resort to infantile behavior, she would remain composed.

"Your friend said you found a solution to the problem you raised, Señor Santana."

Her eyes challenged him across the distance.

He held her gaze. "Call me Rafe." The words

surprised him, both the gruffness with which he spoke them and the fact that he had voiced them at all.

She glared at him, wondering at her sanity for coming into the woods alone. Then she recalled Zolic's comment that it was her name which Rafael Santana found repugnant.

"Certainly," she replied in icy tones. "If you will call me Marina."

With difficulty he averted his eyes, breaking their silent, furious line of communication. He stared toward the burbling river.

"I have decided to allow you to pursue your . . . ah, mission. You may search for the shipwreck."

"And your conditions—what are they, señor?"

His eyes narrowed on her; his mouth had lost its smile, the one she had glimpsed at the cantina and again after they arrived here at his camp.

"Only one," he answered. "That a representative of my government come along."

Jumping to her feet, she glared down at him, hands on hips.

He pulled a large chunk from a tortilla and dropped it in his soup, then another. He took a bite.

"The *Espíritu Estelle* belongs to my grandfather."

He swallowed the spoonful of soup and wiped his mouth with the back of his hand. "The cargo belongs to my government."

"How do you know it does?"

"How do you know it doesn't?" He watched her struggle to contain her anger. "Sit down and eat."

If she sat down, she knew she would throw the bowl of soup in his face. Pivoting, she walked to the riverbank.

"What is so important about that cargo?" he called after her.

She watched water lap at the exposed roots of a cypress tree. It looked cool, but that was the only thing that looked cool. Finally her breathing steadied, but when she felt him come up behind, she tensed.

"What do you know about the cargo?" he asked.

She shrugged. "The wreck occurred in 1839. My grandfather had been engaged to haul the cargo from Veracruz to New Orleans. The ship went down in a hurricane. Tata and his crew almost lost their lives."

"How does that make the cargo his?"

Without looking at him, she explained. "I have the note President Bustamente signed promising to pay my grandfather two hundred thousand dollars when the cargo was delivered to New Orleans."

"It wasn't delivered to New Orleans."

Marina inhaled deeply.

"What is so important about that cargo?" he repeated.

"Everything."

"Do you know what it is?"

She shook her head.

"I am willing to strike a bargain," he said at last.

She turned to look at him through the diminishing light, questioning.

"I come along. Saying we recover anything, you can take your grandfather's two hundred thousand dollars from whatever belongs to Bustamente's estate. Everything belonging to the government of Mexico, I keep."

Pursuing her lips, she turned back to the river.

"What do you say?" he prompted.

She inhaled a deep breath. What choice did she have? Two hundred thousand dollars would more than pay the taxes. That's all she wanted.

"Shall I enumerate your options?" he asked quietly, as though he had read her thoughts.

She gritted her teeth against an outburst. "The Federales," she spat.

"They are good at finding runaway ships off our coast. Even those who try to evade them."

Silently she stared into the swirling water. *What choice did she have?*

"Fair's fair," he argued, his voice low and soft. "After all, this is—"

She whirled toward him. "All right. All right. You may come along, señor, but—"

"Rafe," he corrected.

They stood so close she could hear his labored breath; or was it her own? His eyes held her mesmerized. Daylight had faded fast here in the glen, yet she could still see the intensity in his eyes, hear it in his voice. As for herself, she felt torn into two parts, half anger, half . . . what? What was this strange, unsettling feeling he caused inside her by merely looking into her eyes?

"Marina," she countered.

She watched his solemn expression soften and his lips curve into that hint of a smile. Before she knew what he had done, his hand caught her face; he held her jaw cradled in his palm, his thumb brushed the edge of her bottom lip.

She stood deathly still, scarcely breathing.

Rafe had touched her without thinking, but he stopped himself from going further. Her pulse beat at a rapid clip beneath his hand. She was affected by him, he could tell that.

He also knew if he tried to kiss her she would slap his face. And he did not intend to have his face slapped twice by this lady. Certainly not the first time he kissed her.

Dropping his hand, he grinned. "When do we leave, *capitán?*"

She willed her heart to still, her mind to steady, her thoughts to return to the problem at hand—

The problem of the *Espíritu Estelle*, she corrected. Strains of guitar music floated into the glen from the direction of the cantina. Crickets chirped and the river gurgled along on its journey to the sea. Strangely, she thought how she had not noticed these sounds before.

"I should be getting back," she said.

Rafe began repacking the bucket. "When do we leave?" he repeated casually.

"As soon as my uncle arrives to give us the correct bearings," she answered.

Galván Cortinas, a handsome young man near her own age Marina judged, awaited them at the cantina.

"At last we meet, Cousin Marina," Galván greeted her, bowing low over her hand, while his eyes remained fixed on her face. "We were not warned that you inherited your grandmother's legendary beauty. I am afraid every caballero for miles around—"

"Thank you, Galván," Marina interrupted, fidgeting self-consciously. When her shoulder bumped against Rafe Santana's chest, she tensed, and he cleared his throat, causing her cheeks to flame. Removing her hand from her cousin's clasp, she ran her fingers inside her collar.

"Papá was unable to make the trip," Galván continued. "This is harvest time and all hands are needed in the fields."

"Then I will intrude," Marina objected.

"No, indeed. Mamá and Bianca are anxious for your arrival. I must forewarn you, though, they intend to keep you with us until after the festival of Corpus Christi."

"Your father knows the location of the shipwreck?" Rafe asked.

At Galván's curious expression, Marina realized she had not introduced this representative of his own government.

"May I introduce Rafael Santana, your Minister of—"

"Don Rafael!" Galván pumped Rafe's offered hand. "We have much to talk about. Much. Papá said only yesterday for the hundredth time how he must have you inspect the ruins on Vera Cruz."

"El Tajín." Rafe's voice held such awe. Marina questioned him.

"Reported to be one of the most magnificent examples of pre-Conquest architecture in the country," he replied, his voice light with enthusiasm. "I will show you. Then you will understand why it is so important that I collect my country's artifacts."

"Don Rafael," Galván insisted, "please accept my invitation to come with us tomorrow when we return to La Hacienda de Vera Cruz. My family would never forgive me were I to let an opportunity to entertain you slip by."

Marina watched excitement fire Rafe's eyes. He nodded, opened his mouth to speak, and she interrupted.

"I will not be able to come this time, Galván. As soon as I learn the location of the shipwreck, I must begin recovering its cargo. Time is of the essence."

Galván nodded. "So your grandmother wrote, but I am afraid Papá is the only person who knows much about that. He and an old man who lives on the hacienda."

"La Hacienda de Vera Cruz is not to be confused with the state of Veracruz or the city of Veracruz," Galván began early the following morning after he, Marina, and Rafe were settled inside a heavy coach headed west from Tecolutla.

Galván had spent the night in the other suite of staterooms on board the *Stella Duval*, the suite belonging to Marina's grandparents. Somehow Rafael Santana had wrangled his way aboard, too, sharing the suite with Galván.

Actually, she knew well enough how Rafe managed an invitation to spend the night. It was the way Galván treated him. She could not turn away a respected member of the government, one to whom Galván showed such deference.

Before dawn Cookie prepared an enormous breakfast again at Galván's suggestion, since they would not arrive at the hacienda before midafternoon. With the sky turning a brilliant orange behind them, they set out in what Marina had at first taken for a stage coach. The emblem on each door, Galván explained, was the

Cortinas family crest.

She thought how Rafe had called her a bored little rich girl and cringed, but a surreptitious glance told her he took it all in stride. As though he rode in style every day of the week and Sunday, too, she reflected.

He was a strange man, this Don Rafael Santana. An enigma. At times arrogant and rough, at others gentle, like the evening before when they sat on deck listening to guitar music from the cantina, and to Galván telling stories of her great-grandfather who had moved back to Mexico in the 1830's and re-established the Hacienda de Vera Cruz, bringing it to its present position of esteem in the country's vanilla business. Although Rafe had not entered the conversation directly, he had listened, smiling, relaxed, interested.

A couple of times she had caught him looking at her, a faraway look in his eye, as though he were searching for something—or someone. The other lady named Marina?

It was after his second such perusal that she excused herself to retire. Rafe Santana was her enemy. The future of Los Olmos rested on her remembering that. If she began to like this man, if she so much as let herself become curious about him, he could take everything away from her—and from her family.

"Such a vehicle is necessary here in the wetlands," Galván was saying about their mode of transportation. "At times during the rainy season even this is not high enough nor strong enough to pass along the roads."

"When is the rainy season?" she asked.

Beside her she felt, then heard Rafe laugh. Galván grimaced. "I am afraid we are in the middle of it, cousin."

"Then I should not have left Tecolutla. Time is—"

"Of the essence," Rafe finished.

She turned on him, glaring at the mockery in his voice, only to find his eyes gentle, that appealing smile tipping the corners of his lips ever so slightly.

"Do not worry, *capitán*. If I have to hire a mule to carry you through the mud, you will get back to the *Stella Duval* on schedule."

As soon as she was able to tear her eyes from his arrogant smile, she looked away, staring out the window at the now gently rolling, still lush terrain. He could not know how important this mission was to her. If she told him, he would only mock her, still. He would never consider the ranch of one family—a foreign family—of more importance than his treasured artifacts!

If Galván were not here beside them, she would have slapped him! And the look in his eyes told her he knew it.

Although he sat at a discreet distance on the bench, his shoulders were broad, and they brushed her sleeve. When he shifted positions—she knew it was intentional—his shoulder crushed the sleeve of her camel traveling suit, nudging her own shoulder, sending warmth along her arm.

When she shifted her own position, he straightened immediately, making her move obvious. At least to herself.

Unaware, Galván continued talking about the family, filling her in on the last three generations of Cortinases, and she strove to listen and to remember.

"You have two brothers?" she asked, trying to recall her grandmother's discourse on family history.

"One brother, Manny, and one sister, Bianca. Bianca is near your age, cousin, but I am afraid she is going through that infantile stage before becoming a woman. She will no doubt not even see you with Don Rafael present."

His bluntness caught Marina off guard, and she turned to see Rafe's own surprise reflected in his eyes. He recovered quickly.

"I shall look forward to meeting this sister of yours, Galván. Bianca, you say her name is?" But his eyes held Marina's, his attention on her alone, as though they were the only two people in the coach. She squirmed at the unwanted attention.

"Do not worry, Galván," she retorted, "Señor Santana has a way with women guaranteed to arouse ire in a lady, not passion."

Chagrined at her own behavior, Marina felt her face flush. This dreadful climate, she thought. It was not much cooler away from the coast. She started to change the subject to the weather, but Rafe interrupted her.

"Rest assured, *capitán,* I am as well versed as the next man in the ways of courtship."

Marina felt her heart thump in her throat. She concentrated on the multitude of flowers passing her window, feeling herself as red-faced as the most brilliant of them. Although she was sure her high collar was about to choke her, she managed with a great deal of effort to keep her hands folded primly on the lap of her traveling skirt.

At length Rafe had Galván talking about the ruins called El Tajín and Marina's mind was left to sway along unattended with the coach.

She untied the ribbons, removed her bonnet, and proceeded to fan her face and neck. She could feel strands of hair straggling around her ears and forehead.

The arrogance of this man! The *cabrón!* No matter his high governmental position, his lack of proper breeding clearly showed.

She fanned harder, faster, inhaling the cool breeze whipped up by the wide straw brim. But the gentle movement against her cheek reminded her quite suddenly of his hand cupping her jaw . . .

And of the look in his eyes when he had done so. She had been sure he was about to kiss her. And if he . . . if he had kissed her, it would have been . . .

It would have been like nothing she had ever experienced before. Burt Wilson's kiss would not have counted. Not after that.

It would have been her first kiss.

Rafe watched her from the corner of his eye. He had deliberately turned the conversation to El Tajín, knowing he had best ignore her and quickly. He realized the direction of their thrown barbs, whether she did or not.

Por los dios, she was beautiful when she was mad! Her eyes blazed, inflaming him with their green fire. He could not help but wonder about the first Lady Marina. Was this the effect she had had on the conqueror Cortés?

He eased into his corner of the coach so he could watch her more openly while keeping up the conversation with Galván. That she was as affected by him as he by her was evident. He grinned. The rapid clip at which she fanned herself was likely to rip the brim off her hat.

Already whisps of shiny black hair wafted about her face, kissing her cheeks, her eyebrows, as he wanted desperately to do.

He stared back at Galván. "How much further?"

"We should be coming to Papantla soon. We will stop there to pick up mail. After that, an hour more."

They began to arrive at the Hacienda de Vera Cruz just after noon. The sun shone down from a clear blue sky, and the heady aroma of vanilla filled their senses. Marina studied the tall trees encased as they were in vanilla vines. Workers scurried like ants around the plants.

"Vera Cruz means true cross," she said. "What a strange name."

"Not strange, cousin. It is the name Cortés gave the place not far from here from which he began his march to the Valley of Mexico. His march of Conquest."

"The Conquistadors. One of them was our ancestor. We have his swords and shields at home," she told him.

"Some of them," Galván replied. "Some are still at Vera Cruz."

She glanced at Rafe, expecting a measure of respect; after all, he was the one impressed with antiquities, but he stared, inattentive, out the window.

Following his line of vision, she caught her breath. "It looks like a palace out of *A Thousand and One Nights*!"

The coach drew to a stop before a white-washed adobe structure three or more times as large as the Los Olmos ranchhouse. Graceful Moorish arches rimmed the perimeter of the house, which was topped by a massive red-tiled roof.

"We are home," Galván told them. A horn blared

68

confirmation from somewhere near the driver's box. Before they could alight from the coach, several people emerged from a pair of enormous carved doors. Between them stretched a good fifty meters of paths lined with palm trees and lush gardens.

Outside the coach, Marina examined the scene more closely. The people who approached them had not actually come through the large doors, rather they had stepped through a small door cut into the bottom of one of the others. She had never seen so grand a house in all her life.

Again she recalled Rafe labeling her a bored little rich girl. She turned to him, straightening the ribbons on her bonnet.

"My home is nothing compared to the size and grandeur of this one."

He cocked his head, a slight grin tipping his lips. "This is your home."

"You know what I mean." She raised her arms to place the floppy brimmed black hat on her head, but he caught it in his hand.

She held fast. He pulled it away.

"Let go. I must—"

He shook his head, holding the hat firmly in his grasp. His eyes pierced her own. "I like you bare-headed."

Her heart leaped to her throat, lodging there uncomfortably. Again she had the feeling he was about to kiss her.

Galván's voice found its way through her muddled brain. "Ah, we arrived after siesta. Here comes the family. Papá, Mamá, this is Cousin Marina."

"Aye, aye, aye!"

69

Marina turned to see a handsome white-haired gentleman approach her with a wide grin and welcoming black eyes. "Marina . . . our very own Malinche! Regardless of your name, my dear, you are every inch a Cortinas."

"Ignacio! For shame!" A portly woman brushed him aside and took Marina by the shoulders. "Aye! He is right. You are the spitting image of our family. Except for those magnificent green eyes. They came from your grandfather."

Marina liked her at once. "*Sí,*" she agreed in Spanish.

"Capitán Duval," Tío Ignacio mused. "He visited once, your grandfather did, before your mother was born."

"Come, my dear. We can catch up on the family inside. You must be famished."

"Mamá," Galván called them back, introducing Rafe to his parents, then the late-comer, Bianca to both of them.

In spite of what Galván had said, Bianca came straight to Marina, clasped her around the waist, then took her hand and pulled her toward the grand house. "Come, Cousin Marina, it is good to have you here. You do not know how boring life can be on a ranch with only two brothers."

"Yes, I do," Marina replied, happily. "I have two brothers myself, and we live on a ranch."

And you are not nearly as old nor as infantile as your brother made you out, Marina thought. Why, Bianca hardly acknowledged Rafe Santana's presence.

They passed through the small door cut out of the larger one to enter an enormous courtyard paved with tile and more colorful vegetation. The same Moorish arches ran along each side of the inner house and across the far end. Tía Luisa took charge.

"Come, come. You must have refreshments and get out of those hot clothes."

She led them through a set of arches, down a corridor and into a smaller courtyard, this one furnished with tables and chairs and, as the other, awash with brilliant splashes of fuchsia bougainvillea, orange and red hibiscus, and white gardenias, their fragrances mingling with the ever-present aroma of vanilla.

Just off this patio an elegant staircase circled upward disappearing out of sight, its wooden banisters supported by delicate wrought iron of the same design as the massive chandelier above it. The floor was tiled in a black and white diamond pattern.

Marina took the offered seat, finding herself tongue-tied at the elegant setting. Which didn't matter, she thought, as Bianca babbled on one side of her—

"Your room is next to mine. I will show you my gown for the Feast of Corpus Christi. Did you bring one? Never mind, Mamá will find something elegant for you to wear."

—while Tía Luis bustled about on the other side, directing maids, handing Marina a cool chocolate drink, delicately flavored with vanilla. A maid passed a tray of light sandwiches and pan dulces. Marina settled back, sighed, and as another maid refilled her glass, she caught Rafe's eye. His smile was in place, but his eyes were serious. She could not guess his thoughts, although for once he was not mocking her.

Tío Ignacio suddenly scraped back his chair. "I am

sorry to disappear so quickly," —he spoke to Rafe— "but I am needed in the fields. Manny awaits me. We will continue our discussion about El Tajín over dinner tonight."

Marina rose quickly. "Tío?" He smiled at her. "I . . . ah, we have come to learn the location of the shipwreck."

"Tonight we will discuss it."

Rafe followed Ignacio into the hallway, with Marina at their heels. "We are a bit pressed for time," he began. "What about the old man who has information on the wreck?"

"Diego Ortiz," Ignacio replied. "Lives over by the ruins. His hijos work for me. They are nearing my age, his sons; the old man is ninety, I should think. He has not been able to work for several years."

"Perhaps I could ride out there this afternoon and have a talk with him?" Rafe suggested.

"Both of us," Marina said. "Tío Ignacio, I do not want to sound discourteous, but Señor Santana is right. We have very little time."

Tío Ignacio studied her at length. "I suppose it would not hurt," he conceded. "You will take care of our new-found relative, Don Rafael?"

Rafe bowed to their host. "With my life, Don Ignacio." For some reason his tone was not mocking, his words not patronizing, and Marina chewed her lip to keep from smiling.

"Very well," Ignacio replied. "You will find horses in the stable. Tell Pepe I said to give you good mounts. I will draw a map."

Propriety prohibited them leaving immediately. They said goodbye to Ignacio and Galván, who was needed in the fields now that his mission to town was complete. They drank another glass of chocolate, ate another sandwich, more pan dulces, and were shown their rooms.

The hacienda was as enormous as it looked from the outside. Marina knew if left alone she would soon lose her way. Her room, across from Bianca's as she had been told, was as large as her parents' bedchamber at Los Olmos. Persian rugs adorned the tiled floors, and the draperies and bedcovers were made of a gold damask trimmed with matching tassels and fringe. The furniture was heavy and magnificent.

"It came from Spain," Bianca told her. "Not with the Conquistadors," she giggled. "They were too anxious to find gold to bring furnishings. Later, though, after the Crown gave them lands and they brought their wives from the islands, they sent for the finest Spanish luxuries for their homes. Tomorrow I will show you around."

If I am still here tomorrow, Marina thought, hoping their visit to the old man would prove fruitful.

Opening the mirror-fronted wardrobe, Bianca produced clothing like Marina herself wore from time to time, *huipils* and other cotton garments, although she had always preferred breeches and boots.

"You look as though you will not survive another hour in your city clothes," Bianca giggled. "Change into a *huipil.* This one has a full enough skirt to allow you to ride side-saddle."

"Side-saddle?" Marina winced. "Do you have a pair of breeches I could borrow? Or is that . . . ah, forbidden?"

Bianca giggled again. "Of course, we wear breeches

for riding. Papá does not like me to expose myself to the workers in pants, but since you will be escorted by such a strong and handsome man, it should be all right."

Bianca left, returning in short order with buff suede pants, a loose white shirt embroidered in red and yellow thread, and a pair of boots she said belonged to her mother.

Marina changed quickly, took up the wide-brimmed reed hat Bianca handed her, and hurried downstairs. She wouldn't put it past Rafe Santana to leave without her. And she didn't intend for him to learn anything about the *Espíritu Estelle* that she wasn't present to hear, too.

Chapter Three

"*Capitán*."

Marina's heart skipped along with her feet when she reached the top of the grand staircase to find Rafe staring up at her. Lounging against one of the pillars supporting the Moorish arches, he pushed away languidly and crossed to the bottom step, waiting, hands on hips, that slight grin tipping his lips. While previously he had called her *capitán* in a derisive tone, this time she could not decide what emotion evoked it.

She held his gaze briefly before deciding it best not to. Was he relieved to have her dressed like a man again? Did he despise the former lady named Marina so intensely he preferred her to wear breeches so as not to remind him she was a woman? One day she would ask him. One day . . . after the ship was salvaged and Los Olmos saved. After that she would ask him . . . if she still spoke to him at all.

He led the way directly from the cavernous house to the stables beyond. When she questioned how he knew his way around so well, he shrugged. "All the old colonial mansions were built to much the same plan."

In the stables, the boy called Pepe had two horses saddled and ready for them. *"Gracias."* Rafe took the machete the youth handed him, secured it to a loop on his belt, then accepted the pistol and gun belt.

Mounting her horse, Marina watched him twirl the chamber of the handgun, return the pistol to its holster, and belt it low around his hips. "Why do you need weapons?"

Rafe stepped into his saddle, took up the reins, and touched the horse's flank with his heels. He glanced at her, his now-familiar grin in place. When he spoke it was with the same tone as before. This time she recognized it.

A challenge.

"You don't expect me to take the prodigal daughter of this fine household into the jungle and let her get snakebit, do you, *capitán?*" He led the way from the vast stables onto a two-rutted wagon road. She spurred her mount.

She would show him. If he thought her no more than a *bored little rich girl,* she would show him! She raced ahead.

The wind blew against her upturned face, cooling her, stimulating her senses. She felt invigorated for the first time since coming to this stifling tropical land. Slowing, she became aware of the country.

On either side rose the familiar jungle of vanilla vines. Riding so close to the fields now she could see the beans—yellow-green pods, some almost a foot long. Workmen in hats much the same as the one she wore tramped from tree to tree picking beans and stuffing them into burlap bags which hung from their shoulders.

She inhaled. The fragrance of vanilla hung over the

area like sweet perfume.

"The aroma comes from the curing grounds," Rafe said. "The beans are dried in a shed over almost cool coals until they shrink and are the color of brown chocolate."

She studied the plants. "I have never seen trees like these."

He laughed, though not in a derisive or patronizing way. "They aren't trees. The vanilla plant is a vine, related to the orchid family. In the wild they grow up any available tree or along the ground. Farmers plant a tree for each vine to climb. Makes harvesting easier and keeps the plants from rotting when we have too much rain."

She studied at him curiously. "Where are you from, Rafe?"

He held her gaze so intently she fully expected him to gloat over her unintentional use of his name. He didn't.

Urging his horse forward, he turned his eyes back to the road. "The mountains, where it is cool and dry and you can see forever." He looked at her then, his smile teasing. "I don't like this humid climate any more than you."

She looked south toward the range of mountains which loomed as a jagged black silhouette on the far horizon. Were those the mountains? she wondered. Was that his home?

Here and there they passed an occasional thatched-roof adobe hut. Rafe examined each in turn. "It shouldn't be much further," he said at last. "The old man is a *tzauririka*—a shaman. Do you know what that is?"

"A curandero?" she asked, thinking of the men and

women who were skilled at treating illnesses. A curandera had lived at Los Olmos when her mother was a girl.

"That and more," he answered. "A shaman has special powers over nature—rain, sunshine, harvests, deer hunts, you name it."

She smiled.

"Don't laugh," he cautioned. "Do not even smile while we are inside his hut. This is serious, deadly serious. You must comport yourself in a solemn manner, otherwise he will do . . . well, one of two things."

She squinted toward him, sure he was teasing—or mocking. His expression like his voice however was grave.

"What two things?" she asked.

"Either he will not see us at all . . . or he will put a spell on us."

"You surely do not believe such nonsense?"

Without replying Rafe pointed to a hut ahead of them on the side of a small rise in the land. Behind it instead of vanilla vines she saw cornstalks and rows of something that resembled squash plants.

"If you want to come inside," he cautioned, "you must take this seriously. We cannot offend the old man. It could prove disastrous, if not for you . . . or us . . . at least for Don Ignacio and his family."

She stared at the small hut. Cactus, palms, and a brilliant array of crimson blooms grew around the house. The dirt path, swept clean, led to a doorway, the door to which was missing. A graying set of deer antlers, the largest she had ever seen, was nailed above the entrance, to either side of which hung long strings of round, shriveled up pods—hundreds of them.

"Tell me what to do," she whispered.

Rafe dismounted and she did the same. He tied her reins along with his own around the ancient hitching rail. "See those pods?"

She nodded.

"That's peyote. They say it puts you in touch with the gods." He shrugged. "Regardless, it is hallucinogenic. If he offers you some—or anything else—take a small portion and hand the rest to me. Don't swallow any more than necessary, but do not allow him to see you reject it."

She swallowed, a reflexive gesture, then immediately stiffened her spine. "Are you trying to frighten me?"

"To forewarn you." He stopped suddenly, searching her person. "What do you have for . . . ?" Her hat was extended by its strap along her back and he studied her hair. "Those ribbons . . ." He indicated the scarlet and yellow ribbons she had used to tie her hair back. ". . . if he asks for tribute, they will do."

"But they belong to . . ."

He silenced her with a frown. "Bianca will understand. Once we get inside—if we do—do not speak."

She inhaled, exasperated at his lengthening list of instructions. He must think her a compete idiot. She started to tell him she had only slapped one man's face in her life.

"I mean it, *capitán*. Even if he speaks Spanish, which I doubt he will, do not say a word in his presence. Especially not your name. Do yo understand?"

She shrugged. Of course she did not understand. He had explained nothing but she knew he wouldn't . . . at least not for the moment.

Rafe unstrapped his holster, unhooked the machete, and rested both on the ground against the outside wall of the hut. He then stepped solemnly across the threshold.

Marina followed in his wake, trying not to cringe.

A craggy voice uttered words in an unfamiliar language. Rafe answered in the same guttural tones, after which he stepped forward. She trailed in his shadow.

Inside it was dark, the only light the shaft from the doorway and the low fire in a pit in the center of the floor. One breath of the heavy incense choked her, and she stifled a cough. *Was it, too, hallucinogenic?*

Peering nervously into the corners of the one-room hut, she saw only shadows. Additional strings of peyote hung from the rafters. The lone occupant was a man clothed in pale colors; he stepped into the shaft of light, revealing straggly lengths of snowy white hair. Indeed he must be every bit the ninety years Tío Ignacio had proclaimed.

Skin stretched like thin leather over his facial bones, giving it a taut, almost smooth, appearance. His voice quavered, the guttural tones strangely gentle. His language was unlike any she had ever heard.

"Sit," Rafe whispered. "Here."

Following his lead, she sat to the left of the shaft of light, legs crossed in front of her, with Rafe at her right elbow. Their knees touched in the semi-darkness. His presence reassured her.

Rafe spoke to the old man, again in the same guttural tones. The old man answered; Rafe spoke once more.

The shaman—Diego Ortiz, she supposed—handed

something across the fire. Two strings, which Rafe dangled between two fingers. Rafe spoke, Señor Ortiz answered, then Rafe reached over and pulled the ribbons from Marina's hair, spreading the length of it across her shoulders on either side.

"Sit up," he whispered. "Hold your shoulders back; pretend they are pinned to the wall behind you."

She did as he commanded. Across the fire she watched the shaman peer at her, his own white hair hanging around his chin and over his shoulders. For a moment she held her breath, mortified at the old man's eyes which stared straight at her bosom!

Rafe handed her one of the strings.

She cut her eyes at him, wishing she could spit in his face. Although his lips remained solemn, his eyes danced with devilment.

"Drop it in the fire," he whispered. "Be sure to hold it by only two finges and let it fall straight."

She complied. Rafe continued to talk to the shaman while tying one knot in the other string, which he then tossed into the fire after hers.

The old man muttered what sounded for all the world like the benediction from a priest in church. Speaking rapidly, he offered Rafe something else.

A pod of peyote.

Rafe held it toward her. "One bite, but don't swallow it. Remove it from your mouth as soon as I distract him."

Her jaws locked, then trembled as she nibbled one corner of the rough pod. The substance was bitter. She watched Rafe eat the rest of it when she handed it back to him. After that the conversation flowed for five minutes or so, although, even if they had spoken in

English or Spanish, she doubted she would have understood a word, so attuned was she to the halucinogen she held in her mouth awaiting the chance to spit out.

Nothing happened, however, and after a while she focused on the conversation once more. Rather, on the gentleness in Rafe's voice, the deference he showed the old man, the dignity with which he sat before him, as though he dealt with a wise and very important person.

Even when he rose to leave, signaling her to follow, he bowed in a solemn gesture of respect; she was certain she had not imagined his sincerity.

Outside, he did not speak until he had taken up his weapons and made some notes in a little book he carried in his shirt pocket. "Did you spit it out?" he demanded, handing her into the saddle.

She nodded.

"Where?"

Stunned at his question, all she could manage in response was to lower her head and stare beneath the top button of her shirt.

He followed her line of vision, raising his eyebrows in surprise, a suggestive manner, one that caused her breasts to ache even though she knew he could not see them.

Suddenly the embarrassment she had felt inside the hut returned. "What was that all about?"

He grinned, then studied the sky. "Later." In an offhanded manner he gave her leg a pat through her thick leather boot. "We're about to get caught in the daily rainstorm." Without further ado he mounted and raced down the lane in the opposite direction from the big house.

Nudging her own horse to follow, she surveyed the sky. While they were inside the hut clouds had gathered and the wind had picked up. She lifted her face to the sky. The breeze felt cool and smelled clean and heavenly, especially after the bitter-sweet odor inside the shaman's hut.

Just as the first drops hit them, Rafe made for the low hanging fronds of a palm tree. Dismounting, he caught up Marina's reins and pulled both horses beneath the sheltering branches.

Without delay, then, the sky opened up and pelted the earth with dense, heavy drops of rain. The palm fronds overlapped in such a way as to protect them as well as if they had been under a man-made roof. She pushed her hat off her head, letting it fall down her back, held there by the strap around her neck.

"Now you can tell me," she reminded him. "What did you and the shaman talk about?" She felt a blush rise along her neck. "I know it concerned me."

He stood close, observing her with a curiously gentle expression. "Señor Ortiz is not accustomed to seeing women in breeches. He wanted to be sure that I knew my companion was not a . . . ah, a man."

Her eyes flashed wide.

"He said he knew the truth because the gods told him." Laughing, Rafe held up a hand to ward off her skepticism. "His words, not mine. He noticed the way I . . . ah . . . In his tribe it isn't acceptable for men to consort with other men, if you know what I mean. He would not have helped us if—"

"How humiliating!" she interrupted "You . . . you . . . ?"

"I assured him I knew the difference, *capitán*. But he

83

wanted proof." He grinned, shrugging his helplessness in the matter once more. "How else did you want me to show him? Could you have come up with a better idea?"

She shook her head quickly, averting her eyes to the canopy of palm branches. They quivered beneath the pelting rain, and she marveled that they afforded such protection. Finally her embarrassment ebbed, and her curiosity got the better of her. "What did the strings mean?"

He didn't answer for a moment, and when she looked, his gaze held hers. His smile broadened, his eyes teased. "Sure you want to know?"

She bit her lip, swallowed the lump in her throat, and answered quickly to cover her renewed embarrassment. "Yes."

"What you call strings are actually strands of *ixtle* cactus. The peyote ritual begins with confessing . . . ah . . ."

She watched him now, forgetting her embarrassment at his own obvious discomfiture. His smile enchanted her; his eyes were warm and playful. Yet she could tell he searched for a way out this conversation.

"Confessing what?" she prompted.

"Ah . . ."—she saw the muscle in his jaw twitch— ". . . carnal sins," he finished.

"Carnal . . . ?" She diverted her eyes, catching her bottom lip between her teeth to keep her mouth from dropping open. "What . . . what did you tell him?"

Unexpectedly, yet in a natural gesture familiar from the night before, he caught her face in his hand. Her eyes darted to his; his delved deeply into hers, tugging at her heart as if with magnets. Her breath lodged midway between her lungs and her throat.

"Do not worry, *capitán*. I assured him you are pure as driven snow . . ."—his eyes caressed her face—". . . the snow atop *Iztaccíhuatl*."

His face dipped close to hers, his breath touched her skin. He was going to kiss her, she knew it.

Iztaccíhuatl. She had heard him speak that word inside the hut. "What is *Iztaccíhuatl*?" She spoke from her lips to his, from her eyes to his.

"A mountain outside the Valley of Mexico," he whispered, for to speak louder would have been senseless, they stood so close. "A mountain peak covered with snow, beneath it a simmering volcano. The name is Aztec for Sleeping Woman."

His words heightened the tension of the moment. With every fiber of her being she wanted him to kiss her, and she could tell he wanted the same and as badly. But she was frozen to respond beyond pleading with her eyes.

And something held him back.

That faraway look she had seen when he looked at her on other occasions glazed his gentle scrutiny of her lips. Suddenly the muscle twitched in his jaw again, he pursed his lips and lowered his eyes. His grin became playful once more, his words teasing. "Get rid of that peyote."

Then he dropped his hand from her face. "Rain's over. Let's go. I want to show you something before we return to your relatives' house."

One good thing about the tropics, she decided, in addition to the beautiful foliage, was that once a day a rain came to cool things off. She rode beside him in silence, grateful that he didn't speak either. Finally the intensity of the scenery helped alleviate the even more intense yearnings which had begun to stir inside her the moment she first encountered Rafael Santana standing on board her ship calling her a bored little rich girl. How would she bear the weeks ahead while they searched side by side for the *Espíritu Estelle*?

Thoughts of the *Estelle* reminded her of their reason for visiting Diego Ortiz. She hoped Rafe had been more attentive to business than she while inside that hut.

"What did you learn from Señor Ortiz?" she asked, then hastily added, ". . . about the shipwreck?"

"Bearings he claims will help us locate it." He glanced toward her, then quickly away, feeling his control wearing thin where she was concerned. "And information on the cargo. As a young man, Señor Ortiz helped load the *Espíritu Estelle* for its fateful voyage."

She turned, eyes wide. "What did he say about it?"

"He claims to have seen inside some of the crates. The artifacts he described sound like pieces from the missing treasure of Axayacatl, including a gold image of Coatlicue, mother of Huitzilopochtli, god of war."

Marina tensed, wary. Rafael Santana intended to claim all the artifacts. What if there was no gold, only artifacts? Would he leave her enough to pay the taxes? No wonder he didn't want to kiss her! If he tried now, she would slap his face. She could not allow it—not either one. He would not take all the cargo, and he would certainly not take her.

Her body, even her heart, did not concern her. She could take care of herself. Yet, how could she stop him taking all the cargo? How would she ever save Los Olmos, and she with a weakness for this man growing inside her as insidiously as a lush tropical garden?

86

She let her eyes roam the countryside in an effort to calm herself—to *steel* herself, she recanted. Pray God there was more aboard that ship than ancient artifacts.

Although it was past mid-afternoon, the sun was still hot. Steam rose from the ground after the rain, and she inhaled the sweet pungence of the earth. The tension which had built between them under the palm tree had now given way, at least on her part, to tension of a different kind, leaving her despondent, feeling betrayed.

Yet, she shouldn't. Rafael Santana had made his intentions clear from the beginning. She might not like his position, but she could not fault him for holding to it. Neither had he forced himself on her, quite the opposite. His desire for her was as evident as hers for him, yet he resisted pursuing it. Forcefully resisted, fortunately.

She would simply have to guard her own feelings, that's all. She sighed, thinking. They must proceed as two normal, intelligent people. As friends—well, perhaps acquaintances. Thinking back on their visit with the shaman, she tried to find a neutral topic to discuss. Then she recalled the ritual with the strings.

"Tell me about the cactus," she said.

Absently he turned to her. "What?"

"The cactus strings? Back at the shaman's hut. You said they are some kind of cactus fiber, but what do they represent? Why did we drop them into the fire?"

His eyes widened a notch as she spoke. Gradually, a smile creased his lips, he chewed the corner of his mouth a minute, then sighed heavily and turned his attention back to the road. "We already discussed that."

"No, we didn't."

He nodded, insistent.

"Well, tell me again. I must have missed something."

He fixed her with a stern expression. "You are getting a bit personal, *capitán.*"

"You did not get personal inside that hut?"

He shrugged. "The fibers are part of the ritual."

"Yes . . . ?"

He raised his eyebrows. "Pure as driven snow . . . ?"

Her mind struggled to recall, while her brain resisted. She felt a flush creep up her neck. "My string . . . was . . . straight?"

He nodded.

"And yours . . . ?"

A portion of their earlier conversation came to her, causing her cheeks to suddenly sting—they must be flaming, she thought—but she was somehow powerless to still her tongue. "The knot . . . ?" The words were repugnant, yet something about the subject fascinated her and she was unable to stop herself. "Carnal sin?"

She saw the muscle tighten in his jaw, the same one as before.

"I told you we could not offend the old man. He demanded penance, goddamnit. Do you know what that means? Forgive—forget. It's over, done with, finished."

She watched him struggle to control his emotions. He wasn't angry, she knew, only acutely embarrassed. And she had caused it. The conversation left her with a strange queasiness in the pit of her stomach.

Nudging her mount forward, she stared at the ruts ahead, wondering what had taken hold of her. She could not recall ever deliberately pursuing such an indelicate discussion. Not before this moment. What was it about . . . ?

When she looked at him, intending to apologize, he had halted his mount and now sat staring straight ahead. Following his gaze all thoughts of the shaman and the shameful things that had transpired inside the hut vanished.

Before her in the distance rose a magnificent structure. "What is it?"

"El Tajín."

The site consisted of half a dozen or more stone structures of various sizes and in various stages of ruin, set in a bed of jungle foliage. They rode around them an hour or more before dismounting. She asked questions as they went, and he replied. She came to think she asked the questions to hear not so much his answers as his voice. The awe in it reflected her own wonderment at the incredible sights which spread from every angle into the jungle.

"They don't look like pyramids," she said after they dismounted. She followed at a safe distance while Rafe swung the machete before them, hacking vines and small shrubbery to make a path through the tangled vegetation which grew on and around the various masses of stone.

"A structure doesn't have to be pointed on top to qualify for the term." He reached a hand to pull her onto a fallen slab. "I just came from Tzintzuntzán where the pyramids are round. I will take you there one day."

She climbed up easily, and he let go her hand, suddenly falling to his knees. She knelt beside him.

"Watch for snakes," he cautioned, but she could tell by his voice and by the intense way he tore at the vines covering a stone wall that his mind was far away from snakes. Taking the pad from his pocket once more, he began to make notes . . . sketches of the inscriptions and estimates of distances. Finally, he sat back on his heels and stared.

"*Por los dios viejos,*" he whispered, studying the strange sculptures he had uncovered.

"The old gods?" she translated. "What is this? Where are we?"

"El Tajín means the place of smoke. It was a sacred city to a race of ancient people. We are just beginning to learn about these former civilizations." Rising, he surveyed the flat stone surface on which they stood. Hands on hips, he turned first one way, then the opposite.

"You mean they—these ancient people—are buried here?"

He shook his head. "We don't think so. According to legends and the few *codices*—books—left by more modern pre-Conquest people, our pyramids are all ceremonial."

"All? There are many more sites like this?"

He laughed. "Yes, Mar . . ." As though struck in the face by the unseen hand of some ancient god, his voice stopped in mid-word, then he continued. "There are hundreds such sites around the country. One, El Tamúin is even closer to Tecolutla than this." Then his voice turned harsh. "Most were destroyed by the Spaniards."

Marina pursed her lips, surveying the area, trying to make sense of this man Rafael Santana and his disturbing mood swings. Was he arrogant, insane, or merely obsessed with the past?

"Take this place where we're standing," he was saying. "It was probably one of their ball courts."

She cocked her head, waiting.

"Most of the ancient sites included a ball court, although, the game doesn't appear to have been played for mere enjoyment."

"What do you mean?"

"Like everything else they engaged in, the ball game was a religious rite. According to the *codices,* the loser and often the winner, too, lost their hearts to the gods."

Marina cringed. "Your tone does not indicate a heart lost to . . . ah . . . to love . . ." The original meaning of her sentence faltered near the end, and she was glad she was not looking at him when she spoke the final words. She felt her lips actually tremble, and she touched her tongue to them, willing her own heart to still.

"Not even love of the gods," he conceded, following her line of vision to the grandest of the structures. Taking up his machete, he hacked a path toward it. "The gods of our ancestors were nothing like the benevolent deity we worship today. No, they required constant attention just to keep the world turning and the sun in the sky."

His enthusiasm fired hers, and she followed with a light step, hanging on his every word . . . at least until he joined them in common ancestry. After that she had a hard time concentrating on his meaning, her mind kept replaying the phrase, *the gods of our ancestors, our ancestors, our . . .*

She returned to reality with a jolt when he stopped at the base of the huge structure and she bumped into him. He was so entranced with the magnificent pyramid, however, he did not notice, except to reach a hand and draw her onto the step beside him.

Other than the broad, extremely steep staircase which led from the ground to the top platform, this pyramid resembled a square-shaped wedding cake, each successive tier being a size smaller than the one below it.

Looking upward she counted seven levels. Hundreds of openings—appearing at first glance to be windows—were carved into the side of each tier. On closer inspection the openings looked more like shelves or niches. Red and blue paint smudged with smoke was visible from some of them. She tried to imagine what it must have looked like when in use.

"What is inside?" she asked, not sure she wanted to hear his answer.

He merely shrugged. "Not bodies . . . or hearts." Then he began to climb the steps, his head erect, his back straight.

Reverently, she thought, wondering again whether he were obsessed or merely enchanted, as she was. She hastened to follow him.

Niches were even cut into the staircase on the level of each tier. At the first one, he knelt to examine the interior, again taking out his pad to jot down information.

She knelt beside him. "What were the niches used for?"

"Some say braziers were put inside them." Standing again, he stared to the top of the giant structure, then looked back at her. "Can you imagine what a sight it would have been? Fires burning from each and every niche?"

Turning her back to the staircase she surveyed the surrounding countryside. Even overtaken by the jungle as it was one could tell that the city of El Tajín had been enormous. "I never knew such things existed."

"If the Conquistadors had succeeded, even this would have been torn down or built over."

"Why?"

He studied her, his eyes now hard. Then he shrugged and continued his climb to the top. She walked beside him, matching his progress step for step. By the time they reached the top, her breath came short, but she was filled with an overwhelming sense of exhilaration. The afternoon was clear and they could see the Gulf of Mexico to the east. She thought of home . . . of the tower at Los Olmos which had been destroyed during the War Between the States, and which her grandfather had insisted on rebuilding in order to prove he could climb to the top with only one good leg, as he said. While not as grand nor as ancient as El Tajín, the Los Olmos tower represented the strength and determination of her ancestors. Again she wondered what Rafe had meant—*our ancestors*.

"Is it like this on your mountain?" she asked.

He studied her a moment before understanding, then he gazed around them. "The mountains are even more magnificent."

She recalled the awe with which he had surveyed the ruins from below, the majesty with which he climbed the stairs. Strangely, she saw him in ceremonial robes, a high priest. "This is probably closer to heaven," she observed.

"Or hell."

His answer suprised her and she looked around the place where they stood. Although the pyramid as a whole was intact, the wall surrounding the top floor lay in crumbled heaps. A brown stain, like rust, smeared much of the surface and trickled in rivulets from sluices cut down each corner from top to bottom. Like a cold wind his words combined with earlier things he had said, chilling her.

"What kind of ceremonies did they hold here?"

He held her gaze so long she was not surprised when he refused to answer. "You would have to know the ways of these ancient people to understand."

"You are the expert. Explain their ways to me."

He turned slowly making a complete circle, staring into the distance at every step. When he faced her again he peered into her eyes. When he spoke, it was as though he lectured in a classroom. "The Mexican pyramids are truncated, flat on top, to provide a platform for the altar. Obviously the priests wanted to be as close to their gods as possible before interceding for their fellow humans."

Again she examined the ruins at their feet, trying to imagine them as they had been in ages past. Finding herself in this ancient place with Rafe Santana, a place which obviously meant so much to him, affected her in a way she had not been prepared for. Standing at the top of this magnificent temple she saw them strolling the streets below hand in hand, friends, not enemies . . . lovers.

Now the lecturer, he was cold, almost indifferent, when she knew he could be warm. What held him back? What triggered his mood changes? Challenged by the enigma of the man, she stepped toward him, stopping close. She lifted her face and stared into the depths of his black, black eyes, much the way he sometimes peered into her own.

"What did they pray for, our ancestors?"

He stared back at her. She saw the vein in his neck throb. "Basic things," he answered. "Light and air and water. They believed the sun died every evening when it sank below the horizon and in order to bring it back to life, they had to feed it."

His eyes held her mesmerized. She wanted him to kiss her . . . wanted it more than ever before. This time he would. She knew it. "What did they feed the sun to make it rise again?"

"The most precious thing they had to offer . . ." With a tortured slowness he clasped her face in one hand, while with his other he caught at a loose strand of her hair, smoothing it behind her head. ". . . a living, beating human heart."

She was too conscious of his lips descending gloriously toward her own for his words to register in her brain. She lifted her hands tentatively to his chest and leaned forward.

"Marin—" His words halted abruptly.

Suddenly she saw his eyes glaze as before, watched the same muscle in his jaw twitch. But before he could release her for yet another time, she tore herself from his hands and ran to the other side of the temple. Inhaling deeply, she tried to calm her racing heart.

"I'm sorry," he said behind her, his tone light once more. "That was a dastardly lesson in ancient history."

She whirled to face him, hands on hips, glaring at him across the small distance of the temple floor. "Ancient history be damned! What is it with you? Tear out my heart and offer it to your precious *dios viejos* if you must, but get it over with. Do not torture me first. It isn't—"

"What are you talking about?"

She glared at him, appalled at her outburst. Willing herself to hush, she continued in a rush of words. "Marina!" she shouted. "It's my name, isn't it? Marina! Every time you start to kiss me, you stop suddenly. My name stops you. Marina! Zolic said Marina is a name from your past. Well I . . ."

95

While she ranted, he stared at her. When she mentioned his assistant, he spoke. "Zolic talks too much." Stuffing his hands in his pockets, he stepped to the edge of the platform and glared toward the Gulf of Mexico.

"Who is she, Rafe Santana?" Marina pursed her lips, holding her tirade inside, waiting for an answer. When it did not come, she crossed to stand at his shoulder, staring at the side of his face. She saw the muscle twitch in the side of his jaw. "Who is she, this lady named Marina who has such a hold on you that you cannot kiss another woman when you want to? And I know you want to."

Gradually, as if moved by the gentle breeze, he turned to face her. In slow motion his arms encircled her, drawing her near, pressing her tightly to his chest.

His heart beat wildly against her cheek. Tears formed behind her squenched eyelids. Why had she done this? Why did it matter so much . . . one man . . . one kiss?

After what seemed an eternity, his arms loosened and he clasped the back of her head in his hand. She relaxed against his palm and he lowered his lips . . .

This time she did not leave the matter in his hands, but lifted her face and stood on tiptoe to reach his descending mouth.

The instant his lips covered hers she knew she had been right that first time—was it only this morning?—when she had thought if he ever kissed her it would be like nothing she had ever experienced before.

His moist lips enveloped hers, stroking across them with such urgency her whole body responded. She did not know when her arms circled his neck, but suddenly her fingers were in his hair. Suddenly her arms stretched across his broad shoulders, drawing him near, while she nuzzled herself against him . . .

With the help of his hands which stroked her back, at length cupping her to himself; his tongue entered her parted lips and probed sensuously into the depths and crevices of her mouth bringing her unbelievable ecstasy and untold torment at one and the same time.

Finally he drew their faces apart an inch or so. "One day I will tell you about that other lady," he whispered. "But for now . . . trust me, love, she is no threat . . ." He kissed her softly—". . . not to you."

Marina sighed, feeling safe and secure and light-headed; satisfied, yet tormented by desperate yearnings. She stared up at the clear blue sky searching . . . searching . . .

"What are you looking for?" he whispered, kissing her once more deeply, sensually, leaving her weak and trembling and very, very happy.

When he inquired again, she smiled. "I was looking for elm trees, but I don't suppose they grow on top of the world."

He grinned. "If you think this is the top of the world, you are going to love my mountain."

She snuggled against him, holding him close, hoping against all hope this wasn't some lost dream from ancient times. "I can't wait for you to meet my grandfather. He told me about you, but I didn't believe him."

Chapter Four

By the time they arrived back at the big house on the Hacienda de Vera Cruz the sun sat on the horizon like a giant golden orb. She recalled what Rafe said about the Aztecs—that they believed the sun died each night when it set.

Thank heavens she knew better! Never had her life held the promise of so much joy and happiness! Of so much love. She could not bear it, were this night to be the end of her world instead of the beginning.

Earlier today they left the big house strangers, separated by a rift of misunderstanding. Now they returned, not as lovers, but as two people standing on a threshold of expectancy, on the brink of a wonderful discovery.

Though unspoken, the promise surrounded them as with a warm cocoon seen in the depth of their eyes, felt in the touch of their lips, forged from the fire kindled inside them. No words of commitment had been spoken. None were necessary. The time was not right.

Surely this must be the ember of which her grandmother had spoken—an ember from which love could grow. She knew without being told that these feelings were but a translation of the ardor she had witnessed between her parents and between her grandparents all her life, witnessed and longed for and finally given up for lost.

Now without a word having been spoken she felt it, too. And whether he realized it or not, Rafael Santana had been fired by the same ember. She had seen it in his eyes, felt it in his touch, without a word having been spoken. Not even her name. But that did not matter.

He didn't have to speak her name, when his every glance set her head reeling. Her name didn't matter, only the elation bubbling inside her at the lingering feel of his embrace, only the weakening sense of relief that she had not agreed to marry Burt Wilson, thereby condemning herself to a lifetime without such a love. She must save Los Olmos, of course.

Now she had a personal reason for saving Los Olmos. Now she had a future to anticipate afterward.

They had spoken little on the way back to the big house. Spoken little, but communicated much. The afternoon sun had cast their shadows like wobbling revelers ahead of them, while they took turns pointing to a laborer balancing a basket of vanilla beans on his shoulder, to a mockingbird singing from a ceiba tree, to an eagle soaring overhead. Occasionally they stared deeply, searching into each other's eyes, then quickly diverted themselves with yet another sight or sound.

After a while her giddiness subsided and she was able to chance speaking without her voice trembling.

"What did you mean . . . *our* ancestors?" she questioned.

Rafe smiled easily, his eyes warm when they touched her face. "We are mestizos. Not pure Castilian."

"We?"

"You may claim only your Conquistador heritage, but it is unlikely the blood of your ancestors has remained unmixed with Indian blood since 1591, the year of the Conquest."

"You are descended from the Conquistadors, also?"

"And from the Indians they conquered," he added firmly.

Around them the fields emptied of workers. Some men trudged home, weary from the day's labors; some walked briskly, as though the best part of their day lay ahead. The rest of her day could not possibly be better than what had already transpired, she thought.

Not until they arrived back at the big house, did she discover how right she had been.

Although Marina had worried over being late for dinner, her fears were allayed when Tío Ignacio met them in the central patio. He clapped Rafe on the back, his eyes alight with questions.

"What did you think of El Tajín? Was I not right? A site that needs exploring, eh?"

"No doubt about it, Don Ignacio. My department is definitely interested in the project."

Their host motioned Rafe to a chair, then took note of Marina. "Tía Luisa and Bianca are dressing for dinner, my dear. Perhaps you would like to join them."

Rafe's hand had remained lightly touching her shoulders while Tío Ignacio spoke. Feeling her stiffen at their host's not so subtle attempt to send her from the room, his fingers trailed down her spine to her waist, where they lingered, pressing gently, teasing.

Were she to look, his mouth would be creased with

that tantalizing grin, she was sure of it, and his eyes would glint with devilish humor. But she kept her eyes on her handsome uncle. *Are all Mexican men incarnations of arrogant Aztec gods?* she wondered.

"Certainly, Tío. I shall be happy to rest my mind from the rigors of this day." She endeavored to reply in a syrupy-sweet tone, offering Rafe a smile to match.

He merely grinned, as she had suspected he would, almost serious, yet teasing. But when she moved toward the staircase, he dropped his hand from her back, catching her fingers in a most natural gesture, while his eyes caressed her face with a sensual intensity that weakened her knees. When he squeezed her hand she had trouble tearing herself away.

Tío Ignacio appeared oblivious to their silent communication. "By the way, my dear, this message from your first mate arrived while you were out."

Taking the folded paper, she thanked her distant uncle, then headed for her room. She could play their game. If they wanted to reserve certain conversations for male ears only, she would keep her business to herself, as well.

When she opened it in the privacy of her room, however, Nick's dispatch bore an ominous warning, one she knew she would share with Rafe as soon as she dressed for dinner.

Word has spread of our intent to salvage the Estelle. Others are outfitting rigs to search for it. Someone tried to hire Pedro Ybarro, but Zolic convinced him to wait a few more days. We heard of a man who claims to know the location of the shipwreck; Zolic has gone to find him, while I provision the Stella Duval. We will be ready to sail immediately upon your return. It is not advisable to await the arrival of Giddeon and Serita.

Nick'

Studying the gown Tía Luisa laid out for her to wear to dinner, Marina calculated her chances of convincing Rafe to return to Tecolutla tonight. Slim, she realized. With the support he would undoubtedly receive from Tío Ignacio, none.

Quickly she donned the white cotton skirt and waist. The skirt consisted of three white tiers embroidered with brilliant blue flowers. A matching ruffle on the waist encircled her shoulders, and a blue sash completed the costume.

No sooner had she pinned her hair in place than a knock came at the door. Tía Luisa entered at her call bearing a magnificent pair of filigree silver earrings.

"They're lovely!" Marina hurried to the looking glass to slip the wires through the pierced holes in her earlobes. She tipped her head from side to side, smiling when the long earrings tickled her bare shoulders.

"They are yours, my dear," Tía Luisa told her. "Come now. Let us go downstairs. You have yet to meet your cousin Manny."

Bianca joined them in the hallway. "I will wear the earrings to dinner," Marina said, "but I cannot accept them as a gift."

"Nonsense, my dear." Tía Luisa insisted. "We have plenty to share, and they are part of your heritage, too."

A rush of femininity surged through Marina at the thought of Rafe's reaction to the flirty earrings and fancy dress. He couldn't call her *capitán* in such

102

a costume.

Scanning the broad expanse of black and white tiles below them, she descended the stairs half-listening to her aunt and cousin, her mind on Rafael Santana. She hoped for a moment alone with him to explain Nick's message, but when she reached the bottom step, he was nowhere to be seen.

Neither were the other men.

Lifting her skirts she stepped into the tiled foyer and tried to stifle her disappointment. The filigree work of the silver earrings whispered against her shoulders.

"Fetch the men from the study," Tía Luisa instructed a servant.

Marina straightened the ruffle around her shoulders. She could not give in to gloom this easily, she admonished. No promises had been made. None whatsoever.

"The men are not in the study, señora. They have gone into the fields."

"The fields?" Tía Luisa sighed. "I should have expected as much. Ignacio cannot resist showing off his crops at the slightest interest. Now dinner will be late."

"They are not looking at vanilla beans," the servant responded. "That old shaman, Diego Ortiz, is dead."

Marina gasped. "He couldn't be! We visited him . . ."

As one Tía Luisa and Bianca stared at their guest. "You visited that evil old man?" Bianca's eyes were round with disbelief.

"He was not evil . . ." Marina stopped her denial, recalling the old shaman's eyes upon her bosom. "I mean, Rafe was with me."

"I should have credited Don Rafael with having more sense," Tía Luisa fumed.

"How did he die?" Marina asked the servant.

The woman shook her head. *"No sé. No sé."*

Marina frowned at the woman's vigorous protest of knowing nothing. "You must know something. How did you find out about his death?"

But the woman shook her head again, this time pursing her lips.

"Old age, I am sure, dear," Tía Luisa replied. "Do not concern yourself. When the men return, we shall pry the gruesome details from them." She issued orders to the servant. "We will take our sherry here in the patio. The men will return soon."

The men did not return soon, however, so the three women dined alone. After which Marina's distant relatives proceeded to show her about the home of her Conquistador ancestors, trying to make light of the whole affair.

But Marina could tell Tía Luisa did not take the matter lightly. Indeed, Tío Ignacio would surely be greeted by a blistering tongue upon his return.

Marina was struck by the irony of the situation. All her life she had heard stories of her family in Mexico, had dreamed of meeting them, of seeing the plantation granted by the King of Spain. Now that she was finally here, she was unable to devote more than a small portion of her attention to them, for the larger share remained with the old man she had visited, on the strange occurrences which had transpired during that visit, and on the proud and arrogant, warm and sensual man who called himself a mestizo and who fired her blood as hot as braziers would surely fire the niches at El Tajín. A man who could not even speak her name.

When at last she had seen practically the entire house, carried on over Bianca's lovely fiesta gown, patterned in the current French vogue she was told, and assured her aunt she would visit her great-grandparents' graves on the morrow, Tía Luisa called for chocolate to be served on the patio, where no one spoke of the men returning soon. When Tía Luisa finished her cup of foaming vanilla-flavored chocolate, served hot this time, she rose and informed the girls it was past everyone's bedtime.

Dutifully they traipsed upstairs. Bianca hugged Marina in the hallway outside their bedroom doors. "I am so glad you have come. Tomorrow we can ride into the hills, and I will show you my favorite place in all the world."

Marina returned her cousin's embrace. She hadn't revealed her plans to leave early the next morning. She did not have the heart to argue in the light of the old man's death, nor did she know what to expect when Rafe returned.

She had no intention, however, of going to bed without learning the fate of Diego Ortiz, nor without showing Rafe her message from Nick. So after giving Bianca and Tía Luisa time to fall asleep, she tiptoed into the hallway carrying a lamp and a volume of poetry by the new Mexican poet, Manuel Gutiérrez Najera.

No light showed from beneath Bianca's door, she noticed, relieved, in passing. Downstairs she settled once more into a chair in the central patio where she could catch Rafe before he went upstairs to bed.

But Najera's poems, lovely and musical as they were, did not prove stimulating enough to keep her head from nodding, and try as she did to stay awake she soon drifted off to sleep, assuring herself she would hear their bootsteps on the tile floor.

She awakened however not to bootsteps, but to a

soft tickling on her neck. Disoriented, she saw only a fuzzy shape before her, but when she lifted her hand to rub her eyes awake, she touched someone else's firm, yet amazingly soft cheek. Her eyes flew open; her breath caught at the sight of Rafael Santana peering at her from a distance of not over six inches.

"I will pass on a midnight snack, Don Ignacio," he called over his shoulder. "Go ahead without me."

The sound of bootsteps disappeared in the direction of the kitchen. She felt a gentle tug at one filigree earring.

"What have we here? A little mestizo asleep in the patio?"

Her brain was fuzzy, not from sleep now, but from the nearness of him. She blinked her eyes to see him better. Placing her palms on his chest, she felt his heart throb beneath one of them.

He fingered a silver earring. "Pretty."

She moistened her lips. "They belonged to my Conquistador ancestors."

He studied her embroidered dress in the dim lamplight. "Tonight, *capitán,* you are every inch mestizo." His breath touched her lips, and she ached for him to kiss her.

"What happened to the old shaman?" she whispered.

Rafe's muscles stiffened beneath her hands. Leaning forward, he placed his lips firmly against her forehead. A wayward strand of her hair lay between his lips and her skin.

"What happened?" She pushed his chest, wanting to see his eyes when he answered. But he held her close.

"He died." His words whispered against her temple.

Marina wriggled away from him, straightening

herself in the chair. "What do you mean, he died? He was strong as an ox. His heart would not quit beating just like that. Not in the few hours since we visited him."

She watched the muscle tighten in the side of his face. Reaching, he clasped her face in both his hands. His eyes were so hard she flinched. At his words, she trembled.

"It would if it were ripped out by an obsidian blade."

They left the Hacienda de Vera Cruz the following morning amid pleas from her distant family, filled themselves with an emptiness of dread mixed with sorrow. Rafe gained Tío Ignacio's assurance he would send marigolds to place on the bier of the old shaman.

Tía Luisa insisted Marina return in November for the Day of the Dead, in order to place marigolds on the graves of her ancestors.

This is the Day of the Dead, she thought.

She still could hardly bear to think on Rafe's horrifying revelation the evening before of Diego Ortiz's death. As soon as she could speak following his disclosure, she had begged him for an explanation—not macabre details of the deed itself, rather the reasons behind such savagery, and who the perpetrator could have been.

But Rafe had remained stoic, refusing to speculate other than to assure her the event had taken place in the shaman's hut, not at El Tajín, which was her first thought.

"The murderer is likely some demented thief," he added.

She immediately recalled the impoverished state of the old man's hut. "Whatever could a person have thought to steal from him? And why such a . . ." In spite of herself she shuddered to even speak the words—". . . such a gruesome method of . . .?"

Still kneeling on the patio floor beside the chair, Rafe had pulled her to his chest, implanting his lips in her mass of black hair. His heart thumped steadily against her cheek and she felt secure in his arms. Curious, she thought, with him a virtual stranger.

"The peyote was gone," he had replied to the first part of her question. The second part, he left unanswered.

"Peyote?" She stirred. "A man's life for peyote?"

Rafe had tightened his hold, soothing her with strokes of his hands, which dipped beneath the bodice of her costume in the back, warming her bare skin, binding her to him as with some ethereal tether. As long as his hands continued their rhythmic kneading, she could keep the dastardly deed they discussed at bay.

"The peyote fields lie far to the northwest," he told her. "Ortiz and his tribe make a yearly pilgrimage to gather a supply to last from one trip to the next." He inhaled a deep sigh. "Small doses of peyote are generally harmless. Misused, however, it has been known to cause a particularly violent kind of madness."

The night had ebbed as they talked and soon they heard bootsteps re-enter the hallway from the kitchen. Don Ignacio took the stairs without a word.

"Where are Galván and Manny?" she had asked.

"Their rooms are in another wing. As is mine." He scooped her in his arms and rose to his feet. "Get some

108

sleep. Tomorrow I will help you understand these things."

Speaking, he had deposited her on her feet, absently smoothed the ruffled blouse across her shoulders, then bent and kissed her soundly on the lips. "I'm sorry I missed dining with such a pretty little mestizo."

Suddenly she recalled the message from Nick. "Wait." She withdrew the folded slip of paper from where she had tucked it beneath her sash. "We must discuss this tonight."

Carrying the paper to the lamp, he read the brief message, glanced overhead at the already lightening sky, then spoke. "We will leave at first light, if you are—"

"I will be ready."

Tío Ignacio would not hear of sending his long-lost distant relative away on horseback, so they departed the Hacienda de Vera Cruz in a fine carriage drawn by a matched team, driven by a Vera Cruz vaquero.

The driver climbed to his box, and Tío Ignacio stomped toward the house calling for Manny, whom he was sending along as the family escort, since he was the only family member not to have had the opportunity to meet Marina.

Tía Luisa suddenly recalled the lunch she had ordered packed for them. She sent Bianca to fetch a servant to fetch the basket, then unable to trust that nothing was forgotten, hastened to the kitchen herself.

Marina settled onto the plush leather seat beside Rafe. "I feel as though we have journeyed into Hades and are lucky to be escaping."

He turned his back to the coach window and stared deeply into her eyes. "It wasn't so bad as all that, *capitán,*" he whispered. "Not *all* of it."

Her eyes held his. "No," she whispered. "Not all."

His gaze drifted over her proper Victorian blouse and camel traveling suit. Lifting a hand, he fingered her bare earlobe. "Must we leave the little mestizo behind?"

She smiled in spite of her gloom. Rummaging quickly through her tapestry satchel, she withdrew a cloth packet, unbound it, and held up the filigree earrings. "I have no intention of letting you forget my Conquistador ancestors."

Rafe cocked his head, watching while she attempted to slip the wires through the holes in her earlobes. When she was unable to do so without a looking glass, he took them from her hands and proceeded to thread the slender pieces of sliver through the holes himself.

His hands were too large for the task. His knuckles skimmed her face, his fingers tickling her ear and cheek in the process. By the time he finished and sat back to admire his handiwork, her senses fairly cried for his touch. Her eyes searched his. Quickly, he leaned forward and brushed her lips with his own just before Manny opened the door and entered the coach amid renewed goodbyes from the Cortinases.

They pulled into Tecolutla four hours later, Marina's ears ringing with her cousin's recitation of the family history and of the vanilla business. From time to time Rafe had been able to divert the conversation to Diego Ortiz, quizzing Manny about any laborers on the hacienda who would have committed such a crime. The young man could offer little by way of explanation, other than the fact that their Indians had lived at Vera Cruz for centuries and nothing of the sort had ever happened before.

"Peyote is insidious," Rafe mumbled.

Manny shrugged. "Along with magic mushrooms, poppies, and dozens of herbs."

Rafe agreed. "Some of the others have medicinal applications, though, when used by knowledgeable persons."

Marina listened to them, more conscious of Rafael Santana's overwhelming presence than of the conversation. The ride was long and uncomfortable and every time he shifted positions, his knees grazed hers, sending warm tingles along her skin. When now and again his shoulder bumped hers, he took advantage of the situation to nudge her a fraction longer than necessary, as though to assure her he was affected by her presence, too.

Once she awoke from a nap to find her head against his chest and his arm draped casually around her shoulders. She lay, eyes closed, for a time, enjoying the feel of his heart beating against her cheek. Finally the yearning to respond to his nearness became so great, she sat up in defense of her own actions. *If only Tío Ignacio had not seen fit to send an escort!*

Rafe lifted his arm when she stirred, resting it along the back of the seat, not touching her now, but near enough to be a constant reminder of what might have been. "Your head was bobbing like a *gallina borracho*. I didn't want you to crack your neck."

"I felt like a drunken goose, too," she laughed. "Drunk on too little sleep." *And too little of you.*

111

Nick met them at the gangplank of the *Stella Duval*. "Zolic isn't back yet, but I expect him before nightfall."

Manny returned to the Hacienda de Vera Cruz without so much as taking time for a meal, saying his father needed him in the fields, and Marina and Rafe climbed the gangplank.

Before they left for the Hacienda de Vera Cruz the day before, Rafe had moved his belongings into the only unoccupied officers' cabin. With the new twist in their relationship, having Rafe near excited . . . and troubled her. Until her grandfather arrived, she was captain of the *Stella Duval*. In charge of the ship—and its mission. A mission in direct conflict with Rafe's own goal.

When they came aboard, Nick stared hard at Rafe, then turned eyes on Marina. "I need a word with you . . . before Zolic returns."

"Is there a problem with my assistant?" Rafe asked.

Nick hesitated, started to shrug, and Rafe spoke again.

"Let's hear it." He turned to Marina. "Why don't we go below . . . ah, *capitán?*"

She shot him a warning, then with a heavy sigh nodded toward the companionway. "Follow me."

She led them to the Captain's dining room with a stiffened spine and a gnawing in her stomach. How would she ever manage? Moments before she had ridden beside him desperate for his love. Now she faced him as captain of this vessel, and his jesting tone worried her. Would she be able to convince him that she ran this ship? That she was in charge of this expedition?

When she motioned toward the chairs around the

112

table, Rafe reached to pull hers out, but she stopped him with her hand on his. The mere touch of his skin shot fiery streaks up her arm, followed by aggravation at his . . . at his . . .

Piercing him with a steady gaze, she wrested the chair from his hold. *At his what?* His arrogance? His devotion? Or merely his polite behavior?

Obligingly he released the chair and seated himself to her left, in the place she indicated with a curt nod. His slight grin confirmed her first impression: His arrogance was unequaled by any man she had ever met.

As was his devastating attack on her senses.

Nick poured coffee all around before seating himself to Marina's right.

"What's the problem with Zolic?" Rafe asked again.

Nick stared into the steam arising from his coffee cup. "It might not be anything, Don Rafael. I . . . well, fact is, he makes me uncommonly edgy."

"How?" Marina asked.

Nick frowned, keeping his thoughts to himself.

"What did he do while we were away?" Rafe asked.

"He is . . . well, señor . . ."

"Fact of the matter, Nick," Rafe assured the first mate, "I'm not overly fond of Jesús Zolic, myself, but he is a necessary part of this expedition. Unless, of course, he has proved himself unfit."

Nick shook his head. "I wouldn't say unfit. He is . . . Well for one thing, he sits on deck cross-legged, playing spooky music on an instrument he carved out of reeds."

"That's precisely what I mean," Rafe explained. "The instrument is a reed flute of a kind played by old Aztec priests and holy men. As I understand the custom, learning to play those reed flutes advanced a person along the road toward becoming immortal."

"Immortal?" Marina frowned at the ridiculous nature of this conversation.

Rafe grinned at her, a bit self-effacing. "I know it sounds far-fetched. But the truth is, Jesús Zolic is Mexico's leading authority on pre-Conquest Aztec culture. He will know immediately whether the cargo on board the *Espíritu Estelle* is genuinely Aztec." He returned his attention to Nick. "Anything else?"

"Well, he eats peyote, and I—"

"Peyote!" Marina gasped.

Instantly, Rafe clasped her hand, holding it where it lay on the table. She met his serious eyes.

"I will allow no one on board who—" she began.

"Hold on," he said. "I told you taken in moderation peyote is relatively harmless. Zolic has likely been eating the stuff all his life. I've never known him to abuse it."

"How would you know?" she challenged.

"You mean, how could I tell if he abused peyote?"

She nodded, unable to keep her apprehensions at bay.

"If he consumed too much, we would all know it. In addition to acting noticeably drunk, he would be anxious, his speech would be slurred. He would hallucinate." Rafe turned back to Nick. "Did you notice any of those signs?"

The first mate shook his head. "I have only seen him eat the stuff when he plays that flute."

"I know your concern," Rafe told Marina, "but it's unwarranted in this case. Peyote use is common. As long as he doesn't abuse it . . . well, we need him."

114

"You are certain?"

He held her troubled gaze. "I would never endanger . . ." At length, he drew his eyes away from hers and swept the room. "I would not endanger this crew. We'll keep an eye on him. He may act the lunatic, but . . . well, one of his ancestors was an Aztec priest and he sometimes goes overboard in his obsession."

She entertained the notion of asking him who was calling the kettle black, but with Nick in the room decided discretion was the better road to tread, especially with the long hours and days—and nights—ahead of them.

Zolic returned before they finished their coffee, bringing an end to the conversation. As usual he was charming and Marina wished she had studied more of Mexico's history before she journeyed here. With Zolic an expert, perhaps she could persuade him to teach her something about her own ancestry. Her chance at such an education came sooner than she had expected.

Nick was eager to set sail, so Marina, Rafe, and Zolic followed him to the chart room. On the way Marina discussed with Nick the pilot charts Giddeon had obtained from the United State Hydrographic office showing the path of the hurricane that had sunk the *Estelle*. She walked at Nick's shoulder, followed by Rafe, then Zolic. She spoke a bit louder than necessary, wanting Rafe to be aware of her involvement as the expedition's captain.

Nick, however, was the acknowledged shipmaster, charting the courses, then keeping to them. The chart room was small, too small for these four people, two of whom were overly conscious of each other's every move, so as soon as she felt her position had been established, she excused herself to change clothes.

Once she got back into her pants and boots, she assured herself, Rafe Santana would cease treating her with the deference a lady expected in the parlor.

Her own—her parents'—suite was warm and welcoming. She passed through the small office and parlor into the sleeping chamber where all the amenities of home were provided—or as nearly as one could expect.

Struggling out of her traveling skirt and waist, she recalled the opulence of the Hacienda de Vera Cruz and with it the horrors which had transpired during her visit. Except for the few hours when she returned to her bedroom the night before, this was the first time she had been alone since receiving the news of Diego Ortiz's death.

She slipped off her chemise and petticoats, poured water from a pitcher into the brass basin set in a walnut cabinet, dipped a cloth into the water, then stopped. On impulse she found a bottle of her mother's gardenia scented toilet water and splashed a good measure into the basin, telling herself the fresh scent would help her feel cleaner, what with the humidity and all.

Another good thing about wearing breeches, she thought, donning a fresh chemise and bloomers, was the minimum number of undergarments required. A woman would have to be crazy to wear corsets and petticoats in this climate.

The loose fitting linen blouse felt good after her high-collared proper waist. Absently she pulled her hair into a taut knot at the top of her head, securing it with steel pins and an ivory comb.

She was almost out the door when she recalled her rebozo. After she had attained a certain age—actually the edict had more to do with body development than years, she realized later—her father decreed that in order to go without a corset in front of the vaqueros, she must tie a scarf around her shoulders.

It was not her shoulders which were in question, her mother quickly assured her when Marina had failed to grasp the intent behind her father's demand.

She sighed, securing the light woolen wrap in a knot over her bosom. It would be hot, but better hot than . . .

Back on deck she realized her spirits had revived considerably. The familiar surroundings and her own comfortable clothing gave her a feeling of security, even though she was hundreds of miles from home.

When she reached the doorway to the chart room, Rafe glanced up from the maps he and Nick still discussed. Like dry brush in a firestorm, her determination that he see her as a captain in man's clothing incinerated at his bold appraisal.

Nick grunted a greeting, his attention on the charts, while Rafe stared straight into Marina's eyes, holding her mesmerized by the raw desire she saw there. Methodically his eyes left hers to peruse her body from head to foot, intently, as though he strove to memorize every detail.

Heat rose quickly within her. She shifted self-consciously from one foot to the other. Her breasts chafed against the soft pleats of her chemise; awkwardly she tugged at the knotted ends of her scarf.

The movement brought Rafe's attention back to her eyes, where he acknowledged her discomfiture with his infuriatingly arrogant grin, practically suffocating her with silent, sensual suggestions. He moved around

Nick, never taking his eyes from her.

She swallowed. "I will leave you two to your work. I did not intend to disturb you."

At her last words, his eyebrows raised a notch, and she saw the muscle in his jaw twitch.

Spinning, she fled to the poopdeck above the cabins. Whatever was she to do? She must get hold of herself. She must. And she must convince Rafael Santana to keep his mind off her and on their expedition.

Picking up binoculars, she scanned the distant horizon. She would talk to him. That's it. She would explain how his conduct was making her position as captain of this vessel untenable. He could either behave himself or he would have to go.

"How was your visit to the Hacienda de Vera Cruz?" Zolic's voice boomed like a cannon through her agitated senses. When she turned, his gentle smile relaxed her.

"Hello, Señor Zolic. The trip was . . . actually, it was a devastating experience."

"Hummm . . . ," he commiserated. "Sometimes families do not live up to one's fantasies of them."

"My family was fine. While we were there an old man was murdered."

"Oh?"

She studied him a moment, considering, then barged ahead. The opening offered, she seized the opportunity to set him straight on the rules of the *Stella Duval*.

First she explained about the death of Diego Ortiz. "The evidence points to theft. Señor Ortiz was in possession of a great quantity of peyote, which was taken at the time of the murder."

Jesús Zolic favored her with a concerned expression.

"May I speak frankly?"

She nodded.

"Peyote is an hallucinogenic cactus. It has been used in rituals for more generations than we know. Taken in small amounts it can relieve many . . . ah, shall we say physical needs—hunger, thirst, as well as more carnal demands. I'm sure you can see the benefit of this in a dry land where food is scarce and a person's . . ."

He shrugged. "I will not bore you with details, but suffice it to say peyote has practical applications. It also has a religious aspect, enabling the user to perform dramatic mental feats; some say it is a way of communicating with the gods."

Marina rested her arms on the rail, waiting, hoping she would not have to ask the question she wanted answered. Zolic did not disappoint her.

"Most people of Indian heritage who seek greater knowledge of the gods use peyote from time to time."

"The gods, Señor Zolic?"

"I use the term loosely, meaning nature." He confronted her, eye to eye. "I also use peyote on occasion. I am a student of the culture of my ancestors."

Reaching into one of his trouser pockets, he withdrew a slender reed, notched at intervals along its length. Placing the instrument to his lips, he began to play a haunting melody. "This is one of the revered instruments of the Aztecs." He extended the small reed to her.

She turned it over in her hands.

"By the simple reed one was brought nearer to a state of divinity." His tone reminded her of a traveling preacher she had heard one time in Victoria.

"You seek divinity, Señor Zolic?"

"I seek knowledge, Lady Marina."

Spoken in his resonant voice, carried on a tone of reverence, the name shocked her. *What would it sound like, spoken by Rafael Santana?* Indeed, the name, intoned now, filled her with a sense of majesty . . . or was it Zolic's near regal bearing?

She held her chin high. "Tell me about the lady named Marina."

"That is best left to Santana."

"No." Her eyes searched the sea, seeing instead Rafael Santana's glazed expression when he thought of her namesake. "He cannot speak of her, and I must know the truth."

"Ah, so that is how it is? I should have suspected."

Marina bit her bottom lip to still its sudden trembling. *How what was?* she wondered. But she could not bear to ask. Then Zolic began his tale.

"The truth about the original Lady Marina is difficult to decipher from the legend which has grown up around her."

"The legend will do."

"Yes. That is what we are dealing with, is it not?"

She shrugged, hugging her arms about herself, unsure what they were dealing with, hoping Zolic would tell her, hoping she would not regret hearing.

"Very well. Lady Marina, then. She probably was of mixed Aztec, Mayan blood. High class, some say of noble birth. Her name was Ce Malinalli, an unlucky name given in the Aztec custom according to the position of the stars at the time of her birth. Reports have her as intelligent as she was beautiful, and that must be fact, since much of her life is written in the history of the Conquest."

Zolic's gentle beginning gave way to emotional tones, at times awe-filled, at others very close to abhorrence, as when he mentioned the Conquest. Marina listened intently to both his words and to his tone of voice when he continued.

"Who knows the reason, but as a young woman, she was sold into slavery and was given to Cortés along with a bevy of other young women to pleasure his men. That was when her name was changed."

Here, Marina noticed, Zolic's voice became harsh, faltering with suppressed anger.

"The high and mighty Spanish priests cared nothing for the lost souls of the Indian maidens, only for their soldiers' salvation. They demanded the young women be baptized with water and given Christian names before the men were allowed to . . . ah, to bed them."

Where before Marina's clothing had clung to her skin, stuck there by the hot damp air, she now felt prickles keen along her arms. She clasped her hands about herself; her heart pumped beneath her arm.

"Do not feel sorry for her," Zolic demanded. "From that moment on Ce Malinalli ceased to exist; in her place, a traitor was born. Some excuse her performance as an act of self-survival. More accurately, it was her cunning nature. Her beauty and intelligence helped her work her way into the presence of Cortés himself. She became his counselor and interpreter—she spoke several Indian languages and soon learned others, as well as Spanish. Then there was the carnal side to their relationship. A cunning woman knows how to foster herself on a man who can act as her weapon. She even bore the *great* Conquistador a bastard son. But above all, Malinche, as she is known today, was the strategist behind the Spaniards' destruction of Tenochtitlan, our sacred city. Some among Cortés's own men gave her credit for the success of the Conquest. She is the traitor of all things Mexican. She is our national Judas! She stole our heritage!"

Marina had listened, enthralled as the story unraveled. When Zolic came to the end of his recitation, his revulsion rang clear in her ears, and she felt herself sway with the magnitude of his anger, with the revelation of what this meant to her—and what she in turn meant to Rafael Santana.

"Now I come bearing her name, following in her footsteps, seeking Mexico's national treasures." She spoke into the wind and her words were tossed back like stones, where they sank to the bottom of her heart. "Don Rafael Santana, Minister of Antiquities, faces a modern-day Marina."

"You would have to know him to understand how important his work is to him," Zolic said. "It comes before all else."

Before all else. Her head reeled. "You have known him long?"

"Since our days at the University of Mexico. He is filled with the past, Marina. Obsessed, is a better word. His one aim in life is to restore the treasures lost in the Conquest, or what is left of them. And you my dear, like the first Lady Marina, stand in his way. I am afraid he sees you as a reincarnation of the original."

That night when she dressed for supper, she considered changing into a flirty costume and the silver earrings Rafe called mestizo. She decided against it, however, hoping by wearing breeches she could

122

disassociate herself from the original Lady Marina. Zolic's story had depressed her beyond her worst expectations. At the same time, she argued, it gave her ammunition with which to fight her ancient foe . . . and his.

Cookie served a meal of roast chicken and baked squash which they had purchased, Nick told her, from an Indian woman nearby. She cringed at the bare mention of an Indian woman. She must talk with Rafael Santana soon. She could not run a ship, much less keep him from taking the cargo while their personal feelings were in such turmoil.

Ordering a round of sherry with dessert, she listened to talk of the coming voyage. When everyone had finished, she excused the table, then turned to Rafe who sat at her left elbow, as he had done earlier in the day.

"May I see you on the poopdeck before you retire?" She strove for an emotionless voice, for strength of tone, for a businesslike approach.

"By all means, *capitán.*" He waited until she rose from the table before he rose himself, making no attempt to escort her from the room.

On deck the night air hit her face with a humid blast, albeit somewhat cooler now that the sun had set. She strode across the planks and climbed to the higher deck without pausing; Rafe matched her stride. Her mind spun in reels, her stomach swirled, and her arms trembled. How would she ever manage?

Reaching the rail, she lifted her face to the dark sky. Wisps of clouds hung low, leaving a space of darkness between them and the stars higher up in the heavens. She thought of Los Olmos and for a moment wished herself there.

Rafe stopped beside her. She felt his eyes on the side of her face. She clung to the rail until she could force herself to look at him.

Her breath caught at his nearness and she took a small step backward. "We must get something straight—two things."

His eyes pierced hers. When she didn't continue, he spoke. "I'm listening."

She swallowed, took a deep breath, and prayed her voice would not tremble. "First, I am the captain of this ship. Second, I am not Ce Malinalli."

He stared at her, not the slightest sign of a smile on his lips, no hint of teasing in his eyes. The only movement she saw was the clenching of his jaws, then the familiar twitch. His eyes bore into hers, but she could not read his thoughts. Finally, he relaxed.

"So, which do we tackle first?"

"Neither, as a joke," she retorted.

Turning away from her, he rested his forearms on the rail and stared out to sea. She wished she knew what he was thinking.

When he spoke, it was to the sea. "You object to me calling you *capitán?*"

"Yes. At least, in that arrogant tone of yours."

He turned his head without moving the rest of his body, studying her over his shoulder.

"I was unaware of my arrogance, *capitán.* Explain it to me."

"You know perfectly well what I mean. Your male superiority. Your derisive tone of voice. Taking charge of everything. Pulling out my chair—you would not hold a chair for any other captain."

"In other words, I am not to treat you like a lady?"

"On board this ship I am not a lady, I am the captain. For you to act otherwise undermines my authority."

He faced her fully. "I never intended to undermine your authority. However"—his eyes devoured her face; she watched his jaw twitch—". . . I am hard pressed to forget you are a lady."

"I know," she conceded. "As soon as I realized the problem, I changed into breeches. That way you will not notice . . ."

Her words faded at the look on his face, one of utter astonishment. "What did I say?" she asked quickly.

With infuriating slowness his eyes traveled her body from the scarf knotted at her bosom to her tiny waist, across her tight belly, and down, down, down . . . then back to her questioning eyes. Of a sudden he drew her to him. "*Por los dios, capitán,* do you not know how you tempt me, wearing that get up?"

She felt his heart beat against her and knew her own echoed his in its frenetic pace. For a moment she gave in to his comforting presence—for a moment. Then reality returned.

When she stirred, he drew her back and lowered his lips to hers. Just as their flesh touched, she jerked away.

"Wait. Please, Rafe. We must settle this."

"All right," he said, disgust clear in his voice. "What else do we need to settle? You are the captain. I will not undermine your authority. I will treat you with the deference you demand . . . deserve. In fact, if it will satisfy you, I will avoid you . . . while in the presence of others."

His hands tightened around her arms. "But damnit, you called me to this empty deck in the middle of the

125

night." His gaze melted into hers. "Now you stand here with . . . with the moonlight dancing in your eyes, with your lips begging me to kiss them." His voice softened, then became increasingly husky. "And *capitán,* those doeskin breeches fit your hips like a thick coating of hot butter."

His hands found the knot of her scarf. ". . . and this scarf hides . . ." As he spoke his hands slipped beneath the scarf and cupped her breasts through the thin layers of her chemise and blouse.

Mesmerized by his words, inflamed by his touch, she was unable to tear her eyes from his, unable—or unwilling—to ease her body away from his welcome handling.

"You cannot have the treasure, Rafe Santana." The words came out much weaker than she intended. She tried to stir her anger. Wasn't this exactly what she meant when she called him arrogant? But his eyes caressed her, as did his hands, which supported her breasts while his fingers rubbed tantalizing circles around her nipples.

"What treasure?" he mumbled lowering his face gradually, his eyes holding hers captive.

Her heart beat out of control against the edge of his hand; he could feel it, too. Of course, he could. He knew exactly what he was doing to her. But she was powerless to stop him. It took enough strength to keep her lips from reaching for his.

"The cargo on the *Estelle.* You cannot have it."

"What if that is not the treasure I want?" His lips were so near hers she felt his brandy-scented breath whisper hot against her skin. Still his eyes would not release her.

Her body swayed against him, and she felt herself drowning in the desire in his eyes. She might as well have been swept overboard, as much good as her struggling mind was doing saving her from his seduction. Or was she seducing him? Why else had she called him out here, except for this?

"What other treasure . . . ?" she whispered before she even knew she had done so.

His eyes burned even hotter at her teasing and she felt a thrill rush through her body at having pleased him.

"You," he whispered. "You, my little mestizo." But before he covered her lips with his, she regained a measure of sanity, struggled free, determined now to settle the misunderstandings between them.

"I want you to say my name."

At her words, he froze. His loving gaze turned to stone. He dropped his hands from her breasts.

Instantly she regretted the change of mood—missed his loving touch, ached at the chasm created between them by the mere mention of that long-ago lady. "You need have no fear of me," she whispered. "I am not a ghost from the past."

"I never said you were," he snapped.

She sighed. "No, but you cannot even say my name, and that is ridiculous. It isn't fair for you to treat me as though I am a reincarnation of Ce Malinalli."

He had turned toward the sea; now at her words, he glanced over his shoulder, a retort ready. But the sight of her . . . her serious eyes, her troubled expression . . . stilled his lips. Lifting a hand, he stroked her cheek and ran a thumb over the outline of her lips. "Well, aren't you?"

Opening her mouth she touched his thumb with her tongue, sending spirals of electricity down the length of her body. His hand trembled against her face and she saw the muscle in his jaw twitch and she knew he experienced the same anguished, yet wonderful sensations she did.

"Would it help if I told you why I need the cargo?" she whispered.

As in slow motion, he pulled her against his chest, and she felt the familiar beat of his heart, an erratic beat that told her he cared as much as she did.

Determined, she drew her head back and began her story, telling him about the Burtons and later the Wilsons wanting Los Olmos. How they were now trying to accomplish through the courts what two generations earlier they had failed to gain by force. In a straightforward manner she told him that the only way to save the land was to pay taxes which had already been paid, and the only way to do that was to salvage the cargo on the *Estelle* to raise enough money. When she finished, she lay her head back against his chest and reveled at the feel of his strong arms and the beat of his dear, dear heart.

"Salvaging cargo from a sunken ship is a long-shot at best," he said. "Why don't you sell this vessel? The *Stella Duval* would surely fetch enough to pay the taxes."

"You don't know much about ranching," she sighed. "In lean years—drought, flood, or blizzard—cargo we haul on the *Stella Duval* provides our only income."

"Still, there must be a better, more reliable way to save a ranch than finding sunken treasure in the middle of the Gulf of Mexico."

128

She looked at him when she replied, her words forced through stiff jaws. "I can marry Burt Wilson."

For an eon his eyes held hers, soft and hard, pleading and caressing, branding his expression into her brain.

"I said . . . *better.*" He kissed her then, covering her mouth with his lips, devouring her sweetness, tormenting and thrilling her with the stroking, caressing rhythm of his lips.

When she clasped her arms about his neck, her breasts burrowed into the taut muscles of his chest, bringing an ache to her nipples. Grabbing fingers full of his thick hair, she pressed the length of her body against his.

Clad as she was, only two layers of cloth separated her thighs from his, her belly from his, and as he pulled her body closer a rush of heat deluged her. She moved against him, resisting when he slipped one hand between them. But when he again cupped her breast, the sensual ache inside her only increased, and she moaned into his lips.

Lifting his face, he stared at her with such longing, her heart throbbed. He watched the fire in her eyes beg him to love her. Fumbling with the closure on her blouse, he finally managed to slip a hand beneath the fabric. At his touch, she gasped, filling his hand even fuller with her bountiful figure.

He watched the pleading increase in her eyes, as his thumb found a nipple and teased it to a firm peak. Then slowly he lowered his face, found his way through her garments and captured it in his mouth.

She shuddered at the intense pleasure this brought, coupled with an equally strong and unfamiliar yearning. Her heart pounded against his mouth, she could feel it herself; she knew he must be able to. Twining her fingers in his hair, she pressed his face to her aching breast, clutching him to her, willing him to never stop, while at the same time, other parts of her body wept for a consummation she could only imagine.

As though anticipating her need, he slid a knee between her legs, lifting her onto his thigh. Unconsciously her body responded, as his stroking leg sent spirals of ever increasing desire through her system.

Suddenly her reeling head cleared and she opened her eyes to the stars above. "Rafe," she whispered, surprised by the huskiness in her own voice, "See, Rafe? I am flesh and blood . . . a living woman. I am not a ghost . . . nor a reincarnation of someone else."

Cupping her buttocks with one hand, he lifted her sensuously along his thigh. His lips tugged at her breast.

"See what you do to me, Rafe? No ghost could respond to you like I do."

Slowly he set her back on her feet, bracketing her legs with his own. He moved his face to hers and pressed her tightly against the length of his most uncomfortable body.

"No other *woman* could respond to me as you do," he told her between labored breaths. "Nor I to any other woman. Never like this."

She knew then she had lied when she told him she could marry Burt Wilson. She could never marry Burt Wilson, not even to save Los Olmos.

Not now.

Not after Rafe Santana.

Chapter Five

They sailed the following morning and for the next week Marina Cafferty had trouble keeping her mind on the cargo of the *Espíritu Estelle* and off the man who intended to steal it from her.

That he had already stolen her heart was no longer in doubt, at least to her mind.

That she longed to *give* him her body was equally undeniable.

The ember that sparked when first they met grew inside her now by alarming degrees, and she lay awake long into the night filled with an emptiness she did not understand, aching in a way she had never done. She had even taken to leaving the door to her suite unlocked, in case he came to her in the night.

But he did not, of course. For no matter his arrogance, Rafael Santana was a gentleman. She knew that. And the *Stella Duval*, though understaffed for the original voyage, now teemed with people, what with the addition of Jesús Zolic and Rafe himself, and the arrival of Pedro Ybarro and his salvage crew the evening before they sailed.

No, Rafael Santana did not come to her in the night, and their few stolen moments only added to her craving for more of this man and the wild and primitive passion his mere presence engendered inside her.

The hard-won restraint required to work beside him day after day, however, proved a blessing in disguise, for it allowed her to become acquainted with Rafael Santana the person, quite apart from Rafe Santana the lover for whom she yearned. Although enlightening, however, her increasing knowledge did not diminish the mystery of the man. In many ways it only added to the enigma. Such as the first time he examined Pedro Ybarro's diving equipment with Ybarro's crew working well within earshot.

Marina had come to think of Rafe as possibly the most arrogant man she had ever met, often wondering from whence came the softness he showed on occasion. But the man who examined the diving equipment was an inquisitive little boy exhibiting no sign of pride or haughty behavior.

She smiled yet, recalling how he lifted the diving helmet with its self-contained breathing device over his head. As it settled onto his shoulders, he had dipped his knees mocking the heaviness. His eyes glinted from behind the glass port; bringing his face close to hers, he grinned in delight. She saw his lips move, heard his mumbling.

Struggling with the apparatus then, he had removed it from his head, oblivious to his tousled hair. Her fingers twitched to smooth it back for him.

"How does this contraption work?" he questioned Ybarro, who along with his crew checked the equipment they had strewn about the deck.

Ybarro shrugged. "Just does."

Undaunted, Rafe hefted the compressed-air container which a diver strapped to his waist. "Everything is so heavy, the mask, this metal container. Obviously the diver sinks to the bottom, but how does he come back up?"

Ybarro raised his face and Marina had trouble not laughing at his quizzical frown. "Do not worry, Don Rafael. We have yet to leave a man on the bottom of the sea."

Ybarro's truculent reply did nothing to dim Rafe's curiosity. He traced the air hose from the container to the opening in the helmet with his fingers, frowning in concentration. "I'm impressed." He turned his attention to the force pump used to compress air. "Amazing."

"In your search for antiquities, you have never dived?" Marina asked.

He shook his head. "In fact, I've spent so much time in old ruins I haven't even sailed as much as most men."

"Practically everyone at Los Olmos is a sailor," she said. "My grandfather, of course, and Nick's father, who was one of his mates aboard the *Estelle*. My own father was a Federal Marine Corps officer stationed in the Gulf of Mexico during the War Between the States."

Rafe cocked his head. "I thought Texas was part of the Confederacy."

"It was, but my family is a motley group, part this, part that, a mixture."

His eyes softened at her words, becoming playful. "I am glad to hear that, *capitán*."

133

"Even Conquistador," she challenged.

His arrogance returned in full force. "And Indian."

Suddenly she knew that if she could unravel the mystery of Rafael Santana's aversion to the Conquistadors, she might also find a way to destroy—or blunt—his arrogance.

At present she had little time to worry over such things, for it took all hands to sail the vessel and to determine the exact location to begin diving. Nick converted true headings to magnetic and had Zolic and Rafe help him adjust the binnacle globes.

Fortunately the weather held to warm and clear. This time of year was noted for hurricanes, a fact her grandfather had warned her about before she left Los Olmos.

"Watch the sky," he had admonished. "At first hint of bad weather return to port. You life is more valuable to us than any old piece of land. We can always start over somewhere, so long as we are alive and healthy."

The fifth day out Zolic was sure they had found the right location. Checking charts and compass readings, then adjusting them with the figures Rafe had obtained from the old shaman and Zolic from his source—a fisherman, he said, whose nets had hauled in a rusted piece of the *Estelle's* hull with their catch—the crew concurred.

The sixth day dawned with a brilliant exhibition from the rising sun. Marina waited for Rafe at the rail on the upper deck where they would greet the sunrise together, as had become their custom, their private moment alone before the ship came to life. She stared, transfixed by the multi-hued splendor, thinking how frightening it would have been, living in pre-Conquest

Mexico where people believed the glorious sun died every night when it set.

Then she felt him. Clasping her shoulders from behind, he kissed the nape of her neck, showering her with a wave of golden sunbeams every bit as magnificent as the sun itself.

"Good morning, *capitán*," he muttered against her neck, kissing his way to her face, nipping an earlobe with his teeth, finally claiming her lips in a sound, arousing kiss. After which, he turned them to face the sunrise.

She snuggled against his chest, reveling in the beauty of the moment. "I will never witness a sunrise again without realizing how lucky I am."

He rested his chin atop her head and stroked her arm through the sleeve of her soft linen blouse. "For someone who hasn't been fed in over three hundred years, the old man appears mighty healthy."

"That's fortunate," she sighed. "I don't have a heart to spare." Overcome by an urgency deep inside, she lifted her face to his. Their gazes held, vibrating with the tumultuous beat of their hearts. "I've given mine already."

His lips covered hers, devouring, exploring, teasing her with wonders unknown, with promises she knew instinctively she had been born to experience . . . with this man. Every night after she went to bed, she thanked her grandfather for telling her about him.

"So have I." He smiled at her sunbathed face, vibrant with anticipation—and desire. "Never dreamed when I did it would be to the captain of a sailing ship."

The clanging of Cookie's breakfast bell interrupted them. Rafe spoke softly into her face, his voice husky.

"I am going to be in serious trouble if I don't get away from you soon."

She snuggled shamelessly against him. "Me, too."

Suddenly he took her face gently in his hands, and when he spoke this time, it was to address a different matter.

"There's something I have to say."

She listened, puzzled at his serious tone.

"If we find the *Estelle* today, I . . ." His eyes held hers. "Whatever we find down there, saying we find anything at all, we will work it out. I know you are worried, but don't be. No matter what we find in that shipwreck, we will work things out. Do you understand?"

Tears stung her eyes. Still flushed with passion, her body went limp in his hands. Quickly, he drew her tightly against the length of his body.

"No matter what it is," he repeated, "we'll work it out. I couldn't bear to lose you, not ever, not for any reason."

A flurry of excitement soon gripped the entire crew. The air practically hummed with it, and after breakfast no man straggled to the deck where the diving would begin.

Pedro Ybarro took charge of his three-man crew—Juan DeLeon manned the force air pump, while Pedro's two brothers, Carlos and Gordo, prepared to take turns diving. Gordo would go first; Carlos helped him dress.

"It reminds me of the ritual of dressing the matador," Rafe said in hushed tones.

Garbed in a rubber-coated canvas suit and rubber-ized boots, Gordo began to resemble his name, though he was far from overweight beneath all the equipment. Marina recalled Rafe's observation that the diver would sink to the bottom, wondering herself at the prospect.

Gordo looked to Pedro for last minute instructions, while Carlos attached the metal air canister to his belt, then checked the air hoses. With a curt nod and a slap on the shoulder, Carlos indicated everything was in order.

After which Gordo himself slipped the heavy metal and glass helmet over his head and Carlos, assisted now by Pedro, secured and checked it.

The first dive did not produce treasure. It did, however, confirm that they had discovered a shipwreck. Gordo returned from the dive, ecstatic, describing what he had seen as soon as Carlos unlatched and removed the diving helmet, ". . . timbers from a hull, iron spikes, bands that possibly fit around trunks."

"Nothing else?" Marina asked, her mouth dry.

He shook his head and Pedro spoke up. "If it's the hull we found, we're too far inland. Let's move this rig. By nightfall we may have found what we're looking for."

"Nightfall?" *So soon?* Pedro's words whirled through her brain as all hands manned the lines and the ship glided further east. How happy Tata would be. And Rafe.

And she herself, unless . . . He had said they would work things out, but what did that mean? Would he give her enough of the cargo to pay the taxes, even if they found only artifacts? He had said her share would come from the Bustamente estate. What if nothing belonged to the Bustamente estate?

Carlos made the first dive at the new location, with Gordo now attaching Carlos's air tank, checking Carlos's hoses, securing the helmet around Carlos's neck. Then Carlos dived into the placid sea, and the crew stood by, waiting . . . fantasizing . . .

Worrying.

Feeling Rafe looking at her, her eyes darted to his. He held her troubled gaze, clapping her about the shoulders, a friendly gesture, not romantic here in front of the crew, his hand rough against her arm. He intended to reassure her, she knew, yet . . .

His words echoed through her brain: *We will work things out . . . we will work things out . . . we will . . .*

How could they work things out? How could they possibly, when their purposes were at such odds? She should never have let him come along. She should never have fallen in love with him . . . never . . .

"It will work out, *capitán,*" his husky voice assured her. "Do not worry so much."

She clasped him about the waist, the crew be damned.

As before when the diver surfaced all eyes peered over the rail, hoping for a glimpse of his face through the port hole, hoping to see him wave a prize over his head—a chunk of gold, perhaps, or the image of some ancient deity.

This time they were not disappointed. It was obvious from their first glimpse of his eyes through the glass.

"He's found something!"

"For sure and certain!"

"What do you suppose it is?"

Anxiety quickened Marina's pulse. She felt glued to the deck and could not budge to get a closer look.

138

Instinctively, she knew she did not want to see.

"What is it?" someone asked in a befuddled tone, after which, she dared peek toward the surfacing diver.

"Oysters," Rafe said, his soft voice not quite masking his expectancy.

"Attached to a piece of the hull," Nick acknowledged.

"The hull of what?" Marina asked.

"Could belong to any ship that sailed during that era," Pedro agreed, scraping oyster shells from the wood.

Two additional dives that morning added no more credence to the discovery.

"It's an oyster reef," Carlos informed them. "An enormous one. Built up around a shipwreck."

"We'll make it out," Pedro said. "These things sometimes take months."

"I don't have months," Marina objected.

"Other times it is only a matter of days, señorita," he shrugged. "After siesta, we will dive again."

After siesta! No one had exerted himself enough for siesta. She wanted to demand the crew work through the afternoon. Wanted to, but she dared not, even though she was the captain.

In this hot, humid climate the divers needed time to recuperate. She must not push them. Scanning the sky, she inadvertently caught Rafe staring at her. His brief shake of the head infuriated her, as if he were telling her not to ask the men to forego siesta.

Turning on her heel, she fled to the companionway to avoid making a fool of herself.

He followed, caught her arm, and held on when she shrugged to dislodge his grip.

"Like Ybarro said, it takes time. But you cannot

139

deprive the men of siesta."

She squinted at him, then averted her head. "I do not intend to—"

"I know you, *capitán,* you were—"

"After one week you *think* you know me. You don't!"

"Five and a half days, as of high noon."

Whether it was his tone of voice, soft and understanding, or the fact that he had kept track of the time since they met, she was not sure. Whichever, his words brought tears to her eyes. "I don't mean to be difficult."

"You're not. You are edgy like everyone else—only more so." Turning her toward him in the narrow passageway, now vacant of anyone except the two of them, he caressed her face gently with his eyes. "You have more to be edgy about . . . *we* have," he added, kissing her tenderly, yet fully.

The noon hour miraculously passed, and Pedro Ybarro himself cut short the required time for siesta. Marina's spirits lifted a measure, although she was not exactly sure why. Nothing had changed. Nothing.

Just as Carlos prepared to jump into the water for the first dive of the afternoon, a ship was sighted steaming toward them at a fast clip. Pedro called his brother back to the deck.

The cutter belonged to the Federales, a fact which gave everyone additional cause for concern.

"We are doing nothing wrong," Rafe assured the group. "As a representative of my government, I will handle them."

As it turned out it was the Minister of Antiquities for whom the Federales had come. They brought an urgent message which he discussed at length with Capitán

Jaminez of the Federales, then with Zolic, and finally with Marina herself, leading her toward the opposite end of the deck, away from the eyes and ears of the crew and Federales.

"I have to go back with them," he told her. "There's trouble at a place called Xico."

"Where is that?" she asked, wanting instead to beg him not to leave. At the same time, this could be what she had prayed for. If they found the cargo before he returned . . .

"In the mountains," he answered. "Not far from the port of Veracruz. It won't take long."

"Can . . . ah, can't Zolic go in your place?" she protested, quite against her will.

"I suggested that. Capitán Jaminez says the messenger was adamant. It's an uprising of sorts; the Federales think I can talk sense to the Indians."

Her eyes had widened while he spoke, and he hastily added, "There's no danger. Grave diggers stole Xilonen, their corn goddess, and they believe their crops will fail unless she is returned."

"What can you do?"

"Convince them I will get her back for them."

"Can you?"

"They think I can move mountains," he chuckled, cupping her face in the palm of his hand. "You know better, of course. But it would be a perfect time to show you my mountain. Will you come with me?"

If he had expected to see fear in her eyes, he would have been disappointed, but as he told her earlier, he knew her well by now, and what he saw was what he had expected—excitement . . . briefly, before reality dimmed it.

"I can't leave the ship. Not now."

"Nick can handle things. Pedro was right . . . salvage efforts take time. We'll be back within two days. Nick can run the ship that long."

"I know, but . . ."

"But what?"

She bit her lip, wondering how to speak her mind without offending him. "I need to be here when the cargo is brought up."

"For that matter, *capitán,* so do I."

"You have Zolic."

"And you have Nick."

Their eyes locked—hers confused, his now begging.

"Please," he whispered, nipping her lips with his. "We won't be away long . . . only a couple of days, three at the most. The Federales will take us to Veracruz. We'll catch the train . . . it will take us very close to our destination."

She pursed her lips, thinking, desperately trying to condone such an obvious disregard for duty. "My grandparents could arrive any day."

He tried to read her thoughts, her fears, but he couldn't. His own he knew well enough.

"How would they feel about it? I mean . . . about me taking you off into the hills—the two of us, alone, no *dueña*—me, a stranger?"

Her heart labored to beat, reminding her of an engine trudging slowly, deliberately uphill. She gazed deeply into his eyes, into his glistening, glorious black eyes. She heard her grandmother speak of embers, Tata of love falling out of elm trees. Finally, she clasped her arms around his neck and brought his face close to hers. "They would . . ." She paused, searching for the right word.

"Understand?" he questioned, doubtful.

She smiled. "No, I think they would be very happy."

They left within the hour; it took that long to convince Nick that Marina would be in safe hands, what with Rafe being the respected Minister of Antiquities, and accompanied as they were by a force of Federales.

He didn't like it; she could tell that by the way he stood on deck grim-faced, hands stuffed in his pockets, watching her ride away in the Federales' cutter, refusing to return her wave. He couldn't very well have kept her from going, however, short of tying her to the mast, and in the end they both knew it.

"Pack light," Rafe cautioned. "But expect cold weather?"

"Cold?"

"Cold, not cool. And we may have to walk the last few miles over a rocky trail . . . up hill."

So she wore her boots and a fawn-colored split skirt which she hoped would not show dirt too badly. In a small satchel, she packed a change of underclothing, an extra linen waist, and her hair brush. Not until they were aboard the Federales' cutter waving goodbye to the *Stella Duval*, did she recall her white voile nightgown and wish she had brought it along.

No sooner had the thought entered her brain than her body responded, her breasts chaffing against her chemise, her mind recalling Rafe's lips there, and she felt a blush rise along her neck. Fortunately Rafe was engaged in earnest conversation with Capitán Jaminez, otherwise he would have been sure to notice.

For he had been right earlier, she conceded to

143

herself. In the short time since they met, he had come to know her very well; more often than not he anticipated her emotions before she even knew she experienced them.

Pray God the problems between them worked out! He said they would, and she wanted to believe him. But then the Indians at Xico believed he could move mountains, and like he said she knew he could not.

The only thing she knew for sure he could do was light her own soul and body as with fire from the sun itself.

Evening had fallen by the time they sailed into the harbor at Veracruz, and even though the Federales secured a carriage to take Rafe and Marina straight to the depot they had an hour's wait for the next train to Mexico City.

"Time enough to eat," Rafe told her, securing them a second carriage and directing the driver. The restaurant was nice but not pretentious, noisy, and aflush with people in festive dress.

"I will embarrass you," she whispered after they were seated at a table Rafe specifically requested. He had been greeted by a good dozen well-dressed men, some lovely ladies, and all the waiters. She smoothed straggling strands of hair from her face.

"Leave it." Reaching, he fingered a wisp dangling over her forehead. "I like it a little mussed . . . like you . . ."

He didn't complete the sentence, not in words, his eyes did it for him.

A waiter materialized, greeting Rafe as a long lost friend, and Rafe ordered. *"Sopa de camarónes, huachimango a la Veracruzana, y cerveza para los dos."*

The waiter bowed, left and Rafe stared at Marina across the flickering candle in the center of their small table. "We'll start with shrimp soup," —his words were totally unassociated with the light in his eyes, which in itself brought tingles to her skin—"followed by red snapper. They have a special sauce for red snapper. I hope you will like it."

She smiled. "I will."

"And beer . . . I didn't know what you drink, so I ordered . . ."

"Cerveza is fine."

"I don't want you to think me arrogant . . . for ordering . . ."

"I like beer."

"Tell me about Burt Wilson."

The question, accompanying as it were, their order for dinner, stunned her into momentary silence. At length she shrugged. "There is nothing to tell."

Rafe plucked one of the red roses which surrounded the candle in the centerpiece, reached across the table, and stuck it behind her left ear. Twisting his head, he scrutinized his work. "You need your mestizo earrings."

She smiled, discomfited by the attention they must be drawing, enthralled nonetheless by this handsome though disarmingly prococious gentleman who took her breath with his sensual teasing. His next words, she knew, were not in jest.

"There must be something to tell. You were engaged to him."

"No," she insisted. "There was nothing to it. It was . . ."—she shrugged—". . . different."

"Different? How?"

"Different." She flushed at his intense scrutiny,

wondering how crazy he would think her should she tell him what Tata said about elm trees. "We were friends, that was all. We aren't even friends anymore."

He demanded an explanation, of course, which she supplied.

"So his proposal for marriage surprised you. Why?"

She squirmed under his questioning, but for some strange reason, she wanted to talk about it, wanted him to know the truth, however simple and ridiculous that truth might sound when she spoke it.

Their shrimp soup came and the beer and he continued at his probing while they ate.

"I didn't want to marry him, I told him so. But he convinced me."

"Convinced you how?"

"By assuring me that . . ."—alarmed at the words she was about to speak, she dropped her eyes to her soup and concentrated on extracting a plump shrimp— ". . . that love takes time to grow," she finished quickly.

For the longest time he remained silent, and she dared not raise her eyes. When at last she did he was staring at her.

"Well?" he questioned. "He could be right."

She frowned across the table, surprised at his response. He agreed with Burt Wilson? Rafe, who fired the very pores along her arms with a mere look? Rafe, who set her soul ablaze with a need she no longer even questioned?

"A fire must have something to start from!" she retorted, swallowing a gulp of cerveza. "An ember," she quoted her grandmother, ". . . something."

Her empty soup bowl moved under the hand of the waiter; she watched a steaming platter slip into its

146

place, a fillet of fish covered with a red sauce.

She felt rather than saw the waiter leave the table. Tentatively, she picked up her fork and started to eat the red snapper. Still, Rafe did not speak.

One bite, two. She wiped her lips with her napkin. Another bite.

"There was no ember between you?" His voice was so soft she would have missed his reply had her ears not been attuned for it.

She shook her head, wiped her lips, self-conscious now since her outburst, unable to look at him.

"How did you know?"

She swallowed the fish in her mouth. Curiosity took hold of her self-consciousness, and she looked up. "What?" His eyes held her captive.

"How did you know there was no ember?"

She shrugged, wondering how to explain such a thing. Did he not understand, for heaven's sake? "There just wasn't."

"You had no . . . ah, no *physical* contact?"

Her eyelids flared at his suggestion.

"No, no." He held up both hands. "I didn't mean . . . ah, I meant kisses . . . kisses. He did *kiss* you?"

Quickly, she lowered her eyes. "Once."

"Once?"

Suddenly she could take no more. She faced him again, furious this time. "I have had enough of your arrogant questions. It is *my* personal business. Just leave it alone."

She tried to take another bite, but the cheese had cooled, and so had her appetite. She placed her silverware in her plate, and immediately a waiter took it away.

"Dessert?" Rafe questioned, his voice light, friendly.
As if nothing had happened! "No, thank you."

"I'd like some sopapillas. Will you share an order?
And coffee? It's good here—fresh. We're surrounded
by coffee plantations."

Coffee plantations? How could he think of coffee
plantations, while she . . . ? She nodded, not knowing
what else to do. She certainly couldn't storm out on
him. She had no place to go and no way to get there if
she had.

Mariachis strolled the room with their guitars,
playing for first one table, then another. When she and
Rafe entered the restaurant she had thought it a
romantic idea; now she hoped they would not come to
this table. No, she *prayed* they would not stop here.

"How could you betroth yourself to a man you had
only kissed one time? I mean, since there was obviously
no—what did you call it?—no ember ignited during
that first kiss?"

"I told you I didn't want to marry him," she replied,
weary of the discussion, weakened by it.

"But he convinced you that you would *learn* to love
him."

The sopapillas came—a platter heaped with little
fried puffs of sweet tortilla-like dough, sprinkled with
powdered sugar, and drizzled with honey. The waiter
placed a small empty plate in front of each of them.
Rafe lifted a sopapilla onto her plate, then licked the
honey off his fingers.

She felt queasy and tired and very, very confused.
Why was he pursuing this subject so relentlessly?
Didn't he know what she meant? Did he not know how

it felt to be consumed by fire . . . a fire started by a sudden and inexplicable ember . . . brought on by a stranger?

"How did you know you wouldn't? Learn to love him, I mean?"

"Rafe, stop. I'm tired of this conversation. Obviously, you have never experienced such a thing or you would understand. It is like . . ."—suddenly she thought of an explanation Jorge often used, Jorge who lost his eyesight in the war—". . . like trying to explain to a sighted person how it feels to be blind. Impossible."

He studied her in an almost innocuous manner, although the twinkle in his eyes should have warned her, she realized later. "So, his kiss . . . his one kiss . . . did not ignite an ember . . . because there was no ember."

"Finally you comprehend," she retorted.

"What was it like? That kiss?"

"Rafe!"

"I want to know," he insisted. "I realize it's a bit personal, but—tell me."

She gritted her teeth, recalling her exact thoughts about that one, miserable kiss. How could she tell him that? How could she tell anyone? Yet she knew well enough that he would hound her through the next three days and even back on the *Stella Duval* if she did not put an end to his ceaseless questioning.

"Like kissing a cold tortilla, if you must know." She bit off a piece of sopapilla, in her anger a larger bite than she had intended. Honey dripped from her lips, down her chin.

He laughed. A hearty, resonant, all-the-way-from-the-gut laugh.

She reached for the honey with her fingers. "It was not funny," she insisted, recalling how she had cried all night.

Suddenly his hands were on hers, scooping up the dripping honey. "I'm sure it wasn't," he answered, his voice sober, soothing—confusing after his persistent pursuit of the answer he had then laughed at.

Her eyes found his, and he held her gaze, while he dipped a corner of his napkin in his water glass and proceeded to wash her chin. She was beyond caring what the other customers thought. They were his friends, after all. Not hers.

"But I had to know," he continued. "I'm sorry if I sounded arrogant, but ever since you mentioned that you could marry the bastard to save Los Olmos, I had to know if you really would. No," he corrected, "I had to know if you *wanted* to marry him."

"Well now you know," she answered, finding it difficult to speak around the lump rising in her throat. "I didn't, I don't, and I never will."

Her body trembled. Her shoulders burned, and she felt like the candle in the centerpiece, melting down to the core.

Finished with her chin, he sat back and sipped his coffee. "Drink up. We have to be going soon."

She studied him, wishing she felt as relaxed as he looked. The coffee soothed and at length she decided she could speak without her voice trembling.

"Now it's my turn."

He looked at her grinning. She thought she detected a bit of wariness in his eyes. Well, he had better be wary.

"And don't dare say we are out of time until I finish,"

150

she admonished.

Deliberately he took out his watch, perused it, then winked at her. "Ten minutes?"

"Tell me about the women in your life."

He pursed his lips, his eyes zeroing in on hers.

Quickly, she amended. "No. I know you have experienced more than one simple kiss, and that it would take more than ten minutes to relate all your conquests, besides which, I don't even want to know—"

"What do you want to know?"

Did she detect relief in his voice? Hopefully she could pierce it as easily as he had pierced her own tranquillity a moment before—and discover some answers in the process.

"One question." She watched his face for every reaction, not at all sure she trusted him to tell the truth. "Since you are obviously past the marrying age, why . . . ah, why have you not married?" The moment the question left her lips, she thought of another, even more pressing one—what if he already was married?

He straightened in his chair, then leaned toward her. Holding the coffee cup in both hands, he rested his elbows on the table and stared deeply into her eyes.

"First, I'll answer the question you did not ask. I am not married. Never have been."

She caught her lips between her teeth, unnerved at the alacrity with which he read her mind, or seemed to. "And the question I asked?" she prompted.

He studied her a moment longer, perused the table, then looked out at the crowd.

If she had wished to merely unnerve him, she had succeeded, she saw that in a minute. What she really wanted, though, was an answer to her question. *Or did she?*

"Perhaps I should amend my question. Who is the woman you have waiting? And why are you out running around like this?"

He flashed her a grin. "There is no one waiting for me, much to my mother's regret. If she had her way, I would have been married off years ago. As you said, I am past my prime."

"I said no such thing. I asked—"

"I know—I will answer. I owe you that." Again, he looked away from her. "I'm not against marriage. I used to think it would be a nice way to live. But I've never met a woman who would share my lifestyle."

"They told you so?"

He shook his head. "No. I never found one . . ." He fidgeted, took out his watch again, looked at it, snapped it closed, then cast her one of his slight familiar grins. She could tell he was self-conscious. Well, he deserved it.

"Actually, *capitán,* I never met a woman who would drink beer with me . . . before you."

By the time they boarded the train, her emotions had quieted down and they talked easily again . . . friend to friend, except for the ache deep in her belly and the tingling up and down her arms. She ignored them as best she could.

When Rafe found an empty place toward the end of the sparsely populated car, she settled herself on the bench seat next to the window.

Hefting their bags to stow in the overhead rack, he grinned. "Something else I never found in a woman— one who could travel as light as . . ." He weighed their

152

traveling cases in separate hands. ". . . lighter than? . . . myself."

As the train lurched forward, he sank down beside her and their journey began . . . a journey to where, she did not even know. All she knew was that she liked where she was at that very moment, liked the dreamy feeling that suffused her sitting next to this man.

"Tell me, Rafe Santana, what else do you require in a woman, besides that she drink beer and travel light?" Her voice teased, and he laughed easily.

"Well, let me see . . ." Suddenly, he faced her, staring deep into her eyes. She swallowed back a lump at the intensity she knew he saw there.

Then he averted his gaze to the pitch blackness outside their window. "She must like to climb pyramids. I climb a lot of pyramids."

For a moment she was transported to the top of El Tajín, lost in the magic of his kiss, of his embrace. Although few passengers sat around them on this late evening run to Mexico City, there were too many to pursue that kind of thinking. Forcibly she diverted her attention.

"In other words," she began, "when you find this woman, you do not intend to leave her in . . . ah, in a hut in your village while you traipse around the country looking for antiquities?"

He chuckled. "No, *capitán,* I would not leave a wife at home in a hut in my village. Why go to so much trouble to find one if I don't intend to share my life with her?"

She studied him, knowing his teasing was not that at all, knowing hers wasn't either. The need for him grew inside her, numbing her arm where it brushed against his even through the layers of clothing that separated their skin. She knew she should change the subject, but a thrill from somewhere deep inside urged her on, that and the need to know everything about him. "In your travels around this vast country, you must surely have found many women who enjoy climbing pyramids."

He shook his head. "Climbing pyramids was only an example—a taste, if you will—of the hardships a woman would encounter in a life with me."

"Such as being allowed only one light-weight traveling bag?"

He nodded, grinning. "Among other things. Although I cannot imagine a woman who would willingly leave behind her perfumes and laces and ballgowns."

"Tell me why you think a woman would need a ballgown on top of a pyramid?" she demanded, cocking her head, teasing, testing, probing.

"My point, exactly."

"Either you don't have a very high regard for women, Don Rafael, or you have not met very many."

He laughed. "You are wrong on both counts, *capitán*. I do indeed have a high regard for women, and I have met many . . . very many."

At her grimace, he laughed again. "I consider three sisters, three sisters-in-law, and a doting mother *many*."

Her eyes widened.

"And all of them out to marry me off to each and every other sister, cousin, and society woman in every town from the City of Mexico to Madrid."

She sighed in an exaggerated fashion, shaking her head in mock disbelief. "Such resistance!"

"Regardless of what you think, I'm not that arrogant. Other than, brief encounters . . . those ladies have no more wanted me than I wanted them."

"Brief encounters?"

He straightened himself in the seat, scanning the car in an absent-minded fashion.

"There have been many . . . brief . . ." Her voice trailed off at the image of him in the old shaman's hut, the knot in his string . . . carnal sin he had said . . . brief encounters? Were they one and the same?

A challenge lit his eyes when he turned to her. "Now, as you said in the café, it is my turn. You know my requirements in a woman. What would you require from a man . . . a husband?"

She returned his bold stare, hoping her trembling did not show. "I have already told you."

Holding her gaze, he moistened his lips with his tongue, sending messages spiraling through the tense space between them. "Yes, I recall," he said in a too quiet voice. "Someone to light an ember."

After a tense moment that felt more like an eon, she nodded, then quickly tore her eyes from his, surveying the room herself this time. "So you see, our requirements are of disparate natures."

He didn't reply immediately, but squared himself in the seat, then slouched down, propping his feet on the empty seat facing them. One arm slid beneath her along the back of the seat. His fingers traced her ribs on the far side, tickling, causing her to flinch.

"I don't think so," he said at last. "I think we want exactly the same thing, you and I."

She did not reply. There was nothing left to say. He had said it all. And it was all true. She lay her head back on the seat and propped her own boots on the opposite cushion, letting her split riding skirt fall gracefully around her leather-clad calves. Silently she feasted on the multitude of complex emotions assailing her—peace and chaos, confusion and understanding, and something wonderful and soft and painfully demanding which she dared not put a name to, lest it vanish into the night.

"Don't get too comfortable," he suggested. "We are almost there."

She blinked open her eyes. "At Xico?"

"We can't make Xico tonight. We will stay at . . . at a place I know."

Stretching above her, he pulled their bags from the rack where he had previously placed them. Sitting down again, he rummaged through his own, larger one. "Put this on." He handed her something that looked like a brilliantly hued blanket. "A poncho."

"I know," she answered, "but . . ."

"You are not cold?"

His eyes found hers then, and he grinned. "When we step outside into the cold mountain air, you will need more to keep you warm than . . ." His words trailed off in the huskiness of his voice. She watched the muscle in the side of his face twitch, just before he slipped the other poncho over his own head.

Outside the air was bracing. She stretched her stiff muscles, staring at the inky black sky which glittered with millions of bright, shiny stars. The moon winked from high overhead. Four hours since they left Veracruz, and it felt like no more than a few minutes.

"Is this your mountain?" she asked recalling his promise to take her there.

"Not the one I meant." He led her across the

boardwalk, their bags slung over his shoulder.

"Welcome home, Don Rafael!" the station attendant greeted them in Spanish.

"*Hola, Pepe.* Can you rouse Benito, Alberto, and Jaime for me, *por favor?*"

The attendant scurried off, and Marina smiled. "So this is your home."

He shrugged, ushering her toward the depot office. "One of many, *capitán.*" Inside the crude building, he motioned her to a seat. "We have a good hour's ride, yet. I will try to secure a carriage . . . or wagon."

She cocked her head. "Is that how you usually travel?"

"No, but—"

"Your usual method will suit me."

His eyes danced in challenge. "Without even hearing what my usual method of transportation might be?"

She nodded, returning challenge for challenge.

"In that case, we will take horses. I keep several in the stable here."

She sighed. *At least she hadn't talked herself into an hour's walk at midnight—although . . .*"I would rather ride a horse than sit on a wagon seat any time."

A young boy—eight or nine years at the most, she judged—burst into the room. "Don Rafael!" He caught Rafe around the waist. Rafe bent and tousled the boy's hair.

"Sepio, I need a favor." He led the boy toward the doorway, speaking rapidly and directly to his face. Marina was able to catch neither his words, nor his meaning.

The boy however seemed to, for he nodded, sprinted to the door, but Rafe caught his arm. Digging into his

157

pocket, he pulled out a wad of bills, which increased the boy's excitement.

"*Andale,*" Rafe told him. "*¡Andale!*" He turned to Marina. "Ready?"

By the time they walked the three or so blocks to the stables, she knew what he meant about the weather being colder in the mountains.

"I wish it were daylight so I could see where we are," she said.

"After this we will travel by day. Midnight isn't the safest time to be on the road, but . . . well, you heard the Federales, I am needed . . ."

"I know," she whispered beneath her breath, then added quickly, "I don't mind. I'm enjoying the trip."

At the stables several horses stood in the aisle between the stalls, saddled and stamping in the lantern light. Three men held the reins.

"Benito, Alberto, Jaime, meet Señorita Cafferty. She is coming to Santa Elena with us."

The men greeted her and she returned their "*Holas,*" much of her attention directed instead to their dress, specifically their crossed bandoleers of shells, the pistols at their hips, and the rifles in saddle scabbards. For a moment her throat went dry. *What in heaven's name was she getting herself into?* Then Rafe spoke and her fears vanished at the security he instilled in her with the mere tone of his voice.

He grasped her waist, lifting her into the saddle. She didn't tell him she had not needed an assist since she was three years old and figured out how to lead her horse to a stump from where she could climb up. She did not say as much, because his hands felt wonderfully sensual and warm on her body, even through her layers

158

of clothing.

"I can use a rifle," she said.

"No need," he replied, offhandedly. "The bandits in these hills have never yet preyed on a group—only single riders and sometimes those traveling in pairs."

"Even so I would like to be able to defend myself."

Without another word he disappeared around the end of the stalls and returned thumbing shells into a rifle, which she then stuffed expertly into the empty scabbard at her knee.

The men joked among themselves during the next hour, but she and Rafe spoke little as they wound in and around the hills, climbing ever higher and higher, sometimes emerging into high mountain valleys which appeared only as a vast blackness in the night, sometimes riding single file up a narrow trail.

But they had no need to speak, she thought. Already tonight they had talked enough to straighten out many things between them.

And many remained to be settled. Vividly she recalled for the first time in hours the cargo of the *Espíritu Estelle*, the largest mountain looming yet ahead of them in the days or weeks ahead.

Finally, after passing many huts and several small villages of adobe houses, they came to what looked in the dark like a walled city, one found in pictures of medieval times. Walls of varying heights were topped by towers, three that she saw, all different, imposing.

"Where are we?"

"Home," he said.

"Home?

"Our destination for the night, *capitán*," he replied. One of their riders dismounted and swung wide the

159

heavy wooden gates, allowing them to enter the compound.

"What is the name of this town?" she asked.

He chuckled. "It is only a house, not a town . . . the Hacienda de Santa Elena."

She scanned the walls, while he took her reins and held his arms toward her. Without hesitating she slid from the saddle into his arms. "It's huge," she mumbled.

He squeezed her a moment, then turned to the men who had accompanied them. *"Buenas noches y gracias,"* he thanked them, bidding them good night.

"De nada," each in turn assured him. "For nothing—you are welcome." They disappeared in the darkness, leading Rafe's and Marina's horses, as well as their own.

Rafe ushered her toward a portico in the center of the largest portion of the building. Their feet had barely touched the bottom step, when the oversized wooden doors creaked open, and a large woman came toward them carrying a lantern.

"Don Rafael! Welcome—"

At sight of her Rafe dropped Marina's hand and bounded up the stairs embracing the woman. "Consuelo! Sorry to roust you from bed this time of night." He reached for Marina, pulling her up beside him.

"This is Señorita Cafferty. You prepared a room for her?"

"Sí, y un baño y pozole. Sepio dice . . ."

"Pozole?" Rafe questioned. "Chuy must be home. He is the one you cook pozole for."

Consuelo nodded happily.

"Is he . . . ?"

"He is fine, *hijo*. Do not worry. Tonight the bulls did not get him; tonight he was the winner. The governor awarded him two ears and one tail."

Rafe sighed; when he spoke, Marina heard relief in his voice. "*Y Ma . . . ah, la señora?*

"*Doña Alicia es en la cuidad,*" Consuelo replied rapidly—"Doña Alicia is in the city." "*De la familia, solamente Chuy es en casa.*"

"Only Chuy is home," Rafe echoed. "I will see him tomorrow. *Gracias,* Consuelo. You run back to bed. I will show the señorita her room. You gave her . . . ?"

"*La alcoba de Sophía,*" she supplied.

"*Bueno,*" he agreed. "Sophie's bedchamber is good. The señorita can see to her own bath . . ."—he winked at Marina—". . . unless she prefers to rough it, while I whip us up something to eat. *Buenas noches, Consuelo.*"

The woman handed him the lantern. *Buenas noches.*

"*Gracias, Consuelo,*" Marina called after the woman. The words stopped her, for she turned beaming eyes on Marina for the first time since they were introduced. After a moment's inspection, she responded in a cheerful voice, "*Bienvenida, Señorita Cafferty.*" Welcome." Then she padded down a darkened corridor and out of sight.

Rafe led Marina across the cavernous foyer to a wide stone staircase. She stumbled after him as in a dream. "These are friends of yours?"

He cast a strange grin back at her before replying. "You might say . . . off and on."

She hurried to keep up with him. "But this is an hacienda—built by the hated Conquistadors," she accused, unable to resist the chance to tease him about a subject he usually approached with such rancor.

Tonight his response was different.

He squeezed her hand. "I knew you would give me a hard time. But I also thought you might welcome a soft bed."

His tone was light, his words probably not intended to incite passion, she decided. Nevertheless, they did.

"La Hacienda de Santa Elena," he continued, "was built by one of Hernán Cortés's own lieutenants. It is one of the oldest, grandest . . ."

The second foyer at the top of the stairs opened onto wide dark hallways in three directions. Rafe pulled her along without missing a step. *He must be very familiar with this place,* she thought, confused not for the first time by the complexities of Rafael Santana.

With hardly a pause, he pushed open an ornately carved wooden door and led her into a room which fairly glowed in the light of several lavish lamps and one huge chandelier. Her breath caught in her throat.

"You are certainly full of surprises," she whispered. "If this is what living on the trail with you is like, I'm certain you will find more applicants than you can guess."

Striding across the room, he tossed her satchel to a bench at the foot of an elaborate four-poster bed and proceeded to a wardrobe which he flung open and began rummaging through.

"Use anything in here you wish. Sophie won't mind."

Sophie won't mind? Anxiety stirred to life within her.

He tossed something that looked like green silk onto the rich wine-colored bedspread, then continued to search through the wardrobe.

Sophie won't mind? Alarm pounded through Marina's veins with heavy thuds, reminding her of their horses hooves clopping across the rocky trail earlier tonight.

"Who . . . ah, who is Sophie?"

The question brought his head out of the wardrobe, which she had expected it would. He stared at her a moment, then hedged . . . at least, that is what she heard in his voice.

"Sophie . . . ?" His eyes studied her face. "Sophie is Chuy's sister."

Marina felt her knees grow weak. Quickly she turned, scanning the room to disguise her emotions. In one corner she saw a tub with gleaming brass faucets. *Running water this far from a town?* What was this place? Who lived here?

When he emerged from the wardrobe, his voice was apologetic, but his words were not the ones she needed to hear. "I'm not very good at choosing . . . ah, things. If you would rather have something else . . . look in the wardrobe."

He crossed to the door. "I'll leave you to bathe . . ." —*did his voice sound nervous?*—". . . will twenty minutes be enough?"

Mutely, she nodded, staring at the strange woman's clothing on the bed.

"Good." He grinned. "In twenty minutes I will return, bearing food."

She bathed, not because she wanted to, but because she was unaware of her actions. Confusion ranked closely behind despair in her mind, caressing her as the rose-scented lather caressed her skin. Intended to soothe, the warm water only irritated, burning her skin like the thoughts of Rafe Santana and this . . . this

163

Sophie . . . burned her heart.

By the time she dried her body and reached for the clothing he had chosen, anger grew rampant within her, increasing by the moment. The idea, after cajoling her deepest secrets in such an arrogant manner! The idea, bringing her to a room he had shared with . . . with someone . . .

Chuy's sister, indeed! Who the hell was Chuy?

The gown was of the purest silk, a rich, vibrant turquoise. Its delicate fabric slipped over her skin, chafing. The robe matched in color, but was heavier and trimmed with an offsetting shade of cream.

The latest in European fashions, she heard her cousin Bianca exclaim over her own fiesta gown. Sinking to a plush stool at the dressing table, Marina took up a silver handled hairbrush, gave it one look, and tossed it across the room. She could at least use her own damned brush, she hissed to her reflection in the mirror.

The sight before her brought her senses to a halt, however, because it was immediately obvious why Rafael Santana had chosen this particular gown—the color matched her eyes to perfection. Did it match Sophie's eyes, also?

Incensed, bewildered, and most of all, hurt, she jumped to her feet. She would not wear this . . . this dreadful garment.

And he would not *seduce* her here . . . here in this room where . . . not in this room . . .

Nor anywhere—

"Sorry," Rafe called from the open doorway. "I knocked, but you must not have heard."

164

She stared at him aghast. He had bathed, too. His hair was still damp and a bit mussed . . . No, she cried inside, mussed was his word, not hers, not after . . . He wore a loose fitting shirt, one so white it caused his dark skin to shimmer beneath the golden glow of the lamps, and his eyes to sparkle like black diamonds, and his smile . . .

"This tray is heavy." He motioned toward the table where she had tossed her towels.

Quickly she hurried across the room, reacting, not functioning, she thought, striving desperately to control her mind and her body. She clutched up the towels and turned away. She heard the tray connect with the table.

Then he touched her, catching her arm, twirling her to face him. "The color is perfect," he murmured. "I knew it would be."

"It's Sophie's," she said without intending to.

He nodded.

She glanced around the room, to the bed.

"Everything is Sophie's."

"You don't like it?"

Her heart beat so violently against her ribs it hurt. Her mind raced so fast she could hardly think what to say next. "Why?" she finally managed.

"Why, what?"

She stared into his confused eyes, then quickly squinched hers shut. "Why?" she pleaded.

His hand cupped her jaw, sending shafts like lightning flashing through her. She wanted to pull away but was unable to move her limbs. When he spoke, his voice was husky.

165

"I thought you wanted . . . *we* wanted . . . I mean . . . the ember, love. You know I feel it, too . . . we both do."

Anguish, bitter and cold, filled her as with some evil concoction. She tore away from him and raced across the room.

He followed, reached for her arm, and she flinched. "The ember—" he began.

She turned on him then. "Do not speak that word! Obviously you haven't the slightest idea what it means. It is not something . . . something you pass around from woman to woman. An ember burns between . . . between *two* people, for God's sake, not among a menagerie!"

"Menagerie?" His voice lifted at the end of the sentence, as though he were beginning to understand, but she rushed on, giving him no time to explain.

"You bring me to this house—to this room—Sophie's room . . ." Desperately, she flung the robe wide, holding the lapels with trembling hands. "Sophie's gown!" She turned to stare in horror at the bed. "Sophie's bed! You planned to make love . . . to *seduce* me in Sophie's gown, on Sophie's bed, where you and she—"

Fiercely he grabbed her arms and pulled her against him, her head pinioned to his chest, his face buried in her hair.

"*Por los dios!* I didn't realize you would think such a thing. I'm sorry, love, so sorry . . . so—"

She wriggled to be free of him.

"Look at me." He clamped her distraught face in his hands forcing it to his. "Open your eyes. Let me explain."

166

Refusing, she squinched her lids more tightly.

"I never made love to Sophie! Not in this gown, not on that bed, not in this room, not anywhere. I love Sophie dearly, but only for what she is. Sophie is my sister."

Gradually, Marina opened her eyes. Her pulse still raced so rapidly her vision seemed blurred. The horrifying scenario she had envisioned refused to release her. Tears formed and rolled from the corners of her eyes.

Rafe bent and kissed them away. "This is my home." He grimaced, self-effacing. "I wanted to wait a while longer before springing my *noble* ancestry on you. Now I'm sorry . . . so sorry."

She stared at him unable to find her voice.

He kissed her again, gently. "Do you not know how madly I love you? How insane I am for you?"

"I thought . . ." she began, but her voice trembled and she stopped.

His lips covered hers, caressing, soothing, loving.

Slowly she felt him slip the robe from her shoulders. It fell to her feet. Then his fingers eased the thin straps of the gown over her arms and he shoved and pushed until it, too, fell in a heap on the floor. Gently, he lifted her out of the pile of silk and carried her from the room.

She clasped her arms around his neck and buried her face in his shoulder.

"We are going to *my* room," he offered unasked, striding down the long corridor, turning a corner, and at last pausing before another door, which she heard him push open.

He kicked it closed behind them and crossed the room.

She looked around, inhaled a deep tremulous breath.

Without letting her go, he flung back the covers on a massive bed. He stared at her, pain etching lines in his skin. Reaching she stroked the corner of his eyes.

"I am so sorry," he repeated.

She kissed him quickly on the lips, watching his eyes flame, savoring his admission that he felt the ember, too.

When he lowered her to the bed, his eyes caressed her unclothed body. Then they lighted with a familiar twinkle and his grin broadened. "I never intended to make love to you in that gown . . ."

Chapter Six

". . . nor in any other gown," he added, disrobing quickly.

She glanced around the room—a masculine room, heady with the scent of Rafael Santana, cluttered with his charts on the walls, his books here and there, fragments of pottery and stone, some recognizable, most not in the dim glow from the one lighted lamp and the blazing fireplace. This was *his* room. And she was much more comfortable here than in the feminine one to which he had first taken her, even without the misunderstanding.

She felt his eyes on her and turning her head held his gaze. Although she lay securely ensconced in the thick mattress and clean-smelling sheets, she thought for a moment she might swoon. She recalled thinking of him as a high priest when they climbed El Tajín. Now his body gleamed like burnished bronze, satiny, firm, and molded to perfection. Even his face was majestic, etched with a mixture of grief and passion. Was this how the Aztec priests looked after they had ripped out a living, beating human heart to sacrifice to their gods?

He stretched alongside her. Their bodies trembled at first touch, as though a bolt of lightning had flashed from one to the other, fusing them to a permanent state of togetherness. He clasped her head in his hands.

"I am so very, very sorry, my love."

Lost in the essence of him, she savored his words of love, but though she strove to dispel them, questions barraged her still. Lifting a finger she traced the outline of his lips. "Why did you not want to tell me?"

He kissed her finger as it roamed his lips. "It was crazy, I admit. But damnit, this is our first chance to be together. We have only a few hours, even now, and I . . ."—he shrugged, then continued— ". . . I knew the questions it would raise, and I didn't want to waste valuable time explaining my ancestors."

She watched him intently, feeling his lips beneath her finger, letting the need for him build to wonderfully unbearable heights, like always when she anticipated him kissing her. Tonight she anticipated this, and so much more.

"*Our* ancestors," she corrected, slipping her arms around his neck, drawing his lips to hers. "So let's not waste any more valuable time."

Marina Cafferty considered herself, while not experienced, at least worldly to a point. Certainly, she had known the difference between a real kiss and one that felt like a cold tortilla, and she even knew what the ember of budding love felt like spinning its fiery web inside her.

But not until Rafe Santana stretched the length of his bare skin along her own and proceeded to make love to her with the passion of one of the Aztec gods he

170

so resembled did she have the faintest idea what lay in store this night.

In fact, the skill with which he unraveled the mysterious skein of love drew her into a world so magical she could at times hardly believe it was real . . . it was her . . . it was him.

Primed by their earlier words of teasing and innuendo, their passion needed little stimulation. When she drew his lips to hers, he covered her mouth and soon they returned kiss for kiss, wet and devouring and urgent.

He swept a hand up and down her smooth, warm back, cupping her firm buttocks.

She had known what his lips felt like on her breasts, but tonight was different. Unencumbered by clothing and a lack of privacy, he lingered over one then the other, eliciting moans of ecstasy.

Desperate for more, she wrapped her legs around his, trying to draw him near, but he held her back. "Wait, love. We don't have to hurry that much."

"But I want to," she moaned, clutching his head to her breast. "I want you . . . I can't wait."

"Yes, you can." His hand traced her waist, palmed her flat stomach, and dipped to grasp her lower, cupping his hand around her as she writhed in earnest. "*I* may not be able to," he whispered, nipping at her lips, her eyes, her nose, "but you can. Let me show you."

With that he delved inside, gliding slowly, ever deeper into her inner core. She gasped. Her eyes sought his.

"How is this, love?"

Spasms of pleasurable agony drew her head back to

the pillow. He followed pressing his lips to hers, kissing her deeply, and his fingers rhythmically matched his kisses.

Her hands clutched his shoulders, and soon she kneaded them in the same primitive rhythm. Her pores throbbed to the ancient tune. "Oh, Rafe," she gasped, "do something. I'm on fire."

"The ember," he murmured, shifting himself over her, nudging her legs apart with his knees. She felt his hand leave her body and he lowered himself, entering her slowly.

"Hurry," she whispered, pulling his face to hers. Instinctively her legs wrapped around his hips and she tried to pull him closer.

"Slowly, love," he whispered. "Slowly . . ." Speaking all the while, he entered her at slow intervals, finally reaching the barrier he had dreaded to find. He had hurt her emotionally tonight, he hated to hurt her again.

"Rafe, please don't stop. Not now."

He breathed against her cheek. "I have no intention of stopping, love. But I don't want to . . ." Quickly then, he thrust, felt her tense at the break through. He stopped. After a moment, he looked into her eyes. "Is it bad?"

She held his desperate gaze until the flash of pain subsided, then she clasped her legs more tightly around him. "No, please continue . . ."

In spite of the situation, he grinned at her. "Aye, aye, *capitán*." He saw her smile, but mostly he saw her urgent, agonizing need grow as he resumed the course they had set for themselves. *When?* he wondered, thinking quite possibly the magic between them began the moment she slapped his face on board her ship.

"The fire is growing, Rafe," she breathed into his face, reaching for his lips, moving her hips in rhythm with his own. "It isn't . . . an ember . . . any more. It is . . ."

"A volcano," he muttered.

She gasped at his word, and he felt her shudder in his arms, felt her body quake beneath him. "What is her name?" she whispered. "Sleeping Woman?"

He allowed his own body to crest, then finally collapse beside her, their bodies damp, their arms and legs entwined, their hearts pounding to the same ancient, primitive drum beat.

When he could, he raised himself on one elbow and kissed her face. "I think Sleeping Woman just woke up."

She snuggled closer to his beloved body. *And it took a god to do it,* she thought. But she didn't say it. Rafe Santana was arrogant enough as it was.

The next time she opened her eyes to his tender kisses, it was morning. The heavy draperies had been drawn back to allow the morning sun to pierce the room with great shafts of golden light. The bed lay in shadows just beyond.

"How do you feel?" He ran a hand gently over her face.

"Wonderful, how did you think?"

"I was afraid you would be stiff and sore," he admitted. "Do you feel well enough to ride all day?"

He was dressed, while she lay as she had fallen asleep, covered only by a light sheet. She lifted it now, inviting him beneath. "Love me first."

His eyes fairly burned into hers, then they drifted over her body, following his stroking hand across her breasts, her midriff, her stomach, stopping to linger but a moment at the soft patch of curly hair, before returning to a breast where he plied her nipple between his fingers.

His lips kissed hers, then dipped to her breasts where he tantalized her only an instant. "You are hell to resist." His husky voice betrayed his need for her, but he tossed the sheet across her body. Striding the table, he poured a glass of orange juice and brought it to her in bed.

Sitting up, she pulled the sheet around her breasts. "You abstain from making love in the mornings?" She sipped the orange juice.

He sat beside her on the bed. "I promise never to refuse your offer again during our long and promising future. However, unaccustomed as you are to . . ." He grimaced. "Dammit, don't look at me like that. It's already difficult enough not to act the arrogant bastard you think I am and jump into bed with you."

"You think you know what is best for me?"

"You're damned right." He nipped her nose with his lips. "In this case. Now, get dressed so we can leave." He nodded to her clothes and satchel on a dark chest. "If we reach Xico before noon, we can be back by dark. And I expect your offer to be good for evenings, too, *capitán*."

He brought her a cup of coffee and took her empty glass. "I'll rouse Chuy while you dress . . ." He leered seductively at her sheet-clad body. "If I'm not gone before that sheet comes off . . ."

Before he could leave, however, she called him back. "When did you get my clothing? And the breakfast? Who . . . ?"

"Servants," he answered. At her worried look, he added, "I retrieved your belongings from Sophie's room last night, then locked the door so the maids wouldn't find you gone this morning. I locked our door, too. They left the trays outside in the hall." He shrugged. "I figured you wouldn't want your first night in this house marred by gossip—since you will be running the staff one day."

With that he closed the door on her open mouth, wide eyes, and multitude of questions, leaving her to dress and wonder what lay ahead for them. From the sound of things, he thought he had it all figured out.

He was right about one thing, he was an insufferably arrogant bastard. But he had said he loved her, and she knew that might very well prove to be the chink in his armor. Stories she had heard about her grandfather painted him a much similar sort of man—before her grandmother worked her magic on him.

When Rafe returned she was ready and they left the house without seeing anyone until they reached the stables, and then only the groomsman who held the reins to their horses while Rafe strapped on a holster and pistol, then assisted her into the saddle.

Leaving the stables they crossed riding yards and a large expanse of landscaped acreage. She stared around, disappointed to be leaving so soon. "I wish I could have seen everything."

"You will." He led the way through the massive wooden gates they had entered the evening before and up a steep road lined with glossy green-leafed plants

175

tended by a bevy of field hands, hacking away at weeds, trimming branches. "You may even be like my mother one day, heaven forbid, and want to spend much of your life in the city."

She shook her head in amazement, for he had responded as matter-of-factly as if he had been talking about the weather. For a man who had yet to speak her name, he certainly had her future mapped out. That fact created a whole different kind of turmoil inside her—warm and wonderful and frightening.

Giant trees shaded the road, interspersed at intervals among the plants. "These must be coffee plants," she ventured.

Rafe nodded. "The way we make our living. That and horses and a few fighting bulls for Chuy."

"I want to see your horses, too," she said. "We raise cattle and only enough horses for ranch work. When my grandmother was young South Texas was overrun with horses. They strayed from—"

"I know," he interrupted. "Our horses came from the same place—*our* ancestors, the Conquistadors. There were no horses on the continent before the Spaniards came."

"That should prove the Conquest was of some value," she retorted. "Where would we be without horses?"

He stared at her a time before turning back to the road with a bland reply. "Who can say?"

Since she did not for a minute believe he thought they would be better off without horses, she refused to let him provoke her, but turned her attention to the magical setting through which they rode. The sun was only a couple of hours old and dew still sparkled all around. The abundance of flowers amazed her.

"I've never seen so many flowers."

"Do you have bromeliads at Los Olmos?"

At her frown, he pointed to spidery-leafed plants that grew on the trees. "Bromeliads are parasites," he said. "See how their runners spread over the tree trunks?"

"So many different varieties," she mused, enjoying the array of brilliant colors, knowing the splendor was magnified tenfold by Rafe Santana sharing it with her.

As the road continued to wind its way upward, she suddenly thought of his promise.

"Is this your mountain?"

He pulled on his reins. "Draw up a minute."

Obediently she halted her horse beside his.

"Now look behind us . . . to the far horizon."

Following his instructions her impression that they had been steadily climbing was immediately confirmed. Beyond them lay wave after wave of green-clad hills with the Hacienda de Santa Elena tucked into the middle far below.

"There." He stretched his arm its full length.

The sight took her breath. Far in the distance a perfectly shaped cone of snow reached toward the azure blue sky. "Sleeping Woman?"

He chuckled. Leaning close, he captured her gaze from the wonder beyond them and held her eyes with the intensity in his own. "That is not Sleeping Woman." He kissed her then with such passion she clutched his arm for support.

"*Por los dios viejos*," he sighed against her lips. "What you do to me! I used to have some sense—some purpose to my life. Now you are the only thing on my feeble mind."

She pecked him lightly on the lips, knowing he affected her the same way. "I'm glad," she whispered.

Gritting his jaws, he turned back to the horizon. "Mount Orizaba—*Citlaltépetl,* the Indians call it— mountain of the stars."

"It must surely touch them," she mused. "Can we go there?"

"To Mount Orizaba?"

She nodded.

"Not to the top. The top is nothing but a glacier." He studied her closer. "This is not a test, *capitán.*"

"A test?"

"You are not auditioning for the woman of my dreams." Leaning forward, he kissed her again. "You have already won my heart and soul."

They moved on, enraptured with each other and with the magical setting through which they rode.

"When?" she asked at length. "Last night?"

He studied her with his beloved smile. "Before that." Then he shrugged. "Someday we must sit down and figure it out. I would like to know when I passed your test, too." His glistening black eyes pierced her green ones. "If I have."

She wondered at that statement the rest of the morning. They reached the town of Xico a couple of hours after leaving the compound of Santa Elena, where they stopped beside a town well to get a drink and water the horses.

"What language do they speak?" she asked after several women had drawn water while babbling among themselves.

"Mexicano," he told her. "One of the few remaining

dialects of Nahuatl, the language of the ancient Aztecs."

Her mind worked quite separately from her roving eyes, which took in the few adobe buildings and the church. Perhaps she had been seeking answers to the enigma of Rafael Santana from the wrong source. Obviously, he did not intend to speak about his abhorrence of the Conquistadors. Perhaps his feelings for the Indians would reveal the answers she sought. "Do you speak Mexicano?"

"As well as anyone not born and reared in one of these remote villages."

"Which means . . . ?"

"Which means . . . I know a few words." He entwined his fingers for her to use as a stepping perch in remounting. "Since the Conquest things Mexican— Indian—have been held in such low regard that even the natives themselves rarely admit to speaking those dialects."

She thought about his remarks as they prepared to leave town by the one main road. "Look!" She drew rein in front of the church. "What is that?"

Rafe followed her gaze. "An old idol."

"May we take a look?"

He grinned. "I thought you wanted to get home early."

Her eyes danced, and she swallowed the emotions this disarming, handsome man evoked inside her, emotions made more intense since their lovemaking.

"If that's the choice," she laughed, "we can ride on."

"It isn't." He led the way to the hitching rail in front of the church. "We have time for both, unless you decide to stay for Mass." He raised his eyebrows. "Or go to Confession."

Around them in the patio Indian women swept the stone floor, unheedful of Marina as she knelt to study the bulky piece of carved stone. A head of some sort.

"Who is it?" she asked Rafe.

He knelt beside her and ran his hands tenderly over the rough stone face. "Who knows? If the Spaniards had not destroyed his body, perhaps . . ."

"Everything leads back to that, doesn't it?"

He frowned.

"To the dastardly Spaniards who abused your countrymen . . . although, when the truth is out, the Spaniards are your countrymen."

Absently, he picked at the wax drippings which clung to one side of the idol. "As well as the Indians."

Not far out of town she realized they had done nothing about Xilonen, the corn goddess. "What about the goddess?"

"We're headed for Old Xico."

Old Xico? Everything in his life was old, ancient. What did he want with a modern woman, when he so valued the old, the downtrodden, those he saw as mistreated?

Unfortunately, she was beginning to understand his revulsion of her name. It became clearer every day that the ancient Lady Marina desired better things for her countrymen than they knew at the time of the Conquest.

What had happened to Rafe Santana to cause him to refute this part of his heritage? Jesús Zolic was right—Rafe was obsessed with the past. But why?

A little further on he took a trail which veered to the left off the main road and led up a steep, rocky incline.

180

Dismounting, he gathered her reins in his hands. "We have to walk from here."

She reached for her reins. "I will lead my own horse."

"No need," he replied, taking a step up the road.

She caught up with him. "I may have passed the test, but I can still lead my own horse." This time when she reached for the reins, he let her have them.

"Very well," was all he said.

That damned idol brought this on, she thought, wishing she had never asked to stop for a closer look.

The trail was if anything steeper and rougher than it appeared from the bottom. In places she could tell it had once been paved with cobblestones, but ages, perhaps centuries, of rain and flood had washed away great chunks of stones and underlying dirt. Some places she had to climb using her hands to propel herself along. From time to time she heard her horse's hooves slide.

"Why were you so insistent I come along?" she called ahead, suddenly wary. It was as if the higher she climbed, the clearer her head became. Had she been so physically lost to his charms that she failed to see the issues clearly?

He looked back at her. "Do you want to rest a minute?"

Whereas the question was one of consideration, it was voiced in a noncommittal tone which infuriated her.

"Was it to get me away from the *Stella Duval?*"

Her question brought him to an abrupt halt. "Is that what you think?"

"I don't know what to think!"

Without hesitation, he clamored back down the

trail. Taking her by the shoulders he pulled them down side by side on one of the rocky ledges in the middle of the roadway. While their horses stamped around them, he held her shoulders and spoke directly into her face. "What do you mean—you don't know what to think?"

She swallowed her now-familiar all-engulfing reaction to his nearness. Her arms burned at his touch, even through the wool poncho. "You want that treasure," she whispered.

He nodded.

"I saw how much you want it, in the way you studied the idol back in Xico."

"I never denied wanting Mexico's part of the cargo. What does that have to do with bringing you here?"

"To get me away from the ship."

He sighed, exasperated. His fists tightened around her arms. She thought he might shake her. But he didn't.

"How would that help me?" he demanded. His voice quavered beneath a barely controlled temper.

"Zolic—" she began.

"You forget Nick. Nick will look after your interests."

"But Zolic has Pedro Ybarro and his men."

"How could you possibly think such a stupid . . . ?" His words died like the gramophone back at Los Olmos when it needed winding in the middle of a record. Almost roughly he gathered her in his arms and held her close. "What have I done this time, love? Or failed to do? Last night I acted without considering your feelings. What now—?"

"Nothing," she hurried to say. Pulling away she

gazed into his distraught eyes, feeling her anguish shift immediately to him. She cupped his face in her hand, as he so often did hers. She saw his eyes light, as last night, with a mixture of passion and grief. "It was nothing like that . . . nothing."

"What then?"

Dropping her hand, she clasped her arms about his chest and laid her head next to his throbbing heart. "I don't understand you . . . and I need to."

She felt him sigh heavily and tighten his arms around her. After a while he drew her back and kissed her lips. "Give me time. Please. Just a little time."

She kissed him in response.

"I love you, *capitán*." He held her face in his hands. *"Love* you. Madly, passionately, insanely. I will never do anything to hurt you."

She gazed into his eyes, letting his pledge and his words of love dissolve her fears. She kissed him again. "Then let's go . . . so we can get home early."

The climb got only steeper, but after their talk it became much easier, what with the weight of her fears lifted from her heart—not eliminated, but lifted.

This time when she asked the same question as before, it was in an amicable tone, and he responded in kind.

"I don't want you to fear all Indians because of Diego Ortiz's murder," he told her. "These people will impress you; they're among the nicest I know."

"Tell me about Xilonen. Who could have stolen her? And why?"

"I call them grave diggers. Men who use any means to obtain artifacts, then sell them to foreigners at huge

183

profits. They are so bent on turning a dollar they will do anything to take our national treasures—steal, cheat—"

"Murder?" she asked.

Reaching, he took her hand and squeezed it, an effort to reassure her, she knew. "Even murder. But don't be alarmed. I know where Xilonen is and how to get her back."

He held her hand the rest of the way to the site of Old Xico, and his touch washed—burned, she decided, was a more apt term—every other thought from her brain. Although her boots were scuffed, her hair straggled about her face, and her riding clothes hopelessly rumpled, inside she felt like a queen, or an Indian princess at the very least. With her hand in his she knew she could climb the highest mountain, even dance through the glaciers on top of Mount Orizaba. She felt as though they had already reached the stars.

Before they gained the summit of the hill, Rafe took her reins and tied both horses in a thicket of fir trees. Ten yards or so further, they crested the hill afoot.

She was not sure what she had expected to find at Old Xico, but as was becoming a habit in her travels with Rafael Santana, she was not prepared for the high mountain valley with its acres and acres of corn plants.

The only trouble was everything was brown and withered, dead or dying. A few of the buildings were of adobe, but they were crumbling with age. The others, huts, were built from stone—the stone of the mountain, she realized—or sticks and grass and some timber. Off to one side a bier rose over a smoldering fire, supporting not a body, but a mounded heap of corn. Surveying the camp, she saw several stacks of corn, like hay stacks, the ears shriveled and dry. A wailing, as of the wind, drifted from all directions.

The only people she saw looked as down and out as their surroundings, and as terrifying, when she got a better glimpse. And the wailing wasn't the wind at all, but mourners. A sudden chill passed over her, and she shivered.

Rafe stopped dead in his tracks.

"That damned Zolic! I'll stretch his hide over a—" Interrupting his own words, he searched her face in earnest. "We are not in danger. But don't utter your name, not under any circumstance."

The familiar admonition coupled with his own inability to say the dreaded name, slashed her fear as with a blade of anger. "I won't let it slip if you won't," she quipped in a tone more sarcastic than jocular.

His gaze became stony. "This is serious, love. You must do everything I say."

She shrugged, knowing this particular argument would not be won or lost in the near future, certainly not standing at the edge of this ghastly village. Looking away, she saw an old man shuffling toward them. She gripped Rafe's hand a bit tighter.

"I didn't mean to frighten you," he whispered, returning her grip. "We are perfectly safe."

But Rafe held her hand firmly in his throughout the ensuing conversation, and she wondered whether it were merely to reassure her, or for more urgent concerns—such as expediting a speedy escape. Whatever, she would wait to debate the issue until they were well away from the strange inhabitants of Old Xico.

The man before them could well have been an apparition from a nightmare: long spines of some sort of cactus pierced his ears, his nose, even his cheeks and neck, and along each arm thorns were threaded through little pinches of skin. The punctures were fresh, or relatively so, for blood pooled black and ugly around every entry point. She suppressed a shudder by squeezing Rafe's hand a bit tighter. He drew her closer to his side.

After speaking briefly to Rafe, the old man turned back to the village and Rafe inched his way behind him, keeping Marina close. "The chief," Rafe explained. "We are to follow him to his fire—"

"To eat?" she gasped.

"If we are invited. Perhaps we can settle our business without a meal." He glanced around the settlement.

She followed his gaze, wide-eyed at what had caught his attention. In front of every hut—indeed more arrived by the minute—young women peered at them wearing serious expressions and not much more. An identical halo of flax-colored corn leaves adorned each of their heads like a crown. Strips of colored cloth were tied around their hips forming ankle-length skirts, and as necklaces they wore strands of what appeared to be kernels of corn, dyed in brilliant colors. Other than that they were naked, their bosoms bare.

Marina averted her eyes only to find in her field of vision the men of the village, clothed but pierced to the man of them in the same manner as their chief.

After that she kept her eyes to the ground, fearful even so of what sight might confront her next.

At the campfire Rafe instructed her to sit as they had done in the old shaman's hut; at least here they were outdoors, free of the fumes of incense or peyote.

Talk was exchanged, none of which she understood;

but she did recognize Rafe's adamant tones.

At the chief's summons two young women left the group, only to return moments later carrying platters.

Marina tensed.

Rafe squeezed her hand.

One of the bare-breasted young women knelt before Marina, offering her a gourd cup which sat alone in the middle of the platter. Marina stared, first at the cup then at Rafe, careful not to look at the woman's bosom.

Rafe, however, was being presented the same thing from the other young woman, and he was not shy about observing the entire offering. She cleared her throat.

When he turned his devilish grin on her, it was sheepish, and she implored him with her eyes.

"Sorry," he mumbled.

She glared, wanting to tell him she was too scared to care whether he ogled every bare breast in the gathering. "What is it?" she demanded between clenched teeth.

"Pulque. Drink it. Well, sip it. Too much will make you a little drunk, nothing else."

She took the cup and stared into its dark contents.

"Drink some of it," he repeated. "Then nod your approval to the chief and to the woman who served you. She will go away after that."

Marina watched Rafe take a gulp from his own cup, then perform the required gestures. With effort she brought the gourd to her lips, gripping it tightly in an effort to still her trembling hands. While holding her breath, she took one sip. Bitter, unpleasant, but probably not lethal, she decided. She tried to relax.

The conversation between the chief and Rafe continued, turning to bickering, and the next thing she knew, Rafe had moved his arm around her shoulders. Sheltering. Protecting?

She froze, wishing she knew the language, knowing she might be better off not understanding this conversation.

In an effort to close out the bizarre sights of the village, she had confined her field of vision to the campfire—Rafe, the chief, and herself. Suddenly she noticed a long line of men forming behind the chief.

Robed in white cotton, their flesh pierced with thorns as was their chief's, they approached the fire, their attention riveted on Marina herself. One by one they stooped, peered into her face, studied her body, mumbling all the while to the chief and among themselves.

One lifted a loose strand of her hair in his hands, and Rafe firmly but politely dislodged it.

Her heart thudded against her ribs. Instinctively she covered her breasts with her free hand. "What are they doing?"

Rafe shook his head. "Don't worry. Only over my dead body will they—"

"Then I pray you live, so I can strangle you when we escape," she hissed.

He squeezed her hand. "That's the spirit. You can be mad as hell, but don't let them think you are afraid. Our cause depends on us being in control."

She could have laughed at that, she thought, if her emotions were not already engaged elsewhere.

Haggling ensued between the chief and his men, into which Rafe interjected a word now and then. Mostly, it seemed he let them come to their own decision.

Then the mood changed. The chief spoke—an order, it sounded like. His men glared at Rafe.

The chief spoke again.

Rafe jumped up, pulling Marina to her feet. She scrambled after him.

Her heart pounded so fiercely she could hardly hear above it; the din of angry voices shifted from nonsensical to terrifying.

"Now!" she heard Rafe hiss. Suddenly she knew he had been talking to her.

Her eyes darted to his.

"Get out of here. Run. Don't stop for your horse. I will—"

As through a fog she watched him unhook the thong on his holster, draw his pistol.

"What—?" she began.

"Go!"

She ran. Head down, heart racing, her feet miraculously propelling her out of the village.

Down the hill . . .

Away from danger . . .

Away from . . .

Her legs lasted until she heard sounds behind her; turning she saw Rafe leading their mounts down the hill as fast as the broken terrain allowed.

She stumbled then, but he caught her. Reins in one hand, he pulled her close. "Sorry to have frightened you. We were never in any physical danger."

"No danger?" she mumbled, thinking she must not have heard correctly.

He shook his head.

Her heart thrashed against his. She craned her neck to look behind him. No pursuers.

"I ran, but not from danger?" She heard her voice quiver. "You drew your pistol—"

"Shhh . . . it's over. It's over."

"What did they want?" She pressed her cheek against his still thrashing heart. *No danger?*

"They want their goddess back." He kissed the top of her head. "I assured them she will be returned within the week, but they had a hard time trusting me. I guess they learned I can't move mountains. They wanted to keep you with them as insurance until they receive her."

She stared up at him, aghast. "Me? They wanted me?"

"Shhh . . ."

"Those horrible people—"

"They aren't horrible, love. They are frightened. Their world cannot continue without Xilonen; they are dealing with her loss the only way they know how—actually, their methods have worked quite well for centuries now."

She glanced back up the hill. "Let's go."

They mounted and rode down the hill. After a while her breathing began to steady. "Why do they pierce their skin? And their clothing . . . or lack of it?"

He chuckled. "You mean the bare-breasted beauties?"

"Depends on who is looking," she retorted.

"Usually the young women go bare-breasted only at the harvest festival honoring Xilonen. They do so now in penance, same with the piercing of the skin, hoping to communicate with her wherever she is, hoping she will take pity on them, bring them good crops despite her absence."

"Their customs are strange," she argued.

"Not really. Piercing the skin is a common form of penance. And the other—Xilonen is portrayed bare-breasted. She's the young corn mother, representing fertility and nourishment; without either their crops will not grow."

"It's a cultural difference, I suppose."

He appraised her with warmth in his eyes. "Most people don't even try to understand."

They rode silently, toiling now to find an easy way down the steep, water-eroded incline. "Still," she mused, "it would be dreadful to have to run around bare. I am certainly glad I don't live under those ancient edicts."

"Me, too." His response came quickly, firmly.

Her heart fairly skipped a beat. This was the first time he had admitted that something today was better than yesterday. She did not dare call him on it . . . not yet.

After a while her fears settled, along with the repulsion she had felt at the strange sights, and questions barraged her once again.

"When are we going after Xilonen?"

"We aren't. That's how I convinced them not to keep you. Zolic will retrieve her. Maybe it will teach him to use more caution in the future."

"Zolic stole her?"

"He might as well have—no, that isn't fair. He bought her from some men who assured him that she was not currently in use. We were pleased to have her at first, then we received word that the inhabitants at Old Xico wanted her back. We began negotiating a substitute." He shrugged. "As you probably gathered, they want the real thing."

"If Zolic hadn't bought her, she would be lost."

"Some foreign collector or museum would have spirited her out of the country by now."

They drank at the well in Xico again, bought some tamales from a lady near the church, and arrived back at the hacienda at twilight.

Coming upon it from the hills the compound rose majestically above the sprawling acres of land. Surrounded by fifteen-foot stone walls it made an imposing picture, and ancient, with its stonework weathered to a mottled gray. She felt as though they approached a medieval castle.

"Built by one of Cortés's own lieutenants?" she mused, recalling what he had told her the previous evening, before he acknowledged Santa Elena as his ancestral home.

He nodded, leaving her with a multitude of unanswered questions. But the sun was setting, casting its golden glow over this magical kingdom and inside those walls was a large room with a roaring fire in the fireplace and a soft bed which she had been waiting all day to share with this man.

She had no intention of provoking a change in his amicable frame of mind.

Laborers opened the wooden gates at their approach, and stable hands waited at the portico to take their horses. Lanterns glowed from the exterior entrance and from several windows in the central portion of the palace-like structure.

Consuelo met them in the brightly lighted foyer with word that *cena*—supper—awaited them and that Chuy had been called back to the city.

"His principal *picador* was injured in a *corrida* yesterday. He is not in serious condition, but your brother wanted to be by his side during the surgery."

"I was looking forward to meeting Chuy," Marina said, watching Consuelo pad her way across the jewel-toned Persian carpet and around a corner. "I've never met a matador."

Rafe took her in his arms, his grin devilish, his eyes serious and ardent. "Then I'm not sorry he left. Since this is our last evening alone for a while, I'm in no mood to share your affections."

"My affections lie wholly with you, Rafe Santana. Must I continually reassure you of this?"

Grinning, he kissed her soundly. "Yes, as a matter of fact, and I am past ready for you to begin your next demonstration."

Chapter Seven

Light from wall sconces in the circular foyer glistened from tiled floors and highly polished walnut furniture, casting the adobe walls of the old hacienda house in a mellow hue.

"Consuelo called us to supper," Marina reminded Rafe when he steered her directly toward the broad stone staircase. At the first landing a complete suit of armor stood as though a body were inside, ready to march into battle.

"We have time to remove some dirt and grime," he answered.

Upstairs he guided her down the third corridor, the only one she had not entered: To the left lay Sophie's room where their great misunderstanding had occurred, directly behind them lay his own, to the right where he now led her, the unknown.

Three doors down the hallway he opened the door to a room bathed with the magenta and golden rays of the setting sun. A fire warmed the parlor of the suite. Lamps glowed from polished surfaces. As though decorated to coordinate with nature's evening performance, wall tapestries, floor coverings and upholstery alike were vibrant in rich hues of red and gold, ranging from orange to magenta, accented with brass.

"What a lovely room!" She turned to him curiously. "Who does this one belong to?"

"You." He crossed to a pair of gold-leaf screens which separated the parlor from a sleeping alcove. Behind them rested a tub with gleaming brass fixtures.

He tried the faucets, held a hand under the running water. "There's plenty of hot water."

"*Me?*"

Standing he took her shoulders in his palms and planted a sound kiss on her lips. "You. I told Consuelo to give you a guest suite, preferably this one. Since you will be a regular visitor, you must have your own room—until we are married."

"You told her all that?"

"Mostly."

He kissed her again. "Your things in the wardrobe, along with others we thought you might want. If you need anything else—"

"But we are leaving in the morning."

"But we will return," he mimicked. "Now get your bath so we can eat." He kissed her once more. "I'm near starved to death."

She stopped him at the door with a whispered concern. "The other things in the wardrobe? To whom—?"

"Sisters," he interrupted, coming again to take her in his arms. This time instead of kissing her he held her fast, staring intently into the troubled depths of her green eyes. "For once and always, love, let me settle your mind—you are the first woman I have ever brought to this house . . . and you will be the last."

She kissed his lips with an ardent invitation. "Hurry back. I'm starving, too."

By the time she heard him return she had bathed, dressed in one of the simple embroidered *huipils* from the wardrobe and brushed her hair to a gloss. She had intended to leave it down, but a pair of shell combs amidst the toiletries on the vanity caught her eye. Sweeping her hair to the top of her head, she secured it loosely with the combs, admired the results—it should stay in place until after supper, she decided, and Rafe did like straggling hair. Rummaging in her sachel she found the silver earrings Tía Luisa had given her.

Physically and emotionally exhausting though the day had been, she was unable to sit still. So instead of looking in the vanity mirror to insert the earrings, she carried them with her to the parlor, where she stood before the window, entranced by the spectacle beyond. Absently stabbing at an earlobe with one of the silver wires, she paced to the corner of the large expanse of glass. The view from that angle took her breath with its majesty—Mount Orizaba, inflamed now by fiery rays from the setting sun.

Rafe entered without knocking, and she was so engrossed that she wasn't aware of his presence until she heard the tray touch the tabletop.

Turning gracefully she stared at him, her hands poised at an earlobe where she held the dangling earrings, unaware of anything now, except his mesmerizing effect on her.

He had bathed, too, as before, and wore a loose-fitting white blouse and tight black trousers. She wondered without intent what he would look like in a suit of lights, such as matadors wore, then hastily banished the vision. How glad she was not to have to worry over horns mauling his body.

A mild whiff of his own spicy scent drifted on the air, weakening and exhilarating her at the same time.

"I excused Consuelo, told her we must get an early start again in the morning, so we would find our own supper and retire early."

The way he grinned when he spoke the word *retire* seared her flesh. She inhaled a sharp breath, unconscious of her reaction.

With a slow easy gait he crossed the room, admiring her grooming from head to foot. Almost casually he took the earrings from her hands and proceeded to slip them through the holes in her earlobes.

The contact, so personal, excited her already rampant passions. His knuckles grazed her cheek and his fingers pulled on the fleshy mounds of her earlobes, first one then the other.

His hands trembled against her face, and she watched the muscle in his jaw twitch.

Her mouth dry, she ran her tongue between her teeth and gums to separate them. "Our supper will get cold—like last night."

Finished with his task, his eyes found hers the same instant his hand clasped the back of her head. He drew her lips to his. "I brought it in crocks . . . with covers . . . anticipating . . ."

"This." His lips claimed hers, sweeping her body with a wave of desire. She swayed against him, pressing herself shamelessly, wonderfully to him.

Eagerly returning his kisses, she wrapped her arms around his neck. His silky hair was still damp beneath her fingers, his neck heated under the collar of his shirt. She slipped her hand further, her palm flat against the warm, moist skin stretching across the taut muscles of his back, muscles which tightened at her touch.

Although she strove to attune herself to his every move, her brain fairly trembled inside her head, and when he scrunched her *huipil* in his hands, edging it up and up, past her calves, past her thighs and her waist, she quivered at his touch, their skin separated now only by the light silk of her chemise and petticoat.

She had been tempted to wear the *huipil* without undergarments, but supposing they would dine downstairs, she decided on the minimum she felt required at a dinner for two, attended by Consuelo or other servants.

Rafe's hands found her breasts, bringing a further quiver to her flesh when he grasped one in each palm, working them through the sheer fabric, teasing, tormenting, until she pressed against him, silently urging, begging.

Eager to be shed of her own clothing, she began fumbling with his—moving her hands to his shirt, which she unbuttoned and pulled open. She ran her flat palms over his chest, then slipped her hands beneath his shirt as it clung to his shoulder, intending to remove it.

But before she could entrap his arms thus, he swept her up and carried her to the bed, where he stood her on her feet and stripped the *huipil* over her head, discarding it in a heap on the floor.

Limp and begging she stood before him, watching him study her in the shimmering light before he reached to untie her chemise.

"Hurry," she whispered. His fingers touched her skin, showering her breasts with gentle torment as he untied first one ribbon, then the next, letting the garment gap a bit further each time. "Hurry, please."

"Shhh . . ." He nipped kisses along her face, then stood back to watch the chemise fall from her shoulders at his touch. "You are too fine not to savor, love."

His voice communicated his need quite as clearly as did her own, and she knew if his touch was not her undoing, his husky voice would be.

Then he clasped her face in both his hands, lifted her lips toward him, and kissed her with glorious, wet, and eager kisses. Slowly leaving her face, his hands trailed down her neck, across her chest, capturing at length her breasts where he plied them with his hand in a rhythmic fashion that reminded her of what was to come, increasing her agony even as it brought great swirls of pleasure.

When his hands left her breasts to travel over her midriff, his lips left hers to find their way down her neck, to her breasts where he teased her with his lips until she grasped his head in her hands, holding him closer, and closer still.

His teeth grazed her nipples, sending sweet throbbing sensations to quite another part of her body, the one part which longed yet for his attention.

As though privy to her every need, his fingers finally managed to untie the ribbon holding her bloomers in place. With a flick of his wrists, he sent the filmy garment fluttering to the floor around her feet.

His hands spanned her waist, stroked her skin,

slipped over her hips, cupping them in his palms, as he had once done her breasts. Then he lifted his face tracing his way back to her lips.

"You are so sweet, love, so sweet."

She kissed him greedily, feeling the throb of her heart radiate in all directions. His hands slipped past her hips, and his lips suddenly left hers, to trail back down her chest, his tongue sweeping spirals through the valley between her breasts, past her midriff, stopping to lave her stomach with kisses, while his hands found her stockings and rolled them, one at a time down her legs to her ankles.

When he picked up one foot, discarded the shoe and started to pull her stocking over her foot, she staggered and caught his shoulders for support.

At that moment her body arched forward against his lips and he dipped his face into the curly patch of black hair at the base of her abdomen.

Dropping her stocking, his hands cupped her, bringing her closer and closer yet to his caressing kisses.

Unprepared for such bold treatment, she could but groan her uncertainty, a protest that turned quickly to approval, then to a heightening of passion she had never imagined.

She clutched at him first for support, then finally in an effort to encourage his assault on her very senses. When at last she could stand the torment no longer, she cried out and he lifted his lips, languidly retracing their path up her body while he removed her other shoe and stocking. On reaching her face, he held it in his hands and stared, searching, into her begging green eyes.

Her senses felt abandoned, her breath came in short

pants. With agonizing slowness, his eyes never leaving hers, he withdrew the combs from her hair and dropped them to the floor along with her other items of apparel. Suddenly, his mouth curved in that beloved grin. "Yes, love, you were definitely created for more than cold tortilla kisses."

"Please . . ." Her voice trembled, practically useless, but her hands again began to remove his shirt. This time he let her, while he quickly shed the rest of his clothing.

Stretched together on the plush, satin-covered bed, he leaned both arms alongside her face and nipped her with kisses, laving her skin with his loving.

"Do not misunderstand," he mumbled between kisses, "I am as overwrought as you, but I want it to be good for you. No, what I want . . ." —his eyes, serious and loving, found hers— ". . . what I truly want is for every time to be better than the last, for the rest of our lives."

The sincerity in his voice brought tears to her eyes. How could she have been lucky enough to find a man to love her as much as this man did? A man whose love she could return. And yet so many questions remained. He kept so many secrets, he was such a private man. Could she ever break through the barriers he refused to lower?

"You have our future all planned."

"You bet I do."

"But still you cannot say my name."

He stared steadily at her for so long she began to think he finally intended to cross that dreaded hurdle. When he began to speak, her heart swelled with happiness.

"I have told you how much I love you . . . madly, passionately, insanely, I believe I said."

She nodded.

"Do you believe me?"

She inhaled the deep pleasure she felt with his body next to hers. The ache to become one with him throbbed insistently through her veins. "Of course, I believe you. Why do you ask?"

Again he stared at her a long time, now with that familiar mixture of passion and grief. "Because you have never spoken those words to me."

Now it was her turn to stare dumbfounded at the statement, at the truth of it. Lifting her hand she cupped his face in hers. Her eyes caressed his, the words on her lips. Then she changed her mind . . . and her mood.

"How about a compromise?"

He frowned.

"Until you can say my name . . ." —she smiled, wriggling from under his body, rolling him onto his back, where she assumed his former stance with her arms framing his head—". . . until then I will not *say* the words . . . I will *show* you, like you show me."

Resting on one elbow she watched his eyes glow. His smile broadened. "A bargain, *capitán.*"

When her eyes left his to survey his body, she feared for one instant she might not have courage to carry out such a bold game. Within moments, however, she was so caught up in the magnificence of him, that her inhibitions fled and she found herself gazing at his most intimate parts, stroking his fevered skin, kissing him as he had done her, discovering in the process a new dimension of loving.

For when her hands roamed his taut muscles, her own cried out for him; when she kissed his furry chest, her breasts ached for him; and when she stroked the rigid evidence of his passion, her own body wept for want of him.

Her loving ministrations aroused her own passions to even greater heights and she came to wonder how he had managed such control over his own body when he caressed her, and in wondering she knew the awesome feeling of giving to the one beloved. For in giving, she received.

In loving she knew that she herself was loved.

And now, he knew, as well.

When his muscles contracted beneath her hands, she looked into his eyes, and the raw passion there quickly fired her own to an uncontrollable blaze.

Reaching, he drew her face to his and covered her mouth with kisses. "Now, *capitán,* we will finish together."

This time he entered her boldly and together they rode the wild passions of their desire, much as their ancestors, she reflected, must have ridden the virgin prairies of the New World. And the ending brought not death and destruction, as he claimed, but a wild and glorious understanding of the meaning of life and love.

They arrived back at Tecolutla at dusk the following day, having taken a direct route almost due north from the Hacienda de Santa Elena. As wearing as the long ride was, Marina dreaded to come to the end of it where their future awaited them in tangible terms, ending the idyllic interlude of their visit to the hacienda.

They passed through Xico enroute to Jalapa, bringing to mind one of the most terrifying experiences of her life. Was it only yesterday? she wondered.

"Would you really have left me up there?" She nodded quickly toward the rocky trail which veered to their right. The ordeal still brought a shiver to her spine.

"We were never in any physical danger."

"You said the reason you fought not to leave me was because you didn't intend to return yourself, that you wanted Zolic to retrieve the goddess in order to teach him a lesson."

"I hope to hell it does. Otherwise I may be forced to let him go. His rashness does not win us friends, and as you saw, this work hinges on our credibility among the Indians. If they hadn't trusted me completely yesterday, we would have been in trouble."

"But you said . . . ?"

He perused her face with serious eyes. "I know those people, love. I would never put you in danger."

"You would have left me in that village."

"I didn't."

"That is not the point, Rafe. I have to be able to trust you."

"You did."

She stared at him, curious.

"You trusted me enough to leave—alone—the instant I told you to."

"That wasn't trust," she insisted. "It was reflex—part of my education growing up on a ranch. Every job has a leader, generally the person with superior knowledge, whose instructions must be obeyed at the peril of risking one's own life, or the lives of others, or both.

Obviously at Old Xico you had superior knowledge—at least, you spoke the language. So I obeyed you."

By the time she finished his eyes held a devilish glint. "So you did. I wonder if that holds promise—"

"Don't even think it," she laughed. "I have no intention of obeying anyone all the time. If your plans come to pass, your future will not include an obedient wife."

He halted them in the middle of the open road to plant a sound kiss on her lips. "My plans *will* come to pass, love. And I can think of nothing more boring than an obedient wife."

The country became more wild and rugged before they reached Jalapa, an ancient town built on and around green-clad hills. They entered the town with a light rain falling on their ponchos.

"*Chipichipi,*" Rafe told her, "the native word for this persistent drizzle."

As in every place they had gone, flowers abounded—roses, bougainvillea, even orchids, which grew wild in the jungle along the roadside. Rafe dismounted to pluck one and stick it behind her ear—with a kiss.

After Jalapa, Mount Orizaba was to their backs, and Marina pondered the significance of that. It seemed to her they were leaving the stars behind, coming down to earth as it were, where instead of fantasizing over an idyllic future together, they would face head-on their individual goals in life.

The coffee plantations gave way to other fields. Corn, beans, and various crops grew up the hillsides. "Chilies," Rafe indicated from time to time.

"Look at the scarecrows." She pointed to one of the numerous pole crosses in fields along the way. Bright strips of cloth attached to the arms of the crosses flapped gaily in the wind, bringing to mind some ancient ritual. Rafe's response confirmed that impression.

"The cloth helps ward off eclipses and evil spirits which cause crop failure."

Marina had always considered her family religious. They adhered to the Church calendar, they celebrated Holy Days, and they received Mass and other Sacraments as often as possible given the isolated nature of the hacienda. In her grandmother's youth Los Olmos had its own chapel where daily services were read and where her grandparents were married. When the old house burned, the new one was not constructed with a chapel, but Marina had grown up believing all outdoors to be her chapel.

However, she had never imagined a people so caught up in the religious aspect of nature as those in this land of mixed cultures. When she commented on this, Rafe turned again to the old Indian beliefs.

"They were dependent on nature just as we are, although we sometimes tend to think we control things." He studied her earnestly. "Indian culture is basic—sunlight to grow crops, rain to water them, fire for fuel. People who believe that way have little time for pretentiousness."

His sincerity moved her; yet the images that crossed her mind were the sensual silk dressing gown he had chosen for her to wear, the luxurious accommodations at Santa Elena, and his own suggestion that one day she would run the staff here. He had not forsaken the heritage he denied. And therein lay the complicated mystery of the man.

"Tell me about your brothers," she suggested. Before

they left the hacienda that morning he had taken her on a cursory tour of the palatial home, showing her wings devoted to apartments for each of his sisters and brothers and their families. They walked through the section he intended to take for themselves, until they became masters of the domain and moved into his parents' apartment.

"None of your brothers and sisters want to manage Santa Elena?"

"I'm the eldest son. Two of my sisters are older, but they have husbands with property of their own. It's my responsibility."

"Even if you don't want it . . . the responsibility?"

He frowned. "Why would I not want it?"

Why, indeed? she thought, but she held her tongue.

"I've wondered about your brothers, too," he admitted. "Why are they not the ones risking their necks to save Los Olmos, or even your father or grandfather?"

"Why the little girl of the family?"

He grinned. "I am definitely not complaining. If they had come instead of you, we would never have met. But, yes, I'm curious. Why the little girl?"

"My brothers, Logan and Essie, are away at school—Annapolis. Papa studied there, too. Logan and Essie take after him and grandfather; they are set on spending their lives at sea. It may sound peculiar, but in my family the women have traditionally run Los Olmos. The task fell to my grandmother when her only brother was killed in Texas's war for independence." She glanced at him provocatively. "I believe you called it a rebellion. Anyway, Texas was in a sorry state for a while after that. My great-grandfather moved back to the Hacienda de Vera Cruz, but Grandmother refused to leave Los Olmos. Then my mother came along—she's an only child. Yes, I have two brothers, but my parents would never tie their sons to the land, simply because they are sons."

His face had sobered with her story. When he questioned her further, she knew he wanted more than a mere recitation of family history.

"What will happen to Los Olmos if . . . *when* you leave?"

The question traveled between them on a taut string of passion. The promise of their future lay softly around their shoulders. Reaching, he cupped her face in his hand. His fingers tingled against her temple. His thumb teased her lips, just before he replaced it with his own.

When again they resumed their journey, she answered his question. "Jorge, my grandmother's nephew, owns half interest in Los Olmos. He and his son Miguel love the ranch as much as anyone except my grandmother. We have all been happy there; it is our home, our heritage. But Grandmother, Jorge, and Miguel are the ones who seem to belong to the very soil, itself."

The answer appeared to relieve Rafe, and he pursued it with other questions, until by the time they approached the Río Tecolutla she had revealed everything she knew about her history, including her grandfather's ill-fated voyage, the infamous wager he made in Bagdad which won him the hand of the beautiful and spirited Serita Cortinas, and the way Tata had convinced her grandmother to rebuild the tower atop Los Olmos after the Yankees destroyed it during the war, insisting that if he were to learn to use that confounded wooden leg he needed somewhere other than the flat South Texas prairie to practice.

When she finished, he sighed. "If I tried, I could become jealous of your grandfather, the dashing Giddeon Duval. You worship the man, don't you."

"Yes, Tata and I are very close." She stared long into his questioning black eyes. "You're going to love him. The two of you are much alike—a touch too arrogant on the surface, but warm and romantic underneath."

She could tell her words pleased him, for his eyes softened, caressing her face, bringing prickles to the back of her neck.

"I'm ready for the romantic part," he whispered.

Crossing the river, they headed for the little seaport village. "Actually, I think I'm afraid to meet him."

"Why ever would you be afraid to meet Tata?"

"What if he doesn't approve of me?"

His voice was so quiet, she turned to stare at him. His serious eyes probed hers, seeking an honest answer.

"Of course he will approve of you. What if your family does not—?"

"He's a man of the sea. I know nothing about the sea, except that it's salty." He shrugged, favoring her with a sheepish grin. "And that's about all I want to know."

"The sea has nothing to do with anything, Rafe. Do you remember on top of the pyramid at El Tajín when you asked me why I was searching the sky and I told you for elm trees?"

He nodded, his expression quizzical, waiting.

"Tata is the one who refused to let me marry Burt Wilson. He assured me that contrary to what Burt said, love can fall out of an elm tree and hit a person on the head. His words, I think, were, 'I am not about to stand

209

by—even with only one good leg—and let you marry some gotch-eared gringo who doesn't know his heart from his hind end.'"

He laughed loudly at her words, but when he spoke she could tell he was still not convinced. "You are saying he will approve of me because I love you?"

"And because I—" Biting back her words, she leaned toward him and met his smiling lips with her own.

"I cannot tell you how much you have relieved my mind, *capitán.*"

Although she had known their return would bring to an end the idyllic days with Rafael Santana, she had not anticipated the abruptness with which their magical world would be shattered.

"What is the *Stella Duval* doing in port?" she questioned.

Together she and Rafe raced toward the ship. Marina slid from the saddle and ran for the gangplank, leaving him to see to their horses. Could they have retrieved the cargo with her gone? Disappointment displaced her former ecstasy, and for a moment she wished she had never left.

But if the cargo had been found, Los Olmos could be rescued, and . . .

"No." Nick met her on deck; he was followed close at heel by Zolic. "We found nothing but a few more pieces of oyster-encrusted hull. We aren't even sure—"

"It is the right ship," Zolic cut in. "But our drinking water *somehow* managed to become tainted with salt. We had to leave the salvage to—"

"What's the meaning of this? Can I not leave for—"

210

Rafe's voice boomed from behind her, reminding Marina quite unexpectedly of the first time she had encountered this beloved, arrogant man.

"Couldn't be helped," Nick responded, speaking to Marina in a petulant tone of voice.

"Marina, dear! Thank heavens! We have been so worried." All eyes turned on the sprite figure emerging from the companionway.

"Grandmother! How wonderful! When did you arrive?"

"Just today, dear." Serita embraced her granddaughter. "Fortunately the ship was in port. But where have you . . . ?"

Before Marina could respond to her grandmother's question, Giddeon appeared.

She rushed to him. "Tata. I'm so glad you have come."

Giddeon embraced her protectively. "In the nick of time, so it seems. Your grandmother and I have been uncommonly worried, sugar."

Registering the cause of their concern, she pulled away from his embrace. "You were right, Tata," she whispered. The thrill of sharing her newfound love with him left her lightheaded and a bit giddy. She turned to introduce Rafe.

"You must be Señor Santana?" Giddeon barked over her shoulder.

Marina watched Rafe's expression harden at her grandfather's demand.

Stepping forward briskly, he extended his hand to the elder man. "Rafael Santana, sir. Your granddaughter has spoken of—"

"Where the hell have you been with her?"

"Tata!"

"I had business in Old Xico—an Indian village in the mountains. I thought she would be interested, so I invited her to come along. We stayed at my family's home nearby."

"Your family's home?" Giddeon challenged.

"Yes, sir."

"The Hacienda de Santa Elena, Tata. It was built by one of Cortés's own lieutenants. He was Rafe's ancestor."

"I don't give a damn if he's related to the King of Spain, sugar—"

"Giddeon." Serita stepped to her husband's side, taking his arm. "She is all right. You can see—"

"A damned good thing, too. If her father were here—"

"He isn't." Marina took his arm. "And if he had been on board when I left, I would have gone with Rafe anyway."

Giddeon opened his mouth to reply, but before he could do so, she changed the subject.

"Now what is this about contaminated water? We must hurry back to that site before grave diggers find it."

"We're prepared to sail at first light," Nick put in.

Giddeon and Rafe still eyed each other, a fact no one missed. Serita released Giddeon's arm and took Marina's. "Come dear, I must tell Cookie to set two more places. We are almost ready to sit down to dinner. No doubt you want to change." She looked squarely at Rafe then and extended her hand.

"Thank you, Señor Santana, for returning Marina to us safely. Since you are obviously a member of this expedition and a friend of Marina's, you will please join us at dinner."

As determined as Marina was not to leave Rafe alone with Giddeon, Serita gave her no choice, practically dragging her toward the companionway. Once below Serita scurried around Marina's cabin filling a wash basin, laying out towels, easing the awkwardness with activity, as was her habit.

"How could he?" Marina fumed. "I told Rafe how wonderful Tata is. Only moments ago I assured him that Tata would approve of him. Now . . ."

"Approve of him?" Serita rummaged through the wardrobe pulling out a yellow batiste gown trimmed with a natural colored crocheted lace. "You will want something simple and cool in this heat."

Marina proceeded to strip from her trail-grimed clothing and bathe off at the basin, snatching the garments her grandmother laid on the bed, one by one, unthinking.

"I mean, he never even gave Rafe a chance! He pounced on him like a panther on a kid goat."

"I am sure Señor Santana can take care of himself. Certainly he couldn't have expected to spirit a young lady all over Mexico without her family's knowledge and not face a little heat when he brought her home—especially from the young lady's father or grandfather. Men can be unduly alarmed at such improprieties, dear."

"Doesn't Tata trust my decisions?" Marina fidgeted while Serita buttoned the fitted bodice of her gown up the back. "After everything he said about love and elm trees and wanting me to find the right man, you would think he would at least give Rafe a chance to speak

213

for himself."

"Marina, dear, your grandfather has been worried sick. And I a little, I must admit."

"There was no need, Grandmother." The terrifying scene at Old Xico flashed through her mind, but she quickly squelched it. "Rafe would never let anything happen to me—never. It's like Tata said—"

"Tata talks too much," Serita sighed, giving her granddaughter a hug.

"So I have been told," Giddeon quipped, poking his head through Marina's parlor door. "All decent?"

"Yes, dear."

Marina turned on him abruptly, hands on hips, defiant. "How dare you attack Rafe that way? You didn't give me a chance to introduce you. You didn't wait to find out—"

"Whoa, sugar." Giddeon held up his hands in self-defense. "I may have been a little out of line. If so, I apologize. But you have to look at it from our point of view. We arrived here expecting you to be on board the *Stella Duval* in Nick's care, only to find you had been carried off to the mountains by some lunatic who—"

"Rafe Santana is not a lunatic!"

Giddeon shrugged. "Perhaps lunatic is not the best word. My vocabulary is limited when it comes to a grown man who lives mostly in the past."

"Tata! You don't know him."

"Agreed, but . . ."

"Marina, dear," Serita interrupted, "listen to our side. Even Señor Santana's own man says he is obsessed with the past. That there was a woman long ago named Marina who betrayed the people of Mexico; now you come, bearing the same name . . ."

"And sugar, Señor Zolic claims Santana is so afraid that history is about to repeat itself that he cannot even call your name."

Marina stared from one to the other of her grandparents, disappointment stinging her eyes, the truth of Zolic's claims twisting like a knife blade inside her heart.

"The sound of my name is not important. What is important is how you treat the man I intend to marry."

Chapter Eight

Marina hurried to the upper deck of the *Stella Duval,* grateful dinner had gone so well after the commotion her grandfather had caused when they came aboard, practically accusing Rafe of abducting her. Now she would discover how Rafe had taken the dressing down in front of the entire crew.

Dinner had been a strained affair, with Serita and Zolic carrying the conversation.

"Logan and Stella arrived back at Los Olmos three days before we left," Serita told Marina, then included to Rafe. "They are Marina's parents. Jorge's telegram caught up with them at Annapolis. They and the boys returned home immediately. You know your brothers, Marina. Logan Junior is ready to whip Burt Wilson, and Essie cannot stand to think he might miss being here when we raise the cargo."

"*If* we raise the cargo," Nick interjected.

Serita sighed. "I know—"

"Do you think they will come to Tecolutla?" Marina asked, thinking of her brothers.

Giddeon grunted. "Your papa won't let either of them go after Burt Wilson, says we can do nothing to interfere with Jorge's legal maneuvers."

"I would not be surprised to see them turn up here, though," Serita said.

"Nor Logan and Stella for that matter, saying things calm down at the ranch," Giddeon added.

As soon as Serita dismissed the table, Tata and Nick headed to the chart room, and Marina excused herself to her grandmother, saying the day had been taxing for both of them. Serita looked tired from her trip—or was it from worry over her? Marina wondered, sorry to have caused her such concern, although it was Tata who had raised the alarm. Tata and Jesús Zolic.

Zolic was a strange man. For all his knowledge of Aztec ways, she was beginning to understand Rafe's exasperation with him. He apparently was lacking in social education. She smiled, thinking of the bouquet of roses he brought her before dinner. A peace offering, she knew, although he had not said as much. He had mumbled something about the fragrance purifying the soul, then handed her a little reed flute like the one he himself had played, driving Nick to distraction, while she and Rafe were at the Hacienda de Vera Cruz. The music, he claimed, put one in tune with the senses. He promised to teach her to play it.

She found Rafe at the rail, gazing toward the distant dark horizon. Coming softly behind him, she slipped her arms around his waist.

"Un centavo para los pensamientos de tú."

She felt his heart flutter beneath her hand. He swiveled in place, enclosed her in his arms, and just before he clasped her head to his chest, she looked up into his glistening black eyes . . . his wonderfully playful black eyes.

"A penny for my thoughts, *capitán? Solamente de tú,*" he whispered, repeating in English, "Only of you." Lowering his lips, he kissed her as he spoke.

She returned his kisses eagerly, grateful that he had not been frightened off by her outspoken grandfather. She pressed her questing body to his, running her hands along his shoulders, desperately trying to bring herself closer, then closer yet, as her need for him spiraled.

"Easy, love." He lifted his lips inches from hers. "We are no longer alone."

"But . . . ?" Her gaze darted to the ship's lower decks which lay in darkness now.

"Do you think your grandfather would let us out of his sight?"

"Why, that—!"

Rafe silenced her with his lips, but she could no longer respond to his kisses.

"He wouldn't spy on us, surely."

Laughing, Rafe turned them to face the inky black water. "Surely, he would," he mimicked.

"After all those things he said about love falling out of trees and—"

"He did not tell you to go out and sleep with the first man who came along."

Incensed, she faced him. "He asked you *that?*"

"No, love, not that. But he sure as hell wanted to, I could tell."

"I'm so sorry," she sighed. "And embarrassed. How could he treat you that way? He didn't give you a chance."

"Don't worry about it. I understand."

"You understand? He was mean, cruel—"

Rafe cut off her protestations with his lips, kissing her soundly. "You are his granddaughter. If one of our granddaughters should ever traipse about the country unchaperoned with some arrogant bastard I hadn't even met, spending two days—and nights—alone with him, I'd give him hell, too."

She ran her fingers over his face, hoping in this manner to assuage some of her craving to touch all of his skin . . . with all of hers.

"You would understand, though, wouldn't you? If our granddaughter—?"

"Not until I got to know the gentleman in question."

Marina sighed. "Tata will understand once he knows you. Unless he runs you off first."

He studied her with a curious air. "He won't run me off. But he may never understand, either. Your grandfather does not possess a high regard for archaeologists—not even one whose ancestors rode with Cortés."

She started to tell him it didn't matter what her grandfather thought, but his words suddenly reminded her of her own conversation with Giddeon earlier.

"It's what Zolic told them," she mused, wondering how to correct a misunderstanding in someone's mind.

"What did Zolic tell them?"

"About your . . . ah, your obsession with the past . . . and with the lady named Marina."

"That bastard! I'll have his hide for that, definitely his job, as soon as we complete this expedition."

Marina shrugged. "You can't blame him. In a way . . . it's true."

He turned back to the rail, gripping it with both

hands, staring intently into the darkness. "Not in the way they took it," he hissed. "Even you don't understand."

She slipped her arms about his waist and laid her head on his chest. "I will. Give me time."

And a chance, she thought. If he would try to explain his feelings, it would help. She was no dunce, but neither was she a mind reader. She needed at least a hint before she could draw conclusions.

Obviously Tata did not need that much. She inhaled the salty mist which mingled with Rafe's spicy scent, aggravating her desire to be alone with him . . . to reassure him, to love him.

She could see how he would be angry with Zolic; the man had no right to discuss someone else's business behind his back. Yet, Rafe's aversion to all things Spanish—well, practically all things Spanish, she reflected, thinking of the luxurious hacienda—was common knowledge. If Zolic hadn't told them, someone else would have.

She thought again about the bouquet of roses. From the sound of things, Zolic would be the one needing a peace offering before Rafe got through with him. First the corn goddess, now putting Rafe in trouble with her grandparents. Yes, Jesús Zolic was an exasperating man in many ways.

Tightening her clasp around Rafe's waist she maneuvered herself toward his lips. "My grandparents just need a little time, too. Tata is a fair man."

Returning her embrace, he kissed her face. "He must be, you couldn't love him the way you do if he were not. I hope the rest of your family is fair, too. If they all show up aboard this small ship, I will be considerably outnumbered."

"They will love—"

"Shhh . . ." He silenced her with a kiss, then added "You've already been wrong about that once today."

"They won't be difficult like Tata."

"From my experience a girl's brothers are the most difficult of all, next to her father—"

"No—"

"And her fiance," he finished.

Marina frowned, then she laughed, hugging him close. "You're teasing me."

"I doubt either of us will feel like teasing if Burt Wilson shows up."

"Burt Wilson? He wouldn't come here."

"Hummm . . . and your grandfather will love me on sight."

"Oh, Rafe. Everything will work out, you'll see."

"It's your grandfather I hope comes around soon. I have plans for us in a couple of weeks."

"Plans?"

"I promised my mother I would attend the Independence Day celebrations in Mexico City the middle of September." He cuddled her close, recalling Fernando's message in Tzintzuntzán. That seemed like at least a century ago. "Actually she sent word she would disown me if I failed to show up." Sobering, he stared long into her eyes. "I want you to come with me."

Marina's heart practically sang at the chance to be alone with him again. She couldn't recall ever feeling so confined as since they returned to the *Stella Duval.* "Of course, I'll come, even though it terrifies me to think of

221

meeting your family. We'll bring Tata around before then."

"If we find the cargo in the next two weeks, he won't have a choice. We will invite them all to Mexico City for our wedding."

She sighed against his chest. Again he had things all figured out, or thought he had. It was a lovely prospect, indeed. Yet finding the cargo could work against his plans. If the distribution of it provoked discord, there might well be no wedding, whether her family approved or not. *Pray God, that would not happen.*

"What the hell do you mean, casting aspersions on my character and reputation?" Rafe demanded of Jesús Zolic. As soon as he and Marina said good night, he had gone in search of his insolent assistant. He called the man from his quarters in the fo'c'sle, leading him out of earshot and eyesight of the crew and passengers. He had no intention of sharing his fury at the man with anyone else.

"Aspersions?" Zolic questioned.

"You understand me perfectly. This time you overstepped the boundary between simple stupidity and total ignorance. Obsessed with the past! I should have your—"

"I will not stand by and let you mistreat that girl."

"Stay out of my personal affairs, Zolic. I warn you—"

"And I warn you. If you mistreat her . . ."

"I have no intention of mistreating her."

"No? All you see is her name and Malinche. You live in the past, Santana. You see her as a traitor, whether you know it or not."

"You're demented."

Zolic shook his head, his eyes like pieces of coal. "Then ask yourself? Why can you not even say her name? I have never once heard you speak her name."

Controlling an overwhelming temptation to knock Zolic senseless, Rafe instead turned him loose with a shove that sent the assistant minister sprawling against a hatch cover. "My personal life is just that—personal. What I choose to do—or not to do, and why—is none of your goddamn business. If you were not so valuable to this—"

"You should excuse yourself from the expedition, Santana. Her grandfather agrees. I am perfectly capable of leading the reclamation alone."

Rafe inhaled deep drafts of air, cursing the humidity, the heat, half-listening to the man's ranting. "If you have destroyed my chances for gaining the Duvals' respect—either personally or professionally—I promise you, Zolic, I will slit your chest, rip out your heart, and throw it to the goddamn devil."

"Marina Cafferty does not deserve the likes of you," Zolic spat. "She—"

"If you were so concerned about her, you wouldn't have provoked her grandfather as you did. You have no idea how much that distressed her."

"I would rather her suffer a measure of distress now, than a lifetime of regret."

"You sorry bas—"

"You are the one who provoked her grandfather, the one who carried her off to the mountains without a *dueña* for the sole purpose of seducing her."

"That's a lie and you know it." Enunciating each

word softly and slowly, Rafe managed to keep his raging temper from erupting. What he really wanted to do was punch Jesús Zolic in the nose, again and again and again. But a fight with his assistant on board ship would only confirm Giddeon Duval's adverse opinion of his own character. "I don't owe you an itenerary of our trip, and you are not about to inveigle one out of me. But I will tell you this—the purpose of that trip was to prevent the uprising you incited at Old Xico."

Zolic shrugged his shoulders, his bushy eyebrows narrowed over insolent black eyes.

"Come morning," Rafe continued, "I'm sending you to straighten things out."

"You can't do that. You need me."

"The first thing I need is for you to pacify the inhabitants of Old Xico. The situation you created there could have really put her in danger—"

"I didn't take her to that mountain top. You—"

"If I had known you stole the corn goddess, I would have sent you in the beginning. You lied to me, damn you."

"Now, Santana, don't go—"

"*I* am not going anywhere. You are. Bright and early tomorrow morning, you are going to recover that goddess and return her to Xico."

"But the cargo . . . ?"

"You won't be gone over three days. By that time we may have relocated the shipwreck and we may have recovered some artifacts for you to verify and record, and—"

"Santana—"

"And by that time I *may* have cooled off enough not to demand your heart—and your job."

MORE PASSION AND ADVENTURE AWAIT... YOUR TRIP TO A BIG ADVENTUROUS WORLD BEGINS WHEN YOU ACCEPT YOUR FIRST
4 NOVELS ABSOLUTELY *FREE*
(AN $18.00 VALUE)

Accept your Free gift and start to experience more of the passion and adventure you like in a historical romance novel. Each Zebra novel is filled with proud men, spirited women and tempestuous love that you'll remember long after you turn the last page.

Zebra Historical Romances are the finest novels of their kind. They are written by authors who really know how to weave tales of romance and adventure in the historical settings you love. You'll feel like you've actually gone back in time with the thrilling stories that each Zebra novel offers.

GET YOUR FREE GIFT WITH THE START OF YOUR HOME SUBSCRIPTION

Our readers tell us that these books sell out very fast in book stores and often they miss the newest titles. So Zebra has made arrangements for you to receive the four newest novels published each month.

You'll be guaranteed that you'll never miss a title, and home delivery is so convenient. And to show you just how easy it is to get Zebra Historical Romances, we'll send you your first 4 books absolutely FREE! Our gift to you just for trying our home subscription service.

BIG SAVINGS AND FREE HOME DELIVERY

Each month, you'll receive the four newest titles as soon as they are published. You'll probably receive them even before the bookstores do. What's more, you may preview these exciting novels free for 10 days. If you like them as much as we think you will, just pay the low preferred subscriber's price of just $3.75 each. *You'll save $3.00 each month off the publisher's price.* AND, your savings are even greater because there are never any shipping, handling or other hidden charges—FREE Home Delivery. Of course you can return any shipment within 10 days for full credit, no questions asked. There is no minimum number of books you must buy.

4 FREE BOOKS

TO GET YOUR 4 FREE BOOKS WORTH $18.00 — MAIL IN THE FREE BOOK CERTIFICATE T O D A Y

Fill in the Free Book Certificate below, and we'll send your FREE BOOKS to you as soon as we receive it.

If the certificate is missing below, write to: Zebra Home Subscription Service, Inc., P.O. Box 5214, 120 Brighton Road, Clifton, New Jersey 07015-5214.

FREE BOOK CERTIFICATE

4 FREE BOOKS

ZEBRA HOME SUBSCRIPTION SERVICE, INC.

YES! Please start my subscription to Zebra Historical Romances and send me my first 4 books absolutely FREE. I understand that each month I may preview four new Zebra Historical Romances free for 10 days. If I'm not satisfied with them, I may return the four books within 10 days and owe nothing. Otherwise, I will pay the low preferred subscriber's price of just $3.75 each; a total of $15.00, *a savings off the publisher's price of $3.00.* I may return any shipment and I may cancel this subscription at any time. There is no obligation to buy any shipment and there are no shipping, handling or other hidden charges. Regardless of what I decide, the four free books are mine to keep.

NAME

ADDRESS _____ APT

CITY _____ STATE _____ ZIP

TELEPHONE
(   )

SIGNATURE _____ (if under 18, parent or guardian must sign)

Terms, offer and prices subject to change without notice. Subscription subject to acceptance by Zebra Books. Zebra Books reserves the right to reject any order or cancel any subscription.   049102

GET
FOUR
FREE
BOOKS
(AN $18.00 VALUE)

ZEBRA HOME SUBSCRIPTION
SERVICE, INC.
P.O. Box 5214
120 BRIGHTON ROAD
CLIFTON, NEW JERSEY 07015-5214

Later in his own cabin, Rafe wondered at his patience with the man. Oh, he had been mad, all right. Mad as a fighting bull. But he hadn't really felt like ripping out Zolic's heart; the sorry bastard had already lost his heart—he was in love with Marina. It was plain as the stars in the sky. Zolic would hurt, all right. He would hurt a long time after Giddeon Duval forgot all about his quarrel with Rafael Santana.

Giddeon leaned back in the captain's chair in his stateroom and let Serita remove the boot from his one remaining foot, as she had done for twenty-five years.

"You should have seen them, *querida*. Reminded me of us, all that bridled passion. Between them they generate so much power, we don't even need the sails on this old tub."

Serita slipped his boot off, set it on the floor.

"He certainly is a handsome young man," she sighed. "And the way Marina looks at him—yes, I know what you mean. I can still feel the tingles, the uncertainty, wanting you so badly, not knowing how things would turn out."

Reaching for her, Giddeon clasped his hands about her still trim waistline and pulled her onto his lap. "What do you mean . . . you *still* get those feelings? What about today? Don't I make you tingle right now?"

"Of course, you do," she laughed. "And I definitely prefer the tingles of today. I wouldn't return to those miserable, unsettled times—a few moments of bliss mixed in with hours and days and months of agony." Twining her arms about his neck, she pressed her lips to his in a loving kiss tempered only by the knowledge that they had all the time in the world together. No longer must their ardor of the moment last into the indefinite future.

"But what did you think of this Rafael Santana, Giddeon? You talked with him. Was he agreeable?"

"Agreeable? Yes, most. And honest." He grinned at her, his green eyes twinkling. "Of course, I didn't ask him . . . well, I didn't ask him all I wanted to. Didn't want to force the man into a lie."

Serita nodded, grim.

"Frankly, he didn't sound like a lunatic," Giddeon continued, "although he could be smart enough to disguise the fact, like Zolic suggested. He's forthright, the man is. Says he is in love with Marina. That she's in love with him. And that they want to—no, that they *plan* to be married."

"Did he ask you for her hand?"

Giddeon shook his head. "He asked if that would be the proper thing to do, or if he should wait for the arrival of her father."

"And what did you reply, dear?"

"I told him I had damned-near bungled one such proposal, and I didn't want a shot at another one. To wait and ask Logan."

"You didn't bungle things with Logan and Stella."

"Yes, I did. I still get sick, thinking what would have happened if Logan Cafferty had been killed in that war before Stella had a chance to marry him. And me having refused them before the war even started."

Serita rose and took her husband's hand. "Come to bed, dear, and stop worrying over things that didn't happen. Right now we have to decide how to learn more about Marina's Rafael Santana."

"You're right. We do need to learn something about that young man before Logan and Stella arrive, wanting to know why we let their daughter fall in love with a total stranger."

"They are in love, aren't they? At least, they think they are."

"I'm not the one to doubt it, *querida*. Marina told him what we said to her that day—about love falling from elm trees, and you saying love had to have an ember from which to grow. Well, he sat right there and told me all that, just like we were talking about the weather. I don't know many young men who would talk, man to man, about such romantic gibberish. They would figure it might diminish their manhood or something. Not Santana. He told me all that. Then he assured me he was in love with my granddaughter. But do you know what? He didn't have to tell me. I could see it. That damned ember you told Marina about. It was burning right there in his eyes bright as the morning star when he talked about her."

Serita hugged her arms around her beloved husband. "Thank heavens she did not marry Burt Wilson."

Rafael Santana roamed the deck of the *Stella Duval* like a caged animal. One mishap had led to another until the entire crew now operated with emotions stretched taut as a pole dancer's tether.

One week out and they had only last night located the oyster reef they had found with no problem before he and Marina left for Old Xico. An entire week wasted because the crew somehow managed to loosen the

227

globes on the binnacle, which had then shifted, throw
ing the compass readings off.

Time was running out for the Duvals. They made n
bones about it. The first night after leaving Tecolutl
Rafe began to discover the extent of their determina
tion to claim the cargo. Giddeon had called him asid
after dinner.

"You might as well know, son. Before we lef
Tecolutla I telegraphed our nephew, Jorge Cortinas, t
set legal proceedings in motion to give us control ove
any cargo we bring up from my former ship."

"I wish you hadn't done that, sir. Your granddaugh
ter and I agreed how the cargo would be divided."

Giddeon's expression took on a perplexed air. "You
and Marina agreed? On what exactly?"

"That my government claims any artifacts con
sidered national treasures. That you receive payment i
the amount of two hundred thousand dollars from th
coinage we recover."

"When did you decide this?"

"Before we set sail the first time. It seemed only fai
that you be repaid for the loss of your ship. We arrived
at the amount—"

"I know how you arrived at the amount," Giddeo
barked. "Why in thunder did you not make this ar
rangement public knowledge?"

"Sir?"

"You could have at least advised your own mar
before you traipsed off into the mountains and left hin
in charge."

"What did Zolic tell you?" Rafe questioned, ignor
ing the *traipsed off into the mountains* implication.

"That you intended to remain on board the *Stell*

Duval in order to assure none of the cargo left Mexico."

"He was wrong." Rafe measured his words with difficulty. Although he was positive he had told Jesús Zolic of the arrangement, he could not recall the precise conversation. He knew, however, he would never have left a matter of such importance unattended. He might have lost half his wits to Giddeon Duval's granddaughter, but the half he retained were concentrated on proper procedure for reclaiming Mexico's artifacts. He knew from experience how much a slip-up could cost in time and goods.

"How do you intend to prove what actually belongs to the Bustamente estate?" Giddeon questioned.

Rafe inhaled the salty air, wishing he were in the clear, cool mountains. Wishing he were there with Marina Cafferty—the two of them, alone. But this was the opening he had been waiting for—and dreading. He cleared his throat. "The Bustamente heirs live in Mexico City. At Santa Elena I asked my brother to set up a meeting with them for the fifteenth of this month, the day before our celebration of national independence, and I am . . . ah, required to be present."

"What do you anticipate from the meeting?"

Rafe shrugged. "They should cooperate. I intend to have lawyers from the Ministry present to draw up documents."

"Perhaps I should come—"

"Actually, sir," Rafe hurried on. "I invited your granddaughter to accompany me."

"What . . . ?"

"I . . . ah, *we* would like your approval. This is a special celebration for my country. The Liberty Bell,

229

first rung in 1810 when Father Hidalgo called for the beginning of our War for Independence, has been moved from Dolores to the National Palace. There will be a great celebration in—"

"I'm sure there will be, Santana. But my granddaughter—"

"My family has a home near the National Palace. My mother, sisters, and sisters-in-law will all be present."

Giddeon turned away. "I don't give a damn about all that. Marina has already traveled the breadth of Mexico with you without a *dueña.*"

"I realize that was highly irregular, sir. In fact, were you to whip out a pistol and shoot me dead on the spot, you would be well within the law."

"True."

"And if she were my granddaughter, well, I would probably feel the same as you. I hope after all this, however, if such a thing should happen, I would remember . . . and understand."

Giddeon inhaled. *How well he remembered,* although he had no intention of admitting as much to this brash young man. "I understand. So does her grandmother. As would her parents, were they here. It has nothing to do with understanding, son. It . . . well, things are different from this side of the fence. I've been through it as a father and now as a grandfather—and yes, as a man in love. I can tell you for sure, the love-struck young man does not give as much thought to propriety as does the father and grandfather."

"I admit the situation is . . . unusual, sir, but a formal courtship is impossible. I ask you to consider—"

"Enough, Santana. Enough. I may look like nothing

more than an old man with one leg, but believe me . . ."
—Giddeon tapped his chest with a forefinger—
". . . inside here my heart still beats fast and furious at the thought of Serita Cortinas." He moved his pointing finger to his head. "And inside here I remember well how it was in the beginning—Serita does, too—far too well for any present peace of mind."

Rafe stared into the old man's fiery green eyes, knowing he was seeing not only the source of Marina's own green eyes, but of much of her magnificent spirit, as well. He extended his hand to her grandfather. "I give you my oath, sir. I will protect her with my life, and I will do everything I can to ensure no permanent damage comes to her reputation. She is more precious to me than any gold beneath this ship."

"For your sake, Santana, that had better be true."

That entire first week of searching for the wreck of the *Espíritu Estelle* ended in mystery when on the fourth day Rafe realized the binnacle globes were not in the position he and Zolic had, at Nick's instructions, set them.

"Why did you move the globes?" he asked Nick on one of the rare instances when he ventured to the helm. Since he knew so little about sailing, and with Giddeon Duval the expert, Rafe had decided his cause would best be served by leaving the sailing to the old salts.

"We didn't," Nick answered, and with Giddeon's help this time, the three men reset the globes which allowed for compass deviations according to the metal on each individual ship.

"Before we left the site to get fresh water, Zolic and I

checked everything so we could return with ease. With Zolic's knowledge of the sea—"

"Knowledge of the sea, hell! Zolic knows no more about sailing this ship than I do." Rafe glanced toward a deck chair where Marina sat playing that damned reed flute Zolic had given her.

Giddeon studied Rafe Santana from beneath the brim of his summer stetson. "Makes a man wonder what else the feller might be wrong about."

Nick trimmed the sails, and the next morning they set out for the correct location. A squall had come up during the night, though, and it took all hands on deck and the entire day to change course and reach their former diving spot.

As had become their custom, Rafe and Marina met on deck before retiring. After the squall the sky had cleared and the stars shown bright and near the sea. The ship rocked gently, soothing Marina's disquietude, lulling her into a dreamy mood.

Rafe was not so easily distracted from the recent discoveries.

"That damned Zolic. I know what he's trying to do. He wants to lead this expedition. And I suspect his reason is not to retrieve the cargo on that shipwreck."

"What ever his reasons," she responded, oblivious to his suggestion, conscious only of his arms about her, his breath on her face, warm and faintly tinted with after-dinner brandy, "he is playing into our hands. I heard what Tata said in the chart room yesterday."

"Tata?"

She nestled her head against his chest. "Tata," she repeated. "I think he's coming around."

Rafe chuckled. Since his talk with Giddeon the first

night out, the air had defrosted considerably, at least enough that he and Marina now openly planned their trip to Mexico City. "If this voyage lasts much longer, I'll run out of family history to relate," he told her. "Between the two of them, your grandparents have quizzed me on every Santana going back at least six generations."

"I wish they wouldn't . . ."

"Shhh . . ." He kissed her deeply. "Their questions don't bother me, as long as I am the one they ask—and my answers are the ones they believe."

The following day the divers located the oyster reef again. For two days thereafter however the seas were rough, diving impossible.

At dinner one night tensions ran high. "I hope that really is the *Estelle* down there," Serita sighed. "We are running out of time."

Time was running out for other things too, Rafe thought. The last promise he had elicited from Jesús Zolic was that the man return in time for Rafe and Marina to get to Mexico City for Independence Day. They had only four days left in which to make the trip.

Chapter Nine

Marina pressed her face against the window, observing the countryside she had missed in the darkness the last time they took the train from Veracruz. Although the cars were crowded with people going to the capital for Independence Day, Rafe had secured them window seats from which they could view Mount Orizaba and closer to the City of Mexico, *Iztaccíhuatl* and *Popocatépetl,* the twin volcanoes that guarded the entrance to the valley.

Zolic had arrived the day before they were to leave, bearing another peace offering of roses. This time Rafe saw him present her with the flowers, and she saw Rafe scowl.

"Your senses don't need *purifying,"* he had fumed later. "Definitely not with roses from Zolic."

She had laughed, but inwardly she cringed at the thought of Rafe's reaction should he learn of the conversation Zolic had engaged her in after dinner the night of his return.

Zolic had come to the point in a blunt fashion. "I

don't like you going on this trip with Santana."

"You aren't the only one." She had quipped, thinking he teased. His next words caused her to wonder.

"I'm serious, Marina. The man is not what he seems. I know he has turned your head—with his good looks and charm, I suppose. But you must beware of him."

"Why do you say this, Zolic?"

"Regardless of what Santana says, he sees you as a traitor. You must not forget this. *Malinche,* the traitor who captured the heart of Cortés for her own purposes; *Marina,* the traitor who is trying to capture the heart of Santana for much the same reasons."

"I am not a traitor!"

"I know that, but does he?"

"Of course, he does." Not for a moment did she believe Zolic. "What are these reasons you claim I have?" she had demanded.

"Not I, Marina . . . Santana. He sees you as a threat to his purpose—to keep his heritage alive."

"Then we are after the same things, Zolic, for I am trying to preserve my own heritage, as well."

"They are separate heritages, yours and his."

She had inhaled, incensed with Zolic's badgering—with the truth inherent in his words. She did not want to hear them, especially not tonight, the night before she would travel in splendid companionship with Rafael Santana.

Then Zolic handed her a smooth round stone. "If I cannot persuade you of the folly of this trip, at least take this stone. Carry it with you at all times."

"What is it?"

"A bloodstone. It will protect you, ensure you

remain pure regardless of his attempts to . . . ah, other-wise."

She felt the bloodstone now, lying smooth and round inside her reticule.

"A penny for your thoughts." Rafe's breath blew against her cheek now as he leaned across her, ostensibly to look out the window. His presence sparked a tingle along her spine.

"My thoughts? That I am terrified to meet your family."

"I won't tell you they will love you," he said, "not after our experience with your grandfather."

"That's what has me worried."

"But I will promise you this: They will grow to love you *almost* as much as I do once we are married."

They settled back in their seats, holding hands. She squeezed his fingers for reassurance.

"*If* we are married—" she sighed.

Turning his back to the car, he frowned into her worried eyes. "What do you mean . . . *if?*"

"Your plans are wonderful, but you always manage to forget my mission."

He stared at her long, wanting to kiss away her apprehensions, recalling his pledge to her grandfather not to damage her reputation beyond repair. Kissing her the way he wanted to on this train crowded with revelers would not lend itself to fulfilling that pledge.

"*When* we are married," he insisted. "We will salvage the *Espíritu Estelle* first, then—"

"Not just salvage it. I must have enough profit to save Los Olmos, and it must come before . . . before the Wilsons succeed in foreclosing."

"Why do you think we are going to Mexico City?"

236

His steady gaze held hers, while he considered his reasons for taking her to Mexico City. Independence Day and the Bustamente lawyers be damned. He was stealing time with her. Brief as it would be, he knew he had survived the past two weeks of tender but chaste goodnight kisses by anticipating the next two days of having her to himself.

"The *other* reason . . ." —he responded to their unspoken communication with a wink— ". . . is the meeting to expedite Giddeon receiving payment from any gold we salvage."

"What if there is no gold?" Her fears out, she felt herself on the verge of tears. Her chin quivered, and he instantly reached to cup her face, stilling her tremors. "Grandmother was right," she continued. "Time is running out. What if we don't find it in time?"

"Listen to me, love. We can't do anything about that right now. The divers are working as fast as they can. Your grandfather will keep them on the job while we're gone. When we get back, if there is no gold—or if we don't find it in time, we will find another solution. In the meantime, let's enjoy this trip."

She sighed. He sounded convincing, although not enough to alleviate her fears. On one point, however, she had to agree: this trip was important to them both, especially important if things failed to work out later. "All right."

He pressed a quick kiss to her forehead. "And that solution will not involve you marrying Burt Wilson."

The majesty of the scenery soon took her mind off the cargo of the *Espíritu Estelle*. "I'm sorry. I've tried to be positive in front of Grandmother. It built up—"

"To which the doctor orders a fiesta and two nights

of uninterrupted . . ." He let his sentence dangle seductively, pointing silently to the twin volcanoes that loomed in the distance, their snow-clad peaks piercing the clouds.

"Sleeping Woman." She laughed. "What does the other name mean—*Popocatépetl?*"

When he did not answer immediately, she turned to see a teasing glint in his black eyes. "Smoking man," he whispered. "I can vouch for the validity of that name, too."

They had traveled by horseback from Tecolutla to Veracruz where they took the train. The two hour wait in Veracruz allowed Rafe time to make some purchases he had planned, but had not known how or when to execute. After a couple of hasty inquiries, he had spirited Marina into a custom dress shop.

"*Sí, señor,*" the owner responded, "I have some very pretty *chinas* created especially for Independence Day. I will show you." She scrutinized Marina's figure before leaving the salon, to return with a garment similar to the one Tía Luisa had provided for the dinner at the Hacienda de Vera Cruz—the dinner which never came off because the men had been called to investigate the murder of Diego Ortiz.

Except this costume was even more festive, Marina thought, fingering the five tiers of sheer white organza lavishly embroidered with multicolored flowers. "It reminds me of the tropical flowers along the way."

"Try it on," Rafe had encouraged.

"It will fit, señor," the proprietress assured him. She held the bodice against Marina's chest, spreading the ruffle as it would drape low across her shoulders.

Rafe picked up the fringed sash. Its brilliant green,

designed to bring out the green in the dress, accented Marina's fiery green eyes as well. "Are you sure you like it? We can look at others—"

"I love it," she said again. "But you cannot . . ."

His eyes pierced hers in a look she knew all too well. Unless she wanted to create a scene here in the dress shop, she would have to voice her objection to him buying her such a personal gift later . . . after the dress had been purchased.

"I brought suitable costumes," she insisted.

"No, I want you to wear this for *el Grito.*"

"Then I will repay you when we return to the ship."

Outside she reproached him. "It's improper for you to buy me something like this. What will that woman think?"

He squeezed her arm, ushering her toward the depot, the brown wrapped package under his other arm. "If you wanted a proper courtship, you should have stayed in Texas."

"That is not what I meant. I wouldn't change anything—well, almost nothing. Certainly nothing about you . . . or us. But Grandmother and I chose perfectly suitable clothing—"

"European clothing," he retorted.

"No. American clothing."

"Foreign, nevertheless."

"You're crazy, like Zolic said."

Stopping in the middle of the walkway, he swung her around to face him. "You can wear anything you want any other day of the year, love. But this is Independence Day—Mexican Independence Day. You do like the *china?*"

She had nodded, wanting to kiss him then, to reassure him, he had sounded so plaintive. That of course would have been even more improper than him buying her a lovely fiesta dress. "Thank you."

When they reached Mexico City the depot swelled with Independence Day revelers alighting from trains which arrived every few minutes from all parts of the country. Rafe located their bags, then suddenly hailed a thin young man very near Marina's own age who searched the crowd with a desperate look on his face.

"Fernando, over here."

The young man's eyes lighted with relief. When he approached, Rafe introduced him as Fernando Zamora, an assistant at the ministry.

"Did you set up my meeting?" Rafe inquired. "Do you have a carriage?"

"The meeting is in half an hour," Fernando replied, "and the carriage is at the curb."

"We will take it to our meeting with the heirs." He handed Fernando their bags. "I want you to take these to my mother's house. Tell her I am bringing a guest."

A curious smile crossed Fernando's face.

"A dinner partner," Rafe amended.

As soon as Fernando departed, Rafe hurried Marina toward the carriage his assistant had indicated.

"I hope you don't mind not freshening up before the meeting."

"Not before meeting the heirs." She removed the duster she had worn over her traveling suit, smoothing wrinkles from the gray serge skirt. "I would like to meet your mother in a more presentable fashion, though."

"It won't matter," he assured her. "Everyone else will arrive in the same condition. Besides, you couldn't look anything but beautiful even if you tried."

The carriage traveled at a variable pace depending not only on carriage traffic but on foot traffic since the city teemed with people.

"This is the Zócalo." Rafe swept his arms to indicate a huge square to their left. Marina peered out the window.

"It's the largest plaza I have ever seen."

"One of the largest in the world. See the building trimmed in red volcanic stone, *tezontle* it's called? That's the National Palace where the celebration will be held tonight. See the Liberty Bell?" He pointed to the center portal of the building, where she saw workers atop scaffolding.

"President Díaz had it moved here from the cathedral at Dolores where Father Hidalgo first issued *el Grito* in 1810, his greeting to rally the fight against foreign rule. The President will ring that bell tonight, and the plaza will be full of our people . . . Mexicans."

"Where is your office?"

"There . . . in the National Palace. I'll show you tonight. After *el Grito,* the President is hosting a reception in the rotunda."

She scanned the square, awed by the grandeur of the buildings. "Everything is so old and magnificent."

"Likely the structures Cortés built them on top of were magnificent, too. Only we will never know."

"Here?" She recalled him saying the Spaniards destroyed many of the pyramids.

"The Aztecs' major temples stood right here. In fact the most important one is thought to have been directly beneath that *magnificent* cathedral."

The meeting was held on Calle Madero in what Rafe said was the home of the Marquis of San Mateo de

241

Valparaiso—an elegant mansion built from the same red volcanic stone as the National Palace and many other buildings along this street. It lasted all of ten minutes and left Marina more frustrated than before.

"How could they deny the cargo was ever shipped, when we have Tata's document?"

"They didn't deny it," he corrected. "And their assertion that the former president had nothing to do with the artifacts is probably correct. I've heard rumors for years that an aide to President Bustamente took advantage of the situation to steal some of our national treasures."

"But Bustamente's name is signed to this paper—the paper he gave Tata."

"Like they claim, the aide could have forged the document and Bustamente's signature. A good lawyer can perhaps get Giddeon a fee . . ."

"That takes time!"

The carriage slowed, veering toward a curb, but Rafe called to the driver, who immediately whipped up the horses and they proceeded around the block.

"Where are we going?" Marina stared at the mansion where they had briefly paused.

"That's my mother's house. I thought you might like a little more time to digest the meeting before we join the throng inside."

"You called it a townhouse." She gazed through the window of the cab. "It's a palace . . . and this is a city."

Rafe grimaced. "We have a large family, and Mother likes to entertain, especially now with her husband in the government—"

"And her son."

"She does not entertain for me," he replied firmly. Adding, "The house is rented."

"It's huge."

Taking her gently by the shoulders, he turned her to face him. "Pretentious," he corrected. "Don't worry. I don't like it anymore than you—"

"You belong there."

"And you . . ." —cupping her face he lowered his lips to hers— ". . . you belong wherever I do, right beside me." He deepened his kiss as the carriage rocked along the rutted road, feeling her respond, laughing softly at last when the pitching ride bumped their faces against each other.

The second time around the block, Rafe signaled the driver to stop. "Are you ready?"

She nodded. Ready to return to her own world, she thought dismally.

The multifarious world of Rafael Santana had opened once again, revealing an entirely new and unexpected aspect. Although the Hacienda de Santa Elena had been grand on an even larger scale than this house, it had not appeared overly pretentious, as he called it. The same was not true for the city residence of the Minister of Finance and his family.

The coach had but rolled to a stop when the door was opened by a liveried footman costumed in red and gold. Rafe escorted her up the grand expanse of steps to the carved front door which was opened by a similarly uniformed doorman.

Animated babble punctuated by occasional strains from violins filled the air; elegantly clad bodies belonging to the same voices filled the spacious rooms opening left and right off the wide, also crowded, foyer. Glimpses of dark carved furniture appeared when the guests shifted positions. Above them the walls stretched to high ceilings and graceful arches adorned with gold-leaf carvings.

Crystal and glass chandeliers of proportions to fit the palatial house hung at intervals, while multi-armed candelabras graced the banisters of the bold staircase which branched to either side from a landing accented with an enormous painting. Marina suppressed a shudder, suddenly feeling every bit the unsophisticated Texas ranch girl.

In defense, resentment stirred inside her. This home belonged to Rafael Santana's family; these people, most of whom paused to greet him, were his friends. Why had he kept it all secret? Why had he not prepared her?

She would never fit in here. Never.

"Don't let this fussy stuff worry you," he said at her shoulder. "We won't live like this." He took two glasses of wine from a silver tray passed by a black and white uniformed servant.

"Have some madeira. I'll introduce you to Mother, then we'll go dress."

Suddenly a woman nearer Rafe's age than Marina's burst through the crowd, hugged Rafe, then smiled at Marina. "Mother is looking for you, Rafe. Is this . . . ?"

"Señorita Cafferty," Rafe introduced, "my sister, Sophie."

Marina's eyes widened a notch; she smiled hesitantly. "Marina," she corrected.

Immediately she knew what Rafe had meant by European clothing. Every woman in the room was gowned elegantly in peau de soie, brocade, velvet, or chiffon, trimmed with lace or feathers or fur or spangles, some with all the above.

"Marina, how nice to have you. Let me find Moth—"

"No," Rafe interjected. "Stay with us. As soon as I introduce Mother, you two can go find our clothing."

Sophie's eyes lighted with the same devilment Marina had seen in Rafe's. Her voice was playful, but her words rang with an ominous knell.

"I would rather not be around when Mother finds you, *hermano*," she teased her brother. "You have wrecked her dinner plans, and you know how—"

"Rafael, there you are! Late but present." A tall woman swept down upon them, stopping short of embracing Rafe. Not beautiful, her features were nonetheless striking. Her black hair, parted in the middle and swept back over each ear to form a perfect knot at her nape, was adorned with combs of carved ivory, matching her rich satin gown.

"Mother, may I introduce Señorita Cafferty?" He turned to Marina. "My mother, Doña Alicia."

"My name is Marina, señora," Marina whispered, wishing this one time she had been named anything else in the world. The fleeting displeasure that flashed across Doña Alicia's controlled features reminded Marina quite out of context that Sophie had not been startled by her name.

"I'll show Marina her room," Sophie added quickly.

"Her *dueña* is to be put in the adjoining room," Doña Alicia said.

"She doesn't have a—" Rafe began.

Marina interrupted. This was her battle and she intended to fight it. If he had prepared her, she would never have come to such a home unchaperoned. Since he hadn't, he deserved whatever his mother dished out.

"Unfortunately, Doña Alicia, I have no *dueña*. I am in the city on business, and the necessity for haste prevented me finding a traveling companion. Your son graciously consented to serve as my escort."

As she spoke, Marina watched the color drain from

Doña Alicia's powdered face. When she finished, the woman stared, speechless. Sophie took Marina's arm.

"Come. I will show you where to dress. Your gown has already been pressed. Excuse us, Mother."

Rafe squeezed her fingers. "Take your time. I'll meet you right here. You won't have to look for me."

Sophie pulled her toward the stairs. "Don't let Mother bother you. She will come around."

Marina recalled telling Rafe the same thing about her grandfather. She still believed it about Tata. But she would have to wait for proof concerning Rafe's mother. At this point, she had her doubts.

"She really has our interests at heart," Sophie was saying. "As soon as she gets over the fact that she had no voice in the matter, she will accept you graciously."

At the landing Marina turned to glance back at Rafe. He winked. Beside him his mother talked without seeing her.

"How did you know about me?" Marina asked Sophie, suddenly curious. "I mean, you are the first person in Mexico who hasn't cringed at my name. And you knew . . ."

Sophie laughed. "Chuy. He came back from the hacienda crazy with curiosity. He said your name is Marina and Rafe told him . . ." Pausing she studied Marina a moment, as though considering whether to continue.

"Rafe told him . . . what?" Marina prompted.

Sophie giggled. "Well . . . let us say, my brother Rafe is no longer a target for Mother's matchmaking."

"Is this some cruel joke, Rafael?" Doña Alicia wailed.

Rafe sipped his wine. "No."

"How could you do this to me? Marissa de Valle is in the sala even now, expecting to be your dinner partner."

"I warned you not to waste your matchmaking skills on me tonight."

"You have lost your sense of reality, Rafael, rummaging around in ruins and villages. You do not realize the scandal you have brought upon our house. And your father with his position."

"You met Marina. How could that sweet, beautiful girl cause a scandal in your house?"

"No *dueña!* Does she not have parents? How could they allow her to travel across the country unchaperoned with a male companion? Are they from some village . . . ?"

"Shhh . . . I should warn you not to say something you will regret. Marina Cafferty is your future daughter-in-law."

Doña Alicia scanned the room in a desperate fashion. "You have lost your mind. What will my friends think? How do I explain such a breech of etiquette?"

"You won't have to explain anything you don't reveal, Mother."

The elegance of the mauve decorated guest room to which Sophie showed her came as no surprise to Marina, only the gown pressed and hanging from a brass hook on the opened wardrobe door.

"Here's the tub," Sophie called from behind a screen, this one paneled in a sequence of pastoral settings with sheep grazing on a hillside and flowers blooming beneath a spreading oak. Certainly not a rendition of any scene Marina had viewed since she had been in Mexico.

"I'll leave you to dress."

"This gown isn't . . ." Marina's words died in her muddled thoughts. The changeable moiré taffeta costume, the color of a pigeon's throat Grandmother claimed, was lovelier than she had recalled. It certainly was not European, being designed by a dressmaker in Corpus Christi, and it was every bit as elegant as any gown at the soiree downstairs. She had agreed on the *china* without knowing the type of party they would attend. Surely . . .

Sophie fluffed the white mousseline de soie at the waist and the pleating of appliqué lace which formed the high collar and vest. "Mother decided this one was best suited," Sophie explained. "In fact, she was quite impressed. But if you prefer some other . . ."

"No," Marina decided quickly. "This is the one I should wear."

While she bathed, Sophie fetched them each a glass of wine, then she helped Marina drape and pin her hair in the fashion of the day.

"I can't tell you how relieved I am to meet you," Sophie gushed. "My husband Rudy insisted you must be the daughter of some Indian chief. They're always pushing their daughters off on Rafe."

"I'm relieved, too," Marina admitted, thinking back to the Hacienda de Vera Cruz, to Sophie's room there, to the green silk gown and her own dreadful misunderstanding.

"We will become great friends," Sophie predicted foraging through the wardrobe. "We girls must stick together, when the men are with their mistresses."

248

Marina glimpsed her own gaping mouth in the looking glass, but before she could respond, Sophie withdrew her head from the wardrobe, holding a stiff lace aigrette, still talking.

"Everyone is dying to meet you. I know they will all be pleased. And with the parties going on you won't catch Mother alone again for a couple of days. By then . . ."

"We must leave by tomorrow night," Marina whispered, stunned yet by Sophie's off-hand revelation concerning mistresses, a problem she had never given thought to.

"See? Things will work out. Mother will have until your next visit to come around." She held the aigrette against Marina's hairdo slanting the puff over one ear. "What do you think?"

Marina studied the fancy hair adornment. "Rafe wouldn't like it."

Sophie shrugged. "Very well. But you cannot dress to please a man, Marina. They either have extremely poor taste, or they don't even notice what you are wearing."

Marina followed Sophie toward the grand staircase, thinking of the *china* still tied in its brown wrapper. Regardless of what Sophie thought, Rafe had exquisite taste. And she didn't hold much hope for him not noticing her change in costume, either.

At the landing she paused, searching the crowd for him, for the teasing glint in his eyes. When she found him however there was no teasing glint.

He stood in the foyer talking to several men, all around his own age. But while the others were attired alike in dark cutaway and four-in-hand, Rafe Santana wore a native costume of loose-fitting white trousers and shirt, tied at the waist with a brilliant red sash, like her own green one . . . lying in its brown wrapper, back in the bedroom.

"Mother will die . . ." Sophie was saying. But her words faded from Marina's hearing when Rafe caught sight of them.

For a moment he merely stared, then thrusting his wine glass into a companion's hand, he bounded up the stairs, coming to an abrupt halt in front of Marina. He glared from her gown to her face.

"Where did this dress come from?" He turned to Sophie. "What happened to that brown package?"

"Rafe," Marina began, "please. This is my own gown; your mother had it pressed for me. It fits the occasion perfectly—"

"It does not begin to fit the occasion." Grasping her and Sophie each by an arm he ushered them back upstairs to the second floor, out of view of the guests below.

"Where is the *china* we bought in Veracruz?" he demanded again. "You told me you liked it."

"I love it. It's beautiful, but tonight—" The disappointment in his eyes left her weak.

"Tonight of all nights is no time to promote foreign—"

"This dress is no more foreign than I am. If you are so against foreign things, *I* will leave." Twisting her arm, she attempted to pull away, but he held fast. Sophie tried to help.

"Rafe, Mother thought—"

"Mother can go to hell. I won't stand by and let her . . ."

Marina's anger flared. "You will not put me in the middle of a feud between you and your mother."

250

He glared into her fiery green eyes. "You aren't in the middle. At least, I didn't think you were. I thought you were standing beside me."

"I am, but—"

"Then change your clothes. This is *Mexican* Independence Day. Tonight we are part of the people. I'm not about to sit on that balcony with you dressed like a foreigner."

"On the . . . ?"

Instead of answering, he proceeded to usher her down the hallway, but she dug her heels into the carpet and brought him to a halt.

"I can manage on my own," she told him, embarrassed now at the thought that he might follow her into the bedroom.

"Do you need my help?" Sophie asked. "Shall I call a maid to press your costume?"

Marina shook her head. "No, thank you. The biggest help you can be . . ."—she cut her eyes toward Rafe, an apologetic grin on her lips—". . . is to cool him down."

"How dare you treat her like that?" Sophie accused after Marina disappeared into the guest room halfway down the corridor. "Mother has unnerved her enough without you imposing your idiosyncratic biases—"

"They are not idiosyncrasies, and they are not biases. And you can tell Mother to keep her hands off that girl in there." He nodded toward the room where Marina had disappeared. "I love her and I intend to marry her and Mother is not going to hurt her."

"Rafe—"

"Nor will I allow any of you to turn her into one of those simple-minded clothes-horses you are always

251

pairing me with."

Below them the dinner bell sounded its first call. Rafe glanced anxiously toward Marina's room. "What did Mother do about Marissa de Valle?"

"As adept as our mother is at finding solutions to social dilemmas, need you ask? She dispatched a carriage to fetch Senator Garcia. He had sent word earlier that his wife was ill and neither were coming, but . . ."

Rafe grimaced. "Anything to balance the dinner table." He turned accusing eyes on Sophie. "You go downstairs right now and see that she isn't expecting that damned old senator to escort Marina."

"You know Mother runs her own parties." Sophie smiled, seeing Marina walk tentatively down the hall gowned in the embroidered *china*. "My God, Rafe, she radiates fire and passion. The senator will be most pleased—"

"Go," he ordered, unable to take his eyes off Marina. By the time she stood before him, Sophie had scurried down the staircase.

From his look Marina could tell his anger had evaporated into barely-concealed passion. He studied her at length, finally cupping her face in his hands, bringing her lips to his.

"I'm sorry I was so . . . arrogant."

Her heart beat at a rapid clip beneath the multi-colored embroidered ruffle encircling her shoulders. "I was only trying to please . . ."

His gaze merged with her own. "You please *me*, love. You please me more than I can ever tell you."

He drew her toward a balcony which ran the length of the house in the back and overlooked a charming garden. A heady fragrance of roses and hibiscus wafted through the cool night air. Sculptured plants, in the European mode she thought, encircled a pool that sparkled in the light of a multitude of small torches anchored in the ground randomly about the area.

"Wasn't that the dinner bell?" she asked.

"Before we go down, I have a gift for you." He dug into his pocket and withdrew a small wooden box from which he extracted a pair of elaborately fashioned gold earrings.

She watched his eyes dance when he held them against her face. They were so long they nipped her bare shoulders.

Then, as he had done at the hacienda, he fitted the wires through the holes in her earlobes, grazing her cheek, her neck with his fingers.

"When did you buy these?"

"I didn't." She watched him bite his bottom lip, concentrating on finding the pierced hole, then on latching the hook. "They belonged to my grandmother. Actually to my great-great-great—I'm not sure how many greats—the wife of the Conquistador."

"But . . . ? I can't wear—"

"They belong to *me*. My great-grandmother gave them to me." Finished he stood back to admire his work, gently fingering the filigree tips, teasing her bare shoulders in the process.

"These earrings—so family legend holds—were made from the first piece of gold taken from their very productive mine. My grandmother, for whom they were made, was Indian."

His voice was husky, sincere, and loving. But the reality of his words washed all traces of passion from her body.

"What will your mother think?"

253

His eyes held hers, turning grim.

"I can't wear them downstairs."

"Why not?"

"I won't allow you to use me like this."

"I'm not—"

"Yes. You are. I don't pretend to understand this vendetta of yours. Whatever disagreements lie between you and your Mother, I will take your side. I will always stand beside you. But on my first visit to her home, I will not be made a spectacle of—I won't. You can't expect—" Lifting her arms, she began to unfasten the earrings.

"Whoa . . . hush . . ." Quickly, with fingers as gentle as his voice, he stilled her hands. "Wear them, please. We won't go downstairs. We will slip out the back. This dress—these earrings—they don't have anything to do with getting back at my mother. But I can see now how it might look like that to you."

"And to everyone downstairs," she whispered.

The second bell to dinner sounded. He kissed her soundly, then guided her toward a staircase which led into the garden. "Come on."

"But the dinner?"

"They won't miss us," he assured her. "And you will have plenty of chances to attend Mother's dinner parties." He grinned sheepishly. "You can even wear that beautiful gown I made you take off a while ago. But never on Mexican Independence Day."

"I will never understand you," she sighed, leaning back in the carriage he had found for them.

At the bottom of the balcony staircase he had located a servant and sent him to whisper discreet instructions to his mother not to wait dinner on them.

By the time they were ensconced in the carriage Rafe had returned to his most attentive, gentle self. "Even before I met you I told her not to invite a dinner partner for me tonight. Then I sent word by Fernando that I was bringing a guest. She had plenty of warning."

"I didn't expect an exuberant welcome, but then neither did I expect to be chastised for traveling without a *dueña*. That was short-sighted. I should have—"

He grasped her face in his hand, turning her lips to his. "The only choice was not to have come at all. And that, love, was no choice. If I hadn't gotten you off that ship and all to myself, I would have been in danger of taking you to bed in your grandmother's own cabin."

His teasing suggestions warmed her, but suddenly she recalled Sophie's discussion of mistresses and her blood turned cold. "So the truth is out. It's my body you want."

He grinned avariciously, lowering his lips to hers.

She moved her face before he made contact. "My body. To use for your own *carnal* purposes. To clothe in a traditional costume and flaunt in the face of your family."

His eyes narrowed. Her voice was playful—yet, somehow it wasn't.

"You are . . . serious?"

"Very serious."

"But you can't believe that. I love you. I've told you so over and over."

"I'm beginning to think Zolic is right. You don't know what you want . . . who you are. You're struggling against some unseen, unknown enemy. For a while I thought it was only I who am confused. Now I realize you are, too. If you don't understand yourself, how will I ever be able to?"

"I can't be as bad as all that."

"No? One minute you dress me in your sister's silk negligee, the next in a native costume. One minute you scorn everything Spanish, the next you are telling me I will run the staff at the hacienda. Taken together none of it makes sense."

Rafe slumped back against the seat of the carriage. He closed his eyes, thinking, thinking. She was right. He had explained nothing. How could she understand? Finally, he leaned out the window, barked a command to the driver, then faced her solemnly. "I will explain. If by sunrise tomorrow you don't understand me, you never will."

His eyes bored into hers inside the dimly lit carriage. His jaw twitched.

Staring at the throbbing vein in his neck she felt his own heart beat. She kissed him softly on the lips. "I'm listening."

During the next hour they toured the ancient city with Rafe as tour guide. Turning off Madero they entered a grand boulevard.

"*Paseo de los Hombres Ilustres,*" Rafe told her. "This leads to Chapultepec Castle where the Emperor Maximilian and his Empress Carlota reigned; the same castle your United States Marines stormed in 1845, killing six of our very young soldiers."

"Rafe, keep to the time period in question. The United States Marine Corps has nothing to do with Indians and Spaniards."

Her voice was teasing and he grunted. "Right. Well, this boulevard is a case in point. Maximilian built it so he could have a straight shot at his offices in the

National Palace. Can't you see his royal carriage traveling down this splendid boulevard? I am told there is nothing finer in Europe. He imported a *French* architect to design it."

At intervals the carriage detoured around traffic circles, each with a statue in the center. "Those must be the illustrious men for whom the boulevard was named," she mused, peering out the window in an effort to identify one as they drove past.

"Christopher Columbus," Rafe supplied. "Italian, Portuguese, Spanish, you choose his nationality."

"In the United States we have statues to foreign heroes, too. But I have never known anyone who was as bitter as you about them."

"I suppose I am bitter, but not in the way you think. You were right when you said my feelings are ambivalent; I can see how it wouldn't make much sense to you." He pointed toward the castle on top of the hill, but made no attempt to have the driver stop. "Regardless of how it seems, I'm proud of my Spanish heritage. I would be even more proud, though, if both cultures— Spanish and Indian—could be respected, as the revolution intended."

Before she could answer, he tapped the top of the carriage, called instructions, then sat back. "You saw the scene at my mother's house. Even on this important national holiday those people will not allow themselves to identify with their past."

Marina stared out the window at the passing park, a lovely place with flowers and trees and fountains.

"Chapultepec Park," he said.

"Your mother and her friends are celebrating, Rafe. You should give them credit for that."

"Why? Because they don't pass up a chance for a

party? It's the spirit of the day they are missing. And the chance to promote unity for our country."

They rode an hour or so. For a time she thought they were headed back to the Zócalo, but soon she began to doubt it. "Won't we miss the celebration?"

"We have plenty of time. The President won't give *el Grito* until eleven o'clock. Besides, I told you I intend to spend all night if necessary. Look out the window. That's the University of Mexico. Did you know it's the oldest university in the New World? It was founded in 1551."

"Did you go there?"

He nodded. "But I had to rebel to do so. Our prominent citizens send their sons abroad to be educated. My parents were scandalized."

"Scandalized? For attending university?"

"It's hard to believe, isn't it? Do you see my point? Those people at my mother's house tonight are the most influential citizens in this country. Yet they look on everything from our art to our culture to our university as second-rate."

He stared at her intently now. "I will wager that every woman at that party wore a gown made in France or Spain. If not, their seamstresses used European designs and fabrics."

Marina fingered the ruffle on her blouse. "Except one."

He raised an eyebrow in self-mocking fashion. "Except one. Did you notice their complexions?"

She frowned.

"Dark skin is not acceptable. The darker the skin, the more Indian blood. That was the first thing I noticed out of kilter, my mother powdering her face to make it lighter."

Struggling to understand, Marina found herself becoming more and more confused. "How did you know that was the reason she powdered her face? Did she tell you?"

The carriage rocked to a halt, but inside Rafe sat still, staring into Marina's face, wondering whether he was doing the right thing. Knowing he had no other choice.

"I'm going to share something with you I have never shared with another soul on earth. I hope it will help you understand—I don't want to deny my Spanish heritage; I want to be able to claim my Indian heritage with pride. And I want the same for every person in my country."

He helped her alight into a lovely glen which bordered a lake. Revelers abounded, of course. Every place in the city was crowded today. They walked toward the lake, where she saw canoes decorated with flowers.

"This is Xochimilco. The Aztecs built the City of Mexico on a lake—they called it *Tenochtitlan*. The town was connected to the mainland by a series of canals. These are the only ones left."

While he engaged a canoe, Marina stared around. People picnicked under the trees, sipping wine and cerveza; children played; and on a blanket in the distance lovers were wrapped in an embrace. The air was sweet with the fragrance of flowers. Guitar music drifted softly, and looking for the source, she saw a roving band of mariachis. It was lovely . . . magical. She felt as though she were moving through a dream; she prayed it would not become a nightmare.

He guided her to one of the canoes which he handed her into before climbing in himself.

"You may get your dress wet."

"It will dry."

Silently he pushed off, paddling into the center of the canal; she trailed her fingers in the water.

"I've never seen so many flowers in my life. People use them everywhere."

"The Indians even wore them into battle," he told her. "Covered their shields with flowers, adorned their headdresses. It must have been a sight to behold."

She watched him row, dark skin glistening against his snowy white shirt, highlighted now by the magenta glow of the setting sun. He was handsome and determined . . . and extremely vulnerable.

Feeling her eyes on him, he grimaced. "I may be making a mistake taking you here. I feel like we have known each other forever, but . . . but in reality we haven't. I have no idea how you will react to what I'm about to reveal."

Her heart quickened. At this moment she knew she loved him more than she ever had. When she asked him to open his world, she had not known how difficult it would be. Anticipation built and warred with anxiety inside her. *Pray God I can understand and accept his revelation,* she whispered.

Canals branched off the main waterway and soon she was completely lost in the maze. The silk embroidery on her dress sparkled in the last rays of sunlight and when she moved her head from side to side, the earrings tickled her skin. "Thank you for my dress," she said. "And the earrings. They are perfect for a canoe ride at sunset."

He grinned. "I didn't realize we would be taking a canoe ride when I bought the dress. In fact, I've never taken a girl on a canoe ride before."

Guitar music from passing boats drifted toward them. "I'm glad. It's awfully . . . romantic."

His slight grin brought a lump to her throat. The shoreline all looked alike, lush with trees and greenery and flowers. About the time she decided they must be traveling in circles, a village appeared before them.

Rafe headed straight for it, docked, and helped her onto the pier. She had a feeling of stepping back a hundred years or so in time. The small village was comprised of only a couple dozen white-washed adobe huts. Although the streets were dirt, hibiscus and bougainvillea blossomed in profusion around every dwelling, giving the entire place a festive air. The few people about were men dressed much like Rafe, in white shirts and breeches but without the sash. They all wore woven-palm sombreros.

Her curiosity growing by leaps and bounds, she skipped to keep up with him, feeling his hand damp around her own. When he stopped at the doorway of the hut furthest from the dock, she recalled their visit to the old shaman.

Her heart pumped faster. Wherever was he taking her this time?

The first difference between this visit and the one to Diego Ortiz came in the voice that answered Rafe's call—a feminine voice, albeit cracking with age.

Rafe's fingers trembled around Marina's arm; she glanced quickly to his worried eyes before he ushered her into the earthen-floored hut. Everything was immaculate. The interior walls were white-washed as those outside, a painted border of brightly colored flowers encircling them. The room was warmed by a corner fireplace, in front of which sat a frail woman dressed in black, her legs crossed, again calling to mind

Diego Ortiz.

When Rafe spoke, Marina recognized one word: *abuelita*—little grandmother. She listened to their conversation without understanding—either the language or the circumstances.

The old woman stared at Marina through small black eyes from a face as marred by age as the landscape through which they had passed between Veracruz and the City of Mexico.

"Sit down." Rafe indicated a mat, and when she had seated herself across from the old woman, he followed, sitting beside her.

He held one of her hands tightly in his own while he explained. "This is my great-grandmother . . ."

Marina's free hand went automatically to her ear.

". . . who gave me those earrings," he finished.

The old woman's eyes lit up, whether at Marina's gesture or at Rafe's words, Marina could not guess. But when the woman reached a frail hand across the distance separating them, Marina immediately grasped it in her own. At Rafe's next words, her thoughts stood still.

". . . my mother's grandmother."

Chapter Ten

They did not stay at the old woman's hut over half an hour, but it was a half hour Marina knew she would hold in her heart the rest of her life.

The old grandmother did not speak English; rather she and Rafe conversed in a musical language much like the one he had said was shunned today, while she served them a thick chocolate drink. Pride glistened in her eyes when she looked from Rafe to Marina, taking in their native costumes, resting time after time on the golden earrings, welcoming Marina with a warmth that quickly eased the rejections from both Doña Alicia and Tata.

When they rose to leave, the old woman presented Marina with a finely woven white wool rebozo.

"She says it is cold over there with the Spanish," Rafe said.

"Yes, *abuelita.*" Marina spoke directly to the old woman, using the term of address Rafe had used earlier. Rafe translated in a hushed tone. "It is much warmer here with you."

Marina hugged the old woman, and they left with tears in their eyes.

Strolling arm in arm toward the canoe, Marina felt more complete than she could ever recall. She loved Rafael Santana beyond her wildest dreams, and it was on her lips to tell him so. Yet, she had saved those words, and she would save them still to share with him in a private place.

"Thank you for bringing me here. I understand so much now . . . and am left with many new questions."

At the dock he spread his hands about her waist and lifted her toward the canoe. Before lowering her, he kissed her tenderly. "Now our questions are the same."

"Yes."

As he pushed out into the canal, she turned for one last look.

"You must not say a word about this to anyone," he cautioned. "I'm the only person in the family who knows my mother's secret."

Marina stared at him, aghast. "Not even your father?"

"Not even my father."

"Or your brothers and sisters?"

He shook his head. "I learned it by accident while I was at university. I always knew things were not exactly right, so it didn't come as a shock, only as a shame that she would hide her past." He concentrated on the rowing. "Now you know the origin of the rift between my mother and me. She lives in fear that I will expose her secret to her pretentious world. Of course, I won't . . . not ever."

The sun had set and the evening was cool. Marina pulled the woolen rebozo about her shoulders, marveling at the warmth it afforded. Was it only the wool? Or was it something much deeper . . . and stronger?

"I hope that proves I'm not obsessed, as Zolic claims."

She smiled. "Now we are both obsessed."

"Do not misunderstand. I don't want to live in that village nor to give up the luxuries my family has worked for. I suppose what I'm trying to explain is that the Revolution should unite my people, not divide them."

By the time they arrived back at the Zócalo the crowd was so thick they had to walk the last several blocks. Food vendors ringed the square on three sides, selling a variety of native foods. Rafe seemed determined she try everything: tamales, tacos, quesadillas, buñuelos.

Musicians played every instrument from guitars and violins to shells and gourds, creating a cacophony of sounds punctuated by voices babbling in Spanish and languages—dialects, Rafe said—she could not interpret.

At last she understood his insistence they wear traditional dress. Few people roamed the plaza in ordinary clothing or fancy European costumes as he termed them.

"The parades are tomorrow, and more fiestas. Tonight is *el Grito*." He shouldered his way through the crowd at the entrance to the National Palace, pulling her behind him.

The honored guests, including government officials and their wives, were to sit on the second floor balcony from where the speeches would be given and from where President Díaz would deliver *el Grito*.

"Benito Juárez issued his *Grito*—the call for independence—in 1810, but nothing much in the way of independence has come about, except a few revolutions." Explaining, Rafe dragged her up the staircase through throngs of people, greeting them with nods as he went. "Several delegations of our leading officials went abroad to secure a throne for Mexico. They approached Napoleon who sent us an emperor— Maximilian."

By the time they reached the balcony, the speeches had begun, although the boisterous crowd below milled inattentively.

Rafe escorted her down a row of well-dressed— European style, he would say—couples to their places beside his mother and father. Marina tried to smile even though Doña Alicia scowled at her son, then apprised her future daughter-in-law with equal displeasure. When her eyes fastened on the gold earrings, her mouth dropped open.

"Rafael, you . . . !" she hissed, but the speaker finished at that moment, and the crowd applauded— those on the balcony, leastways—drawing attention back to the ceremonies.

Marina watched Doña Alicia's face take on a pallor which would eliminate the need for powder should it become a permanent affliction. She felt suddenly sorry for the woman. How sad to live with such a fearsome secret . . . how sad to consider her own grandmother a threat.

In the hush before the next speech began, Rafe's father leaned across his wife to speak to Marina. "My son Chuy tells me you have relatives in our country."

Marina nodded feebly, watching a grimace contort Doña Alicia's face.

"Imagine that, my dear?" Don Agustín addressed his wife. "Entertaining a long lost relative of the Cortinases over at Vera Cruz."

"What do you mean?" Doña Alicia turned a frown not on her husband, nor even on Marina, but upon her son.

"Sí, señora, es verdad," Rafe concurred. "It is true; her family is related to Don Ignacio. Her parents and grandparents run the family's Spanish land grants in Texas."

Doña Alicia perused Marina with added interest. She took in once more the native costume and finally the dreaded earrings, at which point loathing etched her face, a loathing Marina now knew shielded fear. Doña Alicia turned away abruptly. "I should have credited Luisa with better sense than to send a girl off unchaperoned . . . and in native—"

"Señora," —Don Agustín's voice chastised— "you do not give your son due credit. Although it is highly irregular, I admit, for a young woman to travel with a male escort, your son is a respected government official. I am sure the Cortinases recognized this fact when he visited them not long ago."

Doña Alicia's eyes lightened a bit. "You were a guest at La Hacienda de Vera Cruz?"

Rafe nodded. "As for our native costumes," he added, "you should know by now that on this day I intend to demonstrate my feelings for our people—*all* our people." Deliberately he stared into his mother's eyes. "And the earrings, señora, are a symbol of that . . . nothing more."

That was all that could be said, Marina knew. Her own inclination to assure the woman she would never reveal the secret would only serve the opposite. The image of the little woman in the immaculate hut flashed through her mind, along with regret that Doña Alicia could not allow herself to acknowledge her own grandmother. The twinkle in those old eyes and the smile on those wrinkled lips would do much to assuage the self-inflicted turmoil in the señora's life.

The conversation had taken place in hushed whispers during the following speech, which now ended. Immediately, Rafe pulled Marina to her feet. "This is it, *el Grito*."

The cheering that commenced when President Díaz took the podium intensified when he waved the red, white, and green Mexican flag high above his head. At his shouted greeting, the cheering changed into chants of the same.

"*¡Viva la Independencia! ¡Viva Mexico!*" The enormous square reverberated with the calls. "Long live Independence! Long live Mexico!"

Beside her Rafe waved their clasped hands in the air, shouting, too. And soon she herself was caught up in the spirit of celebration, calling *el Grito* along with him.

The Liberty Bell pealed, resounding with clear melodic tones through the tumult of rejoicing people. Marina peered through the swaying bodies, watching the President pull the lever to ring the bell. Rafe's arm went around her shoulders, and glancing at him, she saw the splendid light in his eyes, the joy on his face. She slipped an arm around his waist, convention be damned.

"Look!" he whispered as the first fireworks exploded in the night sky forming a sparkling canopy above the Zócalo.

He kissed her then, square on the lips, and she responded with all the passion of the moment. Inside, her senses flared as the fireworks themselves—the moment was magical, one of magnificent communion—she with him and he with her.

Lifting his lips, he watched fireworks flare in her eyes. "From this moment on, my love, you belong to me."

She caressed his face with her eyes. "And you, Rafael Santana, belong to me."

The President's reception followed in the rotunda of the National Palace which was so crowded Marina could hardly get a good look at the building itself. Rafe's parents disappeared into the crowd, but his brothers and sisters sought them out, one after the other, and they were especially welcoming. So much so, she suspected them of attempting to atone for their mother's rejection.

That none of them knew the origin of Doña Alicia's behavior saddened Marina. The dear little woman across the canals was their great-grandmother, too. They had a right to know her. When she said as much to Rafe in a rare moment before greeting other family members, he had replied by shaking his head.

"As long as my mother is alive, I will keep her secret. After she is gone, I will tell them."

What he did not say, of course, but what they both thought, was that in all likelihood by then his *abuelita* also would have gone on to the world of the gods.

Although Rafe's brother Chuy, the matador, was the last to find them, he immediately became Marina's favorite.

"I'm anxious to see you fight the bulls," she told him.

"Tomorrow after the parades and before the dances I fight in the corrida. You . . ." —he studied Rafe a moment before adding with mock reluctance— ". . . both of you will be my guests in the Governor's box. I will dedicate my fight to you, Marina."

"Whoa, now," Rafe teased. "She's my girl. Only after she is my wife will I allow you to shower her with such attention. By that time it will be too late for you to steal her away."

Marina's heart fluttered at his teasing, because she knew it wasn't teasing. She knew also that no matter how handsome the man or how bravely he fought the bulls, no one could steal her heart from Rafael Santana.

Chuy grinned. "We will see, brother. When Marina learns of your obsessions, she may consider you too eccentric for her taste. A simple matador might be a welcome substitute."

Marina laughed. "I have already discovered a few of his eccentricities."

"And he has not run you off yet?"

"Not even with his reluctance to speak my name."

Chuy embraced her in a brotherly fashion, speaking in conspiratorial terms. "My brother Rafael does not fancy himself another Cortés, Marina. It is his *machismo*. What I suggest as a cure—"

"Enough," Rafe laughed. "We have more intelligent people to greet tonight. Be off with you, *hermano*."

Chuy bowed over Marina's hand, brushing it with his lips. "Welcome, Marina. I speak for the family when I say we are delighted the eldest son has such splendid taste in women."

She glanced at Rafe in time to see his grin broaden and pride sparkle in his eyes.

"The invitation still stands—for both of you. Be my guests at the corrida tomorrow."

"Sorry, brother. Another time. Our train leaves at sunup."

"We aren't staying for the parades?" she asked after Chuy had left.

"We have work to do, love." With a hand to her elbow, he ushered her through the crowd and up the staircase they had used to reach the balcony for *el Grito*.

"But Independence Day isn't until tomorrow."

"Tonight was the important part. Next year we'll take it all in. Right now we have a treasure hunt to complete."

On the second floor of the National Palace he led her past the doors to the balcony and to a corner suite of offices at the end of a long corridor. Once inside he passed through the outer office and began to light the lamps in a much larger room. She followed him, fascinated.

"So, this is where you work?" The outer office through which they passed appeared in the dim light to be neat and sparsely furnished. She identified two desks and a wall of glass-fronted cabinets.

The second room was larger, furnished with heavy walnut furniture—a desk, several chairs, a credenza— and two brown leather sofas flanking a low, square-shaped table littered with paperwork. The same sort of glass-fronted cabinets as in the outer room lined the walls. She walked toward one, inspecting the contents:

pottery of various designs, some whole, most only fragments, rocks, also of varying shapes and sizes, and
stone, feathers, jade . . .

Rafe went immediately to a cabinet where he began
rifling through a stack of papers. "Draw back the
draperies if you like. The Zócalo is still crawling with
activity."

The draperies were insulated and heavy. Behind
them she discovered a wall of floor-to-ceiling French
doors. When she threw open the center pair, the sounds
of revelry intensified. He was right—the plaza was full
of people. Stepping onto the balcony, she studied the
sky. Now instead of fireworks it was lighted by millions
of stars.

"Come look. The sky is magnificent."

"Give me a minute," he called back.

Wondering for the first time what he was about, she
returned to the office. "What are you looking for?"

"This!" Triumphantly, he pulled a folder free, closed
the cabinet doors, and thumbed through the papers
inside. "A description of Axayacatl's treasure, recorded by one of Cortés's own men."

"The treasure Moctezuma gave Cortés?"

At her despondent tone of voice he glanced up. Their
gazes locked. The want for him was there. He could see
it in her eyes, in the almost imperceptible quiver of her
lips, in the throb of the vein in her neck.

His body reacted; he ached to reach for her. But the
hurt was there, too. The hurt—and the fear.

"This list will help us determine whether any of the
items are fake. A lot of fakes were made. Unless they
are the real thing, they are not national treasures. Our
agreement extends only to national treasures."

Her eyes widened while he spoke; she pursed her lips.

"We will work things out, love. I promised you that. I mean it."

Desperation flooded her senses which only shortly before had been soft and sensual. She wanted to cry *How? How will we work things out? How?*

Instead she turned and ran to the balcony, crying inside, *Why? Why? Why?*

Why had this special day deteriorated into reality? Even his mother's rejection was no longer a threat. And the depth to which he had opened his world to her had caused her to forget her own mission—the one divisive element remaining in their lives.

The one thing which from the beginning had been the most threatening of all.

She gripped the cold iron rail of the balcony with tight fists and felt him grasp her shoulders with warm tender hands. Inside she screamed at the torment wrought by her own conflicting emotions.

When he turned her to face him, she saw her own need reflected in his eyes . . . in his desperate plea for her love. Suddenly she recalled the way he had looked earlier today in the canoe—the vulnerability. She thought of the enormous part of his life he had shared with her—with her alone.

"Tonight . . ." His voice was husky and it drifted away into the melee in the plaza beneath them, into the wanting in her eyes.

Then they were in each other's arms. His hands slid around her, clutching her to him, warming her against the chill of the night. Their hearts pounded furiously as one.

Tonight, she thought. *Tonight* was all they had, all she could be certain of ever having. Tomorrow she could worry over the cargo. *Tonight . . .*

"Tonight," she whispered, lifting her face to his. Their lips met hungrily. She nuzzled against him, and he broadened his stance, entwining her legs around his own, pressing her close to his already tormented body.

For a moment all else in the universe vanished—all else except their racing hearts, their fiery emotions, their desperate longings.

"*Por los dios,*" he muttered against her lips. "How I want to make love to you."

With her hands she teased the length of his back, feeling his muscles contract. "Let's do."

He grinned. "Sure you won't accuse me of bringing you up here merely for my own . . . ah, *carnal* purposes?"

Her gaze held his as she recalled her earlier words. "After what you shared with me this afternoon, I will never think such a thing again."

"Then give me a minute to lock the door."

The suggestion recalled where they were. She hesitated. "Should we . . . ? Someone might . . ."

He kissed the words from her lips. "No one will come looking for us up here, not with a fiesta going on in the Zócalo. Anyway, my door locks from both sides."

When he returned to find her still gazing at the starlight sky, he scooped her in his arms. "But if we proceed on this balcony, we will definitely draw an audience."

Throwing her arms around his neck, she kissed him urgently while he struggled to carry her inside and close and lock the balcony doors and draw the draperies, all with one hand.

Alongside one of the sofas, he stood her on her feet and bent to sweep the papers off it. "Sorry about the housekeeping. I give strict orders for no one to touch a single sheet of paper in this room."

She tugged at his shirt, drawing the tails from the waistband. "Am I to assume everyone is required to obey your *strict orders?*"

Reaching for her blouse, he did the same. "You bet, arrogant bastard that I am."

Rapidly then they undressed, each helping the other, until they stood together, clinging, warming, all softness and deliciously firm muscles.

"You're cold," he whispered.

She shook her head against his chest. "You set me on fire."

While his hands roamed her body, his lips found hers again. "You do . . . me . . . too," he mumbled between kisses.

They moved in shadows, bathed in the radiance of the soft golden glow from the lamp on his desk—he stroking, kissing, loving, she boldly exploring, expressing her love with her hands instead of words.

Although she wanted to speak the words now, as she had wanted to earlier, she knew the time was still not right. Those words were all she had left to give. And she would give them only when their future was certain, their differences resolved, when they could be one in purpose as well as in spirit . . . and in body.

Lowering himself to the cool leather sofa, he pulled her on top of him, hoping to spare her the shock of cold meeting hot as happened when his own heated flesh touched the cushions.

Her legs straddling his, she leaned forward, her hair teasing his face, her lips seeking his, her breasts tantalizing his chest. Reaching, he grasped them in his hands, accelerating her spiraling need for him.

Arms folded across his chest, she studied his face playfully. "Speaking of *carnal* purposes," she whispered, her lips bedeviling his as she spoke, "do you remember our conversation the day we went to El Tajín?"

His smiling eyes searched hers. "I remember a lot of things we said . . . and did . . . that day."

"Specifically what you told me about the peyote ritual?"

He grinned. "What about it?"

She licked her lips, then ran her tongue around his own. "The string. You said it represented penance for . . . *carnal sin.*"

His eye turned wary. "Yes?"

"Tell me about the knot in your string?"

He blinked once. "Right now?"

She nodded.

Suggestively he opened his legs beneath her, rubbing his taut body against the base of her abdomen.

"This very minute?"

She nodded.

His hands cupped her to him. Her breath caught in her chest at the consuming urgency growing within her. Moving her hips, she struggled to accommodate him.

With a suddenness she had not expected, he caught her around the waist and lifted her, adjusted the angle, then set her down on top of him. She gasped as he entered her body. Quickly, he clasped her to him, chest to chest, lips to lips. He kissed her deeply, desperately.

By digging an elbow into the pliant cushions and using the force of his muscles, he managed to turn them until she rested beneath him, her back to the now-warm leather. "First things first, love," he whispered. "You did ask me to make love to you."

"Hummm . . ." she mumbled, returning his kiss, passion for desperate passion, while he proceeded to fulfill her first request with vigor and determination, bringing them both to the glorious pinnacle much sooner than they had planned.

Clinging together afterwards, they stretched the length of the sofa, relaxing in each other's arms. He nuzzled his face in her hair, and at length she felt his muscles shudder in one last signal of release.

"So?" she asked a while later. "What about your admission of carnal sin? Or should I say . . . *who?*"

Cradling her head in the crook of his elbow, he lavished her face with kisses. With his free hand he plied her breast almost absently.

"You beat all, do you know that? I've never heard of a woman who would ask about a rival while in the throes of . . . in the throes of wicked passion." Favoring her with his special grin, he then proceeded to kiss her soundly.

"It isn't wicked." She studied him with a curious grin. "And I don't for a moment consider her—even if she was a mistress—my rival."

His eyes widened, and he laughed heartily. "Me? With a mistress?" Suddenly his eyes danced. "Are you saying you take me for granted?"

She merely stared sweetly into his eyes.

When he spoke again, all hint of teasing was gone; only gentleness and sincerity remained. "You had better. For you have no rival and you never will have— not for my body or for my attention or for my love. Any occasion when I gave my body to another woman is in the past and is not worthy of being discussed in your presence."

He loved her again then, taking full advantage of the love she gave so fully, giving himself as fully in return. He recalled the night she questioned, the night with

Chief Aztlán's daughter. He recalled thinking that what was lacking in the experience was his desire for control.

Now he discovered he had been wrong. In loving Marina Cafferty, he did not control as much as share. They loved together, as a team, as partners, as they would share their entire lives. How lucky he was to have found such a woman, a woman he could love with all the passion increasing daily inside him.

She filled him with so much life he knew he would wither and die were he ever to lose her. Quickly he banished such a thought. He had to get busy and find some way to keep his promise to her—his promise to work out their differences concerning the cargo on the *Espíritu Estelle*.

By leaving the next day at dawn, they arrived in Tecolutla a couple of hours before dusk, bedraggled and road-weary, but still giddy with happiness.

They had finally left his office the night before after convincing themselves that they could not possibly spend the night locked away there, at least not under the terms of Rafe's pledge to Giddeon Duval to protect her honor with his life. Returning to his mother's house, they had slipped up the back staircase.

She slept alone in the luxurious guest room, and although her mind reeled with the events of the day, her body was exhausted and she slept soundly until a maid awakened her with orange juice before dawn.

"Jugo de la naranja," the maid told her setting the tray of fresh-squeezed orange juice and an assortment of pan dulces on a table beside the balcony window. "Don Rafael said you must leave for the depot in half

278

an hour."

"Thank you." She climbed from bed and searched for her valise. She wished he would have come himself to kiss her and hold her in the early morning privacy before the household stirred. Already she dreaded the days ahead when they would be confined to the *Stella Duval* together, yet separated by grandparents and conventions.

Dressing hastily in the traveling suit she had worn only yesterday when they arrived, she packed her valise, then recalled the golden earrings. She must be sure they were packed well in their little box.

Her search uncovered the bloodstone. She turned it over in her hands. What had Zolic told her about it? Oh, yes—it was supposed to keep her safe from Rafael Santana.

She laughed.

"Now I know why I love you so much."

Rafe's teasing voice settled over her like a mantle of silk. Embracing her from behind, he lay his face alongside hers, kissing her cheek. "I like my women cheerful before the break of dawn."

Protesting the jocular though arrogant statement, she had started to turn in his arms, when he saw the bloodstone.

"What is that?" he asked.

"A blood—"

"I mean, what are you doing with it?" Releasing her, he took the object from her hands and glared at it.

She hesitated briefly. "Zolic gave it to me."

"When? And why?"

"The day we left to come here. Why do you ask?"

"*Why* did he give it to you?" he repeated.

Recalling Rafe's reaction to the reed flute and later

279

to the roses, she wondered how much she could tell him without arousing his anger, knowing all the while she would never keep secrets from this man, especially not after the day before when he had revealed the deepest secret of all. "He said it would protect me from those who would do me harm. That—"

"Zolic told you that?"

"Among other things."

"What other things?"

She clasped her arms around his chest and held him close. His heart beat against her face. She felt his arms tighten, fitting her to his body. "What other things?" he asked again, this time in a quieter voice.

She laughed against his chest. "Well, it didn't work . . . fortunately . . ."

He held her back to stare curiously into her face. "What other things?"

"That it would keep me pure . . . regardless of . . . of *your* attempts . . ."

His hands slipped to her shoulders, where they tightened almost painfully. His eyes clouded, as his thoughts left the room. "That bastard! He—"

"Rafe, it doesn't matter. Let him think whatever he wants. We will be finished with the expedition soon. He can't harm us."

"Jesús Zolic is an expert on Indian culture. He knows damned well what a bloodstone is used for— and it is not to *protect* someone."

"What then?"

"It's a rather vicious method of effecting curses."

"Curses? On what?"

"Whom?" he corrected. "Curses are put on people, generally. Sometimes on crops or the like, but in this case . . . the *whom* is exactly what I intend to find out as soon as we see Zolic."

"You don't believe—?"

"In curses? No. In the evil of the people who claim to effect them, yes."

"But Zolic isn't evil. You said yourself—"

Rafe drew her close. "I know. The man isn't evil, he is socially inept. I suppose I should be grateful, since it's my girl he is trying to steal."

She kissed him quickly. "Remember what you told me last night?"

He raised an eyebrow, waiting.

"You have no rivals, either. Not now, not in the future."

His devilish grin set her senses reeling. When he spoke the sincerity in his husky voice made her wish they could take a later train.

"I know that, love, but it sounds good to hear it."

The train ride from the City of Mexico to Veracruz on the coast took four hours, winding its way through valleys and over mountains. Again, they had a beautiful view of Mount Orizaba.

"There's our star," she told him.

"Yes," he said. "Watch closely now, we may be able to see the San Miguel stone." He indicated the countryside along the rails, rather than the mountains in the distance.

Again she had the window seat and he leaned across her to study the landscape outside. His nearness warmed her. She knew it always would.

"There," he motioned, after a few miles of silent communication.

"What is it . . . the San Miguel stone?"

"An ancient idol—carved in the shape of a jaguar."

She stared at the huge object. Bouquets of flowers

and heaps of corn ears lay strewn around its base.

"Jaguars were considered powerful gods in the old days. I've seen this one up close, and believe me his demeanor is fearsome."

"Los dios viejos?" she whispered.

"Hummm . . ." He planted a small chaste kiss to her temple, then continued. "The corn and flowers, of course, are offerings. We aren't far from Old Xico. I would wager that corn is in thanksgiving for Zolic's having returned their goddess."

She watched the jaguar disappear in the distance. "He looks like he is covered with snow, but there's no snow on the ground."

"Candle wax."

"Why is he sitting way out here?"

"He faces the Mountain of the Star, which was one of the most sacred places in the known world. The first rays of every sunrise touch Mount Orizaba before lighting any other part of this country."

"Amazing." She turned back to the seat and he settled down beside her.

"What's amazing?" he whispered, unable to keep from holding her hand, even here in this public car.

"I think of the Indians' world as having been limited. I'm amazed they would know that the sun touched this particular peak before any other."

His hand tightened around her fingers. "Spoken like a true Malinche."

"Malinche? The woman who prefers all things foreign? You can't put that out of your mind, can you?"

"I don't intend to ever forget it, love. I thought you understood that."

"I do, but sometimes you sound as biased as those you accuse."

He shrugged. "On this particular route it's hard to be objective."

She stared out the window, waiting for him to continue.

"This is the route of Cortés. Or very nearly. Several places along here the tracks cross his trail of Conquest."

"She traveled with him here? Doña Marina?"

He nodded.

"This is where she helped him gather support from other Indians—those whom the Aztecs had conquered?"

"Yes," he answered, wondering how she knew that. "She convinced the Indians Cortés was a god, one of the most benevolent of their former gods who had disappeared—Quetzalcóatl. They called him Feathered Serpent. According to legend he would return from the east. Benevolent he was not—not in the incarnation of Hernán Cortés."

"She bore Cortés a child," Marina continued, quietly reciting the story Zolic had related to her. "A child who could be considered the first mestizo . . . the first of a new race of people. Your race and mine."

He shrugged and this time when he squeezed her hand it was with an entirely different emotion than before—reverence. Lifting her fingers to his lips, he held them there a long time, staring deeply into her adoring green eyes. Somehow he knew this woman, his own Marina, was a healing gift from the gods.

At the cantina in Tecolutla, José's wife fixed them a picnic which they took to the river to eat under the trees while they read the messages that had arrived since the last boat came to shore for supplies.

José said his son, Enrique, would take them out to the *Stella Duval* in his boat as soon as he returned from Poza Rica where he had gone to sell chickens.

"Grandmother was right," Marina told Rafe, reading a message from her mother. "My brothers, Logan Junior and Essie are on their way."

Rafe cleared his throat. "I want you to get word to your cousin Jorge to start proceedings to collect Giddeon's fee from the cargo when we find it. We don't have time to locate the heirs of Bustamente's aide."

She nodded, already scanning the second message. "Do you have fiestas every day of the year?"

"Why?" —

"An invitation from Tío Ignacio and Tía Luisa. They want all of us to come to Vera Cruz for the Feast of Saint Francis on October third, fourth and fifth." She read silently a moment, then added. "Oh, Rafe. We must attend. They're cleaning up the grounds around the major structures at El Tajín. They will hold the festival there."

His face brightened. "Send our acceptance."

Chapter Eleven

Two days after Rafe and Marina returned from Mexico City, the divers brought up the first of what turned out to be several loads of cargo from the *Espíritu Estelle.*

It had taken Marina the entire first day back to lose her self-consciousness in the presence of her grandparents. A guilty conscience, she knew. Neither of them questioned her, and she offered no explanations, other than to confide to her grandmother Doña Alicia's disapproval of her traveling without a *dueña.*

"I was afraid of that," Serita sighed. They had been in Serita and Giddeon's private salon at the time. Immediately after patting Marina's hand in a comforting manner, she had risen, refilled their teacups, and given in to a display of anger such as Marina had rarely seen.

"That woman does not even know you! How dare she treat you like—"

"Grandmother, it was my fault. I broke social conventions by traveling unchaperoned. Besides, when she discovered our relationship to the Cortinases of the Hacienda de Vera Cruz she lightened up a bit. I could tell she was impressed."

Serita reached across the table to clasp her granddaughter's hands. "It is *you* she should have been impressed with. You, for yourself alone."

"To be fair, she has a lot on her mind," Marina answered, wishing she had not brought up the subject. She had wanted to share some of her trip with her grandmother, and this seemed the least harmful to her own reputation, other than the story of Rafe's *abuelita,* which she was sworn not to tell anyone. "You never know the secret disappointments and fears of another person."

"You are right, dear. And I'm afraid you are also right about bringing a good deal of this upon yourself. Unfortunately, you inherited your nature from your mother and from me. Neither of us paid much heed to convention, when we were your age." She stared at the closed porthole as though seeing into the past.

"You were right, too," Marina told her. "You and Tata. I can't wait for the fiesta at El Tajín. I will show you . . ." —briefly she paused, feeling herself blush at what she had started to say, but she continued— ". . . on top of the magnificent pyramid at El Tajín is where Rafe kissed me. Well, to be honest, I had to make him angry before he would go through with it. I had begun to wonder why it mattered so much; then immediately I discovered the answer. It was like you and Tata said—the ember and the elm tree."

"Hummm . . ." Serita mused. "We did put a lot of romantic ideas in your head, dear. I hope it works out for the best."

"It will! Of course, it will. It did for you and Tata."

"We were lucky—and we worked awfully hard at it." She stared frankly at Marina. "We all have skeletons in our pasts, dear. Many of them should remain locked away in the privacy of our own hearts. But I want you to know one thing: Your grandfather and I understand your affection for your young man. Our only concern is for you; we don't want you to be hurt. We want to be sure his intentions are honorable."

"His intentions are most honorable, Grandmother. We are going to be married as soon as the cargo—" Abruptly her mood changed. "If the division of the cargo doesn't ruin things, we will be married," she corrected.

With a heavy sigh Serita crossed to the porthole. "The *Espíritu Estelle* has been buried at the bottom of this sea for over fifty years. Perhaps we should leave it. No cargo is worth risking your future happiness."

"Grandmother, you taught me to be true to myself. Well, you may not understand this—it may be crazy—but I have always felt that one of my purposes in life is to preserve our heritage. Saving Los Olmos is the way I can fulfill that purpose. And salvaging this cargo—"

"A saved heritage will be a cold bed partner!" Serita snapped.

That night in the privacy of their bedroom, Serita confided the conversation to Giddeon. "I'm the one to blame, Giddeon. I have always had a fanatical streak of stubbornness where Los Olmos is concerned, but I had no right to pass it along to Marina."

Giddeon chuckled in her ear. "Never thought I would hear you admit to your *fanatical streak of stubbornness, querida.*"

287

"I'm serious, Giddeon. The situation is serious. Look what we have done to her. First, we fill her head full of romantic nonsense, then we—*I*—cultivate an impossible love of the land inside her. Now the two are in direct opposition. Very likely she will have to lose one in order to fulfill the other. And I am to blame."

"I understand your fears," he told her. "I have them, too. She's our little girl—no, she's our little girl's little girl, which burdens us with a dual responsibility. But I don't agree that we have ruined her life. She seems on the verge of having the very best of lives."

Serita frowned, ready to object, but he silenced her with a kiss. "Look at Marina, the woman. She is strong and passionate . . . and I would have to say intelligent in her choice of a mate."

"But—"

"It won't be easy for her, I agree. Perhaps it shouldn't be. It wasn't easy for us. Nor, for that matter, for Stella and Logan. It'll take work and determination . . . and a lot of love, if they are to settle their differences. But when all is said and done, they will emerge stronger."

Tipping her chin, he stared deep into her worried eyes. "It made us stronger, didn't it, *querida?* All that hard work and anxiety—and passion."

The following afternoon Marina's anxieties changed to leaden dread.

Giddeon himself was at the rail when Gordo signaled Pedro to hoist the cable. The day before they had established beyond doubt the identity of the wreck below the sea—Carlos had brought up a timber which, when the oysters had been hacked away, read: . . . *itu Est.* Since then anticipation had run high.

The scoop was laden this time, everyone at the rail could see that. After watching the winch strain a moment, Giddeon turned to the chart room, where Rafe and Nick studied maps.

With the excuse that he might find the information useful at some later date, Rafe had asked Nick to teach him to read the charts. His motive, of course, was to relieve both himself and Marina of some of the agony caused by their close—yet unbearably separated—proximity.

"He's coming up with a heavy load," Giddeon called.

The instant Rafe understood, he went in search of Marina. Whatever Pedro hauled up, Rafe intended to stand beside her when she learned of it.

"More oysters," she whispered, leaning over the rail, with Rafe standing at her shoulder.

"Gordo must think there's something more," he replied.

Unable to look at the rising mass of oyster shells, Marina watched Pedro work the winch. She concentrated on the muscles protruding in ridges along his neck, on the sinews running the length of his hands, disappearing into his shirt sleeves like steel rails. From her peripheral vision she saw water drain from the large metal scoop; she heard it splash back to the sea.

She saw Zolic standing close to Pedro, peering over the side of the boat. Zolic, who had made himself scarce since the tongue lashing Rafe had given him over the bloodstone the night of their return.

Across from her she saw Serita standing beside Giddeon; watched her clutch his hand; saw him respond. Suddenly the scoop cleared the rail and landed with a thump. She jumped.

"Easy." Rafe reached for her hand, squeezed her fingers.

She jerked her head toward him. His gaze, intense yet soft and comforting, held hers. "Whatever it is, we will work it out," he whispered.

Around her sounds, voices now, buzzed. She looked at her grandparents, their eyes alight with wonder. She looked at Nick, his eyes reflecting Serita and Giddeon's excitement with an added touch of melancholy. His own father had been Giddeon's crewmate on the ill-fated voyage, but he had died ten years ago. Nick would experience the retrieval of this legendary cargo for both of them.

Her spirits revived with the reminder of what the reclamation meant to those she loved. Yes, even to Rafe.

Pedro dumped the load of oysters onto the deck. Giddeon approached them reverently. Kneeling, he began prying them apart with his fingers.

Serita handed him a trowel.

"Be careful," Rafe cautioned. "Gold is soft."

Giddeon nodded, concentrating now, seeing sights no one else aboard the *Stella Duval* had ever seen, feeling emotions no one else would ever feel.

Suddenly the jangle of metal clanged like a cathedral bell. Serita gasped. Marina felt her heart surge in her chest. Her eyes darted to Rafe's.

He pulled her to his side in a rough embrace. Rough and warm, gentle and firm, steady . . . and permanent. His eyes glistened; his words reverberated through her veins: *I told you things would work out.*

Giddeon cupped the oyster shells in his hands . . .

oyster shells with the brilliance of gold shining among them.

"What is it?" Serita asked.

All eyes turned to Rafe, whose eyes were trained on Giddeon's hands . . . on the shiny gold and opaque shells. "We won't know until we clean it up."

Zolic added his assent. "Gold, that's for sure. Like Santana says, we won't know whether coinage or jewelry until it's cleaned."

Speaking, he seized the jumble from Giddeon's hands, sat cross-legged on the deck and, using a pen-knife he took from his pocket, began to pry the shells from the gold. Like vultures hovering over the carcass of a dying calf on the Los Olmos range, the crew stood in a circle around him, all eyes trained on the work in progress.

"Move back and give me some light," he said once.

"What are you finding?" Rafe questioned.

Zolic concentrated on the mass in his hands, merely shaking his head, not answering in words.

Anxiety grew rampant in every one. Even in Zolic, Marina noticed, as the man tossed aside one heavily encrusted section and began hacking at another.

Giddeon picked up the discarded shells, turned them over in his hands.

Rafe stared at the clump in Giddeon's hands. "Wait a minute," he barked. "Stop. You're ruining them."

Zolic jerked his head up. Anger flushed in his round black eyes. "Gold is gold, Santana. You can't *ruin* gold."

"You can destroy artifacts."

In the ensuing silence Marina's heart sank. Rafe scooped up the shells Zolic had tossed aside.

291

Giddeon offered him those he still held.

"Bring them along," Rafe told him.

"Where are you going?" Giddeon inquired.

Rafe stopped. His eyes found Marina's. From his expression, she knew the gold to save Los Olmos was the furthest thing from his mind. His eyes glowed with excitement. "Look in my cabin," he told her. "Bring that list we found in my office in Mexico."

When he moved toward the chart room, Giddeon stopped him. "Why not use the table in my salon? The light is good, and I have a magnifying glass handy."

Rafe followed Giddeon, and the crew followed him as children had followed the Pied Piper from their homes. On what dreadful new path of discovery, Marina wondered.

By the time they reached Giddeon and Serita's suite, and he had deposited his handful of treasure on the tarp Giddeon spread over the teakwood table, Rafe's mind had cleared enough that he knew how to proceed. He asked for soft brushes, small pliers and chisel, and hot water and cloths for polishing.

His initial anger at Zolic's irresponsible handling had dissolved the moment he got a good look at the gold. Descriptions from the journal of one of Cortés's lieutenants flashed through his brain, flushing him with the prospects of this discovery.

Specifically, a necklace fashioned from dozens of golden spheres, each one etched with the likeness of a different Aztec god. Legend—and written accounts, as well—held that Moctezuma had given Cortés such a necklace. No such necklace had ever surfaced.

Which was not peculiar, however, since the necklace was not one a man—a Spaniard—would have worn himself. Cortés could have given it to Doña Catalina, his true wife in the eyes of the Church, who herself could have carried it back to Spain. It could have been handed down through one of his two sons by Doña Catalina. It could have stayed in Spain.

Or, it could have been lost that harrowing night the Spaniards ran from Tenochtitlan for their lives, losing much of the Aztec treasure in the canals where they sank themselves, drowning beneath the weight of their armor—and the treasure which they were reported to have stuffed inside their clothing.

Perhaps Cortés had carried the necklace with him that fateful night. Perhaps he had lost it beneath the *ahuehuete* tree where he sat and wept for his fallen comrades—for his stupid fallen comrades who chose to sink to the bottom of the canals rather than part with their stolen treasure.

Perhaps the Lady Marina had picked it up. Perhaps not.

Perhaps a peasant had found it and bought himself a year's worth of freedom from its sale.

Perhaps . . .

"What are they?" Holding the list of artifacts, Marina spoke quietly at Rafe's shoulder from where she had watched him, thinking herself and worrying.

When finally he became aware of her presence, he glanced up, and she saw the light of conquest in his eyes. "Come look, love."

His voice was quiet, filled with awe, and she knew he was a million miles away from this ship, else he would never have used such an endearment in front of her grandparents. The hairs along her neck stiffened with foreboding when she focused on the gold disks in his hands.

He slipped one arm around her waist drawing her near. "Can you make out the symbols?"

She stared at the squiggly lines that wove like the canals in the City of Mexico across the surface of the brilliant gold disks. She thought quite suddenly of the story Zolic had told her. Had her own dreams drowned in those canals that fateful night along with the greedy Spaniards?

Later that evening when they met in their customary place on deck before retiring, the focus of their lives had somehow shifted. Temporarily, she hoped.

Pray God, it would be temporary.

His gentle hands seemed to grasp, his quiet voice to admonish, and worst of all, his sincere plans for their future seemed hopeless.

The evening meal had been torture. Listening to the conversation, Marina had suddenly felt as though she were the only person present who cared about saving Los Olmos.

And she didn't even plan to live there! At first she wondered at her grandparents' jubilation. They should have been as devastated at the discovery as she was.

Later, of course, she understood. This expedition was the culmination of a life-long dream for them. The ship's sinking had brought them together. If carried far enough, such reasoning led to the inevitable conclusion that the sinking of the ship was the reason she herself was here . . . here on earth, not merely here on board this vessel standing in the embrace of the man whom she loved, yet to whom she was incapable of responding.

"It was only the first load, love." Rafe buried his face in her hair, inhaling the intoxicating scent of her. Try as he might, he could not feel remorse at the wondrous discovery they had made today. And why should he?

"There will be plenty more chances to find enough gold to pay those taxes."

"I doubt it." Breaking free, she turned toward the rail. She wanted to run to her cabin. She wanted to be alone. But she loved this man. And she did not want to act like a spoiled child who had failed to get her way. Yet her spirits remained heavy and she was powerless to change them.

Rafe sighed beside her. "Both divers estimated the oyster reef to be enormous. The odds are in our favor to—"

"Do you not recall what the heirs said?"

"I explained that," he argued. "They know nothing about the artifacts. One of Bustamente's aides was responsible for the theft. If you wanted to be reasonable, you would also recall that far from denying the existence of coinage, they claimed any cargo belonging to the estate of their former ancestor. That means not only belongings, but money. *Gold coinage.* Do you hear?"

"Yes, I hear. But that doesn't mean—"

"It doesn't mean the coins had to be in the first damned load we hauled up."

"You don't have to get angry," she objected.

"I'm not angry. *I* am happy. *You* are angry."

"I don't have time to be angry or happy. Time is running out for Los Olmos."

He jerked her around to face him. Their eyes met.

He watched tears form in hers, tears which washed away his anger as suddenly as ocean waves wash sandcastles from the shore. He pulled her into his sheltering arms.

"It will work out, love. Didn't I promise you? Please believe me."

She stood quietly in his embrace. His heart beat against hers; his body warmed her body against the chill of the night. She had intended to wear the rebozo his grandmother had given her, but she forgot to.

"You don't have to believe me right now," he soothed. "Just don't give up. Not on the cargo . . . not on us."

She left after a passionless goodnight kiss, reviling herself for not sharing his joy over the day's discovery. She had tried, tried hard. But even at supper when he related the story of the necklace the only part with which she could identify was of the *Noche Triste,* the sad night when Cortés sat beneath the *ahuehuete* tree crying for his lost men. And she had returned to her suite after supper filled with the sadness of it all.

Now she returned to the same suite, suffused not only with the same sense of sadness but an added measure of anger at herself for ruining Rafe's pleasure.

Jesús Zolic touched her arm just before she closed her parlor door.

"I must speak with you, Marina."

She stared at him, waiting, recalling Rafe's claim that the man was in love with her.

"I am truly sorry for your disappointment."

"Thank you, Zolic. Tomorrow is another day. Another load." She paused to close the door. "Perhaps tomorrow we will find what we need."

"I do not speak of the cargo, Marina. I speak of

Santana. His reaction to the golden disks did not surprise me, but I can see where you would—"

"On the contrary, Zolic, I'm happy for you and Rafe. That necklace is a prize for the Ministry of Antiquities."

"Ah, but that is the thing, Marina. Sometimes Santana is—how shall I put it?"

"If you're going to tell me Rafe is obsessed, you are mistaken. In Mexico City I learned the truth. He is dedicated, Zolic. Dedicated to his quest."

Zolic sighed. "If you say so, my dear lady. I see he has convinced you of such, whether it is true or not. Fortunately it is I who will verify the artifacts; I who will keep the records. I had hoped to enlist your help."

"My help? To keep records?"

"Yes. It never hurts to be cautious. Not when priceless items are at stake. Men who appear perfectly honest have had their heads turned when faced with enough capital to set them up for life."

"Do I understand you? You are saying Rafe Santana would *steal* the artifacts he is so anxious to gather for the ministry? You must not know the man, Zolic. In addition to his dedication to his profession, his family is wealthy—"

"His family, yes. But not Santana personally. You would have no reason to know this, but the wealth belongs to his mother, who is forever on the verge of disowning the man. One day she will carry out that threat. Then where do you suppose the Minister of Antiquities will be? In the gutter without a peso to his name, unless. . . . You get my point, I am sure."

"Your suggestion is clear, Zolic. And inaccurate, as well. Goodnight."

Chapter Twelve

As scoop after scoop of treasure-laden oyster shells were retrieved from the sea, Marina's spirits rose and fell like waves lapping the sides of the *Stella Duval*. After that first day, however, her fears waned beneath Rafe's enthusiasm, and she never gave in to utter despair again.

The retrieval process, as Pedro had forewarned, was painfully slow. Often a day's worth of work provided nothing more than oysters for Cookie's stew. Early discoveries, however, convinced all aboard of the monumental significance of their efforts.

The artifacts dazzled Marina. Rafe slipped a necklace of alternating gold and turquoise nuggets around her neck.

"An Aztec princess, three hundred years later," he muttered. Watching her eyes sparkle with their own green fire, he knew his first impression had been correct—if the Aztecs had seen Marina Cafferty's eyes, they would not have called turquoise the fire stone.

One load contained three collars made of the purest

gold—worn by both men and women, Zolic assured her. But the artifact which identified the entire cargo was discovered in the third scoop brought to deck: a two-headed serpent. Its turquoise mosaic body coiled in successive loops with a head at each end, both open mouths exposing vicious fangs and teeth fashioned from white onyx.

"How can anything so threatening be so lovely?" Marina mused.

"This is it," Rafe whispered. "This is the proof we have been searching for." Sitting at the table in Giddeon and Serita's salon, he studied the now clean serpent. His eyes strayed to the list of artifacts he had taken from his office, then to Marina. "This is definitely part of the treasure Moctezuma was reported to have given Cortés."

She was happy. He was elated. And the search continued.

The next load contained one golden disk, so large it grazed the sides of the scoop. The inscriptions on it looked like more squiggles to Marina.

Zolic, who had recorded every item in a book, drawing, measuring, and describing each in turn, explained the disk.

"The Aztec world was destroyed four times before the Conquest. Each epoch was called a sun." He indicated to the four sides of the disk. "Each *sun* is represented here by the symbol of its destruction." He pointed to the four figures positioned in a square around the center of the disk. "The first epoch was destroyed by jaguars, the second by wind, the third by fiery rain, and the fourth by water. We were in our fifth sun at the time of the Conquest."

His forefinger jabbed the center of the disk from where a malevolent face peered menacingly. "That's old Tonotiuh, the sun god. See his tongue—it's a sacrificial knife, dripping with the blood of his victims." His finger moved to either side of the sun god's face. "His fists—claws is a better word—grip the hearts of his victims."

A shudder ran through the group. "I hesitate to ask what the other symbols represent," Giddeon said.

"It's complicated," Zolic replied. "Briefly, they are symbols of all the epochs. An Aztec century lasted only fifty two years. The history of the Aztec race is recorded here: dates, times, events."

Although most of the discoveries thereafter were not as gruesome, Marina knew it was not because the stories behind them were less ghastly, but that Zolic did not provide the details. One particularly grisly artifact was a human skull that had been overlaid with a black onyx and turquoise mosaic, the original teeth still intact.

Rafe appeared oblivious to the gruesomeness of the find. His elation stemmed from the fact that the skull, too, was on the list of treasures presented to Cortés by the Aztec ruler.

Finally they raised a load containing two dozen gold coins. Not Aztec coins. Not disks used for adornment.

"Mexican specie minted in 1824," Rafe proclaimed.

The euphoria that coursed through Marina was not even dimmed by the discovery, in the same load, of a hideous obsidian knife whose multi-stoned mosaic handle depicted a jaguar with his teeth bared.

Zolic stroked the still brutally sharp obsidian blade with a forefinger. "A sacrificial knife."

300

Marina's eyes felt glued to the coins.

Giddeon beamed at her. "See, sugar? I told you we would strike pay-dirt."

She smiled weakly, for her body felt totally useless at the moment. Her eyes found Rafe's. His intense stare held hers. He did not speak in words. He didn't have to. His beaming face told her everything she needed to hear.

That night she held him close and had trouble keeping tears from her eyes—tears of joy . . . tears of hope. The coins were not enough, of course. But Gordo had assured them the oyster reef extended many meters further.

"I told you so, *capitán*," Rafe whispered, showering her with his wonderfully exciting grin.

Her eyes held his. "The worst part was knowing the rift it would cause between us if there had been no money."

His smile faded while she spoke; his eyes softened to a determined sort of pleading. "If I lost you, I wouldn't want to live. I might as well die at sunset like—"

Her fingers stilled his lips, his words. "Let's not speak of death—not after the gruesome things we have seen and heard the last few days. Did you see Zolic holding that knife? The blade is still so sharp it could have slit his finger open if he had—"

"Now you hush up." He lifted her face, lowering his. "This isn't the time to talk about Zolic, either. I haven't had a real kiss in almost a week."

She surrendered to his lips, to his arms, wishing desperately she could surrender to the demands of his body, and hers. He was right, she knew, when he said to live apart would be worse than death. Whatever happened with the cargo from here on out, she was certain of one thing. It would not keep them apart. She could not let that happen.

By the time the day arrived to leave for the Feast of Saint Francis, the entire crew of the *Stella Duval* was ready for a celebration. Along with additional artifacts for Rafe's museum, more gold specie had also been recovered. Still not enough to pay all the taxes, but hope ran high.

In the two weeks since Rafe and Marina returned from the city, Nick and a couple of the regular crew members had taken a boat to shore once for supplies. They returned with news that Logan Junior and Essie, Marina's brothers, had arrived from Los Olmos. Following the instructions she had left for them at Tecolutla, they had gone ahead to the Hacienda de Vera Cruz, where they awaited the arrival of the family for the fiesta.

The first order of business, however, was to determine how best to safeguard the valuables while they attended the fiesta.

Finally it was decided that the risk was too great not to leave someone on board. Since no one wanted to miss the entire two-day festival, Giddeon suggested they take turns at guard duty.

Pedro Ybarro and his men, of course, would be free to attend the fiesta or to go home as they wished. They had not been engaged to guard the cargo, only to retrieve it. Likewise, Giddeon decided, the twelve-man *Stella Duval* crew had no stake in the cargo, therefore, they should not be put in the position of protecting it.

302

"With the distance between Tecolutla and El Tajín close to fifty kilometers or better," Giddeon told them at supper the night before they left the salvage site, "it will be impossible to change shifts more than once a day."

"Seeing how this is a family affair," Nick insisted, "you folks go on ahead. I'll take first watch."

"I will keep him company," Zolic said, bringing a chagrined look to Nick's face, which he quickly stifled with his napkin. Marina smiled.

"Fine," Giddeon replied. "Serita and I will return early the following day to relieve you."

"Let me take guard duty the second day," Rafe offered when Giddeon called him to his and Serita's suite after supper.

"No. From what I understand Don Ignacio expects you to serve as the fiesta's authority on El Tajín." While he spoke, Giddeon opened a safe hidden behind a shelf in a locked cupboard, placing inside the coins they had retrieved from beneath the sea, and which he and Rafe had just recounted.

"Two hundred ten-dollar gold pieces," Giddeon said before closing the door to the safe.

"Two hundred," Rafe acknowledged.

Giddeon locked the safe, replaced the shelf, then closed and locked the door. Turning, he ushered Rafe into the passageway.

"Besides being Ignacio's expert . . ." —Giddeon spoke as though he had but paused in their conversation— ". . . this will be a good opportunity for you to get to know Marina's brothers."

Rafe stiffened, and Giddeon clapped him on the shoulder. His voice was jovial when he continued.

"Like I told Serita, it won't hurt the two of you to have it a little rough at the beginning. It'll make the good times all the sweeter when they come."

He paused so long, Rafe turned to question him and saw the old man nodding his head, lips pursed, his green eyes—Marina's green eyes—dancing to some gone but not forgotten music.

"If I may be allowed a moment of oration from the vantage of my long years, son. All that electricity sizzling between the two of you . . . well, I'd bet the ranch, taxes paid, that it's the real thing. Yes sir, you two have plenty of good times ahead. You'll make it through this uproar from her family—and yours. Marina is cantankerous as an ol' mossyhorn, and you—well, I've seen enough of you by now to know you won't buckle in a strong wind, either."

"Thank you, sir. I appreciate your confidence."

"You're earning it, son. Day by day, you are earning it."

The test in which he was earning Giddeon Duval's confidence was only one of many hurdles left to cross, Rafe discovered the next day, watching Marina dash down the gangplank to greet her brothers.

The boys grabbed her one at a time and swung her around. Then they all huddled together, laughing and talking and gesturing with the abandon of friends long separated.

Her brothers were big, both of them, and close to the same age, although to see them, one would never suspect them of being related. Logan Junior was blond, his obviously fair skin darkened by the sun. Essie was dark like Marina, with the same black hair and olive complexion.

They loved their sister. That was plain to see. But what would they think of him—the man who intended to marry her and take her away?

A hand slipped around Rafe's waist as Serita joined him on deck. When he looked down, her attention was trained on the little group before them. When she spoke, her words brought a chuckle to his lips.

"Don't you worry about a thing, Rafe. They are going to love you."

He started to tell her that was what Marina had told him about Giddeon. Instead he replied quietly, "Given time, I hope."

As things turned out it took a while for the boys to learn of his plans for their sister.

Don Ignacio had sent two carriages to town, not knowing how many guests to expect from the *Stella Duval*. Galván had accompanied Logan and Essie to fetch the guests, and at Giddeon's insistence, Galván rode with him and Serita in one carriage, allowing the brothers to ride in the other with Marina and Rafe.

"Did you bring your dress from Veracruz?" Rafe whispered, handing Marina's valise to the driver, who in turn tossed it to the other driver to strap atop the carriage.

"Yes, and the golden earrings. I loaned Grandmother the silver ones. I didn't want Tía Luisa to think I wasn't grateful." She smiled, infinitely happy, wanting to kiss him. His eyes twinkled back at her, but he moved a step away, afraid she might carry out her secret, though not at all concealed, desire.

"I have barely been introduced to your brothers, let's not start things off on the wrong foot."

She laughed, watching her brothers in animated con-

305

versation with their grandparents, quizzing them, she knew, about the long-mysterious cargo on the *Espíritu Estelle.* "They will love—"

"Shhh . . ." he laughed. "Your grandmother just assured me of the same thing. I'm beginning to think that phrase is the much heralded kiss of death."

The drivers finished securing the baggage and called to Galván, who in turn called, "All aboard!" Everyone found a seat.

Although not exactly the seat planned, in some cases. Logan followed Marina into the carriage, taking the seat beside her. Adroitly, she shifted to the facing bench when Rafe climbed in beside her.

This caused Essie, who tried to enter from the opposite door, to find both seats near him taken by siblings. He hurried around the carriage and climbed in beside his brother.

Logan squinted across the aisle from Rafe to Marina, then back to Rafe.

Essie did not appear to consider the mix-up anything other than miscommunication. "So you are the Don Rafael Tío Ignacio raves about."

Rafe grimaced. "Depends on what he's saying."

"That you are an authority on the ruins. Wow! I have never seen anything like them. That pyramid . . . they call it the Pyramid of the Niches. Tío Ignacio said it has three hundred and sixty-five niches in it . . . exactly the number of days in a year. Why is that?"

Rafe raised an eyebrow as he listened, immediately at ease with this new discovery.

"You didn't tell me that when we were there," Marina said.

"I didn't know it—"

"You visited El Tajín? The two of you?" Logan asked.

Marina studied him. Beside her she felt Rafe's intake of breath.

"Didn't Tío Ignacio tell you we came to the hacienda?" she inquired.

Logan sat very still. Marina watched the facts enter his brain, the equations form, the theories emerge. "He didn't say you came together."

Marina sighed. She hadn't planned to launch into an immediate explanation of her relationship with Rafael Santana. She wanted her brothers to get to know him for himself first. Especially Logan, who had always been impossibly protective.

"Rafe was in Tecolutla when Galván came to get me," she explained. "Galván invited him to come out to see the pyramids. Tío Ignacio had been wanting Rafe to see them for a long time. He wants the Ministry of Antiquities—"

"He told us," Logan interrupted. He stared frankly at Rafe. "Don Rafael, forgive me for interrupting, you were about to answer my brother's question."

Marina could have strangled him. Gladly. Was there no one in her family who would receive Rafe graciously, at face value and on sight? When Rafe spoke, though, his strong voice did not quaver, and her apprehensions dissolved.

"About the three hundred sixty-five niches?" Rafe questioned. "Actually, it's news to me. At this stage we have done no studies of the site, but I'm sure the people who built it will prove to have been as advanced in astronomy as the other civilizations of their time."

"Do you mean . . . of their time around this place?

307

Or of their time in the entire world?" Essie questioned, his interest obvious and sincere.

"Around the world," Rafe replied.

"Tell them what you told me about Mount Orizaba on our way to—ah, about the first light."

Rafe adjusted his hat which he had capped over his knee when he settled into the seat beside Marina. Turning now, he studied her a moment before speaking. "We can discuss pre-Conquest Mexican history any time. Why don't the three of you catch up on the last two years? Didn't I hear you say it has been that long since you saw your brothers?"

"You're right. We do have . . . time." She looked from Logan to Essie. "First, Rafe and I are both interested in what is happening at Los Olmos."

Rafe had settled back in his corner and propped his hat over his face intending to stay out of their way until they arrived at the hacienda. When Marina included him in her statement, he peered from beneath the brim of his hat in time to catch a belligerent warning in Logan Junior's eyes.

Marina continued until she engaged the boys in conversation about the ranch. By the time they reached Papantla she had learned of Jorge's petition, filed with the judicial system in Mexico on behalf of Giddeon.

"Jorge seems to think the best we can hope for is to win a judgment awarding Grandfather repayment for his ship," Logan advised her.

"Rafe said the same thing." She turned to him with a broad smile. "Didn't you?"

Rafe met Logan's gaze an instant before turning to Marina. Noting the plea in her eyes—a plea for help—he sighed. "I figured that might be the quickest way to have a judgment returned," he said, striving for her sake to carry on a conversation which held no immediate interest for him, and he suspected, for no one else in the carriage, except possibly Essie, who still appeared oblivious to the rising tension.

"Your grandfather apprised me of the necessity for speed," he added.

"Yes." Logan spoke in terse tones. "Jorge is an expert on international law. I am sure he will handle *our* problem in the correct manner. Where did you go to school, Santana?"

Marina blinked at the abrupt change in topic.

"The University of Mexico," Rafe answered quietly. "In Mexico City. I understand you—"

"It's the oldest university in the entire hemisphere," Marina enthused. "It was founded in the fifteen hundreds."

Logan settled back in his seat, although he still gave the impression of a fighting cock ready to circle and pounce. "You have certainly become enamored with . . . ah, with this country, Marina."

She glared at him. "I certainly have, Logan. It happens to be part of my heritage. Look out the window. It is your heritage, too."

He shook his head. "Someone has been feeding you pretty stories, sister. You left your heritage behind when you crossed the Rio Grande River."

Furious, she turned to Rafe. "Excuse him. The trip must have been difficult. Surely all semblance of proper upbringing could not have been destroyed by two years on the East Coast."

Rafe's voice was quiet. "I have three sisters, remember? I recognize concern and compassion when I

309

see them."

The carriage bounded through the streets of Papantla, its occupants silent. Rafe focused his attention out the window, but he could feel Logan Junior's eyes on him. He felt Marina's tension beside him, and he sensed her eyes on her brother.

Things were not working out at all as she had hoped. Why did she expect them to, she wondered, at the same time desperately searching for some way to at least neutralize Logan's animosity before they arrived at the hacienda. As things stood he would ruin the fiesta for them all.

Just before the carriage left Papantla behind, she turned to Rafe again.

Helplessly he watched the agitation struggling within her. He ached to hold her, to reassure her, but of course that would only make things worse.

"Isn't this where we stopped for the mail last time?" she asked.

He nodded.

"Could you . . . ah, do you think the driver would stop? I need something to drink."

The words had no sooner left her mouth than Rafe reached outside the window and slapped the side of the carriage. The driver pulled to a halt.

"What do you want? Chocolate? Coffee?" His eyebrows raised, his eyes smiled. "Something stronger?"

"Much!" she sighed. "But water will do . . . and . . ." Her eyes begged him to understand.

"It may take a minute," he told her. "Do you mind waiting?"

Their gazes held in silent communication. *He understood.* Relief brought a rush of tears to her eyes.

Instinctively he moved to touch her face, but he stilled his hand in mid-air.

"I just need a minute," she whispered. And he was gone.

The instant he closed the door, she leaned forward, her face stern, her voice low and determined. "I don't know what you are trying to do, Logan Cafferty, but I expect you to straighten up right now."

"You're the one who needs to straighten up, Marina. From the looks of things Essie and I arrived in the nick of time." He tossed a wicked glance toward the window where Rafe had disappeared. "Day after tomorrow we are taking you home . . . away from that man."

"You just try it."

"What the hell is going on?" Essie demanded.

"Marina's gone and gotten herself mixed up with some disreputable—"

"He is not disreputable."

"What does he do, then, besides dig around in old ruins? Essie and I are going to take you home so you can find yourself a proper husband."

"Whom do you have in mind?" she hissed. "Burt Wilson?"

"You know better—"

"From your behavior today, I know nothing of the kind. Listen to me" —she included Essie, who sat with a not so puzzled expression forming on his face— ". . . both of you. I will say this only once, and you had better understand. I intend to marry Rafael Santana. Nothing can stop me. Certainly not a brother who has turned into a . . . a *cabrón* in the two years since I last saw him. Grandmother and Tata have accepted Rafe, and I expect the two of you to give him a chance, too."

"How long have you known him?" Essie asked.

"Thank you for an intelligent question. The answer is long enough to be certain beyond any doubt that I could never live without him."

"How did you meet him?" Essie asked again.

"He came to the *Stella Duval* to tell me I could not have claim to anything on board the *Espíritu Estelle.*"

Both boys' eyes opened wider.

"We have worked that out."

"How fortunate," Logan barked.

Footsteps crunched in the gravel outside the coach. Marina glared at Logan one last time. "Mama taught you how to act like a gentleman. I expect you to use that training the next two days." She looked from one brother to the other. "If you don't give yourselves a chance to know Rafe, it will be your loss. And if you don't give him a chance to be a part of my family, your loss will be *me!*"

By the time they reached the Hacienda de Vera Cruz, the air inside the cab had cleared, if not actually settled.

When she finished speaking, Rafe had cleared his throat outside the door. She called him in, and when he handed her the cup of water she took his hand instead, drawing him onto the seat beside her.

He studied her a moment. "Are you all right?"

She lifted their clasped hands to her lips, holding them there while she smiled at him. "I made an announcement while you were gone. Now, I want to reintroduce you to my brothers—as the man I intend to marry . . . very soon."

He could see the torment in her eyes still, hear the tremor in her voice. Her lips warmed his hand and sent a deep need for her spiraling up his arm and through his

312

system. All he wanted was to be alone with her, to hold her, to comfort her, to love her. What was it her grandfather had said only last night? That they had plenty of good times ahead? Well, he was ready for them.

"Soon," he echoed, speaking to her. Then he turned to her brothers. "I am in love with your sister—for many reasons, some of which you know since up to now you've spent more time with her than I have." Pausing, he turned to Marina and winked. "And she loves me. As she said, we plan to be married, soon. But not before I speak to your father and gain his approval."

By the time they reached the Hacienda de Vera Cruz the fiesta was in full swing and Rafe had won over one of Marina's brothers. After the announcement of their marriage plans, Rafe reconsidered his refusal to discuss ancient Mexican history. At this point it seemed the safest topic all around. Essie's eyes lighted as the revelations of an advanced and cultured civilization unraveled.

Logan Junior, however, remained stoic. The sensible New England part of his heritage, Marina thought, observing her morose brother, wondering how she would manage to convince him to give Rafe a chance.

As it turned out she had help. After the briefest of greetings and refreshments, Tío Ignacio and Tía Luisa prepared to shuttle the group to El Tajín in carriages specially decked out with flowers and paper streamers.

Serita ventured a request that held them up momentarily.

"Since we won't return to the big house until dark,

could I visit the graves of Papá and Mamá before we leave?"

Instead of being somber, the family cemetery exuded an old world elegance and a sense of beauty and peace. Surrounded by flowering shrubs, the graves were marked with a variety of headstones, ornate crosses, regal scroll work, and a couple of shrines. Tía Luisa led the way to two plots in a far corner. Serita kept pace, motioning her little family to join her.

Giddeon stood with her briefly, then stepped aside to wait beneath a ceiba tree, its seed pods hanging like festive ornaments from the branches. He watched his wife gather her grandchildren to her side, along with her soon to be grandson-in-law, whom Marina held tightly by the hand.

After a moment Logan Junior broke away from the group and came to stand beside his grandfather.

"What are you going to do about that?"

Giddeon followed the boy's gaze to Marina and Rafe.

"About what?" he countered.

"You know. Him."

"What about him?"

"Marina said—he did, too—that they are planning to get married."

"They said the same to your grandmother and me."

Logan braced his shoulders. "Well, she can't do it. I'm taking her home tomorrow."

Blond and fair-skinned, Logan Junior favored his father, whom Giddeon had always considered himself lucky to have as a son-in-law, business partner, and friend. From an early age Logan Junior had tried to imitate his father in all ways, some ways coming more

314

naturally than others, like now. Giddeon recalled Logan the father's attempts to protect the young and headstrong Stella Duval during his courtship with her. He had learned he couldn't do that. Now his son was trying the same tactics with his sister.

"What do you have against the man?" Giddeon asked.

"Everything! For starters, who is he? Where did he come from? She has only known him a few weeks, and we less than that. She doesn't know what she's doing. He has cast a spell over her with all his mumbo-jumbo and his rugged appearance. He is different from Burt Wilson. That's all she sees."

"Could be you're right," Giddeon nodded. "I don't much think so, though. I like the man. He is forthright, sincere—about his work and about Marina. I'd swear to his integrity. Fact is, I wasn't prepared to like the fellow either, not at first. Of course, when we arrived, he and Marina were off in the mountains. By the time they returned two days later—"

"He took her . . . to the mountains? Who chaperoned? What did you do about it?"

Giddeon groaned at his slip of tongue. "There wasn't much I could do, Logan. I didn't know about it until . . ." He recalled the Mexico City trip he had known about well in advance. "You see, love is—"

"Love? Are you daffy, Grandfather? Papa would put a stop to this."

Giddeon turned stern eyes on his grandson. "No, I don't think he would. Actually, I don't think he could. They are a determined pair, those two." Giddeon sighed. "You know the stories about your mother and father during the war . . . how Stella led the cotton trains from Alleyton to Matamoros, how your father risked his life and his commission in the Marine Corps to try to protect her."

"I've heard all that. What does it have to do with . . . ?" He nodded toward Marina and Rafe.

"You didn't hear *all* of it. For over a year while they each pursued separate missions for different sides of that war, they found numerous times to be together—unchaperoned. Your grandmother and I decided at the start that their determination—desperation is probably a better word—to be together was more important than the fact that they were breaking a bunch of society's conventions."

"That was war, Grandfather."

Giddeon placed a comforting arm around his grandson's shoulders. "No, son, that was love."

The grounds around El Tajín had been cleared with machetes and cleaned so that it was almost impossible to recognize the place, except for the majestic Pyramid of the Niches. Along a central space between several edifices—an avenue, Rafe called it—booths had been set up by neighboring Indians selling food and art work of every rhyme and description. Giddeon and Serita spent a good part of the day with Ignacio and Luisa, letting them show off the plantation that Serita had always longed to see. Giddeon himself had visited once long ago, before Stella was born.

And before he came to his senses about loving Serita Cortinas, he thought, watching Marina and Rafe, with Essie and Bianca at their coattails. He studied Logan Junior, wishing he wouldn't spoil Marina's happiness.

Thinking about Rafael Santana, hoping he wasn't wrong about the man. Desperately hoping as much.

That night in the luxurious room Luisa had assigned to them, Giddeon lay propped in bed watching Serita flit around, her long hair brushed and flowing, as beautiful now as when it had been pure black. Her nightgown, richly embroidered in white on white, fell in soft drifts over her gentle curves.

"You had a good day, didn't you, *querida?*"

"Hummm . . . a perfect day."

"Then come to bed. Let's end it with a perfect night."

Laughing, she joined him, but her mind was still on the day, on the family whom before today she had known only through stories and letters. "Luisa insists we return for the Day of the Dead. The ceremonies are lovely, and I would like to be here this year . . . for Papá and Mamá."

"My one regret has been not getting you back down here before they died," he sighed.

"No, Giddeon. No regrets. I could have come. You know I would have if I had wanted to badly enough."

He laughed. *"Sí, querida.* Still, as your husband . . ."

"As my husband, I'm asking you now. It's less than a month off. Can we afford to be away from Los Olmos that long?"

"We'll plan on it. I have a feeling we may still be here, anyway—for one reason or another."

She studied him. "Legal actions or a wedding?"

He smiled. "Perhaps both." Then he recalled Logan Junior and his smile faded. "I wish he wouldn't ruin things for her," he finished after relating the conversation he and Logan had at the cemetery.

"He can't ruin things. Marina will be disappointed if

he doesn't come around, but . . ." Quickly she slid across the bed and into Giddeon's embrace. She felt his arms tighten around her, warm and comforting and dependable.

And still exciting after all these years. "What I wish is that Logan Junior would fall in love." Lifting her face she spoke with her lips close to Giddeon's. "Desperately, passionately in love. Only then will he understand."

Giddeon squeezed her closer. "If he doesn't fall in love, I hope he never has a daughter. He would never understand a daughter who possessed even one drop of fiery Cortinas blood."

Chapter Thirteen

Even though Marina dressed quickly for the second day of the Feast of Saint Francis, by the time she hurried down the winding staircase at the Hacienda de Vera Cruz, her grandmother and grandfather had already left for the *Stella Duval* to relieve Nick and Zolic.

Rafe met her at the bottom step, his eyes appraising, his offered hand warming hers. "I thought you intended to wear the dress from Veracruz today."

"Tonight," she answered, "for the lighting of the braziers on the pyramid."

Reaching, he planted a quick but definitely not chaste kiss on her lips, singeing her skin with the heat of his own. "Tonight," he whispered, his voice rich with promise.

As on the previous day the fiesta began with Mass in the hacienda chapel, read by Father Bartolomé from the parish in Papantla. Arriving just as the service began, Rafe and Marina squeezed into the family pew beside her brothers and cousins.

The smell of candle wax and incense accompanied by the familiar Latin words of the Mass filled her with longing for her parents. If only they had come.

"We could be married right here," she whispered in Rafe's ear. "Right now . . . today, if Mama and Papa had come."

She felt his reply—a chuckle and the tightening of his hand around her fingers. She saw it in the glow of his eyes in the dimly lit chapel.

Then he glanced down the row at the still implacable Logan Junior. "Perhaps not today. We still have a few natives to convert."

More people attended the fiesta on this the second day than the day before since word had spread of the beauty of El Tajín and of the Minister of Antiquities who could explain the mysteries of the place.

Marina's hopes of stealing a moment alone with Rafe Santana faded as the hours passed. She sat beside him on the edge of the ball court and listened for the umpteenth time to the story of the game played by ancient people. The words were familiar, the voice beloved, and she was gripped by the knowledge that she would never tire of either.

"How do you know all this?"

The question was asked by Logan Junior, but unlike his belligerent tone of yesterday, today he sounded more like a student questioning an instructor in whose intelligence he had not quite decided to place much credence.

Rafe answered in an amiable manner, firmly in command of his subject, yet not forcing it down Logan's, nor indeed anyone's throat.

"The Indians kept records much as we do, although

they transmitted their information through drawings and symbols rather than in words. We are still deciphering much of it."

"You mentioned their books yesterday," Essie said. "What were they like?"

"We call them codices. In pre-Conquest times, before the Spaniards arrived with printing presses and European paper, paper for a codex was made from the bark of amate or wild fig trees. The bark was beaten into long strips that were then folded like a screen; the text was painted in symbols. I have some well preserved codices in my office; I'll show them to you one day."

"What Rafe forgot to say," Marina put in, "is that the first printing press in the New World was used in the City of Mexico in the 1500's. He showed me the—"

"Going back to the ball game . . ." Rafe interrupted, returning to the previous subject. Later he drew her aside.

"Go easy on promoting Mexico's *firsts* when Logan is in the crowd. You should have seen his eyes harden when you mentioned the first printing press."

"I don't care," she retorted. "If he doesn't—"

"Shhh . . . you *do* care. You're put out with him, that's all. If we handle things right, he will come around. He has to learn I'm not a threat . . . other than in the fact that I plan to take his little sister away from Los Olmos, and away from him."

The highlight of this year's fiesta would come at dusk with the lighting of pottery braziers which had been placed in the niches of the great pyramid—all three hundred sixty-five of them.

The second most important event was planned for

just before lunch. In truth, Marina suspected that to Rafe the morning ceremony was more important than the lighting of the braziers. While clearing the grounds, Tío Ignacio's workers had unearthed an ancient idol carved from sandstone. Tío Ignacio had steadfastly refused to give Rafe so much as a peek before the unveiling when he planned for Rafe to stand before the crowd and explain the discovery. "Smacks of witchcraft," Rafe had complained the day before.

"I hope I can identify it," he confided to Marina now. "After the commotion Don Ignacio has made over my position the past two days, it will be embarrassing if I can't."

Marina smiled. It was on the tip of her tongue to quip, *I'll love you anyway.* But she didn't. This was not the moment she awaited—the private moment when she would first utter those words and he would never ever forget the time or place. Instead, she sighed. "Let's climb the pyramid today."

Her suggestion immediately transported him to their first trip atop the Pyramid of the Niches, to the way she had prodded him into kissing her . . . to the feel of her lips, of her body, the throbbing of her heart against his.

"Do you think I could take you to the top of that pyramid without . . ."—his eyes glistened in sport, yet not in sport—". . . without *at least* kissing you?"

"I hope you couldn't."

"Then we will wait for nightfall after the braziers have died down and the dancing has started. If Logan were to see me kissing you in broad open daylight, my case with him would be set back to ancient times."

"Is it a date then . . . for tonight?"

His lips curved in his intoxicating grin. "No,

capitán, it's a promise."

By now the crowd had grown to several hundred revelers, along with various entertainers: jugglers, acrobats, mimes. Musicians strolled the grounds playing every kind of stringed instrument Marina had ever seen and some she had not even imagined. Food from the booths sizzled on braziers, filling the air with mouthwatering aromas. They tried them all: cakes made from maize, fowl prepared in a mole sauce spiced with chocolate and chilies, everything imaginable from chicken to beans to seafood wrapped in tortillas, fried, seasoned with chilies and more chilies.

"This is like a county fair," Essie enthused. "Except for the costumes."

Indeed the costumes left no doubt as to the country's Indian heritage. Entire villages formed companies of marching, chanting creatures more resembling fowl than men.

"I've never seen so many different colored feathers," Marina told Bianca.

Several groups wore enormous headdresses of feathers, colored ribbons, and flowers interwoven to resemble giant pinwheels that were in turn attached to caps and strapped to the wearers' heads. The costumes ranged from simple brightly colored mantles, to elaborate mantles decorated with feathers, to brilliantly embroidered skirts and shirts. Almost every woman wore fresh flowers in her hair. And nearly all had earrings resembling the gold ones Rafe had given her, although she didn't see a pair as lovely.

Tío Ignacio caught their attention, beckoning Rafe to the table he had placed on the ball court for the unveiling of the idol. Rafe studied the setting. "Don

323

Ignacio is in the wrong business. He should stage theatricals."

"The better to serve your cause," Marina whispered. "You need all the support you can get from these people."

He nodded, catching up her hand. "Come with me."

"This is your show. I am a spectator. Go."

While Tío Ignacio recounted the finding of the statue, Marina took a seat Bianca had saved for her on the first row of the old bleachers. Tía Luisa sat between the girls, their brothers ranging to either side.

"It gives one an eerie feeling," Tía Luisa sighed. "Sitting in the very place where our ancestors' ancestors sat centuries ago on their own ceremonial days."

"Sí, Tía," Marina whispered, her attention riveted on the cloth-covered object and on the man who unwrapped it. He was nervous, she could tell. Not so much at being unable to identify the idol, now, as at the awesome task he performed.

"Do you think he will know what it is?" Essie asked.

Marina shrugged. "The odds are against him. Much remains to be learned about the ancient people. The Spaniards destroyed most of what they found. Of course, from their point of view, the pagan idols had to be destroyed to make way for the Lord God, Our Lady His Blessed Mother, and Christianity."

"But Rafe is an expert. I'll bet you a new saddle with silver fittings he identifies it."

At his worshipful tone, Marina tore her attention from Rafael Santana. "Rafe is an expert, yes, but experts are not omniscient."

As it turned out Rafe was lucky; he admitted as

much to her later. The pieces of the idol were large, the work on it intricate, the goddess a familiar one out of the literally hundreds it could have been.

"She is called the Goddess of the Jade Petticoat." He spoke to the crowd, but his glistening eyes held Marina's. His excitement thrilled through her. Lost in his work, he was at once confident and vulnerable—a quality she had seen but one other time in him—in the canoe on the way to the house of his *abuelita*.

"One legend claims that," he was saying, "at the death of the Fourth Sun, she provided a bridge to heaven by persuading the rain god to flood the earth with water. She then turned men into fishes so they could swim through the rain water to heaven. That's why generations of our ancestors were buried with a piece of jade in their mouths. They used it to pay their fare into the other world."

Afterwards Rafe stood for an hour or more, holding the pieces of the goddess in place while visitors filed by to view her. Logan Junior tagged along last in line.

"How did you know all that?" he asked. "Did it come from . . . what did you call the books?"

"Codices," Rafe answered. "No, not all of it. A lot of our information comes from tales handed down generation after generation. That's why I refer to them as legends." He shrugged, smiling at Logan as though the young man had never entertained an adverse thought against him. "Legends allow each person to believe what he chooses."

Marina watched Logan scrutinize the statue of the goddess. She was a lovely creature, seated cross-legged with her shoulders thrown back. Marina thought suddenly of Rafe's instructions inside the hut of the old shaman, Diego Ortiz. This lady did not need to throw her shoulders back to be identified as female.

Her intricately carved clothing included a tall hat with a bow tied neatly over its brim, enormous round earrings, a skirt complete with belt and sash, but nothing covering her bare and also intricately carved bosom.

Logan's eyes strayed to the goddess's endowments, then quickly away. Marina diverted his attention.

"That must be the reason jade was more valued than gold, since it provided their ticket to heaven," she said.

"One of the reasons," Rafe agreed. "On the practical side, jade is a harder substance than gold, easier to work. They could carve it in greater detail."

While Tío Ignacio helped Rafe rewrap the goddess piece by piece and pack her in the wooden crate his workers had built for her, they discussed which crafts-man would be capable of restoring such a priceless piece of art. When they finished, Rafe cleared his throat.

"You know my plans for the museum, Don Ignacio. Can we expect to have your goddess as a focal point?"

Ignacio chuckled. "I wondered when you would get around to that. The answer is yes, definitely. But I would consider it a favor if we could keep her until the museum is built."

"Of course. You've already proven your desire to see her preserved. I know you will guard her well."

Immediately then Don Ignacio gave the call for siesta, and the crowd dispersed in the time-honored tradition of people who inhabit tropical climates, spreading mats in the shade of ceiba and palm trees, napping, minding children, a few drinking pulque they

326

brought from home in pottery jugs.

The Cortinas family retired to the big house, their special guests in tow, along with their newly unveiled goddess. Upon arriving they found Nick and Zolic in the patio at the foot of the circular staircase, sipping tequila, Nick morose, Zolic pacing the black and white tiled floor in agitation.

Nick's face brightened when he saw them. "We'd almost given up the fiesta."

After the introductions, Tía Luisa directed the two new guests to their quarters for siesta and shepherded the girls upstairs to the bedchambers. "We will meet here at four o'clock and travel together for the evening's festivities."

Marina cast Rafe a wistful goodbye, then hurried to her room to change clothing. Not unfamiliar with the custom of siesta—in her grandmother's youth the practice had been adhered to at Los Olmos—she nonetheless did not intend to waste one minute of this day alone, unless it was alone with Rafael Santana. She smiled to herself.

Downstairs the men were not eager to conform to the custom, either. At Rafe's suggestion, Don Ignacio unwrapped the goddess once more for Zolic's inspection.

"I would like him to verify my identification," Rafe told their host. "Zolic is the expert."

Later, after Don Ignacio disappeared into the interior of the mansion with his goddess, Zolic made straightway for the grounds of El Tajín.

When he was barely out of earshot, Nick turned to Rafe. "The only thing that man's an expert on is peyote. He consumed so much yesterday I wouldn't

327

have been surprised if he had jumped into the ocean and drowned."

Rafe frowned. "He hallucinated?"

Nick grunted. "He got so tipsy he nearly spilled a barrel of tar on Ybarro's diving equipment. And he brought his sackful of the stuff along today. He's mixing it with tequila."

Rafe inhaled a deep breath. "I'll be glad when this expedition is over."

The boys, of course, had stopped listening with the mention of peyote, demanding at the first break in the conversation an account of the drug and all it entailed. Even Logan, Rafe noticed, hung on every word.

"How do you know so much about all these things?" Essie asked, his tone indicating a growing case of hero worship.

Rafe laughed, then purposely caught Logan Junior's eye. "I don't know a lot about any of these things. I know a little, because it's my country, like you two at Los Olmos; you will be able to answer my questions about Los Olmos when I visit."

Logan Junior's green eyes turned as cold as carved jade when Rafe's implication registered. "Marina will be the one to show you Los Olmos," he replied, "if you visit. The ranch is her responsibility. Essie and I are going to sea."

Rafe held Logan Junior's stare, soaking in the young man's discontent. So that was it? Marina's plans to leave Los Olmos disrupted Logan's plans for himself; at least, he thought they did. Rafe's spirits rose by degrees. Knowing the enemy's worst fear was essential to winning a war.

Footsteps on the staircase, soft as they were, alerted

328

him to her presence. He turned to see her poised there, looking even more lovely than he recalled in her *china* from Veracruz and the earrings belonging to his grandmother many times removed. *Used* to belong to his grandmother, he corrected as he met her at the foot of the stairs. Now they belonged to Marina, to his own lovely Marina.

Reaching the bottom step, he stopped short of cupping her face in his hand, recalling in time her brothers who watched his every move from behind them. Instead he touched one golden earring, letting his fingers whisper across the soft skin on her shoulder. Her eyes begged him to kiss her, a silent command his body ached to obey. His brain registered their sensual communication, and his heart sang.

Later, in the carriage, he realized their communication did not always extend beyond the sensual, however. In questioning the boys about Los Olmos, Nick provided the perfect opening to address Logan Junior's concern about having to run the ranch himself, but the opportunity slipped by when Marina failed to pick up Rafe's cue.

"Has Jorge heard anything from the law suit he filed in the Mexican courts?" Nick had asked.

"No," Logan responded. "Those things take time, Jorge says."

"Miguel discovered something which may confirm the Wilson's guilt," Essie added. "You recall the tax assessor who disappeared, Marina? Well, Miguel located her grave—unmarked, at that. He's petitioning to have her body exhumed—may have accomplished it by now. The body being hidden away in an unmarked grave and all, Miguel says likely someone knows something. It's just a matter of ferreting out the person who can be persuaded to talk."

"Miguel Cortinas?" Rafe asked. "Isn't he Jorge's son?"

"I told you about him," Marina replied.

Rafe frowned into her eyes, prompting her to speak the words he knew would be better received coming from her lips. "Didn't you say he is one of the Los Olmos heirs?"

Obviously, Rafe decided, she did not yet suspect Logan's concern, for instead of responding as she had to him about how Miguel would gladly run the ranch when Giddeon and her father retired, she launched a recounting of the family tree. "His grandfather was Grandmother's brother. Together they inherited the hacienda."

By the time they reached the grounds of El Tajín siesta was over, the fiesta in full swing again.

"Hurry," Galván encouraged. "The pole is already in place for the Voladores."

"We missed the blessing of the pole," Bianca said as the Cortinases of Vera Cruz hurried the Cortinases of Texas to a spot where they could view a ritual ancient to this particular place before their Spanish ancestors arrived.

"This dance is a mixture of pagan and Christian customs," Bianca continued.

"You missed the offering." Zolic materialized so quietly at Marina's elbow that when he spoke she jumped.

"What offerings?" she inquired.

"To insure the performers' safety," he responded, "a live turkey is put into the hole before the pole is raised."

Essie spoke into the ensuing gasps, unmoved by Zolic's revelation or unaware of it, Rafe wasn't sure which.

"That's no pole," the boy enthused. "It's a tree trunk. Why it must stand a hundred feet in the air."

"Near enough," Rafe murmured. He watched color drain from Marina's face as five men clad in brilliant red and white climbed the pole by way of pieces of wood slashed up its length.

Around the base of the pole, Indians—Totonacs Bianca said—chanted to their own accompaniment of flutes and drums.

Once they reached the platform on top of the pole four of the men tied ropes around their waists, while the fifth man, the captain, took the center position and began to play a flute and a drum simultaneously. With his playing, the chanting and music on the ground stopped abruptly.

"He is the sun," Zolic told Marina. "The other men represent the other elements necessary to life: earth, air, fire, and water."

She held her breath, wondering what to expect, but the wait was short. Suddenly the four men fell from the platform and the crowd gasped in unison, even though Bianca informed them that most of the group had witnessed such a performance every Saint Francis Day their lives long.

As birds the four men spiraled toward the ground, while the captain remained on top, spread-eagled over the center pole, as though he alone kept it in place. Held securely by the ropes attached to their waists, the four men glided in graceful arches around the pole.

"They will make thirteen circles," Zolic told Marina.

331

"Thirteen?"

The men dipped closer and closer.

"Four times thirteen makes fifty-two—the number of years in our century."

"The Totonacs . . . were they part of the Aztec kingdom?" she asked.

"No, no," Zolic replied. "They helped Cortés defeat the Aztecs. Carried his cannons over the high mountain passes; some of them froze to death on the journey."

After the men flipped gracefully to their feet, the captain returned to the ground, where they all received well-earned applause. The crowd milled, and Rafe and Zolic spoke of the new goddess and what discoveries might still lie hidden here at El Tajín.

Twilight approached and the food vendors lighted candles in clay lanterns, *luminarias,* Bianca told Marina. As time neared for the lighting of the niches, everyone drifted in that direction, although the sight would surely be visible and breathtaking from a great distance.

Tío Ignacio rounded up dozens of young men to help with the lighting ceremony, including Logan Junior and Essie. Groups of people still flocked around Rafe, besieging him with questions, each of which he took seriously and tried to answer, noting in the little book he carried in his pocket any questions he could not immediately provide answers for. Watching, Marina thought of their future, of the now unheard of mysteries they would solve in the years ahead, of the wonders they would share, and her heart thrilled with an urgency to get on with their lives.

Zolic took her elbow. "While Santana is occupied,

let me show you something at the pyramid."

Although she had no intention of wandering far from Rafe's side, she trailed Zolic to the very steps she and Rafe had climbed that day which seemed so long ago, yet actually was not over five weeks back.

"Did you notice the flutes the voladores played?" Zolic asked.

"They were like the ones you gave me."

"Do you still have yours?"

"I left them on board the *Stella Duval.*"

Withdrawing his hand from his pocket, he held his fist toward her. "Here is another one."

With her palm up she waited for him to place the flute inside, but he lowered his fist, then clasped her hand in his, the flute inside both their palms.

"Tonight is a special night, Marina. The culmination of both a pagan and a Christian festival. If you play this flute while you watch the fires on El Tajín, the music will enhance the magnificence. Your senses of sight and sound will merge into a glorious union."

She pulled to free her hand, and he released it without a struggle, smiling amicably. Then nodding toward the stairs he moved forward. "Come, let me show you what I mean. You know there are three hundred sixty-five niches in this pyramid. But do you know how many steps lead from the ground to the altar on top?"

"No," she answered, surprised to find herself standing on the third step. He had walked ahead, and striving to hear his voice through the din around them, she had followed unaware. She searched the crowd behind them. Rafe was still absorbed in conversation.

"Come with me to count them. You will be sur-

333

prised . . ." —he laughed, enticingly— ". . . but I won't. I will tell you the strangest story you have yet to hear, after I prove my point."

"I shouldn't—"

"Why? The acolytes are still lighting the braziers. We will be up there and down before they finish."

Still she hesitated.

"Come, Marina. You are not afraid of me?"

"No." She laughed. "Certainly not in this crowd."

"Not any place, I hope." His wounded tone plucked at her conscience. "Nick must have told you about the peyote." he continued. "Don't believe all you hear. He and I—well, he is a fine man, valuable to you in Texas I am sure, but our personalities are in conflict."

She smiled, anxious to return to Rafe.

"Like Santana and I. We have disagreements time to time. But our deepest passions lie in the same . . . area, so we work together in spite of personal differences."

Later, she thought how it must have been his openness that lured her to the top of the Pyramid of the Niches. A place she had had no intention of going with anyone except Rafael Santana. In short order, however, they stepped onto the platform of the temple itself.

"How many steps?" Zolic quizzed.

"Fifty-two." Her voice ended on the high note of awe.

"The sacred number," he agreed.

Without further ado, he sat on the top step and pulled her down beside him. In front of them lay the sprawling compound of El Tajín, shrouded in growing darkness now. Like swarms of fireflies, lanterns flickered from booths and tree limbs. An enchanting sight.

334

She spread her embroidered skirt over her knees and clasped her arms about them. This is where Rafe would bring her later. This is where she would kiss him goodnight.

"The story of the Unblemished Youth illustrates the basic teaching of the Aztec religion," Zolic was saying. "The most beautiful young man in the entire kingdom was chosen for the honor. For a year he was prepared to become a god, gowned in fine array . . ." —he paused to finger the delicate embroidery on her skirt— ". . . given seven pure women as his brides, seven handsome servants to bring everything he desired, while high priests taught him to purify his senses."

Fumbling in a pocket, he withdrew a flask. "The incense of purity." Tipping his fingers to the mouth of the container, he smeared a sweet-smelling, oily substance on her bare arms, then dabbed some on her shoulders.

Just as she began to protest, he corked the flask and returned it to his pocket.

"The Unblemished Youth's only task was to become as pure as a god. To this end he learned to play certain melodies on the flute—to play them perfectly, of course." Producing another flute, he handed it to Marina.

"Let me see how much you have learned."

Smoke drifted toward them. She glanced behind her in alarm.

Zolic tugged on her arm. "It is nothing. The braziers near the top have taken hold. Give me a few minutes more, then we will go."

"No." She tried to rise. "I must go now. Rafe will be looking for me."

He pulled her back to the step. "You have no need for Rafael Santana. He has turned your head from your mission; you have become weak and we must correct that."

"Let me go, Zolic." She twisted her arm, pulling away from his hold, but he jerked her back.

"Only a few more minutes. Do not be impatient, Marina. Impatience will interfere with your purpose."

When he unsheathed his penknife, she felt her heart flutter. Immediately, she chided herself for fearing Zolic, and for coming up here with him in his intoxicated state.

She fought to free her arm. "It's time to go."

Again he held her fast. "Do not be afraid, Marina."

"I'm not afraid," she hissed. "I am embarrassed. Everyone will—"

"Sit still," he commanded. "I don't want to hurt you. One drop of blood. Only one . . ."

Before she could stop him, he slit the tip of one of her fingers.

"What . . . ?" Her eyes wide, her heart pounding, she stared warily at him, scooching down a step.

As though unaware of her protests, he sheathed the blade with one hand, still gripping her arm as in a vise.

"What did I tell you? That didn't hurt. One drop of blood to purge the impurities from your soul."

Dazed she watched him lift her finger to his lips and lick the blood away.

She jerked to free her hand, angry now.

"Play your flute," he demanded. "Let me judge your progress."

"Zolic . . ." she objected.

336

"Play it, Marina. Time is short. You will never purify yourself by—just play it, will you?"

"No." She struggled in earnest to free herself from his grip. "Nick was right. You have consumed too much peyote. You're intoxicated."

"Sit down," he ordered, jerking her to the platform.

Tears stung her eyes. She was mad and angry. And a little frightened. Why had she followed a drunken man to the top of a pyramid in front of half of Mexico? What had happened to her good sense?

Suddenly she realized that although the night sky had darkened, the area around them glowed as bright as day. The braziers were flaming. The people below stared in awe.

They hadn't seen her—not yet. But they would.

"Now look what you have done," she accused. "We're stranded up here, a spectacle for all to see."

"Yes," he mused. "The better to teach you the behavior of the gods, my dear lady."

Rafe had been so swamped with questions from those interested in antiquities, so excited at what their interest meant for his work that he lost track of time . . . and of Marina. When someone shouted that the braziers were lit, he reached for her hand, but she was not beside him.

Neither were her brothers nor any of her family, so he went in search of them.

"Where is your sister?" he asked Essie when he located the boy standing with Bianca at the base of the pyramid.

Essie shrugged. "We just finished lighting the braziers. Isn't it the most spectacular thing you've ever seen?"

Rafe stared at the flaming pyramid. Indeed it was breathtaking. A sight to remain in one's memory, a moment to share with children and grandchildren.

But where was Marina? The woman with whom he had intended to share this spectacle? The woman who would tell the stories along with him? Where was she?

Looking left and right, he stared into the mass of packed bodies. Finding her in this crowd would be impossible. Disappointment settled over his enthusiasm.

"Look up there," someone shouted.

"What is it?"

"*Who,* you mean?"

"You're right. Someone is on top of the pyramid."

Half-hearing the commotion, Rafe's gaze drifted to the top of the Pyramid of the Niches. Indeed, some thrill-seeker . . .

He squinted. Edging his way through the crowd, he moved nearer, his attention focused on the top step of the pyramid. Flames danced from every niche, filling the spaces between them with darkness. The stairs leading to the temple had become one black sweep of night. Only by intense concentration was he able to recognize the figures seated on the top step of the platform.

Marina!

And Jesús Zolic!

His mouth went dry. He ran his tongue inside his gums, studying the situation. His immediate reaction had been anger, but before it progressed to more than a stirring the figures moved.

In opposition, Marina moved one way, then jerked back the other; the process was repeated. Zolic was holding her . . . pulling her . . . *That damned Zolic!*

Of an instant images of ancient Aztec priests flowed through Rafe's mind. Zolic's ancestors, Aztec priests who ripped out the hearts of living victims to feed to their fearsome gods. Zolic, who this day was high on both peyote and tequila.

Shouldering his way through the crowd, Rafe gained the staircase leading to the top of the pyramid. Zolic wouldn't harm her, he reasoned. Not Zolic. Hadn't he himself assured Marina, and her grandparents and Nick as well, of the man's harmless obsession?

Beneath him the crowd watched and responded, gasping, gaping.

Zolic wouldn't harm her. He wouldn't, Rafe repeated step after step after step. He would bet his life on it. But the man was crazy and drunk and probably hallucinating.

And it was Marina's life Zolic held up there, not his own.

And even if the lunatic only frightened her—

That was enough.

Chapter Fourteen

"What the devil is going on?" Rafe fell to his knees before Marina, reaching for her hands. He squinted through the smoke and flickering light. "Are you all right?"

She gripped his hands. Her heart still beat wildly, she thought perhaps from the rapid sequence of events, so unexpected, escalating by the moment.

"Why did you . . . ?" His eyes beseeched her, his heart raced from the climb to the top, his mind reeled, bewildered. Marina and Zolic sitting on the top step of the pyramid, as he himself had done with her.

Her earlier request rang in his ears. "I told you we would come tonight after . . ." The strange look in her eyes further complicated his thinking.

He turned to Zolic. Tiny red flames, reflections of the multitude of fires, danced in the man's eyes. He was mad! "Why . . . ?" Studying Zolic's face Rafe frowned at the glistening smudge around his lips. "What . . . ?"

Suddenly he felt it. Opening his hands, he cradled her limp fingers inside his palms. Blood.

Blood smeared her hands and his. When she tried to

340

pull away, he held fast. "What is this?"

"Nothing . . . just . . ." Again she tried to hide her hands.

"You're bleeding. Why?" Without waiting for an answer, he glared at Zolic, seeing once more the man's blood-smeared mouth. At that moment, Zolic lazily ran his tongue around his lips, removing the evidence.

Rafe diverted his gaze, consumed by an anger so fierce he knew he would be hard pressed to control it.

"You bastard! What have you done to her?"

"One drop of blood, Santana, no more. After you defiled her body, I had to purify it."

Rafe felt his breath come even more shallow, as though an iron band had been secured around his chest and was squeezing all life from him. Exactly the thing he wanted to do to Jesús Zolic.

"Get out of my sight." His voice rumbled from deep in his throat, reminding Marina of a volcano. Smoking Man, she thought involuntarily. She cringed against the possibility he might fight Zolic here—on top of the flaming pyramid.

"Get out of my sight," Rafe ordered again. "Now. Before I throw you off the top of this pyramid without even stopping to cut out your heart. Now! And don't ever let me catch sight of you again. You're finished."

Zolic's flashing eyes did not dim a degree at Rafe's orders, whether from insolence, madness, or the mixture of peyote and tequila, Marina wasn't sure. Muttering something unintelligible, he sauntered down the steps.

"What did he say?" she asked, fearing the answer.

"Nothing." Rafe examined her hand, found the flow of blood stemmed. "Are you all right?"

She nodded, inhaling, surprised to feel her breath

341

quiver inside her.

Rafe cradled her head in his hands. "I had no idea he was so demented."

"He's drunk. Drunk men don't think clearly."

"Regardless, he had no right . . . I should have known to protect you from his madness."

"He said he wanted to *purify* my soul."

Rafe inhaled deep drafts of the smoke-filled air, trying to quiet his still racing heart. "Your soul is beautiful." His thumbs brushed the tender skin around her eyes. "Everything about you is beautiful. He will never touch you again. I promise."

The air had become increasingly warm and smoky. Dropping his hands to her shoulders, he started to help her rise, but she stopped him.

"Wait." Her legs were so weak she knew she could not walk down the steps. And Rafe couldn't carry her, not down steps as steep as these. "Can we sit here a minute . . . and share this extraordinary experience?"

Settling on the step beside her he lay an arm around her shoulders and drew her close. Flames leaped on either side, smoke rose into the night sky overhead. Her shoulder trembled against his chest. "An extraordinary experience," he repeated.

"Imagine we are back in the old days, the ancient days, when this pyramid was lighted for special occasions. Do you think they ever had weddings up here?"

He chuckled, surprising himself. "No. I don't know the truth, of course, but in those days weddings were not high on their list of priorities. Their major concern was to keep the sun from dying. I suspect this pyramid was used like all the others, for human sacrifice."

The clamor inside their hearts died gradually, allowing shouts from the ground to reach them.

"Marina . . . are you all right?"

"That's Logan," she sighed.

"Well . . . I'd better get you down these steps before he comes up here and does to me what I threatened to do to Zolic." Rafe rose, tugging on her hand.

She held him back.

When he looked down, her eyes teased. "Don't you remember what you said?"

He cocked his head, waiting.

"That you couldn't come up here without at least . . . a kiss?" She rose to stand beside him.

He stared at her a moment, glanced down at the crowd who waited impatiently to discover the outcome of the drama, then winked, his grin more intoxicating than any substance. "If you don't mind an audience . . ."

"Grandmother called our relationship unconventional. Why change things now?"

Taking her in his arms, he lowered his face to hers. "Why indeed?" he agreed as his lips closed on hers.

His tenderness surprised even Rafe himself. Hungry for her kisses, craving her touch, wild with the fear just behind them, he had felt himself ready to explode.

But when his arms drew her near, he sheltered her with a gentle strength; when his lips touched hers, he stroked her tenderly, firing the flames within them by the very knowledge of the reserves he held in store and by those perimeters of convention they had not yet broken. Lifting his face, he whispered against her lips. "Until later, love."

"Later," she sighed.

For the first time then he noticed how the fire

glistened from the golden earrings that had belonged to his great-grandmother, and from the brilliant embroidery on her *china*. And in that instant he knew this was the moment he would remember; this the moment they would relate to their grandchildren—not watching from below, spectators to the glorious event, but rather as participants, standing on top of the flaming structure with hundreds of spectators gaping up at them, while they only had eyes for each other.

Catching up her hand, he smiled—devilish now—and hand in hand they descended the steep fifty-two steps, proud and regal, relishing this moment which they would hold in their hearts forever.

The romantic spell was broken the instant they stepped onto solid ground. Logan Junior confronted them in the presence of the entire crowd of revelers.

"What do you mean, taking my sister into all that fire?" He grasped Marina's hand. When she flinched at his touch, he saw the cut on her finger.

"What the hell?" Releasing her, he grabbed a fistful of Rafe's shirt. "What have you done to her?"

"Now hold on—" Rafe backed away.,

"He rescued me, Logan," Marina interrupted.

Tío Ignacio, Galván, and Essie gathered around the little group, shielding them from the rest of the onlookers.

"We tried to tell him," Galván told Rafe. "Logan didn't show up until after your man got away. He assumed—"

"Assumed, hell. I know what I saw. And look at this—she's bleeding! What did you do to her, Santana?"

Rafe glared at the agitated young man. "Looks like

there's only one way to settle this." He jerked his head toward the unoccupied side of the pyramid. "Come on. We don't need an audience."

"Rafe." When Marina caught his sleeve he paused. Before them, Logan fumed.

"I'll fight you on top of that damned pile of rocks, if you want. But I will not let you make a spectacle of my sister."

"My, my." Tío Ignacio maneuvered his way between the two men. "You have injured your hand, my dear."

"It is nothing," Marina whispered, her attention riveted on Rafe and Logan.

"Ah, yes," her uncle many times removed continued, "superficial. But we must see to it. You know how wounds fester in this humid climate." As though the two men did not wage a battle around him, Ignacio turned to Rafe.

"Don Rafael, would you be so kind as to take my carriage and escort my niece back to the big house. This hand must have attention."

Logan didn't like it, of course, but Tío Ignacio was persuasive, and Galván and Essie took him in tow until the carriage pulled away from the festivities.

Marina leaned back in the darkness of the carriage, secure in the crook of Rafe's arm. The events of the past hour whirled through her brain, superceded now by Logan's attempt to draw Rafe into a fight.

"I'm sorry about Logan," she said. "He is usually so good natured."

"I didn't intend to start a fight. The words just came out. My anger was still too close to the surface, after Zolic—"

She silenced him with her lips. His arms slid around her, pulling her close, molding her body to his, holding

345

her tight against the bouncing of the carriage, against his fears for her that had yet to dissipate. His kisses deepened and she responded hungrily.

When a bump in the road jounced their lips apart, he chuckled. "I never realized kissing could be such a hazardous occupation."

"Maybe we could stop a while," she whispered into the moist folds of his lips.

"Tempting, love. But what would we do with our driver?"

She laughed. "You did agree our relationship is unconventional."

He kissed her face softly. "I also promised your grandfather not to totally compromise you, which promise I am fast on the road to breaking if we don't slow down."

With his hands on her waist then, he turned her around, adjusting her against him with her back against his chest. Together they looked out the same window. The flames from the Pyramid of the Niches illuminated the sky.

Although he tried to keep his mind off the woman in his arms—or at least, off making love to the woman in his arms—he soon discovered that his body worked quite separately from his brain. For before he was aware he had done so, his hand had slipped beneath the ruffle on her blouse and inside her corset cover, where he cupped her breast in his palm. Warm and full, it only increased his desires, and when she stretched her arms behind her and clasped his head, he knew the road to the big house would be fraught with peril—not to their persons now, but to her reputation.

"Look," he whispered against her temple. "Do you recognize that old palm tree?"

She studied the weeping tree at the edge of a vanilla field. "Our tree. Where you *almost* kissed me."

He squeezed his hand around her breast. "I still remember how badly I wanted to, but . . ."

"But the specter of my ancient counterpart rose between us."

He chuckled against her, recalling the afternoon when they had taken refuge from the rain beneath the sweeping branches of the old tree. "Not counterpart," he admitted. "It was what your name stood for. I was determined not to lose any more artifacts to foreigners . . . and I could feel myself falling under your spell." —she felt him heave a sigh beneath her.

She tried to turn in his arms, but he held her still. "Then I'm losing my touch. You are certainly able to resist my spell tonight."

"It isn't easy," he groaned, teasing her with nibbles to her ear.

She squirmed. "Look. Isn't that Diego Ortiz's hut— with a light burning inside?"

"Hmmm . . . they must have a new medicine man."

"Stop the carriage. Perhaps he can restore my magic." Again she squirmed in his arms. This time he was distracted and she managed to right herself, but her skirts tangled hopelessly over her thighs, exposing the lace ruffle on her bloomers.

Dislodged from her breast, his hand slipped to her knees, where he lifted her legs over his lap, running his hand over the single layer of fabric separating her soft thigh from his warm hand.

"If your magic were any more potent, love, we would be in trouble."

"So you say," she challenged, her face near his, her mouth dry with wanting him. "You are uncommonly adept at resisting that which you profess to want so badly."

He kissed her face, then to make his point stroked his hand up the inside of her thigh, clutching her with a firm grip. "Only because one day soon you . . ." —he squeezed her provocatively— ". . . *all* of you . . . will be mine forever."

Moonlight streamed through the windows of the carriage, highlighting his bronzed arm where it disappeared into the snowy white of her bloomers. She wanted him more than she had ever wanted him.

That probably wasn't true, she countered. Yet, heightened by her earlier fright, and now finding herself alone with him . . .

But he was right. She had already been made a spectacle once today, and once was once more than a lady was allowed.

Besides, from Logan Junior's choleric manner, she wouldn't be surprised should he ride them down, even now.

"It's going to be an interesting *forever,*" she mused, "spending it with a man who cannot speak my name."

His eyes glistened. "And you, *capitán,* have yet to confess your undying love."

She sighed against him, content, unrequited, and desperately in love, all at the same time. At their approach to the big house, he straightened her skirts, then tightened his embrace.

"They are only words," she whispered.

"And what are words?" he added. "When I have four other senses to love you with."

They left for Tecolutla early the next morning—

Marina and Rafe, Logan Junior, Essie, and Nick—in a carriage supplied by Tío Ignacio.

Logan Junior's surliness had not dissipated since the encounter the night before. If anything, his objections to Rafael Santana's presence increased with time.

Rafe ignored him as best he could, but he knew before long he would be forced to take charge of the situation. It was not a chore he anticipated with pleasure.

As it turned out the situation righted itself, but not before things deteriorated a bit more.

Arriving in Tecolutla at midafternoon they found the *Stella Duval* provisioned and Giddeon and Serita ready to set sail with the morning sun.

"Pedro Ybarro brought another set of diving equipment," Giddeon informed them. "With two men diving at once, he figures we should salvage all the chests by the end of the month. That will give us another month to straighten out the paperwork before the December deadline."

"And it means we should be finished in time to attend the ceremonies for the Day of the Dead at the hacienda," Serita said.

"It won't matter whether you finish by that time or not," Rafe told her. "Ybarro and his men will insist on two days off." He studied Marina a moment. "I'm supposed to go to Janitzio, an island in Lake Pátzcuaro for the Day of the Dead observances."

"Am I invited?" she challenged, a gleam in her eyes.

Rafe quickly took in the assembled group—her grandparents would be easy enough to convince, and her brother Essie, probably. But Logan Junior? Rafe saw how he seethed at the mention.

Giddeon rescued the moment, and as it turned out,

Rafe thought later, the entire situation, by his next words.

Giddeon put a fatherly arm around Marina. "By the way, sugar, you have a visitor over at the cantina."

"Me?"

Giddeon nodded, a grin tipping his mouth.

"I don't know anyone around here except—"

"Last I heard, Burt Wilson didn't live around here."

"Burt Wilson? Here?"

Giddeon nodded again. "He and a friend rode in early this morning. Says he won't budge an inch until you agree to talk with him."

At the mention of Burt Wilson, Rafe scowled, Logan Junior bristled, and Marina marched down the gangplank to confront the man. Rafe caught up with her; her brothers trailed in their wake, with Nick following.

Wilson must have seen them coming, Rafe supposed, for two men, closer to Marina's age than he himself, appeared at the entrance to the thatched-roof cantina, where they waited for the group to approach. No question, even before he spoke, which was Burt Wilson. He stood to the front, obviously in control of the situation.

He was an uncommonly handsome man. Rafe felt his hackles rise at the thought of him even speaking to Marina, much less . . .

"Hi." Wilson greeted Marina, his manner casual and offhand, further irritating Rafe. That, and the fact that Wilson's eyes never left Marina's. Cocky and confident, he did not even look to her brothers. Swiping a shock of brown hair off his broad forehead, he grinned in a good-natured way, belying all Rafe had heard about the Wilsons and their attempts to use Marina to gain Los Olmos.

At this moment Rafe Santana stared at a man who appeared to want only one thing: Marina Cafferty. Rafe's eyes narrowed watching Wilson look at her—at the woman he himself loved . . . had loved . . . would love . . . forever. *Cold tortilla kisses from this hot-blooded Texan?*

"What are you doing here?" Marina's voice was steady, Rafe noted, devoid of emotion. Somewhere deep within he sighed in relief.

"I came to talk to you," Wilson said. "We have a lot to work out."

"No, Burt, we don't. I have nothing to say to you."

"Then I have some explaining to do," he replied. His eyes were soft and warm, and Rafe wondered suddenly what Burt Wilson saw in Marina's eyes. He wished he were looking into them to be sure.

"She isn't going to talk to you, Wilson," Logan barked. He had come to stand at Marina's other side.

Ignoring Logan, Wilson reached for her arm. "Come inside where we can talk . . . alone."

Instinctively Rafe caught her hand. He pulled her closer, out of Wilson's reach. "She said she has nothing to say," Rafe said. "And *I* say she isn't going inside that cantina."

At Rafe's tone Burt Wilson's eyes lost their softness. He turned a hard look on the man beside Marina. "Who the hell asked you? Stay out of—"

"Burt," Marina interrupted. "This is Rafael Santana, the man I'm going to marry."

Burt Wilson blinked only once. He appraised Rafe, head to foot, then dismissed him.

"Tell her what you came to say, Wilson," Rafe barked. "We've had a long day, and we are not in the mood for the likes of you."

"What the hell?" Burt quizzed Marina. "You're engaged to marry me."

Marina shook her head.

Wilson's eyes narrowed. Again he scrutinized Rafe. "Who the hell is this fellow? You run out on me, a perfectly good American and come down here for some . . ." His eyes pierced Marina's. "What the hell have you turned into, anyhow?"

Rafe struck first. Only after his fist connected with Burt Wilson's jaw, did he see Logan in his peripheral vision. Wilson staggered, taken by surprise, then he regained his footing and swung at Rafe.

Rafe landed another blow to Wilson's jaw, staggering the man a second time.

"This isn't your fight!" Logan grabbed Burt Wilson by the shoulder, swinging him around so he could hit him full in the face. "That's for mistreating my sister."

Rafe stepped back, took in the situation. Marina stared wide-eyed; Essie and Nick held Wilson's friend by the collar and one arm.

The man struggled. "Let me go. That ain't a fair fight. Two men on one."

"If we let you go, we'll jump in, too," Essie told him. "Then it'll be four on two. You want those odds?"

"I didn't mistreat your sister," Wilson shouted. While Rafe watched, the man rose to the occasion, finding his footing and returning Logan's punches blow for blow.

Logan rocked on his heels, Wilson pulled him to his feet. "I came to take her home with me—where she belongs." He swung a wicked right to Logan's esophagus.

Rafe interrupted, jerking Wilson toward himself, landing a solid punch to the Texan's chest. "That's for trying to take her away from me."

Burt Wilson acclimated himself quickly. Before Rafe's fist could more than graze his ribs, he sidestepped, then came in swinging both arms. Rafe punched back, fist for fist.

Somewhere in the back of his brain, he heard Marina shouting for them to stop. For Burt Wilson to go home and leave them alone.

Alone . . . his attention snapped back when Burt landed a strike at the corner of his mouth, smashing his tongue between his teeth. He tasted the salty tang of blood.

The first part of October was still warm. Heat hung in the humid air, heavy; every breath was hard to come by.

When Logan spun Wilson around again, Rafe stepped back beside Marina, his breath short. He wiped blood from his mouth with the back of his sleeve and watched Logan and Burt through sweat that stung his eyes.

Logan was heaving, too. Blood poured from a cut over one eye and sweat dripped from his hair. That damned Burt Wilson was a bull of a man, his strength concealed within a trim body. Rafe studied the situation. Logan needed help.

When he stepped back into the fracas, Marina clutched at his arm. "Please. Not anymore. Stop this."

Rafe shrugged. "I can't let him kill your brother." With a grin he lunged at Wilson, knocking the man backward, leaving Logan poised with a fist in the air and no place to land it. Logan stood, hands on knees, breathing hard, watching Rafe and Burt Wilson roll on the ground.

Behind them Rafe heard scuffling and the muffled

voice of Wilson's companion. When Logan bent down and pulled Wilson to his feet by his collar, Rafe saw Nick holding the friend with his hands behind his back, while Essie gagged the man with his neckerchief.

Turning back to the fight, he saw Logan strike, watched Burt's knees buckle. As quickly as his own wobbly legs would move, Rafe lunged, grabbed the man with trembling arms and slugged him. Wilson fell to the ground once and for all, taking Rafe with him.

When Rafe looked up, he spraddled Burt Wilson, his chin on the man's chest; the fuzzy image of Logan Junior lay collapsed beside them. The two adversaries exchanged a long, weary look.

Rafe heaved. "You grow 'em tough in Texas."

Logan gasped for breath. "Don't you go forgetting it, either."

Rafe felt his breath steady. "Way things turned out,"—he took a gulp of air, focusing unsteadily on Logan—". . . lucky the fellow came along." He studied the quiet, battered face of Burt Wilson, half the blows caused by his own bloody fists, the other half by Logan's. Looking back at Logan, he chuckled. "I thought for sure I was going to have to do that to you."

Logan grinned, a weak but satisfied smile. *"Try,"* he corrected. "You thought you'd have to *try* to do that to me."

Rafe nodded lazily toward the cantina. "How 'bout instead I buy you a shot of tequila?"

Logan struggled to his feet. "Second round's on me."

Chapter Fifteen

They sailed the following morning and for a month continued to entreat the sea to give up the treasures it had stolen fifty years before.

By the morning after Rafe and Logan's fight with Burt Wilson, the crew had drifted back, eager to learn what treasures awaited them in the oyster bed. Rafe and Logan had stayed at the cantina until late.

Aided by his friend, Burt Wilson left as soon as he caught his breath. "Figure we've seen the last of him," Giddeon mused over supper, after Marina, Essie, and Nick had returned to the ship. "That fight shaped up to be a fortunate thing, giving those two young bulls a chance to vent their anger on someone other than each other."

"Logan wouldn't give Rafe a chance," Essie said. "I tried to talk some sense into him but—"

"Sometimes a man needs a little help removing the blinders," Giddeon told his grandson.

"Rafe understood," Marina responded. "He said he would probably act the same way if one of his sisters decided to marry a stranger without giving the family a chance to get to know him."

"Well, now they know each other," Nick put in. "Nothing like a knock-down-drag-out fight with a mutual enemy to tie two men into friends."

"Speaking of our mutual enemy," Serita broke in, "what do you suppose Burt's visit really means?"

Giddeon studied her a moment, reflecting. "He said he came to fetch Marina."

"If he wanted me, he would have come to the ranch before I left. Grandmother is right. We must consider his true purpose for riding all this way. After all, he has not been known for honorable intentions up to now."

Serita sighed. "No, dear, I am afraid he hasn't. But I didn't mean to suggest . . ."

"Grandmother! Do you know how lucky I am? If Burt's intentions had been honorable I would have . . ." Pausing she searched the faces of her grandparents. "If I had married Burt Wilson, I would have lost . . ." She sighed. "And if his intentions had been honorable, I probably would have married him." She returned her attention to her steamed fish, seasoned with the juice of local limes and, of course, chilies. "Cookie is becoming acclimated to this region," she said, changing the subject.

Giddeon, however, pursued Serita's original question.

"That visit can only mean one thing. That Jorge and Miguel are getting close to solving the case in our favor."

They ate in silence a moment, then Giddeon cleared his throat and spoke again. "Essie, I know you and Logan Junior want to continue on the expedition with

356

us, but—"

"Don't worry, Grandfather. We want to save Los Olmos as badly as Marina or any of you. We will leave at sunup . . ." —he laughed, nodding west beyond the harbor where the cantina lay nestled in its stand of banana trees—". . . if my brother is up to the ride."

The table laughed, and Marina stayed up after everyone else had retired waiting for Rafe, even though her grandmother advised against it. Unless she told him goodnight, she knew she would not sleep a wink.

The moon had started its downhill run by the time the two staggered up the gangplank, arm in arm, singing a bawdy song in Spanish, each trying to hush the other.

When they saw Marina at the rail, they stared up at her, grinning sheepishly, and she knew she had been right to wait. The sight of these two men in such companionship was one more hurdle crossed.

Logan Junior swayed toward her, his serious eyes at last focusing on her own. When he spoke his words swayed quite as much as his body. "Don't worry about a thing, Marina. You won't have to stay at Los Olmos. Miguel can run things." After which he gave her a quick kiss on the cheek and wove toward the companionway. She watched him side-step a tar bucket, then she heard him bounce from wall to wall in the narrow passage leading to his cabin.

"What was that all about?" she asked Rafe.

He steadied himself with a hip to the rail and studied her, his grin a trifle askew. With an exaggerated effort he cupped her cheek in his hand, and she felt its roughness from the fight. "A little unsettled business, settled."

357

His face wavered a bit as he moved toward her. "Thanks for waiting up for me."

"So you two made up?"

"Only took one fight and two bottles of tequila,"— his slurred words reflected at least one of the bottles, she thought— ". . . but yes, we made up." His eyes were glassy, and she could tell it was hard for him to focus, even though he stared deep into her own. She covered his hand with hers. "Your hands . . . ?"

He chuckled in a self-effacing sort of way. "I think the salt and lime juice may have healed them." His breath cloaked her face with the strong scent of tequila.

"Three drunk men in one day," she sighed.

"I won't make it a habit. Fortunately Essie doesn't require convincing. Unless, of course, you have other suitors—"

"No others." She smiled. "I have never had men fight over me before. It was kind of . . ."

His thumb roamed the outline of her lips, stopping her words. "I hope you didn't find it so enjoyable you go looking for men for me to fight. I'm not up to it on a regular basis, neither the fight nor the celebrating afterwards."

She stared into his glazed eyes, wondering whether he even saw her clearly. "I was so afraid for you."

"I'm sorry, Mar . . . , ah, *capitán.*" His grin broadened. "Come morning I will probably be sorrier." Leaning close, his lips brushed hers, sending heat streaking through her system.

"One kiss," he told her. "One goodnight kiss, then I'm going to bed before I make a fool of myself and you wish you had stuck with that pale-skinned bastard from Texas."

358

The following morning all hands arrived at breakfast with a purpose. When Giddeon informed Logan Junior and Rafe of the decision the group had made the night before, both men agreed on the spot.

"We need to see about Mama and Papa, anyway," Logan said. "If things are going well, perhaps they will return with us for the Day of the Dead."

"Wonderful!" Serita rushed to her room to prepare a letter for Stella. "In case they need encouragement from us," she told Essie instructing him to give the letter to his mother first thing upon arriving at Los Olmos.

"In the meantime," Rafe told them, "I will wire Fernando. Perhaps he can expedite matters in Mexico City."

He didn't elaborate and in the commotion of getting Essie and Logan Junior off to Texas and the ship ready to sail on the next leg of the expedition, Marina forgot to ask him to explain.

Her heart swelled when Logan and Rafe shook hands, their smiles revealing the extent of camaraderie that had grown between them in the brief time since they discovered they were on the same side.

"Take care of my sister, Santana," Logan instructed before he and Essie rode away from the pier. "Like I said last night, if you don't, I'll beat the devil out of you."

Rafe laughed, drawing Marina to his side, an arm draped casually over her shoulder. "Don't give it another thought. You just keep that scoundrel from Texas away from my soon-to-be bride."

The extra set of diving equipment proved a stroke of genius, as Rafe enthused after the first day's dive produced twice the usual results. Marina took over Zolic's record-keeping chores, the immediate advantage of which was to keep her in even closer contact with Rafe. While he polished and identified the artifacts the divers pulled up, she hovered nearby with the records.

In the first two days two extra caches of gold coins were raised, doubling the amount they had heretofore collected. After Marina recorded the number and denominations, Giddeon secreted them in the safe in his and Serita's bedchamber with those he stored prior to the Feast of Saint Francis.

The second day out, Marina discovered a discrepancy in the record book. She checked it several times before mentioning her concern over supper.

"How many opal and gold necklaces have we retrieved?" she asked the table at large.

Each person considered her question.

"Why?" Rafe asked.

"How many do you remember cleaning?" she restated.

"Three, I think. I would have to check the records."

"What about you, Tata? How many do you recall?"

Giddeon shrugged. "Same as Rafe. Three. I think."

"I remember three, also," Serita said.

Marina nodded. "I thought so, too. But we only have one."

"The records?" Rafe asked again.

"The records show one," she admitted.

He shrugged. "What's the problem, then?"

She glanced around the table. "We all remember there being three."

"We've recovered a lot of artifacts," he told her. "It

isn't uncommon for memories to conflict with records. That's why accurate accounts are essential to an expedition."

Every day now was filled with the same things—diving, cleaning, recording, and storing. Another part of their routine was the flurry of butterflies in the pit of each and every stomach when Pedro hoisted the scoop and emptied a new load of oyster-encrusted cargo onto the deck.

The excitement of discovery kept them all in a state of intoxication which caused Marina to wonder why Jesús Zolic needed to resort to peyote . . . or even tequila.

One night on deck while she stood in Rafe's arms, she pondered the question further.

"I'd rather not talk about that man and his madness," Rafe responded, sprinkling light kisses across her face. "Besides, you are intoxicating enough for me. Before I met you I drank tequila in the way of other men, for socializing. Now you are all I want or need . . . you are my friend, my lover, soon you will be my wife. You have even taken the place of treasure hunting—you are the only indispensable part of my life."

His lips sealed hers as with a pledge, intoxicating in themselves, moist and warm and questing. His hands held her close, though discreetly because of lack of privacy. Lifting his lips, he watched moonbeams reflect from the depths of her smoldering green eyes, felt their sparks ignite a want in him that spread like wildfire through his body. "You are more precious to me than gold, my love."

Her knees felt weak at the passion in his voice, at the

love in his words. "Tell me about Janitzio. How long will we be gone?"

When he smiled, his devilish grin told her he understood her question. "Long enough to steal some time alone," he whispered.

Finally in defense of his aching body, he turned them toward the rail, where they stared out on the moonlit sea.

"Why must you go to Janitzio?" Laying her head against his shoulder, she clasped his hand as it draped over her arm. "Do you have family there?"

He nodded. "Distant. My great-grandmother's family. They disowned her when she married a *gapuchine*— their term for Spanish-born rulers. I've gone there for the Day of the Dead every year since I met her, in her place, so to speak."

They stood for a time, reveling in the feel of each other, in dreams of what could come of their trip together. "Also," he continued, "just before I received word of your infamous arrival at Tecolutla, I had taken a fake goddess to Tzintzuntzán, near there, to replace an original the Tarascans gave me for the museum. I agreed to check with the chief when I came for the Day of the Dead. If she hasn't performed for them, I promised to return the original."

"A perfect solution. Couldn't you have done that at Old Xico?"

Rafe sighed, recalling how Zolic intended to steal the corn goddess outright. "Possibly, if Zolic hadn't messed things up. As it stands, I doubt I will ever be able to convince them to try the switch."

"How did you convince the people at—what did you call it?—Tzintzuntzán?"

He nodded. "Actually, I only convinced one of them—their chief. No one else knows about it. That's why it is imperative that I return to see how she is doing."

"Well, how did you convince the chief?"

Rafe shrugged. "He was happy to comply, he even gave—" Abruptly, as forgotten memories poured into his brain and out his mouth, he closed his lips over them. Marina Cafferty was too easy to talk to. The chief's daughter had come instantly to mind. The daughter who had been given him as a bride. That, he could not tell Marina.

She had accepted a lot of things—fearsome gods and bare-breasted beauties—but a bride? No matter one in name only and in one person's mind only . . . a bride might be a more difficult thing for her to grasp. It would only hurt her, and for no good reason.

"I've been thinking," —he strove to sound casual— "perhaps you should attend the Day of the Dead ceremonies with your family."

She turned toward him frowning. "No."

"I just thought . . . I mean, this could be the only chance you have to observe that ritual with them."

"Rafe Santana, *you* are my family. No matter how noble you attempt to be, I will not miss this trip with you."

Reaching she closed her lips over his, felt his arms come around her, his body press against hers. She mumbled into his lips. "I intend to spend the Night of the Dead wrapped in your arms . . . and nothing else."

He pulled her close. "A night for living."

A few days later the new diving helmet filled with water, almost drowning the diver. Pedro Ybarro hauled him to the deck, while the scoop fell to the seabed forgotten.

"A simple matter," Pedro sighed, but Marina could tell from the way his skin turned pale that a moment before it had not been simple, far from it. "I should have foreseen such an occurrence. We must have new cables for this helmet. See? A faulty seal."

"I thought your equipment was new," Giddeon said.

Ybarro shook his head. "New to me. Bought from a diving crew in Veracruz." He shrugged. "I do not know how long he used it, the former owner. I should have checked the seals and cables more carefully."

"That means we have only one diver," Serita worried. The December deadline, though not mentioned for days on end, loomed closer with each passing hour.

"Unless I can send to shore for new cables."

"How long would that take?" Giddeon questioned.

Ybarro shrugged. "Not over two days, three perhaps. If you can spare a boat and one crew member, I will send Juan DeLeon. Gordo and Carlos can remain behind to continue the diving so we will not lose so much time."

"Agreed," Giddeon responded quickly. "How soon can your man be ready?"

The two men left within the hour, and after a longer than usual siesta, the diving resumed, culminating in the most productive day so far.

At least, from Rafael Santana's point of view.

The load dropped by the diver when water flooded his helmet had contained a large golden idol. Rafe became excited at his first glimpse, but he held his tongue, taking it below where he painstakingly cleaned and polished every nook and crevice. Marina

sat across from him, mesmerized as much by his enthusiasm as by another ancient artifact.

"Isn't she grotesque?" Rafe held the shiny goddess
for her to see. The admiration in his voice belied his
words, but Marina was forced to agree with his words.
Indeed, as he recounted the story of Coatlicue, mother
of the Aztec's god of war, Marina found grotesque too
mild a term.

Listening, she measured the goddess and recorded
the details, cringing to touch the fearful thing. The
head was carved in the likeness of two rattlesnake
heads facing each other fang to fang. Around its neck a
necklace of hands and hearts had a human skull for the
focal point. The skirt was carved with the plaited
bodies and rattles of more snakes. "Why did they
design such fearful deities?" she asked.

Rafe chuckled. "The mother of the war god had to be
fearsome. Actually, the rattlesnake was an important
symbol to the ancient Aztecs. Legend holds that the
first Aztecs came from caves in western Mexico, few in
number and far from fearsome, looking for a home.
They were guided by gods who told them to settle
where they saw an eagle with a rattlesnake in its claws
sitting on a prickly pear bush. They found such a sign in
the lakes where Mexico City now stands."

The other items brought up, though not as large as
Coatlicue, were equally valuable—a number of gold
coins which Rafe polished, Marina recorded, and
Giddeon stored, along with statues of jaguars, the fire
god and a lovely little man called Xipe Totec with
flowers carved on his head and around his neck, the
god of springtime, of birth and renewal, Rafe told her.

Xipe Totec lost much of his appeal when Rafe

365

pointed out the curled skin around his wrists, neck, and feet. "His garment is made from the flayed skin of sacrificial victims."

"Ugh!" Marina turned her head away from Xipe Totec in time to see Giddeon, grim-faced, approach the table where she and Rafe worked.

"Sugar, I think your grandmother would like your company."

Marina stared at him. "What?"

Rafe looked from one to the other. Marina saw his eyes lock with Giddeon's. "What's happened?" he asked.

"Marina, leave us alone, please," Giddeon repeated.

Later she wondered why she had not insisted on remaining in the room to hear firsthand whatever concerned her grandfather to the point that he would demand a private conference with Rafe.

Whatever it was did not take long, for in no time Tata found both her grandmother and herself and escorted them back to the cabin where Rafe had put aside his tools for cleaning artifacts.

"The coins are missing," Giddeon explained.

All strength drained from Marina's body, more at his ominous tone than at his words. His words made no sense.

He quickly explained.

"All the gold coins we have recovered, until today of course, have disappeared."

"Are you sure?" Serita turned toward the bedchamber where the safe was. "Have you checked the safe?"

Rafe frowned at Giddeon. "I thought you and I were the only two people who knew where those coins

366

were kept."

Marina looked from one to the other.

"Surely you are not suggesting Serita—" Giddeon began.

"I'm not suggesting anything, but before you condemn me, we should make a list of everyone who knew where they were hidden."

"You think Rafe took the coins?" Marina demanded.

"He would not have done—" Serita began.

"Hold on, both of you. Sit down and we'll straighten things out. Or try to." Giddeon turned to Rafe. "I told you it wasn't a good idea to let them know about this."

Marina had come to stand beside Rafe. Taking her offered hand, he pulled her onto his knee, oblivious to his actions. "I intend to marry your granddaughter, Giddeon. I can't very well do that with you thinking me a thief."

"I don't think you a thief," Giddeon retorted. "I . . . well, I don't know what to think. You and I are the only ones who knew about the hiding place."

"Except your wife," Rafe added.

Giddeon looked pointedly at Marina.

"I didn't tell her," Rafe said. "Not that I intended to keep it from you," —he spoke now to Marina— "it just never came up. Your grandfather and I counted the coins, checked the records, and locked them away before leaving for the hacienda. Now they are all gone."

"You are both crazy." Marina's words whispered through her lips. She thought suddenly that her voice would not work without air, and all the air had been pumped from her lungs in one fell swoop. "Is this what treasure does to people? Turn them against each other? Well, I won't stand for it. Nothing is this important . . .

not even Los Olmos."

"She is right, Giddeon," Serita added. "Suspicions between you two will bring trouble to the whole family. We all know neither of you took the gold. So, who did?"

That was not an easy question to answer. Over supper they told Nick about the missing coins, but he had no idea what could have happened to them, either.

"When did you discover them missing?"

"Today when I deposited the latest batch."

"You mean they were here when we returned from the hacienda?" Marina asked.

Giddeon nodded. "The first thing I checked was that safe. Yes, all were accounted for."

"Then they have to be on board. So, come morning we will search until we find them," Serita replied.

Later that night on deck, Marina's head swirled in a daze. "I don't understand how it could have happened."

Rafe held her close. "Neither do I. There is a logical explanation. But what? Who?"

"And Tata suspecting you. It isn't fair."

"Fair or not, I am the only reasonable suspect."

"But you're innocent."

Lowering his lips, he kissed her, warmly, tenderly, whispering, "Thank you," between kisses. But their passion had cooled somewhere between the story of Xipe Totec and the accusations of her grandfather.

"With Giddeon's suspicions, I think you should reconsider going to Vera Cruz for the Day of the Dead."

"No—"

"Hear me out, love. You must resolve these misunderstandings now, before he returns to Texas leaving you with regrets."

A thorough search of the ship the following day, including Zolic's old cabin, turned up neither the missing coins nor the missing necklaces.

Days passed, the boat returned with new cables for the diving equipment, and time neared for the observances of the Day of the Dead. More coins were retrieved, bringing the total in Giddeon's safe to double what had been stolen.

Still the missing coins lay unseen. Although everyone knew they must be aboard the *Stella Duval,* and even though not a day passed without each person conducting additional searches of this or that part of the vessel, day by day the theft was mentioned less and less. Unexpressed accusations lay over the crew like a thick fog, dispelling the excitement for everyone, resurrecting the turmoil which Marina had thought ended when Logan Junior accepted Rafe.

The evening before they sailed for Tecolutla and the Day of the Dead holiday, Serita accompanied Marina to her suite to help her choose clothing for the trip to Janitzio.

"Will you take your *china?*" Serita flipped through the costumes in Marina's wardrobe.

"It's too festive. Regular clothing will do."

"You'll wear your riding skirt and boots, of course," Serita continued, "and the matching jacket—"

"I've decided to go to the Hacienda de Vera Cruz with you and Tata."

Serita sank to the bed, holding one of Marina's petticoats in her hand. "Why?"

"I must . . ." Marina sighed, then began again. "I

369

must try to convince Tata of Rafe's innocence. Away from the ship . . . away from Rafe, perhaps—"

"What about Rafe?" Serita asked. "I am not at all sure he will understand."

"Yes, he will. He suggested it; he thinks this is the best way."

"You mean he doesn't want you to go with him?"

"Oh, no. It isn't that. But—"

"Then you must go to Janitzio. If you love Rafe Santana enough to marry him and spend the rest of your life living in his country, bearing his children, growing old with him, then you must learn to stand beside him when he needs you."

Tears rushed to Marina's eyes and she wiped them away with the back of her hand. Quickly Serita rose and embraced her. "It will all work out, dear. Your grandfather would be the first to tell you, had you mentioned this to him instead of to me, your place is with Rafe Santana."

"Tata knows Rafe didn't take the coins, doesn't he?"

Serita nodded. "We all do."

"And . . . Mama and Papa will approve of him, won't they?"

"I know they will. And in case Logan Junior had not recovered from his bout of jealousy by the time he got home, I wrote your mother our impressions of your young man."

Marina's eyes widened. "The letter?"

Serita smiled. "The letter I sent by Essie. If you recall, I told him to give it to his mother straight away."

Chapter Sixteen

Rafe and Giddeon waited in the companionway for Marina and Serita when they finished packing for the journey to Janitzio.

Giddeon ushered the women into the salon, where they stared at a gaping hole in the wall.

Rafe quickly closed the door behind them.

"What happened?" Serita asked.

"We decided to hide the principal artifacts and all the gold in here." Giddeon indicated the built-in cabinets where not only shelves, but the wall boards had been ripped out. "Everything else will remain crated in the hold."

Rafe handed Marina the record book. "Put this in your valise. We will take it with us."

"Can you two reassemble this wall so no one will know it was disturbed?" she asked, taking the book.

He chuckled. "Giddeon's the captain, he says yes."

Later that night on deck, Marina rested her head against Rafe's chest, anxious for their trip to begin, yet concerned over the problems they were leaving behind.

"How did you think to hide the gold inside the walls?"

"It was your grandfather's idea. We needed a place neither a seaman nor a landlubber would suspect."

"You mean neither Zolic nor Pedro Ybarro and his crew?"

"Zolic is long gone, and Ybarro and his men will be busy with their own observances. If they had anything to do with stealing the coins—"

"Who else could it have been? The only other people on board were our crew from home. They wouldn't steal from us."

Drawing her back, he smiled into her moonlit face. "Don't you think we've talked enough about thieves? Let's think about tomorrow and tomorrow night . . . and the night after that." He kissed her soundly.

They made port before sundown the next afternoon and found Galván Cortinas waiting for them, accompanied by Logan Junior and Essie. Stella and Logan, the boys related, had stayed behind at Los Olmos, afraid to leave the place unattended by family. The three young men clamored aboard to spend the night on the ship.

As it turned out, Logan Junior and Essie spent several nights on the ship.

"Now that we're alone, I have something to say," Giddeon told the family the next morning after Ybarro and his crew had left the ship. "Nick and I will remain behind. Nick with the ship, and I . . . I'm following up on the man Ybarro bought his diving equipment from—see what else DeLeon did when he went to buy new cables. Maybe run down a bit of stolen gold."

The resulting clamor brought Serita and Marina

372

rushing to his side.

"You can't go on such a dangerous trip by yourself. I will come with you," Serita insisted.

"No," he countered. "Absolutely not. I want you to go to Vera Cruz, as planned."

"Not without you."

"Tata, you've never let Grandmother attend something this important alone," Marina admonished. "Rafe and I can check out DeLeon on our way back from Janitzio."

"She won't be alone," Giddeon argued. "Logan Junior and Essie will accompany her."

"Then *I* will go with her, too," Marina retorted.

"You will do no such thing," Serita admonished.

"Well, I won't let you—" Marina began.

"Hold on!" Giddeon bellowed above the din.

"Essie and I will track this DeLeon fellow, Grandfather," Logan Junior offered.

"Absolutely not!" Serita exclaimed.

Nick cleared his throat. "Why don't I track DeLeon? I know him by sight, and I speak the language. We have enough crew to—"

"Then Logan Junior and I will remain aboard the *Stella Duval* with the crew, and you go with Grandmother," Essie told Giddeon.

"Now that's a solution I might consider," Giddeon responded.

Serita's eyes darted to her grandsons. "Are you sure it would be safe?"

"I don't see why not, *querida*. They are seamen born and trained."

After a bit more wrangling, it was agreed. Nick hired a horse from José at the cantina and got on his way.

Logan Junior and Essie remained behind, waving their grandparents off for the Day of the Dead observances with relatives.

Rafe had gone to the cantina to pick up his horses, as well. Marina waited at the bottom of the gangplank talking with her brothers. Essie handed her a letter from her mother, and the boys began teasing her about its contents.

"You had best burn it, Marina," Essie said. "She's blistering your ears. You should have seen her when Logan told her about you and *Don Rafael.*"

"Come on, Essie, you know I didn't tell either Mama or Papa anything."

Essie winked. "Oh, no? Then why is Papa on his way down here right now with his shotgun?"

The boy stopped his banter seeing Rafe stride toward them, leading two saddled horses. "I like him, Marina; he's a fine man. I may come live with you when you get married."

"I thought you were going to sea," Logan scoffed.

"I am. But first I'll see if Rafe has any sisters my age."

"What about Bianca?" Marina asked. "She's—"

"Young," her brothers retorted in unison.

Rafe shook hands with the boys. "Jesús Zolic is over at the cantina. You remember him from El Tajín. I don't expect trouble, but be on the lookout. Don't let him come aboard."

"Zolic is here?" Marina glanced toward the thatched-roof hut.

Rafe tied her valise behind her saddle. "Says he wants to return to the expedition. That he's sorry for how he treated you, that he has stopped using peyote and drinking tequila."

"Why is he in a cantina then?" she asked, feeling Rafe's hands span her waist, assisting her into the saddle.

"Waiting to talk to me," he replied. "Said he didn't want to face Giddeon until he had seen me, after the way he behaved at the Feast of Saint Francis." Rafe studied her a moment, lost in his own thoughts. "I told him that was a damned foolish way to look at it, that I would be every bit as implacable as your grandfather—or more so."

She warmed at his words, finding it hard to worry about Jesús Zolic with anticipation for their trip bubbling inside her. "What did you tell him? About coming back, I mean?"

"I said I would think about it."

Abruptly then, Rafe glanced at the brightening sky. "If we're going to make the evening train at Pachuca we had best get on the road." He handed her the reins, nodded to the boys and climbed up on his own horse.

"Take care of her, Santana," Logan Junior called.

Rafe tipped his hat. "You can bet on it."

They followed the river east out of Tecolutla with the rising sun to their backs. But as Marina had learned, no road in this country led due east, west, north, or south very far. With mountains cropping up at regular intervals, their path was twisting and winding. When she commented on it, Rafe turned in his saddle with a chuckle.

"Want to know how your hero Cortés described our terrain to folks back in Spain?"

"*Cortés* is not my hero, but that's another subject. What did he say?"

He winked at her, sending fiery tingles up her spine.

375

"Wasn't what he said, it was what he did. He crumpled a piece of paper and dropped it to the floor."

She scanned the country, her eyes coming to rest at last on his. He was studying her, his eyes devilish, his familiar grin breathtaking. "A fitting description," she mumbled.

"Now what's this other subject? About your hero?"

Messages traveled between them like streaks of lightning, burning them with anticipation.

She laughed, spurring her mount. "We have a train to catch, remember?"

Like the train they had taken from Veracruz for the Independence Day celebrations, the one they caught at Pachuca was filled to the brim with passengers, each on his way to observe the Day of the Dead with relatives.

Rafe found them two seats together and they squeezed past men, women, children, dogs, cats, and chickens to reach them. "Get some rest if you can," he told her when they had settled back. "We won't stop again until Mexico City where a lot of this group will disembark."

She relaxed against the cushion, heedless of the babble, mindful only of Rafe's sleeve brushing her shoulder, and beneath it his arm, his flesh, his beating heart.

The next thing she knew a familiar face peered into hers, and Rafe was gone. She blinked to focus her eyes.

"You are in Mexico City," the young man told her. "I am Fernando Zamora, Santana's assistant. We met Independence Day."

Recalling, she nodded. "Where is he?"

"Tending to business with the station master. He will return before we pull out for Morelia."

And indeed Rafe did return. Just as the train bellowed and spewed steam and cinders, he slipped into his seat.

"I arranged our passage back to Pachuca tomorrow night after the ceremonies. Figured we shouldn't take time to stay for the fiesta." He winked. "We'll catch it next year."

While the train raced tumultuously over the steep mountain track, pulling, dropping, swerving, the men talked business, and Marina watched the scenery, its hairpin curves and steep drop-offs breathtaking in the early morning sun.

"Thanks for coming," Rafe told his junior assistant. "What did you find out?"

"It's settled. All we have to do is come up with a figure. The money is available."

"Good."

"You think Chief Aztlán will trust me?" Fernando asked.

"He met you. That should be enough. Tell him I arrived too late to come to Tzintzuntzán. That if there is trouble with the new goddess, we will return his old Lady Chaly."

After a brief stop at Morelia, they arrived in Pátzcuaro near noon with the lake spreading before them like a jewel set in a rim of glorious mountains. Already the air was clear and cool. On the lake tonight, it would likely be cold. Opening her valise, Marina withdrew the rebozo Rafe's great-grandmother had given her.

"Thanks again." Rafe shook hands with Fernando. "Oh, and tell Aztlán . . ." —he smiled at Marina— ". . . tell him I will see him next trip, that I will introduce him to my wife. Say I brought her to Janitzio for the observances tonight."

After exchanged glances, Fernando nodded. "Sure."

"Our train pulls out at two in the morning, so I won't see you again," Rafe added. "I will wire instructions for the money."

Leaving their valises with the station master, Rafe escorted her toward a rough wooden pier.

"I won't get to see her?" Marina asked, skipping to keep up with his long stride.

He stopped in his tracks. "Who?"

"Lady Chaly. Whom did you think?"

He shook his head to clear it. "My mind must have wandered. She's in one of the Tarascan *zácatas* up in the mountains. They protect those ancient temples from outsiders, but perhaps one day—"

"Then how did you exchange goddesses?" she interrupted.

He stopped at the pier. "Secretly . . . in the dead of night. A harrowing experience, believe me. For a time I was certain my ancestors would be preparing duck for my return tonight."

She frowned.

"The Day of the Dead. You don't know about the meal?"

She shook her head.

Summoning a boy with a canoe, he spoke rapidly in a dialect similar to the one he had used with his great-grandmother, then helped Marina into the small boat. "I don't guess I prepared you very well for this trip. I'll fill you in on the way to Janitzio." He nodded toward an island arising from the center of the lake.

The trip to Janitzio she soon discovered was to be

combined with duck hunting. Using a spear like the ones they reclaimed from the wreck of the *Espíritu Estelle,* Rafe brought down two large ducks which the boy managed to scoop into nets and deliver dripping at their feet.

"It's the ancient way of hunting," Rafe confirmed at her comments. "For this night, it seems appropriate. We'll take these ducks to my relatives on Janitzio. The women will cook them, then at midnight we'll carry the food and pulque, candles, and flowers to the graves."

"What a quaint custom."

"Not quaint," he corrected. "Practical. The spirits of the departed return to earth this one night each year. We welcome them with their favorite meals. At Janitzio, that meal was usually duck."

The lake was congested with rough hewn canoes similar to theirs. Some of the men fished, using enormous looped nets which they dipped from one side of the boat to the other in a rhythmic maneuver more like a dance than a chore.

Rafe laughed at her suggestion. "The old timers call them butterfly nets. And it's a chore, all right. They are fishing for small white fish, a staple in the diet of the Tarascan people. We'll be served some for supper."

By the time they reached the rocky shore of Janitzio, the tiny island teemed with people, their voices drowned in the melodic tones of church bells. Marina stepped onto the pier. "The bells are so loud and clear."

"It's the water." Rafe paid the boy for the use of his canoe, then escorted her up the cobbled street through the growing crowd. "The bells will ring continually now until midnight."

Indeed they did, finally fading into the back of her

379

consciousness, providing a musical backdrop to the din of the crowds, many of whom stopped to greet Rafe, calling him by the same appellation she used for her grandfather.

"Why do they call you *Tata Rafael* when you are certainly not the age of a grandfather."

He shrugged, self-conscious, she could tell. "A term of respect. They know I'm helping save their way of life."

"All these people can't live on this small island. Where do they come from?"

"Same place we do, everywhere. Families try to gather on this night, if at no other time during the year. I hope one day my great-grandmother will be allowed to return."

"They accept you because they respect your job, but they don't accept her even though she is a closer relative?"

"Not only my job. I never lived on the island, so I was never disloyal to them. When my grandmother was young she lived here, but she left to marry the *gapuchine.*"

"So it works both ways . . . prejudice?"

"Isn't that usually the case?" he questioned.

And indeed Marina wondered later whether the statement had not proved prophetic, for at the home of his ancestors Rafe was welcomed as a returning hero, but she—even though he introduced her with profuse demonstrations and words she could not understand— she was shunned.

The house, one of the numerous whitewashed adobe homes lining the single cobbled street in Janitzio, was larger than it appeared from the outside, opening onto spacious though sparsely furnished rooms and a patio lush with vegetation, even in this high mountain climate.

Guitar and violin music such as she had heard on the street rang inside the walls of the immaculate home.

"My ancestors were taught to build the instruments by a Spanish priest who is revered for his kindness to the Tarascans," he told her. "Don Vasco de Quiroga . . . they called him Tata, too . . . Tata Vasco."

"So the Spaniards treated the Tarascans well?"

"No." His reply was so vehement it startled her. "The most despicable of the Conquistadors, a man named Guzmán, wreaked havoc on these simple fishermen who had even withstood domination by the Aztecs up to that time. Tata Vasco partially made up for Guzmán's evil."

While the men gathered in one room playing their guitars, singing, and talking, the women took the proffered ducks into the kitchen beyond, where they proceeded to clean and cook them.

Marina stayed close by Rafe's side, although not as close as she would have liked, given her growing apprehension. Although no one spoke to her, she had the distinct impression they spoke *about* her. When she ventured a glance toward the kitchen, the chattering ceased, but several pairs of eyes stared menacingly in her direction.

Finally she relaxed, telling herself she imagined things, that her nervousness had nothing to do with the people themselves; rather it must surely stem from the isolation she felt at not understanding the language.

At least she convinced herself of such until the meal was served. Wordlessly the women emerged from the kitchen carrying heaping platters of food to the table. Marina watched the men drift to the table one by one, while the women retreated to the kitchen from where they stared, each of them, at Marina.

She turned away, but suddenly fingers plucked at her rebozo, and when she looked, she encountered the cold black eyes of one of the younger women. Her pulse quickened.

"Go with her," Rafe said.

"Where?"

"To the kitchen. Haven't you noticed that I'm the only man in the room without a plate of food?"

Her eyes scanned the group. He was right. She glanced into the kitchen where the women, ten or twelve of them she supposed, had begun to fix their own plates. Still, their eyes were riveted on Marina. Her mind raced back to Old Xico.

"They will show you what to do."

They? she thought, barely able to quell her rising alarm. From her position, all she could see of the kitchen was the sea of women. Their black garments merged into a dark mass against the pale plastered walls; their black eyes undulated in the golden glow of several clay lanterns. She suppressed a shudder.

"I am to go into that kitchen and bring you a plate of food?" Her voice cracked. "Then what do I do?"

"Return to the kitchen and eat with the women."

At the plea in her eyes, he caught up her hand, squeezed her fingers. "It's the custom, love."

Somehow she managed a smile. Turning toward the kitchen, she chided herself for foolish anxieties. It was the language barrier, she knew, like at Old Xico.

Except these people posed no threat; these people

were Rafe's family.

When she reached the doorway to the kitchen, the sea of black garments parted as the Red Sea, leaving an aisle the length of the table. She moved forward on hesitant steps, feeling as the Pharaoh's soldiers must have, expecting the waves to come crashing down upon them.

Without uttering a word, one of the women thrust a clay platter into Marina's hand, and as she moved down the line each woman in turn spooned food onto it—a thin stew, a thick corn pudding, the small white fish.

She reached the end of the table, her plate—Rafe's plate—heaped with strange yet sweet-smelling food. Then she turned toward the other room, and a large, big-boned woman stepped into her path.

This time Marina did not chide herself at the wave of anxiety. The woman had obviously been carving duck, for her greasy hands still grasped the carving knife, which she now sharpened against a hand-held flint-stone. Her eyes were hard as onyx. The knife flashed in the flickering lantern light, its tip at last piercing a piece of duck to sling onto Rafe's plate. Marina flinched at the gesture, seeing instead the obsidian knife in Zolic's hands.

Rafe had taken his place beside his relatives, and when Marina set his plate in front of him it clattered against the wooden table top. Her only coherent thought was to escape the horrors she felt engulfing her. Without replying to his "thank you," she fled the room, racing through the patio and out the front gates onto the cobblestones.

Dusk had fallen. Lanterns hung from the walls of

homes up and down the street. She looked to the top of the hill, wondering what to do now, where to go. Feeling foolish.

Suddenly the incessantly tolling bells overwhelmed her. With determined strides she started to climb the hill.

Rafe caught her arm from behind, drawing her to a stop. "What's the matter?"

She stared at him, started to speak, and felt her chin tremble.

"It's the custom," he repeated.

"Your custom," she managed, "not mine."

"Their custom," he corrected.

Her brain reeled. Shrugging from his grasp, she walked up the street away from the house. He kept pace.

The woman with the knife flashed through her brain. "Did you tell them my name?" she asked, thinking that would explain the woman's belligerence.

"Of course not. Why would I . . . ?"

"Because they despise me . . . those women."

"They don't despise you, love. How could you think such a thing? I wouldn't have brought you here if—"

"Why did you bring me here?" she challenged. "To teach me to be a submissive wife?"

He caught her chin, forced her to look at him. "I don't want you submissive, *capitán*. I like you . . . *love* . . . you . . . the way you are."

Her fears began to quell at the gentleness in his touch, in his words. Turning her around, he guided them back down the hill, an arm around her shoulders.

When they came to the entrance to his relatives' house, however, he stopped and she tensed.

"I can't go back in there."

"Wait here, then. Let me tell them that we'll meet them at the cemetery. It's almost time."

Darkness had fallen quickly, and a heavy fog now wrapped the island. Marina pulled the rebozo close. She tried to forget the young woman's fingers, but she could still feel them clutching at her shoulder.

Suddenly a single figure bolted from the gate—the large woman from the kitchen. Marina stiffened; her eyes darted to the woman's hand. No knife, only a lantern. Where was Rafe?

The strange, black-clad woman came close to Marina's face, peering into her eyes. Then she lowered the lantern gradually, surveying Marina from head to foot, before her eyes, cold and menacing, returned to stare into Marina's.

"Juana!" Rafe's voice slashed through Marina's already flayed nerves. His arm came around her shoulders, providing much needed comfort. She watched him frown at the woman. Looking back at the woman, she saw recognition turn to fury in the cold black eyes, fury . . . and something else.

Rafe spoke rapidly while the woman called Juana scrutinized Marina. Then without warning Juana scrunched her face into an ugly wrinkled mass. When she opened her mouth Marina dipped her own face into Rafe's shoulder, thinking the spiteful woman intended to spit on her.

Instead only words left Juana's mouth. A string of words. Words which came fast and furious. Marina thought strangely that the Tarascan language no longer sounded musical. Then she thought of Rafe cautioning her never to speak her name. But she

385

hadn't . . . and neither had he.

"Malinche!" Juana cried.

Rafe covered Marina's head with his arms, holding her tightly against him until the sound died away. Finally she felt him sigh beneath her face. "She's gone, love."

Marina stared vacantly at the closed gates to the home of Rafe's ancestors. "Who is she?"

He guided her down the hill. "Chief Aztlán's daughter."

By the time Rafe and Marina arrived, the cemetery was already crowded with people awaiting the return of the spirits of their ancestors. Rafe's family came shortly thereafter, bearing lighted candles, marigolds, jugs of pulque and the duck they had prepared at the house.

They paid no mind to Marina now, as they sang, cried, and talked, sitting on the ground around the grave watching the candles and food.

While the hours droned on toward midnight, Marina sat silent with her thoughts, feeling physically separated from the rest of the group since she could not understand one word they said or sung. The music was beautiful, she admitted, moving from eerie to pensive to festive and back again. She wondered what they awaited . . . whether for the food to disappear or for the spirits to take human form and sit among them singing and talking and eating.

"They're talking of the old days," Rafe whispered. "The stories are wonderful, full of courage and persistence. I will teach you the language so you can understand them."

Although she didn't say it, she thought perhaps this was one experience she would not share with her husband-to-be. After her reception here today, Rafe's trips to Janitzio would likely be without her.

Her mind wandered back to the relatives' house, to her encounter with Juana in the kitchen and later in the street, to the woman's eyes, her recognition of Rafe . . . and more.

The chief's daughter, he had said. Something Sophie told her in Mexico City nagged at the back of Marina's mind. About chiefs pushing their daughters off on Rafe. . . .

About . . .

Then she knew.

As clearly as she knew her own name was Marina Cafferty, she knew. And her heart practically stopped beating. That woman—Juana—was Rafe's lover. Turning her head, she stared at him in the darkness.

They sat as at the shaman's hut and later in his great-grandmother's house, their legs crossed in front of them, their knees touching. Feeling her eyes on him, Rafe turned. He couldn't see her expression in the darkness, but her nearness warmed him against the night chill.

"Are you cold?" he whispered.

"She's your . . ." —a lump came in Marina's throat when the word Rafe's sister had spoken in Mexico City left her lips— ". . . your mistress."

His heart lurched. Reaching, he found her hand and brought her fingers to his lips. "No."

The moment he uttered the word, he winced at the lie. Yet it wasn't a lie. Juana was not his mistress. Not in any sense of the word.

Marina did not respond. She just kept staring at him through the darkness. He couldn't see her eyes, nor make out her expression.

"I said . . . no," he repeated.

Still she sat, unmoving.

"Didn't you hear me?"

"I'm not sure I believe you."

He turned his attention back to the graves. Her fingers felt cold in his hand; she sat stiff and rigid beside him. Around them the crooning of his relatives blended with the droning of the church bells.

He shouldn't have brought her here. He had known better, but his desperate need to have her with him, beside him had overcome his common sense.

His heart pumped. Who was he kidding? It was her body he had thought to have, her body he had yearned for every time he considered not bringing her on this trip.

Now look what he had done.

No! he shouted inside. Clutching her fingers, he brought them to his lips and held them there. It was Marina herself. He loved her—loved her in a way he had never dreamed a person could love. She was a part of him. He would wither and die like a flower pulled up by its roots if he lost her.

The nights on board the *Stella Duval* when they were forced by convention into separate beds had been the hardest nights he could recall in his life. Yes, he wanted her body, but he also wanted *her*—her voice, her face, *her*. Rising suddenly, he pulled her to her feet.

"Let's get out of here."

She followed numbly, wondering where he was taking her, what she would discover next about this complicated man.

No one remained at the dock to row the canoes when

they reached the lake, so Rafe chose one and handed her into it.

"Whose boat is this?" she asked.

He shrugged, shoving off.

"Are you stealing it?"

He stared at her, his guilt turning to annoyance. "Don't you trust me about anything?"

She didn't reply and he rowed feverishly, getting them to the shore at Pátzcuaro in record time. They still had a couple of hours before the train arrived, and Rafe was at a loss for what to do with the time. He could visualize Marina's reaction to their accommodations aboard the train. In Mexico City when he arranged for the station master to send a separate sleeping car for the Antiquities Ministry he had envisioned a long pleasant trip back to Pachuca in the arms of the woman he loved.

Now such a trip was likely out of the question. His relatives had frightened her and she had encountered the very person he had taken pains to avoid, a woman she now thought to be his mistress.

Of all things. When he had never even considered taking a mistress. But how would he explain the truth?

The truth could well prove more damaging than the idea of a past mistress. All the way across the lake, he had worried over how to handle the situation.

Reaching the depot, he still had not the faintest idea. The truth worked best, but . . . ?

"Are you cold? We can wait inside."

She shook her head. Walking to the edge of the platform, she stared across the black water toward Janitzio, still alive with lights and music. "How could I be cold? My emotions have been put to the test the last

389

few hours. First your relatives threaten to . . . to . . ."
—with a sigh, she changed topics— ". . . then your mistress."

Rafe took her shoulders. "My relatives did not threaten you. They may not have welcomed you, but they did nothing to harm you. And . . ." —he stared hard at her now—". . . that woman is not my mistress."

"Juana. You called her Juana."

"It's her name. Juana. Haven't you ever heard the name before?"

"Of course, I have heard that name. It wasn't her name . . . it was her eyes . . ." Recalling the look on the woman's face, she dislodged Rafe's hands and turned to stare once more at the lake. Why did she feel so threatened? She hadn't expected Rafe Santana to be a virgin, for god's sake. What had come over her?

"What do you mean . . . her eyes?"

Marina shrugged, still facing away from him. "The look. It was obvious—"

"What, damnit? Nothing was obvious to me. What was so obvious to you that—that you accuse me of taking a mistress?"

"Don't act so offended," she retorted. "Sophie told me about mistresses."

"Sophie? What the hell did she tell you? Whatever it was, it was a lie."

"I doubt it. She said all men take mistresses. She said she was glad she liked me, since we would be spending so much time together while our husbands entertain themselves with—"

"*¡Por los dios viejos!*" He forced Marina around by

390

her shoulders. "Listen to me. I have never taken a mistress. I will *never* take a mistress. You—you are the only woman I will ever—" He stared deeply into her eyes, beseeching her. "How could you think that? After you, how could I ever want another woman?"

His hands singed her skin where they encircled her arms. The flames leapt straight to her heart, then raced down the length of her body. "I don't," she whispered.

He drew her close, holding her tightly against him. But when at length he tried to lower his lips to hers, she spoke again.

"Who is she then, if not your mistress?"

He sighed. "What the hell kind of look did she give me?"

"I don't know," Marina admitted. "It was . . . well, I've never experienced such a . . ." —she shrugged, baffled— "Do you suppose a woman can always tell when she meets a rival?"

"A rival? I told you, love, you have no rival. You never will." His aggravation worked its way toward anger. "I never claimed to be—"

She smiled, rueful. "Pure as driven snow?"

"No, damnit. I never claimed to be such."

"I didn't expect it. But this . . . this woman—the way she looked at you—it isn't something I can explain. I can't forget it, though."

Releasing her, Rafe clasped his hands behind his own neck and stared up at the black sky, at the multitude of stars. Would they shine as brightly after he told Marina the story of Juana and her father?

"Why don't we sit down over here?" He ushered her to a bench along the depot wall. When they were seated side by side, he took both her hands and kissed her fingers, wondering whether he would ever do that again.

"I'm going to explain this against my better judgment. But first I want you to promise me something— while you listen, please ... please remember how much I love you. There have been other women, but none were important. Before you, I never even professed to love a woman. I never kept a mistress, and I can't imagine a wife who would condone such a thing. To me that would be the height of submissiveness, and I told you, I don't want a submissive wife. I want a partner ..." —he kissed her fingers again— "... and a whole lot more."

Marina clutched her hands around his. Whatever he was about to reveal was heart-rending—for him. Not for her. He loved her, she knew that. She knew he would be true to her. She knew also that this was one secret she must know ... and he must reveal.

"So, Juana is not your mistress. Who is she?"

He stared long into her eyes. "She's ... well ... she's sort of ... Chief Aztlán called her ... a bride ..."

Chapter Seventeen

"Not in that sense!" Rafe stared, his own horror reflected in the horror in Marina's eyes.

Her stomach churned, her voice rasped from her throat. "You told me you weren't married!"

"I'm not—"

"A wife means you are married. At least where I come from it does."

"I didn't say *wife*. Bride isn't even a good word." He gripped her hands tightly, feeling his own tremble. "Look what you do to me. The thought of losing you is terrifying."

The chill of the night trembled inside her. She pulled away. "What *I* do to you? You . . . have a wife."

"Not a wife. She was *given* to me, as a . . ."

"Given?" Marina slumped on the bench, her head propped against the wall of the depot. Her limbs felt useless. Her mind reeled, stupidly. Inside, she felt empty and at the same time full of a suffocating sickness.

"By Chief Aztlán. Remember the goddess, Lady Chaly? How I told you the chief was grateful to me for saving her? That he gave me . . . ? I didn't tell you what, because . . . It's their custom, has been since well before the Conquest. The chief gives his most valuable possession . . . a daughter."

"Like the Aztec priests offered their most precious possessions to the gods . . . human hearts? That's what you did to me just now, you ripped out my living, beating—"

"No, love . . . no. Listen and you will understand. I did not agree to take this woman—"

"Juana! Can you not even call her name? Or is her name equally as hateful as mine?"

"Juana," he complied, ignoring her last statement. Unless he resolved the present problem, it wouldn't matter whether he ever called her own name. "If I had refused Aztlán's gift, the operation would have been lost. I would have offended him."

"Pray God, you do not offend anyone!"

"Listen to me," he repeated. "Let me explain, then when I finish, if you don't understand . . . I will try again."

She inhaled deeply, unable to conceal her tremors. "Go ahead. I'm curious to learn how you think you can explain such a thing as a secret wife."

"It happened only a few days before I came to Tecolutla . . . before I met you. After I switched goddesses I reported to Aztlán before returning to the city. We had agreed that no one would know of the switch except the two of us. Then he insisted on thanking me by offering his daughter. I resisted—*por los dios,* I resisted. I told him I couldn't accept her. I recall how the idea unnerved me."

The cool night air washed over her numb face as

though it were striking someone else's skin. "I doubt you will ever know how much it unnerves me."

Staring at the depot floor, he longed to hold her, to comfort her. "Aztlán countered every excuse I made, assuring me she was a bride in . . . ah, well, for the night only. That I was to . . . ah, to spend the night with her, then I could leave with no obligations on either part."

Marina stared, unseeing, toward the distant lake. "That's what Sophie meant," she mused.

"What else did Sophie tell you?"

"That her husband thought I was the daughter of some chief . . ." Her words faltered to an end, sinking into the thick, charged air between them.

Finally she spoke again. "How many other chiefs have given you their daughters, Rafael Santana? How many wives do you possess? However many it is," she added quickly, "you certainly do not need one more."

His mouth was dry as dust. His heart hurt for the pain he had caused her. "No others. You can believe that. I wouldn't lie to you, regardless of what you think."

She turned to look at him. His face was in shadow, but she could tell it was set in sadness by the elongated shape of it, by the tone of his voice.

"I know," she whispered.

He looked at her.

"Where do you live . . . you and Juana?"

"Live?"

"Live," she repeated. "When you are married, you live someplace. With her father? Where?"

"Nowhere. I told you. It is not a marriage. It never was."

"Then why was she so angry with me? Calling me *Malinche?*" She spat the name as Juana had done, anger spewing from deep within her soul.

Rafe sighed. "Her anger had nothing to do with you and me . . . with us."

"Now, that is something I don't believe."

"It didn't. She was . . ." Dammit, why had he ever accepted Chief Aztlán's gift? Why hadn't he prepared Marina for this visit? "The morning after . . . ah, the following morning Fernando came with word of your expedition. She heard your name."

Marina stared at him now, her eyes swimming with pain. "The night you slept with her?"

He nodded.

"You stayed with her the whole night?"

"What the hell would you have me do? I couldn't very well ride off to Mexico in the middle of the night."

Her mind whirled with images of Rafe's body and that woman's. Juana. How had he been with Juana? Marina thought of his passion and excitement, of his playfulness, his tenderness. Had he been the same with Juana? And Juana? Had she . . . ?

Desperately she threw her head forward clasping it in her hands. Questions whirled . . . questions she never wanted to know answers to . . . questions that would never have occurred to her had she not seen the woman. Juana. Juana.

"One night?" she whispered.

"One night."

"No more?"

Quickly, Rafe knelt before her on the depot floor. Taking her head in his hands, he raised it gently, forcing her face to his. "No more. Not ever again. Not with her, not with anyone. I have told you that all along. There will be no one but you."

She looked into his begging eyes, mesmerized by the truth she saw there—by the love.

In the distance the train whistle blew. Soon it would be time to go.

He thought of the private car, knowing he could not tell her about it now.

"If we do get married and I go into the villages with you, there will be no others?"

He shook his head, solemn. "I love you. On that love I swear there is nothing else in my past for you to fear or dread. Nothing. And I don't intend to marry you and leave you at home."

She thought suddenly of his relatives back on the island. "They hated me . . ."

"No. It was your name—Juana told them. She overheard Fernando telling her father about us being at Janitzio and she went to them."

Marina sighed. "What will happen later? My name will be the same . . . except . . ."

He held her gaze, seeing fear now, fear replacing hurt. Progress? "I know they seem strange and primitive. One day you will discover that they are not. They've been hurt by foreigners, and they are afraid. Afraid and defensive. It is understandable. Emotions are the same—for us all."

She nodded, a slight, almost imperceptible movement.

"They treated me with caution at the beginning. I had to prove myself by becoming their friend. When they discover your sincerity, they will accept you, too."

The whistle blew again, closer now. Iron wheels

397

screamed against iron rails; the platform where they sat vibrated from the force of the braking engine. Inside, Rafe's brain churned with indecision. Finally he knew—if for no other reason, he needed the privacy of the special car to continue his efforts to assuage her fears, to win back her trust.

He drew her to her feet. "That's our ride."

With leaden movements she followed him inside the depot where he retrieved their bags. Outside again, she watched him approach an elderly matron, discuss something, then draw some bills from his pocket and give them to the woman.

When he ushered Marina into the last car on the train, the old woman followed. "Who is she?" Marina asked.

"Your *dueña.*"

The car came as such a surprise that his words did not immediately sink in. Sleeping areas were curtained off on either side of a passageway which led to a parlor with comfortable chairs and a dining table laid with silver and china and a fresh-cooked meal. Turning, she stared wide-eyed, then his words registered in her brain.

Rafe was speaking with the steward, who scrutinized the old woman and Marina, then nodded to Rafe. "I will send a boy to clear the table when you finish."

"No," Rafe instructed. "We are tired. Do not disturb us until we reach Pachuca. If we need assistance, we will ring."

She figured it out after the train pulled away from the station and Rafe left with the old woman. "I will find her a seat in a car up front, then I'll return."

This car was for them—for her and Rafe. This entire

luxurious car. Bouquets of roses everywhere, a bottle of champagne chilling in its silver bucket. Steadying herself, she crossed to the table, where she lifted the silver domes on dish after dish of the elegant meal which included the little white fish prepared in a sauce with the tangy aroma of limes. The little white fish she had watched them catch in butterfly nets only hours before. It seemed like years . . . eons.

Rafe returned to find her peering behind the curtains at the berths which were carefully made up with crisp, fresh-smelling linens.

She looked at him, questioning, but he passed without attempting to touch her. At the table he lifted the same lids she had moments before lifted herself.

"When did you arrange this?" she asked.

Turning he studied her, wary. "In Mexico City." He shrugged in a self-deprecating way. "I told them to send a car for the Antiquities staff . . . and food."

"And flowers," she added, "and champagne."

"At the time, it seemed like something we would enjoy."

Unable to pull her gaze from his, she felt tears rush to her eyes. She tried to blink them back, but her eyelids refused to move, and soon the hot wet tears were rolling down her cheeks, and . . .

Before she knew it Rafe was wiping them away, soothing her with sounds, with the fine touch of his fingers on her face. Suddenly she was in his arms, holding him tightly, molding her face to his chest. But the tears would not stop. Why was she crying? The worst was over. Or . . . ?

"Rafe, will you . . . ?"—she heaved a quivering sigh—". . . will you be required to . . . to sleep with

399

her again?"

"No." His response was quick, firm, definite. "She was given to others before me, and I am sure there are—or soon will be—others to follow."

"What a despicable life."

"It is their way. To them it isn't despicable. Our way would likely be."

"But if she has been . . . ?" Marina's face froze. A look of abject horror contorted her features.

"What is it now, love?"

"She must be . . . accomplished. Was she? I mean . . ."—tears gushed from her eyes— "I couldn't bear to think she was . . . better than I . . ."

He stared at her, dumfounded, thinking what a stupid question. But it wasn't stupid, it was real—a new fear. A fear he might have a difficult time allaying. "It was not the same thing. It was a physical act, nothing more." He drew her head to his chest, cradling it in his hand. Her silky hair soothed his trembling hand; her face against his heart gave him courage, hope.

"I recall at the time wondering why the experience was so unsatisfying." His words whispered into her hair. "Now I know the reason—there was no sharing, no joy, no excitement, no passion. Now, I know why."

Cupping her face in his hands, he drew it to his, kissing away her remaining tears. "There was no love."

She quivered beneath his caressing touch. "When I saw that look on her face, I became frightened," she confessed. "I thought I might lose you, or be required to share you, which would be the same thing. In that moment I knew more clearly than ever before . . ." She searched his eyes, then continued, inspired by the love she saw there.

"I love you Rafe Santana. I love you. I love you."

The words floated as butterflies from her lips, nipping and teasing against his face, fluttering inside his heart. Neither of them moved for the longest time. They stood quietly, still as death, while their hearts beat in rhythm with the train as it clattered down the track. When the moment was sufficiently etched in their brains as to be remembered in its finest detail forevermore, he lowered his lips and closed them over hers.

She responded eagerly, matching his ardor with her own. When at length he moved to lift his face, she pulled his lips back to hers, as if to affirm her own commitment.

Finally he dislodged their lips enough to speak against hers. His eyes glistened with love and the remnants of fear.

"I was frightened, too. Scared to death. For a while tonight I was sure I would never hear you say those words."

Twenty-four hours later the train pulled into Pachuca, and Rafe and Marina disembarked, a little hungry, but otherwise well satisfied.

Once their differences had been settled, Rafe suggested eating, but Marina objected.

"We can eat when we get back to the ship."

With a grin he scooped her in his arms and carried her to the berth, where after drawing back the curtains, they disrobed and fell into bed, clinging to each other.

For a long time, all he did was hold her. Weakened by the fear of losing her, his body felt spent even before

401

he began to love her. His arms quivered when he drew her closer, and closer still, his hands roaming her spine from neck to base, feeling, absorbing, communicating.

Her breasts full and firm nestled into the hair on his chest, burrowing, or so it seemed, to his very heart. When he cupped her buttocks in his palm, she pressed her body closer to the center of his own rapidly growing demand.

Then he raised his lips to hers and tasted her tears and his heart seemed to crack beneath the weight of the pain he had caused her.

In the light of the lanterns flickering from the other end of the car, he watched tears stream down her face. Silently he kissed the wet trails, then each eye in turn. "Are you going to cry while we make love?" he murmured, wanting desperately to soothe, to reassure her, yet not knowing how to go about it.

"Only this time," she replied. "Then never again."

"You are not thinking about—"

"Shhh . . ." She kissed his lips softly, stilling his words. "I'm thinking how lucky I am . . . how lucky we are."

Her words brought moisture to his own eyes. "I most of all."

She shook her head. "No. *We* are lucky. We love each other so much . . . that we will always work out our problems. When something comes between us, we can talk about it . . . and we trust each other. Nothing will ever keep us apart."

He kissed her, lightheaded from her words, from the truth of them. She snuggled against him, working her legs between his, increasing his need for her by the demands of her own body. Then he felt her laugh against his chest.

She met his quizzical eyes with a smile. "Except Tata." Her body squirmed as she spoke. "We had better make good use of this time, because when we get back to the *Stella Duval*—"

"Say no more, love." His lips descended greedily. "Time's wasting."

She did not cry again until it was over. Her delight in his loving dried all tears from her eyes. Her senses seemed sharper now than ever before. The heady, wonderful scent of him intoxicated her. His furry chest seemed softer than she remembered, and when she nuzzled close, her breasts began to throb even before his lips found their aching tips.

He loved her with the precision she had learned to expect, yet reverently, too, and gently. His stroking hands brought shivers to her very soul as they worked her body inside and out into a mass of yearning flesh . . . until she writhed against him in eagerness. . . .

Until she moved her own hands over his body, finding and stroking, teasing and titillating his own quivering flesh. . . .

Until together they moved as one, united in body, in mind and spirit, united as never before. . . .

Until at last their race was won . . . this one, anyhow . . . and they lay sated and together.

At that moment the train reached one of the hairpin curves she recalled seeing the past morning. Without warning the car swerved, throwing them against the outer wall. He clung to her. She laughed. He chuckled. Together.

Together. She squeezed her arms around him, the

events from Janitzio rushing to her mind. The thought that she could have lost him brought a new rush of tears to her eyes. He felt them immediately against his own face.

His hand cupped her face, catching the last of her tears. "What is it?"

For a time she lay silently in his arms, squenching her eyes against the remnants of anguish. Then she looked into his troubled, adoring face. "If we hadn't faced all that, I might never have known how much I love you."

He stared long into her loving eyes. "You will never know how wonderful those words sound to me."

After a while, she smiled. "We've solved almost everything."

He nipped her nose with his lips, spread his fingers through her luxurious hair. "Yes, love. We are definitely on the downhill run."

Her smile turned to a grin. "Except for one more . . ." —she paused purposely, letting his mind catch up with hers— ". . . and that doesn't matter so much any more."

He grinned then, a return of his devilish grin, setting her pores on fire. How she loved teasing him . . . and having him tease her.

"In that case, *capitán,* we may as well forget it. Or perhaps I will have a surprise for you one day. You do like surprises?"

"Hummm . . ." she sighed. *A surprise.* She thought of the trouble they had just passed through and of the surprise she had for him. A baby would be a terrible surprise for two people who didn't love each other. "I love surprises," she whispered. "I hope you do, too."

The only time they saw another soul on the entire

trip was twice when Rafe called for meals. At those times, Marina remained discreetly hidden behind the curtains of the berth. Once, while waiting, she remembered to read her mother's letter.

"Grandmother wrote my mother about us," she told Rafe over the meal.

He raised his eyebrows.

"No, Mama won't be a problem. She's already planning the wedding. Says to hurry home so we can arrange a spring wedding under the elm trees by Los Olmos Creek."

"Hummm . . . spring isn't very soon," he said.

She shook her head, thinking of her great desire to become Rafe Santana's wife . . . of the secret she had for him. "No," she agreed, "spring is not nearly soon enough."

When she finally thought to ask about the old woman he had brought aboard at Pátzcuaro, he had answered, "I paid her fare in exchange for her coming aboard with us. Thought it would give the conductor the idea that she's your *dueña.*"

"What do you suppose he thought when he saw her in the front of the train?"

Rafe shrugged, kissing her bare shoulder. "I couldn't let her ride inside with us; that would have been going too far in keeping my promise to your grandfather."

She laughed, hugging him close, recalling how he often said she was more precious to him than gold.

Well, she felt the same way. She didn't know why she had reacted so vehemently to the encounter with Juana and to Rafe's ensuing confession. The fact he had known other women didn't bother her. She knew—he had proved it by both word and deed—that he loved

405

her and would remain true to her.

The next evening when Rafe called for dinner, Marina came to the table in her dressing gown, which she had worn—off and on—all day. "I'm going to find it hard to put on clothes again."

He held her gaze across the table. "I'm going to find it hard to let you."

In the middle of dessert—a vanilla-flavored flan served with coffee—a thought occurred to her and she laughed out loud.

"What is it?" he asked.

She cocked her head studying him. "I have one more question about this whole sordid affair."

"What else could you possibly want to know. I've answered everything—practically." He waggled his eyebrows, feeling a surge of happiness that they could tease about a subject which had caused so much initial pain.

"The knot in your string at the old shaman's hut. That's what it was for, wasn't it?"

He held her gaze, challenging. "Maybe."

"I don't understand, though. Why would you seek penance for something that was . . . well, in their eyes at least, legal and moral?"

His expression changed gradually from playful to passionate, from jesting to seriousness. "By that time I knew what you meant to me. And anything else by comparison became . . ." —he shrugged— ". . . a carnal sin."

She thought on his answer, knowing he filled her with more happiness than she had ever imagined. She didn't deserve it, nobody deserved to be so happy. "I beg to disagree," she teased. "At that time, you had not even kissed me."

"Regardless, I wanted to. You knew how badly, else you would not have badgered me into it on top of the pyramid."

"You were afraid of—"

"Enough!" Rising, he drew her from the table. "I'm not the coward you make me out." Sweeping her in his arms, he carried her to the berth. "We have time for me to try to prove my virility once more before we arrive in Pachuca."

"Your virility has never been in question, Rafe," she whispered, when at last they lay damp and exhausted. "Nor has my love for you. I love you beyond the ability of any words to convey."

He kissed her soundly. "Your ways are convincing enough, love. But don't stop telling me, too."

They rode into Tecolutla at high noon the following day, laughing in easy camaraderie, counting the days until their next trip together.

"We should finish salvaging the cargo by the end of the week," Rafe informed her.

She turned to him wide-eyed. "Then what?"

"How much are the taxes?"

"Fifty thousand dollars. Why?"

"As soon as we finish the salvage efforts, I will wire Fernando for that amount. He, in turn, will transfer the money to an account Giddeon names in Papantla—or wherever he wants it. The transfer shouldn't take long. We can wait for it at the Hacienda de Vera Cruz."

"Where will the money come from?" she demanded.

"Not from me, if that's your concern. I am not

buying a wife." He turned his beloved grin on her. "But I would if it were necessary, believe me."

"From where then?"

"Fernando, on my instructions, convinced our government that we owe Giddeon for salvaging the cargo—call it a finder's fee—along with payment to be figured on a daily basis for however many days the salvage effort takes."

"Why didn't you tell me sooner?"

"Now don't go accusing me of keeping secrets. I wasn't sure it would work out. I didn't want to get your hopes up. That was why I had Fernando meet us day before yesterday in Mexico City. I planned to tell you at a special time."

She glanced around the sparsely populated town of Tecolutla, her smile stemming from deep inside her heart. "In a special place, I suppose?"

He chuckled. "I figure we've about run out of special times and places for a while. Won't be long, though, until we have the rest of our lives—and we can go any place, just the two of us, alone together."

Those words rang joyously in her ears while they returned their mounts to José at the cantina, paying him handsomely for stabling them.

Alone together. The words sang through her senses when she and Rafe strode hand in hand across the pier and up the gangplank.

Alone together . . .

Then the words sank into oblivion, as though cast to the bottom of the sea, when Tata greeted them on the deck of the *Stella Duval*.

"Some damned thief broke in and stole the artifacts and gold from our hiding place."

Chapter Eighteen

"How are Logan Junior and Essie?" Marina asked as soon as Giddeon told them of the theft.

"Fine. Embarrassed, but fine."

Rafe and Marina followed her grandfather to his quarters, while Giddeon related the details of the break-in, as much as was known.

"The boys saw no harm in going to the cantina," Giddeon said, "since the ship was within sight. It was the peyote that got them."

"Peyote?" Rafe inquired.

Giddeon ushered them solemnly inside his salon.

"They heeded your warning not to let Zolic come aboard, but they thought nothing of drinking with him. He is a personable sort of fellow, after all."

"How did it happen, Tata?"

"While the boys were drinking with Zolic, he offered them some peyote, and they don't recall much else until Nick stumbled to the cantina hours later."

"What do you mean . . . stumbled?" Rafe asked. "What did Zolic do to Nick?"

"Nothing. Zolic never came on board. We don't even know the man was involved. While he was drinking in the cantina with the boys, the thieves gained the deck from starboard, tied up the crew, and"—he waved his arms in a wide gesture—"played hell with everything."

Rafe stared into the still gaping hole in the wall. "What did they take?"

"Without the records we couldn't be sure, except the gold pieces and that goddess with all the rattlesnakes."

"The crates in the hold?" Rafe asked.

Giddeon shook his head. "Didn't bother them. Don't figure they were equipped to haul off such a load."

While they spoke, Marina pulled out the record book and Rafe began calling off the items that were left.

"How do you suppose they found this place?" he mused.

"Nick said we made a lot of racket tearing out those boards," Giddeon answered. "Ybarro must be involved or one of his men, although Nick found nothing tracking them. Nick returned just before the robbery."

Rafe sighed. "We should have found a better way."

"Your idea was sound," Serita insisted. "If someone on board was involved, you couldn't have found a place they wouldn't find. I don't know how we will track down the thieves, though."

When Rafe and Marina finished checking off the few remaining items, she read the list of missing artifacts.

"The goddess Coatlicue, like Tata said, the golden image of Xipe Totec, the large golden disk of the sun"—her hand moved to her neck—"the golden necklace, the first piece we recovered."

Rafe glanced at her neck, their thoughts united,

recalling how Zolic had almost ruined the pieces trying to scrape them clean, how later Rafe had placed the exquisite restrung necklace around her neck.

With a sigh she continued. "One spear thrower, the obsidian sacrificial knife, and all the gold specie, of course." She snapped the book closed. "That's it."

"There go the most important artifacts for your museum," Serita told Rafe, "and our efforts to raise enough money for taxes."

"Not necessarily." Rafe outlined the plan he had revealed to Marina not over an hour earlier.

Giddeon questioned him extensively as to the origin of the money—he wanted none of Rafe's personal funds, he insisted.

"Your granddaughter is cut from the same cloth," Rafe laughed. "Personally, I would have considered it a wise investment, helping save my wife's land, but I respect your position. The money comes from a grateful Mexican government. I swear it . . ."—catching up Marina's hand, he brought her fingers to his lips—". . . on my love for your granddaughter."

After the expressions of gratitude died down, Serita voiced again her concern for Rafe's project. "I'm sorry about the artifacts. The museum is important."

Rafe heaved a heavy sigh. "Don't worry. By this time tomorrow, I intend to have recovered everything."

Marina searched his face. "What do you mean? Where are you going?"

"After Zolic."

"There's no evidence he is involved," Giddeon reiterated. His words halted abruptly. "Except Nick's . . ."

"Nick's what?" Marina prompted.

"The tar," Giddeon said. "We forgot to tell you . . . we found the first batch of gold coins . . . most of them anyhow. During the robbery, the thieves overturned the tar barrel."

"When we cleaned up the mess," Serita interjected, "we found the coins at the bottom of the barrel."

"In the tar," Rafe mused. "A place no one would look."

Giddeon agreed. "My guess is they hoped to mislead us into thinking they had taken the coins in the boat that went ashore for new diving cables."

"Logan Junior suspects the barrel was overturned when they tried to move it off the ship," Serita added.

"Either that or they purposely emptied it on deck," Giddeon continued, "and were interrupted before they could retrieve the coins." His eyes leveled on Rafe, then he crossed the room, his hand outstretched. "Hope you'll accept an old man's apology, son."

Rafe took Giddeon's hand. "No need to apologize, sir. You called it like you saw it." He drew Marina to his side. "But if you insist, I will claim your granddaughter's hand as reparation."

Giddeon laughed. "I'm sure you will have no trouble gaining her father's approval. I might even put in a good word for you myself."

Marina brought them back to the original conversation. "You didn't explain what Nick knows about Zolic."

"Nick said Zolic was mighty interested in that barrel while we were at the Feast of Saint Francis," Giddeon said.

"But that was before the coins disappeared," Marina objected.

"That son of a bitch!" Rafe breathed, then immediately apologized to the ladies. His eyes caught Marina's. "Do you remember the day we met . . . here aboard . . . ?" He saw her eyes dart to his jaw. His hand followed her gaze, rubbing the stubble, recalling her hand slapping his face.

He chuckled. "If we hadn't been so angry with each other, we might have prevented this whole affair."

Still her eyes held his, teasing now.

"The theft," he corrected. "Remember how adamantly Zolic refuted knowing Pedro Ybarro? Yet you . . ."

Marina nodded. "Pedro Ybarro distinctly told me that Zolic had sent him. Yet, Zolic claimed not to know him. I believed Zolic, that Ybarro used his name."

"Why?" Rafe countered. "Jesús Zolic's name would have meant nothing to you . . . not as a reference. Zolic was trying to conceal his relationship with the salvagers. Now we know the reason."

He returned his attention to the salvage efforts. "Time is money to you, Giddeon. Go back to the expedition site as though nothing had happened. I will have José's son Enrique bring me to the ship when I finish."

Marina followed him on deck. "I'm coming with you."

"No." He cupped her face in his hand, rubbed his thumb across her lips, let the softness of her skin send fiery streaks like lightning down his arm and through his body. "Not this time, love."

"You said you would take me every place."

"I didn't foresee this when I said that." His mind whirled with the ways he had hurt her. He saw her on top of the pyramid with Zolic, her finger bleeding from the point of that madman's dagger, on top of the pyramid where she had asked him to take her.

He saw her face at Pátzcuaro—the pain he had caused her with his inept handling of the thing with Juana.

"Not this time," he repeated. "I want to know you are safe. I want you here in the protection of your grandfather and brothers. I won't be long. If my hunch is correct, I will be back by suppertime tomorrow."

Her family came on deck then, and he kissed her quickly but soundly in front of them, filling her with pride that he would so openly demonstrate his love and affection.

She held that in her heart when they set sail, according to his instructions, as soon as Ybarro and his crew returned.

"Don't let them know you are suspicious of them," Rafe had instructed Giddeon. "That way they may make a mistake."

And indeed Pedro Ybarro, Gordo, Carlos, and Juan DeLeon acted with the proper shock at the robbery.

"They are innocent men or accomplished actors," Giddeon proclaimed over supper that night, after they had reached the salvage site. "In either case it will do no harm to follow Rafe's instructions."

The first few hours of the following morning dragged by. Rafe had said suppertime, but perhaps he would come sooner. Then Marina saw Enrique's boat approach.

Rafe, however, was not with him. Enrique had come alone. Nick helped him aboard, while Marina pelted him with questions.

"I do not know the answers to your questions,

señorita. I have come to fetch you for Don Rafael."

"To fetch her where?" Giddeon demanded.

Enrique shrugged. "I do not know. Don Rafael sent a message to my father, requesting the señorita come at once."

"Where is this message?" Giddeon demanded.

Again the young man shrugged. "I did not bring it, señor. I cannot myself read—"

"Fool!" Giddeon raved. "We could have read it. Do you expect me to let my granddaughter go to Tecolutla alone with you unless—"

"Tata, it's all right. I know Enrique. He and his father have helped Rafe and me before." She turned to the boy. "Let me fetch a wrap. I won't be . . ."

"I can't let you do this, sugar."

Marina caught her grandfather's sleeve. "Tata. Don't worry. If Rafe sent for me, it was with good reason."

"No—" Giddeon began.

"You know Rafe would not put me in danger."

"Then we will come with you."

"Absolutely not." She tried to laugh off the suggestion. "I appreciate your concern, but he sent for me, not for my entire family."

When she returned to the deck with her wrap, however, her grandfather had made his decision and had issued orders to carry it out.

The *Stella Duval* had already weighed anchor.

"What are you doing?" Marina demanded.

"Do not worry, dear." Her grandmother drew her aside. "Come below deck. I will explain."

"Do you promise he will take me only as far as the port at Tecolutla?" Marina demanded when her grandmother related Giddeon's decision to return to shore.

Serita nodded. "I will see to it."

As she feared, however, when they reached Tecolutla and discovered her destination would be the old shaman's hut on the Hacienda de Vera Cruz, Giddeon wanted to accompany her.

"No, Giddeon," Serita intervened. "Marina is right. Let her get on her way so she can arrive before nightfall."

They found Pedro with a horse saddled and ready for her journey to meet Rafe at the old shaman's hut, as the message had indicated.

"Where is the message stating this?" Giddeon demanded.

"No, sé," Pedro responded. "I do not know. The word came to me from one of the fieldhands at the hacienda."

Giddeon drew Marina aside. "I don't like it, sugar."

"Tata . . ."

"I would feel a lot better if someone came along. Logan Junior and Essie can ride with you as far as the big house. They will promise to wait for you there."

Finally, in an effort to save time, she consented.

"Neither of you will accompany me beyond the big house."

The boys agreed. Later she thought of her determination and wondered what demon had possessed her. At the time, all she could think of was being with Rafe.

Surely, she worried, surely, if he were injured he would have sought help at the hacienda.

At the big house, she did not wait to speak with her relatives, fearing they too would want to accompany her, and her refusal would waste more time. Time was escaping fast; it was near dusk when she came in view of the shaman's hut.

The sight of it brought to mind the strange man who had lived there and his violent death, and a momentary reluctance to proceed gripped her. How foolish, she reproved herself. Rafe Santana would not summon her to a place where harm awaited.

Dismounting, she hitched her horse at the weathered old rail, seeing Rafe here beside her. The memory of his presence somehow soothed her, while at the same time it hurried her onward. Pray God he was here—and safe.

In the doorway she paused to let her eyes adjust to the dim interior of the hut. And when they did, her reluctance became a premonition. Across the fire sat a hunched figure. No, Rafe Santana would not invite her into harm.

But Jesús Zolic would.

"Come in," Zolic invited. "I have been waiting for you, Lady Marina."

She grasped the door frame for support as the truth sizzled in the moiling panic in the pit of her stomach. Rafe had not invited her to this hut. Jesús Zolic had.

"Where is Rafe?"

"I take it you followed instructions and came alone."

"Where is Rafe?"

Poised for flight the instant she learned Rafe's whereabouts, she scanned the darkened one-room hut. In the center the fire pit glowed, the smoke from its embers smelling sweetly of incense. It seemed only yesterday she had sat beside this very pit with Rafe's knees touching hers. Only yesterday Rafe had tied the knot in the string the old man gave him. The old man who was later brutally murdered. . . .

His peyote stolen.

She squinted against the outside light, trying to adjust to the dim interior, while her eyes darted to the corners of the room. "What have you done with him?"

"Nothing, Lady Marina."

She cringed at the name issued in slurred diction. She longed to look into Zolic's eyes, but the dread of what she would see there held her back.

The glazed look of one demented by drugs, she knew. "Then where is he?" she demanded.

Zolic rose; Marina stepped backward, still clutching the door frame.

Taking up a sack from one corner, Zolic emptied the contents into the fire. It sputtered, crackled, and a sickening odor rose with the smoke. "You are afraid of me." He spoke casually, dipping his face into the rising smoke, inhaling deeply. "Why?"

His hair, usually neatly combed, hung down his neck and over his forehead, forming a dark curtain about his eyes when he bent to inhale another draft of the nauseating smoke. Her stomach tumbled.

"What have you done with Rafe?"

"I have done nothing with that *lunático*. He is not worthy of my time or attention. Nor of yours, I might add. Although I realize it is a little late to worry about that. I have been remiss in your training. I let you stray."

He stepped around the fire pit with limpid movements she attributed to whatever it was he inhaled from the fire. Instinctively she moved away from the door, her heart thudding a warning inside her breast. Judging the distance to her horse, she imagined untying the reins. Would she have time? Could she escape? Or was she being unnecessarily skittish?

"Why did you steal our gold?" She asked the question as much to distract him as for an answer. She certainly did not expect him to admit to the crime, nor to explain the reasons behind it. His answer surprised her.

"For the same reason anybody would steal gold, my lady. That was a foolish question, far beneath your intelligence. But come in and we will discuss it."

"I prefer to discuss it out here."

Later she admonished herself for not moving faster. At the moment he lunged, she had thought him distracted, had thought the distance between them greater.

And she had not credited him with the agility of a jaguar. The instant he grabbed her arm, she flung herself backward, pulling him after her. But not for long. He held his ground, dragged her back inside the hut, and threw her to the earthen floor on the far side of the fire pit.

"Do not struggle," he told her. "I do not want to hurt you." He stoked up the fire and with it her fears.

"Where is Rafe?" With great effort she controlled her voice, restraining her desperate inclination to scream— from fear, from rage, for help.

Only the latter would do her the least bit of good, and even that, she knew, would be a futile waste of energy. This hut stood on the hillside, apart from any other.

"Please tell me where Rafe is."

He brought a gourd cup filled with a dark liquid, and when she refused to take it, he held it to her mouth.

"I am not thirsty," she told him, but her open lips

419

provided the opportunity for which he watched. Clasping her head in one hand, he forced the foul-tasting liquid down her throat. She struggled, kicking at the fire, at him, clutching at his hand, at the cup until most of the substance ran down her face.

"What do you want from me?" she cried.

"Not to frighten you," he soothed.

"Well, you are, so stop. Let me up. Let me go before my grandfather and brothers come."

In the dim light she watched his expression change from one of simple determination to desperation. The glow from the fire pit illuminated the insanity in his black eyes.

What was it Rafe had told her, that years of abusing peyote could lead to permanent dementia? At this moment Jesús Zolic appeared to be a man on a journey from which he would never return.

And she herself was about to embark on a similar journey, she discovered, when she tried to stand and her legs crumbled beneath her.

"What was in that drink?"

"Something to settle your nerves, my lady. Your illicit relationship with Santana has unstrung your nerves."

"What was in that drink?" Enraged within, her voice nevertheless tumbled stupidly from her lips.

"Never mind, lady. It will quiet your nerves. Soon you will begin to float free. Your spirit will fly."

"I don't want to fly." Her brain thrashed in a chaotic fashion inside her skull. Her skin felt clammy, yet perspiration seemed to weep from her pores. Frantically she tried to focus her eyes, but moment by frightening moment the room became increasingly blurred.

She felt his hands on her blouse, and she resisted,

420

struggled against him valiantly . . . but only in her mind. Her limbs were now useless. Somewhere inside she knew this, and her fear grew.

"What . . . are you . . . doing?" she mumbled, while her hands clutched in a limp fashion at her blouse, at his hands.

"I will not harm you."

She stared into his blurry eyes . . . or was it her vision that was blurred? For a moment she struggled to decide the answer to that question. Then she became frantic once more, desperately trying to fight Zolic's hands from her body.

With a start she realized she was nude; then she felt a cold liquid wash over her. The nauseous odor from the fire pit choked in her throat. Except now it did not make her sick. She was becoming accustomed. . . .

"No," her voice wailed inside.

"Be still, my lady. I am almost done cleansing your body. Then we will go."

"Where . . . is . . . Rafe . . . ?" She felt the words reach her lips, but was unsure whether she had spoken them.

By contrast Zolic's voice sounded clearer than before and more threatening, except intermittently when it became Rafe's voice and she relaxed.

Quickly then her senses would return and she would realize whose hands touched her body . . . whose voice spoke soft words to her, and her terror would return also, each time a little stronger than the last.

After a while she began to tremble; she was cold . . . very cold. Then she suddenly awoke, as from a dream, finding herself in the saddle of her horse in the middle of the night with someone riding behind her, his strong body touching hers.

"Rafe?"

Arms encircled her and she felt nude beneath them. Surely no more than a couple of layers of rough fabric covered her skin.

Irrationally she recalled telling Rafe she would have a hard time getting used to wearing clothing again.

"Rafe?" Her voice rasped, burning from her throat.

"Do not be afraid, Lady Marina," Zolic soothed. "We are almost there."

"Where?" Anxiety gnawed like a rat in her brain.

"To our destiny."

The cool night air blew against her body, chilling her, cooling her feverish face. She lifted her eyes skyward, focusing on the stars.

"A lovely night," Zolic mused.

"Where are we going?" She struggled to recall what had transpired since she arrived at the hut. She remembered hitching her horse, finding Jesús Zolic there instead of Rafe, intoxicated on peyote.

"Are you taking me to Rafe?"

"Santana will come. Eventually he will unscramble my riddle, and he will come. He will find you. You can be certain of that."

Finally the need to escape reached her brain. She recalled thinking the same thing earlier. Why had she not done so? Attempting to lift her hands, she found her wrists tied to the saddlehorn. "The drink . . . you drugged me."

"Not drugged," he corrected. "Only a weak potion to settle your mind. If you had not fought against it, it would not have worn off by now."

She had to escape. Surreptitiously she glanced from left to right, but her head was cloaked inside a deep hood which obstructed her peripheral vision. Shifting in the saddle, she did learn, however, that her feet were bare and her ankles had been tied together beneath the belly of the horse, for in lifting one she pulled on the other.

"Why did you tie me?"

"A precaution. I have no desire to bring you harm."

"You keep saying that," she wailed, although her voice was octaves lower than normal. "If you mean me no harm, let me go. My grandfather and brothers will come."

"They will not find us now."

They rode through the night and for a time Marina's brain would hold but two alternating thoughts: the icy cold wind permeating her body and her need to escape.

But her brain could go no further. Try as she might, she could not formulate a coherent plan. And that thought chilled her to the marrow with fear—a frantic fear so encompassing it left room for nothing else. It was the drug, she knew. She was not given to fear.

Neither was she given to being led into a trap, drugged, and abducted. And to what end? For what purpose?

The ominous truth of the matter settled through her fears like lead. Her abduction had something to do with Rafe and with . . . Lady Marina. In terse replies to her questions he had made one thing clear, desperately clear: wherever he was taking her, no one would rescue her.

Unless it was she, herself.

Then the Pyramid of the Niches loomed before them. El Tajín. She should have known. Relief surged into her battered brain. Rafe would know.

He would know, and he would come. El Tajín was

the first place he would look—if he knew to look for her.

When he knew to look for her, she corrected fiercely. Miraculously, her brain began to function. Hope invaded her anguish. Of course Rafe would come. But she must not wait. She must escape at the first opportunity.

Struggling to shake the last vestiges of drugs from her brain, she gave silent thanks for the cold night air that helped clear her mind.

"Why did you tie me, Zolic? I would have come to El Tajín with you. Did you not know that?"

Drawing rein at the foot of the Pyramid of the Niches, he heaved himself from the saddle behind her. For a moment he stood, reins in hand, gazing up the steps.

"You will untie me now, of course."

"Of course, Lady Marina."

Inside she screamed. Terror coursed through her veins at the title, at the foreboding in his tone. Outwardly, she strove to appear calm. Her brain functioned. She rejoiced.

The instant he released her hands, she would grab the reins and be gone. She knew the way to the big house. Her ordeal was over.

Later she wondered why when one thing went wrong, often everything else followed suit.

Zolic slashed the rope tying her ankles first, then he quickly swept her from the saddle, and with another flash of his blade he cut the rope tying her hands to the saddlehorn. His movement was so swift, she thought he intended to cut her hands off at the wrists, and terror of it wracked her body.

In the next moment he whipped the horse on its

rump sending it racing from the compound.

"Why did you do that?" she screamed.

His answer was to grasp her wrists more tightly. "You thought to trick me by pretending to acquiesce," he accused, sidestepping her flailing feet.

When he tried to drag her to the bottom step of the pyramid, she dug her heels into the ground.

"Come now, my lady. This is all your own fault. I explained the importance of perfection, but you did not heed."

She squinted at him through the cold light of the moon. "You are mad."

At that he flung her with a great wrest against the steps of the pyramid. "Not mad, Lady Marina, disciplined. As would you be also had you obeyed my commandments."

"Your commandments?"

Rummaging through a black sack which she now saw hanging from his neck, he withdrew a flute and handed it to her. "It is too late for practice. You must break it and leave it on this bottom step."

"What are you talking about?"

"Penance. Break the flute."

She gasped as in a flash he thrust the point of his razor-sharp blade against her throat.

"Do not cause me to mar your beauty, my lady."

Fear and anger fused inside her body flooding her with weakness. She searched the sky, the countryside around. *Help me,* she wailed inside. *Help me, Rafe. Please.*

But she knew that even if Rafe were to ride up this very moment, the sound of his horse's hooves would alert Zolic. She must save herself. She must.

When she did not comply with his command, he

425

bore down on the blade. Instantly a wet trickle rolled down her neck.

With a fierceness belying her drug-sapped condition, she broke the flute into two pieces and threw it to the step at her feet.

"Try for humility, my lady."

"Humility! You are truly mad!" she accused again.

His eyes danced with it, his demeanor screamed it. His voice, however, carried a calm dignity. "Not mad, destined. You and I, we are destined. Our stars have crossed in the night of time. From this day forward they will shine together through all eternity."

Together, she thought, *together.* "I am destined to live with Rafe Santana. With no one else. Do you hear me?"

With painstakingly slow movements, Zolic raked the tip of the dagger across the skin at the top of her neck, where he pressed it to a point opposite the first.

She dared not move. Not even when he released her arm to dig into the sack again, producing another flute.

"Play it while we walk up seven steps."

She glanced in the direction of the big house, then to the ground around the base of the pyramid. Her body coiled with the first movement to escape.

With a flick of his wrist, he pierced her skin; another drop of blood rolled down her neck. Whereupon he scooped up the blood with his forefinger, showed it to her, then languidly licked it from his finger.

"In the flash of a soul departing this earth, I can plunge this blade through your neck . . . or through any part of your body I wish. Of course, I do not wish to disfigure you, Lady Marina."

She flinched at his words, at the name, at the images he conjured in her mind.

"Now, try to regain a sense of serenity while we walk up seven steps."

At the seventh step she broke the flute and dropped it to her feet, but of course he produced another one. When again she balked, he pierced her skin at the center of her neck, and once more caught the trickle of blood on a finger which he licked clean.

Unbidden tears rolled down her cheeks; she recalled Rafe kissing them away. How would she ever escape this madman?

At the forty-ninth step, she broke the last flute, and Zolic immediately dragged her up the remaining three steps to the platform. The sight here further unnerved her, and she chastised herself for not suspecting as much. Bouquets of flowers, wilted but massive, rimmed the edge of the temple. A huge stone, flat on top, stood in the center of the area. For a moment she wondered how he had carried such a load up the steps, then she saw that rather than stone, the altar was made from several pieces of wood.

Wood would serve as well, she thought, frantic now, determined. She would escape. Jesús Zolic, madman, demented from drugs or from his obsession with the past, was not going to even pretend to sacrifice her to any god—not any time—any place.

This time she was prepared. The instant he turned to his bag, she dashed for the steps. She made two before he caught her arm, flinging her to the hard stone surface of the temple.

Her head hit a step, stunning her, and in that moment he was upon her. Gasping a ragged breath she screamed, flinging her arms, kicking at him with her bare feet, all to no avail. His superior size and strength overpowered her, and his madness only added to that strength.

With one powerful tug, he ripped the cloak from her body, revealing a thin white robe. She expected him to tear the robe away as well, but he did not.

Briefly the image of him undressing her returned, and she recoiled at thoughts of what he might have done. She could recall none of what transpired after he poured the potion down her throat.

Something heavy clung to her neck, and when she asked, he replied, "The golden necklace of the gods, Lady Marina."

She did not go to the altar without a struggle. If her choice was between dying up here with a knife in her chest or falling off the pyramid with Zolic in tow she knew which she would choose. Struggle as she did, however, she only managed to scrape her legs on the stone and receive another pierce from his blade at the base of her throat.

This one he did not stop to devour, however. Instead he flung her backward over the altar, her legs dangling behind, her head and arms to the front of the pyramid.

With her continued flailing and struggling, it took him so long to tie her in place, that afterward both were drenched, each in his own perspiration.

"I am disappointed in you, my lady." Between breaths he traced his blade down her breast bone, severing the fabric of her robe, but otherwise leaving her unharmed.

For the moment, she thought. Her heart beat frantically; she could hear it reverberate in her own ears. Tears sprung to her eyes when she thought quite without design that this might be the last sound she heard on earth.

With two flicks of his wrist, he brushed the robe

apart exposing her breasts to the moon and stars above.

"You can't do this, Zolic," she begged. "Please untie me. Let me go. You are not a murderer."

"I am offering you the highest honor a woman can achieve, and you snivel like an Aztec's slave." He rummaged through his sack, drawing out one object after another.

"Please, Zolic. Rafe will find me. He will come after you. He will—"

"Enough. You have already defiled your body; I do not know what end your soul will reach now. If you had practiced the flute as I instructed, if you had held yourself pure instead of consorting with Santana—"

Of a sudden he leaned over her, peering into her eyes. "Do you carry his seed?"

Her heart, which she knew by now would meet no good end, fairly stopped. Did he know? What would he do should he discover the truth? Tear the babe from her womb?

"No!" she screamed.

Her baby would die, of course, along with her. But she would not have him mutilate her body searching for it. That would only bring more grief to those she loved . . . to Rafe, her baby's father, were he to find her with his baby torn. . . .

Desperately she drew her mind from such things. Desperately she searched her brain for a way to live— not to die—to live.

After a while Zolic sat beside the altar eating peyote, and she began to hope he would become intoxicated enough to forget about her. Perhaps he would pass out.

He dragged out the artifacts from the cargo, one by one, showing them to her: Coatlicue, mother of the war god; Xipe Totec and the gold specie to save Los Olmos. He told her how Juan DeLeon had helped him steal and hide the gold. He turned the spear thrower over in his hands, explaining its use . . . in case Santana did find them, he said, "He will never get close enough to deny me my plans." And he had stared out across the enormous compound as though in his dementia he could see through the darkness.

The moon passed its zenith, dipped toward the horizon, and began to fade beneath the light of day. She began to hope.

Then the first streaks of magenta from the rising sun touched her eyes, and she clinched them shut.

When she opened them Jesús Zolic stood above her, robed in a faded, but obviously once brilliant mantle made of green feathers. In his hand he clasped the same obsidian knife they had recovered from the sea. His eyes, two shiny black orbs, stared in a mesmerizing daze of glazed insanity.

"The time has come, Lady Marina." His voice intoned, as in prayer. "As one chosen by the gods, may you savor the sweetness of death, a sweetness known only through death by the obsidian blade."

The next sound she heard was her own voice, hoarse yet surprising in its strength and volume, screaming to the sky above.

Then from the distance, as an echo of her own cry, another voice came to her—

—as from the other end of the world.

Another voice. A beloved voice.

Calling her name.

"MARINA!"

Chapter Nineteen

After leaving Marina on board the *Stella Duval,* Rafe had headed straight for the hut of the old shaman, Diego Ortiz, in his haste bypassing the big house on the Hacienda de Vera Cruz. The light he and Marina had seen shining through the hut's doorless entrance the night of the Feast of Saint Francis had bedeviled him ever since.

Coming so soon after he banished Zolic, his gut told him that was where the man had gone. Playing the sorcerer fit Zolic's demented brain.

When added to the strings of peyote which had disappeared after the shaman's death and Zolic's endless supply of the drug, the lighted hut only magnified Rafe's suspicions.

A couple of times on the way there Rafe entertained the idea his hunch could be wrong. What would he do then?

He knew Jesús Zolic well, however, and upon entering the darkened hut was not surprised to find his former staff member sitting before the fire.

"Santana. I have been expecting you. What took you so long?" Zolic sneered from where he sat cross-legged, making no move to rise nor to invite Rafe to sit at his fire.

When Rafe did not reply, Zolic continued. "Don't tell me, I know—whoring with that bitch named Marina."

"You bastard!" Skirting the fire pit, Rafe moved toward him. "Get up and give me the cargo you stole."

Zolic glanced right and left. "Take anything you find."

Rafe studied the maniacal glaze in the man's eyes, then made a visual search of the hut. "Where is it?"

"What?"

"Everything. The artifacts—the gold."

Zolic stared into the fire. "What's in it for me?"

Rafe jerked him up by the collar. "Life—maybe."

Zolic laughed in his face. "Still the macho *gapuchine,* I see. Thought that little whore would have worked it out of you by now."

Rafe backhanded him across the face. "I have a deep-seated yearning to whip you, Zolic. Do not tempt me now. I haven't the time."

Zolic laughed again, licking the corner of his mouth where blood had spouted from Rafe's blow.

"You have two choices," Rafe hissed. "Tell me where to find the cargo you stole or I take you to the Federales."

"Charging me with what? You have no proof."

"All I need, as you so often remind me, is my family's position. I can see you imprisoned for life—in a deep, dark cell."

Zolic shrugged. "So you have power? I will grant you

432

that, for now. But one day, Santana, you will pay dearly."

"Where are the goods you stole?"

Shaking loose from Rafe's grip, Zolic readjusted his shirt and sat back down. He cut a plug of peyote and chewed on it, oblivious, while Rafe searched the small hut.

The only thing he found, other than a sleeping mat which he shook out releasing a couple of spiders, was a burlap sack full of peyote. Upending it, he spilled the contents onto the dirt floor—nothing but peyote, a mound of it. "You killed that old man," Rafe hissed. "For peyote."

"Your ignorance is stupendous. That old man would have led you to the cargo before I could get my hands on it."

Rafe gripped his emotions. A tremendous impulse to beat the truth out of Zolic, or to try to, stirred inside him, but he fought it down. In the man's drunken state all he was likely to accomplish was wasted time. And he had no time to waste.

He could deal with Zolic later, after Giddeon Duval paid the taxes. "Like I said, you killed an old man for nothing. I will find the cargo, and when I do. . . ." His words trailed off seeing the black bag hanging around Zolic's neck. When he reached for it, Zolic slapped his hand away.

"Don't touch my Unblemished Youth sack." He withdrew a reed flute, extending it to Rafe with a patronizing smile. "Unless you want to purify your soul."

Rafe scowled.

"No? I agree yours is a hopeless case." Grinning in wicked delight, Zolic juggled the sack a few times, producing nothing but clunking sounds.

"Coins jingle, Santana. Even you should know that—with your highfalutin, thieving Spanish lineage."

"Where have you hidden that damned cargo, Zolic?"

"You are good at solving riddles from the past, Santana. Try this one. Your goddess has gone home. You will find her with an obsidian blade in her heart."

Rafe Santana glared at the madman.

"Come, now," Zolic taunted. "An expert such as yourself. You will decipher the riddle in no time." He yawned and stretched. "Leave me, I need to rest."

Rafe left, exasperated, knowing he could get nothing substantial from Zolic until the man sobered up. By that time he would have sent the Federales to arrest him. He searched the grounds around the hut, the puzzle resounding in his mind. *Your goddess has gone home. You will find her with an obsidian blade in her heart.*

Catching up the reins, he sat his horse a moment, thinking. He had considered bringing Zolic along, but in the man's present state of dementia, he would only slow him down and Rafe felt a growing urgency to return to the ship . . . to be with Marina . . . to hold her close.

Riding away from the hut, he smiled to himself. It was amazing how much his life had changed these past two months. Once a confirmed bachelor, he now knew living alone would be impossible. Marina Cafferty had gotten under his skin and into his heart. With her by his side, he felt whole, complete; without her, even for a short time, as now, it was as though a part of him were missing.

434

Drawing his mind back to the problem at hand, he considered Zolic's riddle. *Your goddess has gone home.* Home? The ancient temples were the earthly homes of the gods and goddesses. Is that what Zolic meant, a temple? If so—if he were not lying through his rotted teeth—which temple? Since Zolic was still in the area, it would be a temple close by. El Tamúin was closer to the ship. El Tajín was closer to the hut. After all that had transpired the last few weeks, El Tajín was the obvious choice.

Too obvious?

Rafe spurred his mount. With the few remaining hours of daylight, he would visit El Tajín, although he did not expect to find the missing deities nor the cargo there. Zolic was more cunning than that.

But when he reached El Tajín he began to wonder. From his horse he could clearly see something rising from the temple atop the Pyramid of the Niches. Was Zolic so high on peyote he didn't know he had given Rafe the key to solving the riddle within the hour?

Staking his horse to a ceiba tree, he figured the answer would be a resounding no. He climbed the steps anyhow, berating the man's stupid riddle, his obsession with the Aztecs, and his use of peyote. Next he berated himself for allowing Zolic to come on the expedition, for thinking the man indispensable, for trusting him as long as he had.

On top of the pyramid, he stared in amazement. Huge bouquets of flowers—actually, large handfuls of flowers—had been placed at intervals around the perimeter of the platform. Flowers? Then he thought of Don Ignacio. Was he perhaps planning another festival?

Rafe stooped to examine a crude altar in the center of the temple. Built from blocks of wood instead of stone, it nevertheless, added to the authenticity of the setting.

Suddenly he smiled, recalling how at the Feast of Saint Francis he had suggested Don Ignacio should stage theatricals.

He must be planning another festival. This time, Rafe vowed, he would bring Marina to the top of this pyramid and he would kiss her the way she deserved to be kissed.

Even though he expected to find no sign of the stolen cargo, he made a cursory search of the premises and was not surprised to find neither gold nor artifacts.

In the last remaining rays of sunlight he searched the rest of the compound. Again he expected to find nothing and again he was not surprised.

Afterwards he rode back to the hut. This time he would bring Zolic along. He would force the man to reveal his hiding places, before he turned him over to the Federales.

Zolic was not at the hut. The fire was banked, and Rafe thought briefly of waiting for his return. Considering Zolic's erratic nature and drunken state, however, his actions were unpredictable and Rafe didn't have time to waste on unpredictable men. A sane man, of course, with a stash of stolen goods would have left the area long ago.

So Rafe headed for the big house. He would discuss the theft with Don Ignacio, then tomorrow he would travel to the ceremonial center at El Tamúin. The temple there could well be the one to which Zolic referred. *Your goddess has gone home.* A home for

Coatlicue, mother of the god of war? Rafe scowled to the darkening sky above. War. What he would like to wage on Jesús Zolic at this moment.

He awakened the following morning in a soft bed in one of Don Ignacio's luxurious bedchambers wanting Marina. Once this was over, he was going to marry her as quickly as the conventions they had not yet broken would allow.

Her absence hung over him this morning like a pall, heavy with premonition. He felt sluggish, as though he had consumed a quart of tequila before going to bed. Since he hadn't, he tried to recall his dreams, but to no avail.

Coffee and orange juice left by the maid did not dispel the feeling, nor did the fieldhand's breakfast awaiting him in the *comedor* below.

Nothing but her presence would fill the emptiness inside him. He knew that now. And he had promised to return to her by suppertime tonight. A promise he intended to keep.

"How do you plan to proceed?" Don Ignacio asked before leaving for the fields.

"Regardless of whether I find anything at El Tamúin, I will return to the *Stella Duval* tonight. Time is running short for Giddeon to raise the money he needs; I can search for the missing artifacts after we complete the salvage."

Don Ignacio offered his hand and the two men shook. "Thank you for putting my kinsman's troubles first. A ranch is certainly of higher priority than artifacts which have lain buried as long as these."

The ride north consumed most of the day and resulted in a dismal failure to find either the artifacts or anyone who had seen Zolic in the last few days. Rafe considered spending the night there, since he could not arrive in Tecolutla in time for Enrique to take him out to the *Stella Duval* until morning. But his heavy spirits had sunk lower than the wreck of the *Espíritu Estelle,* and he knew that even if he had to sleep in his old camp by the river, he would be closer to Marina come morning.

The sun set, the moon rose, and the stars shown in their patterns, much the same as always, he thought. But without Marina beside him, he hardly glanced at them. Alternating between longing to see her and chastising himself for acting the love-sick fool, he arrived in Tecolutla a little past midnight by the stars.

The sight that greeted him awakened his tired brain. The *Stella Duval* was in port, her anchor dropped, her sails furled. Why had they not returned to the salvage site as he advised?

Then his spirits soared. Whatever the reason, it meant he would see Marina sooner. Sitting his horse dockside, he studied the raised gangplank and considered calling to the ship, then decided against awakening them tonight.

He had but drawn rein to ride back into the woods when Nick hallooed him.

"What are you doing up?" he responded to Nick's call.

"Guard duty. Where's Marina?"

Rafe studied the man. "What?"

"Marina? Didn't she find you?"

"What the hell are you talking about?"

Nick leaned over the rail. "The goddam message." Rafe heard fear in the man's voice. "The one you sent for her to meet you—"

Rafe's heart jumped to his throat. "I sent no message."

By the time Nick finished the story, Rafe's body fairly shook with anger—with fear. *Por los dios,* how could he have let such a thing happen? His heels twitched to sink spurs and ride to El Tajín. But his horse was spent from the day's ride. He would never make it in time.

Desperately he forced his mind to work. "I will get a fresh mount from José and leave immediately," he told Nick. "Wake Giddeon. Get the folks to Vera Cruz. Alert the family there; get everyone out searching for her in case I am mistaken—again. I am riding straight for El Tajín."

The only thing that had gone right in the past twenty-four hours was that José awakened easily and he had a fresh horse for Rafe. As he switched saddles, Rafe explained Marina's plight and asked the bartender to aid Nick in getting the family to Vera Cruz.

Then he was gone, riding with abandon, his mind crazed with fear. Zolic's words echoed through his brain and he wondered at his own stupidity that he had not immediately understood them: *You will find your goddess with an obsidian blade in her heart.*

The phrase opened his mind to a rush of guilt, like flood waters sweeping into an already turbulent stream, but he banished it. There would be time enough for guilt later. If he did not save Marina this night, guilt would ride in his saddle, sleep in his bed, sit at his fire the rest of his life.

It was near sunup by the time he reached the outskirts of the ancient city of El Tajín, its structures dark

439

against the brightening sky, pillars of death and destruction rising in ominous display. He left his horse well beyond the ball court and made his way carefully from cover to cover, keeping constant watch on the temple at the top of the Pyramid of the Niches.

Once he thought he saw movement, but he could not be sure. Creeping along the ground toward the bottom of the pyramid, he crouched beside the bottom step, hoping the darkness would cover him should Zolic be on top and should he look down.

The broken flute caught his attention. At first he thought it was a stick, and he carefully removed it so as not to step on it and make a noise. The notches along its side felt familiar, and when he looked closer his breath caught.

No doubt remained. But he did not dare use these steps exposing himself as he climbed. That would give Zolic time to do whatever he had come to do . . .

A chill racked Rafe and he gripped his arms a moment. *Por los dios viejos,* let her be alive and unharmed! Creeping around the structure, he looked for a way up, tried to determine which side would draw the least notice, then chose the back. That would put the rising sun behind him when he came over the top, behind him, in Zolic's face.

Climbing from niche to niche, he pulled himself slowly up the back side of the pyramid, scarcely daring to draw a breath lest he be heard, while at the same time, he tuned his ears to the top, straining to hear any sound foreign to the night.

For the longest time, none came. When he reached the fourth tier, he removed his boots and strung them around his neck by a rope which he took from his belt

440

and threaded through the side straps, climbing from there on in his stocking feet.

Like him the sun inched its way along, casting its brilliant first rays across his shoulders and over his head. He looked up. Two more tiers.

Then he heard her scream.

When the first streaks of the morning sun touched Marina's face, she flinched as though Zolic had slashed her with the obsidian blade he held above her.

Her heart throbbed in her breast, as in an effort to fight back on its own. Every part of her body hurt; the chill to her naked skin seemed minor by comparison. Her back felt broken from being stretched over the wooden altar. Her arms had long since lost all feeling with the blood drained to her hands.

She had screamed so long and so loudly during the night that her throat burned now as though it had been rasped with Zolic's blade. She was sure she would never utter another sound again in this world.

Then Zolic steadied the blade. "The time has come, Lady Marina. You must pay for your traitorous ways."

"No! Help me! Rafe—somebody—please!" The words clawed their way from her lungs searing her throat with their urgency—with their futility.

Then she heard it—the other voice.

"MARINA!"

Rafe's voice stilled her heart and froze Zolic's arm in mid-air.

"Marina! I'm coming."

She stared into the startled eyes of Jesús Zolic, her name resounding in her ears—her name, spoken by the man she loved. It was the first time he had ever called her name, her muddled brain acknowledged. *Pray God, it would be not the last.*

Tears flooded her eyes, poured down her face, dripped into her hair. Tears, when she was sure she had cried all the water from her body during the night.

The muffled sounds of Rafe climbing the back of the pyramid grated through the still morning silence. It was more beautiful than any music to her ears. Then she saw Zolic move to confront him.

"Rafe, he's coming. Watch out!"

Zolic hissed at her, but she did not hear for her struggles to free herself and help Rafe. If he killed Rafe they would both die. Here, together. Now. Before they could start a life together . . . before their baby. . . .

"Rafe, be careful!"

From her spread-eagled position she could see little of what transpired at the edge of the platform, but the sounds sent new fears chasing old.

They scuffled, she heard that, and she knew it meant Rafe had gained the top without being knocked from the edge of the pyramid.

She heard blows being exchanged, which must mean Zolic had not immediately stabbed him with the obsidian knife.

Something clattered to the stone surface of the temple—the blade?

Men heaved, grunted, air swished from one—was it over?

More scuffling, more blows, muttering she recognized as Rafe's voice.

Rafe's beloved voice. Her ears tuned themselves. Never again would she wait until later to appreciate a moment's pleasure. There might be no later time, even now.

Her heart beat so furiously she began to wonder whether it would wear itself out, cheating Zolic of tearing it from her breast. Then suddenly it stopped. Her heart. The scuffling. The blows. And the singular sound which followed chilled her as no mere temperature ever could—as she hoped nothing in her life ever did again.

"Aaaa . . . Eeee . . . eee . . ."

Like the death of a sun the cry waned; the body fell to earth at the foot of the pyramid. Marina heard several repetitions of deeply drawn breaths.

Then Rafe was at her side, kneeling beside her, kissing her face, holding her head in his hands.

"Marina. My love . . . my love . . ." He laid his head on her cold chest. His hot tears wet her skin. Her heart beat against his warm face, as her chest rose and fell, her heart pumping relief through her body and from hers to his.

At length he lifted his head and she saw him shudder at the sight. "It's all right," she told him. "You came."

When they arrived back at the big house the family was out searching for her, a maid revealed.

Rafe carried Marina straight up the stairs, issuing orders as he went. "Warm water, hot tea, soft cloths. And hurry," he instructed.

She wore his shirt over her otherwise nude upper body, since the thought of wearing the cloak Zolic had dressed her in had sent further shudders down her spine. At Rafe's question, she indicated the room Tía Luisa had given her on her previous visit and he carried her there and placed her gently on the bed.

443

"I'll be right back." He kissed her tenderly. "We must ring the bells to let them know you are safe. And I will send someone to collect Zolic's body and the stolen cargo."

The maid arrived, and when Rafe returned, he sent her scurrying from the room, locking the door behind her.

He turned to the bed, where Marina sat, clutching his shirt and staring wide-eyed at him. In an instant he was by her side holding her close, rocking her back and forth. Their mutual fears were still so fresh it was difficult to speak, but gradually his soothing strokes on her back, his gentle voice in her ear, brought her heartbeat back to normal. When she told him this, he drew her head back, cradling it in his palms.

"I'm not sure mine will ever return to normal, love. I was such a fool—"

"Shhh . . . You had no way of knowing how demented he was. None of us did."

He kissed her, soundly but tenderly, and afterward handed her a cup of tea laced with honey, instructing her to drink it slowly.

She complied, watching him pour warm water from a pitcher into a bowl, which he then carried to the bed and proceeded to bathe her face, her hands and arms where the ropes had been tied, and her feet and ankles.

"You're sure he didn't hurt you?"

She shook her head, soothed by his ministrations . . . by his presence.

He started to remove his shirt from her shoulders, then grinned. "Perhaps you had better finish. If I get started . . ."

She smiled, her eyes alight, and he knew even though

she was tired and frightened she would be all right. "Look in the wardrobe," she told him. "Find a *huipil* or something . . . anything except . . . a green silk night-gown."

He held her gaze.

"The family will return soon."

He smiled and she saw the muscle in his jaw twitch. When she finished he handed her a yellow *huipil,* his eyes on her bosom. "I will always be tormented by what he intended to do."

"But he didn't. You saved me."

She slipped the dress over her head, stood, and he pulled it down around her body, then held her tightly against him.

Then she remembered other things. "There is something I should tell you."

He stared lovingly, silently inquiring, into her troubled eyes.

"In the hut he drugged me with something . . . some kind of liquid he poured down my throat. I spit up most of it, but enough got down, that I lost consciousness . . . or, at least, I lost the ability to think. Anyway, when I came to, he had . . . ah, I don't know what he had done, other than undress me—completely. I was wearing that robe . . . nothing more."

She felt Rafe tense while she related the story. She saw his eyes harden into cold black stones.

"He didn't hurt you?" he asked again. "You don't *feel* hurt . . . anywhere?"

"No, just weak as a newborn colt."

He drew her to his chest and held her there. "Then we will forget it. If you are unharmed, nothing else matters. I doubt he did anything to you. Peyote usually

445

stems . . ."—pausing, he held her back and looked into her eyes, finally winking—"*carnal* impulses. And he had consumed enough peyote that he should have been able to join the old god Quetzalcóatl on his own steam."

A knock came at the door, and the maid called through. "Your family is returning, señorita."

"*Gracias,*" Rafe answered. He sat Marina back on the bed. "I will bring them up."

She held his hand, unable to let him go. "Come back with them . . . don't leave me."

He kissed her quickly. "Never again, my love."

By the time he reached the staircase the family had arrived below. The fright in their eyes reminded him of his own fears and of Marina's.

"Doña Luisa, will you send for the priest, *por favor?*"

"The priest?" Serita grasped her heart and leaped for the staircase all in one movement.

Rafe stepped toward her. "Marina is fine," he said quickly. "I asked for the priest—to marry us."

Below him eight pairs of eyes widened as one. Giddeon came forward.

"Now, Rafe, I told you I can't give permission. You will have to wait for her father—"

"Giddeon, with all due respect, I didn't ask your permission. I asked Doña Luisa to send for the priest."

"Let's take our time about this—"

"No. We have taken enough time. Like I promised you, sir, I am prepared to protect Marina's honor with my life, but . . . well, since I don't intend to leave her side again—day or night—" He shrugged. "We have broken too many conventions already, wouldn't you say?"

That night after the family had visited her in her room, after the priest had come and been prevailed upon to perform the ceremony, after the household retired and the bedroom door was locked, Rafe took her in his arms and loved her and held her close.

"What a romantic idea, to be married today," she sighed.

He nipped kisses across her face. "This morning when you asked me not to leave you, I knew I could never do so again. And perhaps we should start considering conventions, since we may want to fit into society one day."

She hugged him close. "Yes, we have broken enough conventions. And if we hadn't married today . . ."—speaking, she drew his hand to her belly, where she clasped it to her bare skin— ". . . in a few months we would have broken another one."

"You mean . . . ?"

She smiled. "I mean you saved two lives today instead of one."

"Por los dios, Marina, why did you not tell me?"

She savored the sound of her name coming from his beloved lips. "Like you, I wanted to wait for a special time."

Author's Note

I hope you have enjoyed the stories of the Cortinas family of the Hacienda de Los Olmos and that you are looking forward, as I am, to exploring new and exciting people and places from our past. My next two books are in the planning stages: the first is a cowboy story I think will be fun to write and I hope you will enjoy reading. Look for it in your bookstore in a few months.

Many excellent books have been written on the Aztec culture of pre-Conquest (also called pre-Columbian) Mexico. One of the best is THE DISCOVERY AND CONQUEST OF MEXICO by Bernal Díaz del Castillo, an eye witness account by a lieutenant of Hernán Cortés.

My personal thanks to author and treasure expert Tom Townsend for help with the treasure sequences.

In case you are curious about Marina and Rafe's baby, I leave you with this last entry to the Cortinas Family Tree:

|

Marina Cafferty
m. Rafael Santana

|

Giddeon Duval Santana
b. June 15, 1891